JAGUAR HUNT

TERRY
SPEAR

sourcebooks
casablanca

Published by Sourcebooks Casablanca, an imprint of Sourcebooks, Inc.
P.O. Box 4410, Naperville, Illinois 60567-4410
(630) 961-3900
Fax: (630) 961-2168
www.sourcebooks.com

Printed and bound in Canada.
WC 10 9 8 7 6 5 4 3 2 1

To Joshua Fowler, a librarian who loves books as much as I do.

Thanks to our librarians all over the world who help to instill a love of reading in us from an early age.

And thanks to all my Facebook fans who shared their favorite animals or foods at the circus and their favorite bubble baths. You make my research a collaborative effort and so much more fun!

Chapter 1

DAVID PATTERSON PARKED HIS CAR AND HEADED INTO the Clawed and Dangerous Kitty Cat Club, a Dallas-based social gathering spot for jaguar shifters. Humans didn't know that the shifters even existed, and the shifters meant to keep it that way. The owners of the establishment didn't restrict humans from frequenting the place, since more business meant more money.

But David wasn't there to support the club. His current task as a Special Forces Golden Claw JAG agent was to follow two unruly teens—jaguar shifter twins Alex and Nate Taylor—and bring them into the JAG branch if they violated one more law, jaguar shifter or otherwise.

This was not the kind of mission JAG agents normally took on—unless the organization felt the teens were at risk, or that they could be a welcome asset to the branch, and the agent was between assignments.

Neither of the boys was supposed to be in a club that served alcohol, which he would let slide if they were only there to watch the dancers in their skimpy leopard-skin loincloths and micro-bikini tops.

The place was more crowded than David remembered the last time he was here. One rowdy group caught his attention. They looked…*different*. Many were in great shape—almost as if they were shifters in the Service. But they were speaking in a smattering

of foreign languages—Spanish, Russian, Chinese—
and some of them wore clothes that were…unusual.
Tights, sparkly tops, and ballet slippers that looked less
like club clothes and more like what a Las Vegas en-
tertainer would wear. The air-conditioning blew their
scents to him. *Not* jaguar shifters.

They smelled of elephants, horses, camels, lions,
tigers, and dogs. *The circus?* Had to be from there.
David was surprised they hadn't changed into everyday
normal clothes, unless they were trying to help promote
the circus.

He wrinkled his nose, glad he wasn't planning to
drink anything here tonight. That was the problem with
being a shifter—the enhanced ability to smell odors. He
noticed other patrons glancing their way, wrinkling their
noses. *Must be shifters, too.*

The jungle music beat shook the floor and tables as
conversations hummed all around him. A few couples
danced on the floor, while others were just drinking
and talking. Piped-in sounds of parakeets and parrots
twittering and calling to each other and an occasional
monkey's howl made the silk leaf jungle sound more
like the real deal.

David's attention returned to Alex and Nate. Though
not as muscular, they were both as tall as David and they
could pass for adults. Alex's hair was blond, his eyes a
dark blue, while Nate was less tan and his light brown
hair shaggier.

One was dressed in camouflage pants, the other blue
jeans, and both were wearing black T-shirts with pictures of differently posed jaguars screen-printed on the
front. The words *Panthera onca*—the scientific name

for jaguar—announced to the world that they were jaguar shifters, though only their kind would realize that's what they were saying.

When David had been that age, he'd felt the same way. He'd wanted to shout to the world that he was a jaguar shifter and damned proud of it, instead of hiding it from everyone who wasn't like him. Since there were more human females than female jaguar shifters, he'd wanted human girls to see him as someone truly special. He'd often fantasized that girls he'd had crushes on were of his kind and not strictly human. Most of his kind were born as jaguar shifters, but some were humans who had been turned, which was not the best of ideas. Though his brother's wife, Maya, had turned her brother's wife-to-be and that had worked out well, despite the trouble it could have caused if Kat had had family.

So he could definitely commiserate with the twins.

The boys grabbed chairs at a table and David sat at another close by. Nate flagged down a server wearing a skimpy leopard-skin dress, cut high on the thighs and low on a very well-developed bust. Red curls bouncing about her shoulders, she smiled brightly at the boys as Alex whispered their drink order.

Grinning, the kids focused on two women who were dancing, breasts jiggling in their teeny bikini tops. David shook his head. The boys were so much like him and his twin brother, Wade, at seventeen.

The server returned with the boys' red-colored drinks topped with lime-green paper parasols, the toothpicks seated in cherries.

David was about to move in to ensure the drinks were nonalcoholic when Alex said, "Okay, listen, Nate.

We did it your way last time and you know how much I objected. This time we can't take a chance with the missing zoo cat."

David sat back down in his seat, listening intently. They had to be talking about the missing zoo cat from Oregon. Maya, his brother's wife, had a cousin—Tammy Anderson—who was looking for a jaguar missing from the zoo.

Nate snorted. "Hell, everything would have been fine with the jaguar if all had gone as planned. At least she's safe for now."

He wanted to hear more of the boys' conversation about the missing cat before he took them in for further questioning, if he felt the situation warranted it, but he saw something quick, big, and muscular in his peripheral vision. The bouncer. Brown eyes, nearly black, muscles bulging in readiness, mouth turned down. *Hell. Joe Storm.*

As much as David didn't want to make this personal, he couldn't help feeling a grudge toward the guy. David still believed that if Joe hadn't stolen Olivia Farmer away from him and promised to marry her—which he had no intention of doing—she wouldn't have committed suicide.

David watched the former JAG agent turned club bouncer stalk toward the boys. He looked eager to teach a couple of shifter teens they weren't welcome at the club until they were of age. David had worked with Joe on a couple of assignments and knew that the bouncer liked women—too damn well, in David's opinion—made allowances for most men, and had zero tolerance for troublemaking teens.

"Hey, Alex, trouble's coming," Nate said. Though David knew from experience that kids had to learn from their own mistakes, he also knew how hard Joe could be on them, and David didn't always agree with Joe's stern methods of enforcement.

Before David could reach the boys and protect them, the bouncer grabbed Alex and Nate by the arms and hauled them through the crowded club toward the back door. "I'll break both your bloody noses," Joe growled. "See if you'll want to come back for more after that, eh?"

Joe never made idle threats. David had seen him rough up a drunken human who had started a fight in the club. Joe had broken another man's nose for harassing one of the club's dancers. Talking Joe out of what he intended to do was *not* going to work.

David lunged from behind and hit Joe in the side of the head with his fist. Joe released the boys at once, but neither of the brothers left the club as David had expected they would.

"Go!" he shouted, just as Joe swung around, aiming to plant a fist in David's face.

David ducked and came around to slug Joe in the jaw, but managed to hit him in the temple instead, knocking the son of a bitch out cold. It was one helluva lucky punch, and it felt damn good, he had to admit. Joe was an ex-marine, ex-boxer, and ex-bartender. He looked like he killed men for pleasure, but right now, it appeared he'd be sporting some major bruises.

Getting the upper hand with him was probably as much a shock to David as to everyone else in the club. The music had stopped and all conversation had died. The teens had vanished.

Cheers went up and David gave a thumbs-up to the club patrons' raised glasses, whistles, whoops, and hollers.

Grinning, he hurried to call his boss, Martin Sullivan, director of the JAG branch, about the boys and the missing jaguar as he headed for the door, still hoping to catch the kids before they disappeared for good.

"Martin, I've got good news and bad. The good news is that the Taylor twins seem to know something about the missing zoo jaguar. I want in on the case with Tammy Anderson. The bad news is that I'm probably about to get arrested. Can you tell her I'm working with her on this mission and to come pick me up from jail?"

Chapter 2

STILL FUMING, TAMMY ANDERSON HEADED TO THE PO-
lice station to pick up her new, currently *incarcerated*
partner for this mission—David Patterson, a fellow
jaguar shifter who worked for the Special Forces unit
known as the Golden Claw JAG Elite Force. Tammy
was in the Enforcer branch, which normally was tasked
to police their shifter kind. *Like now.* Except that "normally" didn't include JAG agents.

How could she get so lucky?

Two of the Enforcers she'd worked with on previous
missions were leaving the red brick building—all smiles
when they spied her. Weaver's black hair curled around
his face in the hot Texas breeze. Krustan walked beside
him, his blond, butch haircut unaffected by the turbulent
air, his blue eyes sparkling.

"Hear you've got a new partner," Weaver said, jerking his thumb toward the police station. "Too bad you
didn't get *me* for a teammate. You certainly wouldn't
see *me* in there."

She raised her brows.

"Not in a cell," Weaver clarified.

"So what *were* you doing here? You could have freed
David Patterson, and I could have been doing something
more important." Like looking for new clues about the
missing zoo cat.

"He's your new partner, not mine. I figure he's yours

to ditch. From past experience, I know you're perfectly capable. The easiest way to do that would be to leave him where he is," Weaver said with a smirk.

She suspected Weaver still held a grudge against her for the last assignment he and Krustan had served on with her—which was just too bad. Next time, they wouldn't leave the cases for her to wrap up on her own. *If* there was a next time.

Krustan chuckled. "If you want me to work with you again, tell the boss. Sylvan would buy your recommendation, but it's the only way I'll be on your team."

Apparently, Krustan wasn't the kind of man to hold on to resentment. Though she suspected that was more because he was still interested in dating her, if she was willing. Which she wasn't.

"Thanks, fellas, but I'll take my chances with the JAG agent." At least he wouldn't know she intended to dump his butt, pronto. How could Sylvan Tolliver, head of the Enforcers, team her up with a guy who'd gotten himself jailed last night?

Maybe David didn't know yet that he was supposed to be her partner. Tammy decided not to say anything. She'd solve the case just fine without him.

She shook her head as she filled out the paperwork in the police station and was about to pay his fine— courtesy of his JAG boss—when she discovered someone else had already done so anonymously. That was weird. While she waited for David to be released, she folded her arms, sandaled foot tapping the floor. She normally thought herself a very patient person.

"He's all yours," the police officer said as he escorted David out of the cell block.

David was darker haired than his brother, Wade, whom she had met. David's locks were shaggier, windswept, and wilder looking, his eyes a pure green that focused on hers. He appeared way too eager to see her. Sure, she had just sprung him from jail, but his look was more a "cat that got the cream" expression, instead of simply seeming pleased she'd come to have him released. That worried her a bit. His brother was now married to her cousin, but that didn't mean anything to her. She didn't know David from the next troublemaking shifter.

David smiled at Tammy, his dimples making him look sweeter than she figured he was.

A year ago, she'd worked on a mission with a couple of other JAG agents who had thought she was wasting their time. They knew their business, and according to them, she was just a handicap. So she didn't figure David would act any differently. Worse, if he couldn't keep out of mischief, why should she risk her investigation while working with him?

As he signed for his personal items and pocketed his cell phone, she studied the olive T-shirt stretched across his impressive abs and pecs. He looked prepared for combat action with camo cargo pants and boots ready to tromp through the jungle—typical attire for a JAG agent headed to South America on a mission. She, on the other hand, was dressed casually for summer—jeans, blouse over a camisole, sparkly sandals—to blend in with the everyday population.

"The cop told me you're Tammy Anderson. You must be Maya's cousin," David said, his eyes shifting over her and again meeting her gaze.

"Yep." Tammy was heading outside when a tall,

well-built man with a handlebar mustache bumped into
her, not watching where he was going as he bolted up
the steps to the station. She took a sniff of the air surrounding him.

Scowling at the guy, David looked like he wanted to
teach him some manners, but Tammy said, "Don't. I'm
fine and you've already been in enough trouble, don't
you think?"

She glanced back at the man as he entered the police
station. He smelled like a lion. An African lion…shifter?
She didn't think anything like that existed.

"Has to be with the circus. *Thought* I smelled elephant, camel, lion, and dog shifters last night at the
club," David joked. "They must work with the animals."

That made sense. The staff at the local zoo that
handled the animals most likely smelled that way, too,
although this guy didn't look like a zookeeper. Not with
the handlebar mustache.

"If you think you can keep yourself out of jail for a
while, you're free to go," she told David and took off
across the parking lot at a quick pace.

Before she realized he was following her—*closely*—he
caught her arm, his large hand strong, his grip tight. She
swallowed an un-Enforcer-like squeak as he promptly
stopped her in place. Her ire stoked, she was *so* tempted
to take him down. She suspected he knew just what she
was thinking, and he'd thwart her before she even made
the attempt. That was the problem with him being with
the JAG and trained in hand-to-hand combat. A wry smile
curved his mouth. For a second, she was transfixed. He
had lips that enticed a woman to sample them—not too
thin or too large, just the perfect size for kissing.

Shaking loose of *that* thought, she glared at him instead.

"What?" she asked, annoyed. "I'm *not* babysitting you. Just freeing you from jail so you can be on your way. And *stay* out of trouble. I've got better things to do with my time."

"We're working together," David said, cutting to the chase.

Damn, he already knew.

"Your boss asked my boss if he could assign one of his best agents on the job to work with you. That's *me*. David Patterson." He gave her another award-winning smile.

She would have laughed at his cockiness if she hadn't been so irritated. Though her boss had told her that David was one of his best agents. "You? I had a lead on where the missing jaguar from the Oregon Zoo might be." Which she didn't. She was fresh out of clues at the moment, but she had every intention of finding some, pronto. And she didn't have to let David know that. "My boss called, saying I had to drop everything to come here. For *you*. On a day when I have no other mission, getting a shifter released from jail is one of those 'other duties as assigned.' But I'm working a case. Springing a *partner* from jail?"

She shook her head. "If you want to work with me, super. You follow your leads and I'll follow my leads, and we'll work together just fine."

She didn't wait for a response. Those were her terms—like it or lump it. She was certain she'd pick up another clue soon. On her own. She'd solve the case, and that would be the end of having to team up with another JAG agent.

She headed for her car, parked as far from other

vehicles as she could manage, not wanting anyone to scratch or ding the new paint job. She didn't hear David's footsteps following her, but she knew he was sticking close to her from the heat she felt radiating from him. She heard his heartbeat thumping. Smelled his hot, sexy, masculine jaguar scent close by. Big cats moved so quietly that their prey would never think they were being stalked—unless the person being followed was also a big cat.

She glanced over her shoulder. Sure enough, he was only inches away. "*Where* do you think *you're* going?"

"With you. I've got a tip. This is going to be one helluva hot assignment."

Narrowing her eyes, she tilted her chin down and gave him a look of disbelief.

"We're headed for Belize. It's...*hot* down there."

Not believing that's all he was referring to, but surprised at his declaration, she stopped. She loved Belize. The jungle, the crystal aqua waters off the coastline, the fact that jaguars still roamed free in the rainforest there. She'd give anything to go there on a vacation—but this was work, and she didn't believe for one moment that the missing zoo cat was there. Too difficult to transport across international borders.

Tammy folded her arms and stared at him skeptically. "Belize."

"Yep. That's where our lead is," David said, hands in pockets, looking smug and...she had to admit, appealing.

"How did you learn of it?"

"Why do you think I was in jail?"

She tilted her head to the side. "You punched one of the bouncers at the shifters' club and knocked him out."

"Well…yeah, there was that."

"Must have been a lucky shot. I've heard Joe Storm packs some deadly punches."

"I'm just that good. So where's your car?"

She wasn't buying any of this. "How did you find out about a lead?" she asked again, more emphatically.

"Okay, if we're working together, I'll share my stuff with you, if you share your stuff with me." He grinned.

He was such a rogue of a jaguar. And damn if he didn't charm her on some level. She had to be nuts. She hadn't realized Wade's brother could be this much of a character.

"I know how you helped my cousins, Maya and Connor, and his wife, in Belize this last mission…"

"But?" David asked.

She bit off the "but" part of the sentence and said instead, "So I wanted to thank you."

He was looking at her as if he still expected her to add a "but" to the declaration.

She didn't want to feed into his all-knowing ego so she turned and stalked off toward her car, figuring she was going to have major problems on this mission. This guy wasn't going to be easy to lose. And she wasn't sure she wanted to.

The fact that she was having doubts? That was really *not* good. But she could do this on her own. And would. As soon as she knew what was going on in Belize.

Chapter 3

THIS WOULD BE ONE HELLUVA SCORCHING ASSIGNMENT, David thought to himself as he walked with Tammy through the police-station parking lot. Yeah, with one fiery-tempered partner, who had a great reputation for getting a job done right. He kept telling himself this was strictly a job like any other. But who was he trying to kid?

He looked her over again. Not only did she have a distinguished standing in her branch for being a top-notch Enforcer agent, she had curves that wouldn't stop, red-gold hair he'd love to run his hands through, and a mouth meant for kissing. Tall, stacked, sexy, dressed in a pair of dark green jeans, same-colored sleeveless silky camisole underneath a whispery-light blouse, and sparkly little sandals; she was a knockout. She also had the most striking blue eyes he'd ever seen—that had caught his attention and held on with fierce determination.

Nothing in the regs said he and his partner couldn't have a little fun on assignment if she was of a like mind. And he was owed some downtime. Martin had said this was an easy task and told him to enjoy the mission while he was at it. David was taking his boss's advice to heart.

This time was going to be nothing like the last four operations David had been on—kill or be killed, dodging bullets, knives, jaguar teeth, and claws—you name it. This one was going to be laid-back, stress-free, no trouble at all. So if he could convince Tammy to have a little fun while they were on the mission, he wouldn't even need a vacation.

Her brothers and his own, all of them in the JAG branch, had made the recommendation to their boss that David work with Tammy. Her brother, Huntley, had called David and warned him that she preferred dating humans to shifters. Her other brother, Everett, had told him that if she didn't like who she was partnered with, she'd ditch him as soon as possible. He'd gone on to tell David that in the past six months, she'd dumped five Enforcer partners, and she had solved all five cases on her own. From the sound of it, she'd been perfectly capable—at least concerning those jobs.

She wasn't losing *him* on this mission though. He was a Golden Claw. And he had some pride.

His brother, Wade, had warned him not to get fresh with her or there'd be hell to pay—since Wade had married her cousin, and he didn't want to get into hot water with Maya.

Never had so many fellow JAG officers warned David about working with an agent from a different branch. He suspected he would have difficulty with her before they even began the mission. Which meant he had to be ready for anything. He loved a challenge.

Keys in hand, Tammy stopped in front of a yellow Jaguar, a 1969 convertible roadster.

He gaped at it. "This is *yours*?"

"Yeah. It's a…*hunk* magnet."

He stared at her for a moment, thinking she meant the car was for attracting all kinds of human males. Since that's what she purportedly dated.

He smiled and winked. "Caught *me*."

She rolled her eyes and unlocked the doors. She wasn't smiling, but he thought he saw a glimmer of one that she was trying darned hard to suppress.

His attention fully diverted to the convertible. He couldn't quit marveling over the sports car's details: the new black leather seats, elegant rosewood steering wheel, and shiny stainless-steel wire wheels. Hell, Everett had told David she drove an old car, and he had envisioned some old clunker. *Not* a hot car like this.

He ran his hand over the black canvas top. "Could I drive it?" He suspected she'd say no—particularly when he saw the expression on her face, raised eyebrows, chin tilted down, the look that said no—but he *had* to ask.

"Nope."

He sighed dramatically and she gave him a quick smile that brightened her expression and revealed just how pretty she was.

A low engine rumble growing closer made him turn to see why another vehicle would be parking way out here when no other cars were. A shiny, new black sedan pulled up next to them.

Fellow JAG agent Quinn Singleterry.

Quinn thought himself a real ladies' man, and David wouldn't put it past him to attempt to hook up with the she-cat Enforcer.

The agent got out of his car, slicked back his long black hair, the muggy summer breeze fighting him for control. His blue eyes sparkled in the early-morning sunlight as he gave Tammy one of his *knock 'em dead* smiles reserved for hot chicks.

"Quinn Singleterry," David said to Tammy by way

of introduction as the agent joined them. "And this is Tammy Anderson."

"We've met," she said. She didn't sound pleased, and for that, David was grateful.

"How'd you swing *this* gig?" Quinn asked, sliding his gaze from David to Tammy. "I told her I was interested in working on this case. Thought I might have a lead or two."

"Did you share them with Tammy?" David asked, guessing Quinn was just trying to bait her to convince her to work with him. He probably didn't have any clues.

"Nah. She said she was working alone on the case. Preferred it that way. I checked out the leads. *Nada.* So, how the hell did *you* get to team up with her?"

"Her boss asked for the best," he said, slapping Quinn on the back. "So Martin picked me."

Tammy shook her head—David noted she was smiling ever so slightly—and climbed into the car, shutting the door behind her.

"What are you doing here?" David asked Quinn, certain his arrival wasn't purely chance.

"I heard she was getting you out of jail. Figured she might want a partner who was a little more reliable. She needs someone who is totally focused on the mission."

"She likes roguish guys." Not that David saw himself that way, but the fact that she had to pick him up from jail made it appear that way. He was certain, from what her brothers had told him, that she was *not* into bad boys.

She started the car's engine, and David's heart skipped a beat.

"Gotta go," David said quickly and gave Quinn a thumbs-up, but before he climbed into the passenger side of the Jaguar, Tammy locked him out, gave them both a wave and a smile—on the wicked side—and peeled out of the parking lot.

Slack-jawed, David couldn't believe she had left him to fend for himself. He'd have to ask Quinn for a ride or call a taxi to get to his car still parked at the club, then grab his bag at his apartment and get to the airport on time. No matter what, the whole branch would know the she-cat had already abandoned her new partner. David could see his brother and hers shaking their heads at him and smiling smugly.

David would never live it down.

Wearing a conceited smile, Quinn didn't say a word as he drove David to the club, but David knew he wanted to. He almost wished Quinn would just say it—the woman was a maverick cat and there was no way to team up with her. David had every intention of proving otherwise.

"Thanks, owe you one," David said as he left Quinn's car, got into his own, and hurried home. As soon as he arrived at his apartment, he texted his boss: Can you locate Tammy for me?

Martin texted back: She just picked you up at the police station. Don't tell me you already lost her.

David chuckled and sent: Unsure if she's going to Belize or not.

Martin: The two of you are supposed to be a team.

David: Right.

Martin: Checking.

David showered, changed, loaded his bag into the car, and drove to the airport.

Martin texted him: Her boss says she's on the same flight as you, and she's already there.

David breathed a sigh of relief.

———

David arrived after first boarding at DFW and hurried to make the gate. He had to admit he was a bit miffed with himself for not seeing what she had intended to do before she did it. As a jaguar shifter, he was usually good at reading the signs—posture, change in scents, eye contact or avoidance. But David hadn't been paying attention to the signals because he was trying to rub it in that he got to work with her instead of Quinn. From everything he'd learned about her, he knew she was smart and savvy, and he was certain they'd solve the case in record time.

Despite the embarrassment of her ditching him—in front of Quinn—David actually enjoyed her game. She had just the kind of flirty sass he liked in a woman, and he wasn't giving up working with her for anything.

Once David boarded the plane, he found her struggling to get a bag into the stuffed overhead bin. He stepped up nice and close to her, pressing his body against hers and leaving his scent on her as she left hers on him, and smiled down at her as he maneuvered her bag in just so. He added *his* bag to the overhead bin and closed the compartment door. She raised one arched brow in response. She didn't move out of his way—as if she was showing him his close proximity didn't intimidate her. She also took a deep breath, proving her interest in his scent.

"Tammy," he said in greeting, unable to keep the grin off his face.

She smiled also and slid into the window seat. Which might have been why she'd smiled. An older gentleman was seated next to her, and she might have assumed that David wouldn't have another opportunity to get that close to her on the flight. Except that David wasn't about to be outmaneuvered. Martin had gotten him a first-class seat, the perfect bargaining chip.

David said to the older gentleman, "She's an old friend of mine. Do you mind exchanging seats with me? Mine's in first class."

The man's face was alight with enthusiasm. "Thank you, young man."

"The pleasure is all mine," David said, casting Tammy a satisfied look.

She chuckled.

He sat in the seat next to hers, surprised she had gotten here well ahead of him, though he'd had to shower after being in jail for the night. He admired her for being able to travel at a moment's notice. Every woman he knew needed days to plan ahead and packed way too much stuff for a trip. Best of all, she'd taken him at his word that the clue concerning the missing jaguar could be found in Belize. Or maybe she had called her boss to let him know what was going on, and *he* had informed her that she needed to go there.

"So what's the deal?" she asked, sounding resigned that she'd have to work with him.

"We've got to bring in two seventeen-year-old twin shifter brothers who are violating our laws. My people have been keeping tabs on them for some time, and they just managed to skip to Belize. My boss wants them brought in before they get into considerable trouble."

Her eyes narrowing, she folded her arms across her chest. "Okay, so if your director wants the teens on his team, why does he need an Enforcer to help bring them in? Sure, we police the shifters so they abide by our rules and human laws, which, if the boys are doing illegal stuff and could land in jail, is a definite reason for picking them up. As you know, incarceration in human jails is out of the question for our kind." She gave David a pointed look. "It's too easy for a shifter to want to protect himself from other prisoners, and the best way to do that is to shift. But since *your* boss wants to recruit them, that puts them in *your* jurisdiction. Because the Golden Claws can do anything that any of the other branches specializes in, it seems to me this should be a JAG team assignment. Not to mention, where's the connection to *my* mission to track down the missing zoo cat?"

He smiled at the reference she made about doing jail time, which he was sure was directed at his recent stay in one, and the way she was still referring to this as *her* mission and not *theirs*. "Alex and Nate Taylor don't do well with male authority figures."

She raised a brow. "The JAG director is a male."

"Right. We'll worry about what happens after we return them there. We needed a woman, who is wild, to help bring them in. If you've ever had to work with a city shifter in the jungle, I'm sure you know what a disaster that can be. Most never visit our natural habitats and don't know the lay of the land or how to survive if they get into trouble. Instead of taking care of the mission, I'd end up having to watch out for the city cat just as much. Sure, their big-cat instincts would kick in, but it's not like working with someone who grew up visiting the jungles, hunted in them, knows what to expect. Hell, the last time I had to do that, I swore I never would again."

"All right. So you needed me…because the boys are in the jungle?"

"Precisely. And you were free."

"Free? As in not doing anything important with my time besides getting a JAG agent released from jail?" She didn't wait for him to respond, though he fully intended to. "I was working a case. Jaguar missing from the Oregon Zoo? Remember?"

"Right. But you were free to travel. Other female agents were already out of the area. The boys know something about the missing cat. Since you were working on that, it seemed only natural that we work together on the case. This way we capture three cats with one net—so to speak."

He suspected she wouldn't like the inference that she was unable to do her job without a JAG agent's protection. Still, when missions were in the wild, *his* boss always sent a team of at least two agents. It was just safer that way.

"How do you know the boys have information about the zoo cat?" she asked.

"They mentioned the missing jaguar at the club." He shared the conversation the boys had with each other with her. "When I called my boss before I met up with you, we talked about the teens, and we assume that's why they skipped the country."

"Because they're involved? Or because they *know* who's involved and they're afraid whoever stole the jaguar will come after them? Or thought you were onto them and would make them pay?"

"We're not sure. I've been keeping tabs on them. I followed the boys to the club and overheard them talking about the missing jaguar. One of the club's bouncers spotted the boys, grabbed each by the arm, and yanked them toward the door."

"Joe Storm."

"Yep." David cleared his throat. "The ape said he'd break both their noses for coming into the bar underage. It wasn't an idle threat, either. The club owners don't want the place closed down. Being a shifter, Joe knew the boys would heal fast. He would have gotten flak for injuring them, but the teens might not have bothered to report it—afraid the whole incident would get back to their parents. I'm certain Joe thought it would be enough of a punishment to deter them from trying to do the same thing later."

"So you decked Joe," she said, "and the boys got away."

"Yeah, but it was all part of my plan."

She looked skeptically at him.

He shrugged. "I rescued them. That could help us in the long run."

"But you said the boys won't take orders from a male authority figure, and that's why *I'm* needed." She sipped from a plastic cup of water. "Why were *you* needed exactly?"

He fought smiling at her and said, "I used to be just like them."

Chapter 4

TAMMY *KNEW* DAVID PATTERSON WAS TROUBLE. IF HE had caused problems growing up, he clearly hadn't changed at all—if picking him up from jail wasn't enough of a hint. And where would that lead when she had to work with him on the mission?

Yet sticking his neck out for the boys was commendable, and she admired David for it. He could have been badly injured. She was glad she'd ended her relationship with Joe Storm, knowing all about the time he'd spent as a boxer, which meant he could really injure a guy who wasn't prepared for the punishment Joe could dish out. She was thankful David had decked him first and hadn't gotten himself killed instead.

She reminded herself that David *had* helped her cousins in Belize during their last mission. With hunters going after exotic cats and Maya, Connor, and his wife getting caught up in it, David and his brother, Wade, had been invaluable in keeping them safe. She couldn't have been more grateful for the brothers' help at great risk to themselves.

She took another deep breath, letting his scent fill her with a warm, tingly feeling. Some men's scents were a total turnoff. David's was provocative, very male, and interested. It made her almost forget she wasn't into that kind of guy.

He pulled down a couple of blankets and pillows from the overhead bin. He handed her one of each, his expression curious—as if he was trying to read her. Their hands brushed, the gesture not meant to be intimate, yet to her, it felt that way. His eyes and mouth reflected a hint of both intrigue and amusement.

"Thanks," she said, and he took her empty cup so she could close up her seatback tray.

He was being such a gentleman, sweet with a hint of sexy playfulness. He leaned his seat back, and she did likewise with hers.

She was always driven on an assignment and wanted closure on the missing zoo cat now, particularly when a life was at stake—in this case, a jaguar's. But she did want to help the boys, too, and ensure they were taken in hand and given proper guidance so they wouldn't end up in jail in the future. Even though David's time with the Service hadn't completely helped him in that regard.

She wished she *could* have some fun on this trip. Where that notion came from, she was at a loss to say. Her work ethic—work first, play afterward—had been drummed into her since she was a small child. They had a job to do, and playing wasn't part of the mission.

"Thanks for getting me released from jail," he finally said to Tammy and handed their empty water cups to the airline hostess as she hurried by with the trash bag. "I sort of missed getting a ride with you, though."

Tammy assumed he was fishing for the reason she had left him behind. She pulled the blanket over her lap. "I figured you and Quinn needed more time to talk. I had to get home in a hurry and pack if I was to make the flight."

"I knew you hadn't tried to shake me."

She smiled a little. That had been her intention, even

though she'd guessed she wouldn't have any success at it—not when he was headed to Belize on the same plane. "Just so you know—this is strictly a job for me, and the first chance I have to solve the mission, I'm doing it."

"Absolutely."

After leaving him behind, she liked the way he'd acted toward her with only good grace and humor. Not to mention the sexy comeback when he was working her bag into the overhead bin, and rubbing against her just to say he was sticking close to her. Then the thought popped in her mind about his bail having been paid.

"I thought your boss would have settled your fine to get you out of jail, but someone beat him to it. Was it a girlfriend?"

David smiled at her.

She didn't want David to act like he was interested in her if he had a sweetheart at home. Her previous shifter boyfriend's unfaithfulness had made her wary of getting back into the dating game right away.

She shrugged. "The donor was anonymous."

"Hmm. I would think Martin would have used JAG funds to pay it since my involvement was all in the line of duty. If my brother had known, he would have paid the fine and been reimbursed afterward, but I doubt our boss told him. Anonymous, eh? Secret admirer?"

She noted that he didn't say whether he was seeing someone or not. Though, if he were, there was no reason for the woman to bail him out anonymously.

"We should do some exploring when we finally get to Belize," he continued.

"Absolutely. We can stretch our cat legs a bit. For now, we may want to get some sleep on the flight."

He settled against the seat. "Sounds good to me."

She liked the idea of running as a cat in the jungle to get some exercise after all the sitting they would be doing on the plane and the bus trip to their destination.

David snuggled against his pillow, patted the armrest, and said, "We can pull this up and you can lean against me if you'd like to get more comfortable."

"That's okay. I can sleep against the window." She imagined he didn't normally offer his fellow agents his shoulder to sleep on. Or his… lap. Unless this was par for the course for him when it came to working with *female* agents.

He waited for her to say something more, probably because she had fought smiling and had lost. She didn't know him and shouldn't ask, normally wouldn't, but something about him made her want to play with him a little. Like a cat with a catnip-filled toy. "Do you propose that to all your partners?" she asked.

He chuckled, the sound dark and sexy, as if he was reading more into the situation than she intended and he was game, not just strictly amused. "I've worked with five over the years. Taken several plane trips with them. And no, not once have I offered."

"Thanks. I'll be fine." She set her pillow next to the window and rested her head against it.

"If you change your mind, the offer still stands." He closed his eyes.

A couple of locks of dark silky hair hung over his forehead. He looked angelic in a rough-hewn way. Knowing he wasn't angelic in the least made him all the more appealing. And that should warn her to take care.

—w—

After the plane trip and the long drive in the rental car
from the airport in Belize City—better than if they had
to rely strictly on bus transportation—David and Tammy
finally arrived at their jungle resort. Their small cabana
sat on short, wooden legs to keep it off the ground, the
surrounding rainforest encroaching on the wooden wrap-
around porch. One wooden chair sat at a corner of the
railing, and two green and blue hammocks hung from
the thatched roof overhead. The building's wooden
walls were well-weathered, as if this particular cabana
were one of the first units the resort had offered to
guests. Still, it was *way* better than tenting in the jungle.

Tammy rolled her regulation black bag through the
small living room, past the couch and single chair, both
upholstered in plain white fabric. A glass-topped table
sat in between them, and a couple of potted plants were
placed near the windows, bringing the jungle look inside. The cabana smelled of humans. No shifters had
stayed here recently. The only "air-conditioning" appeared to be a circulating fan overhead.

While David claimed the first bedroom and unzipped
his bag, Tammy headed down the narrow hall to the
other bedroom and found a queen-sized bed topped with
a mesh canopy to keep the bugs out—much to her liking. An orange hibiscus-patterned bedspread added to
the tropical feel. The bedroom was also equipped with a
ceiling fan, but she didn't think it would cool things off
that well midday.

After dumping her backpack on a dresser, she laid
her bag on a luggage stand, intending to unpack before

they grabbed a bite to eat and explored their options. She unzipped the top of the bag and opened it. A box of XXL condoms sat square in the middle of a pair of black briefs. Momentarily stunned, she stared at them. Until she realized she must have David's bag and not her own.

XXL?

She tried to recall how big his feet were and mentally shook her head at herself. The size of a man's feet, nose, or Adam's apple were not indicators of how well hung he was. Although an Asian study had found some correlation to the size of his index finger…

She grabbed the bag and headed out of the room.

What did he think? He was going to get lucky with the natives?

He better not think he was going to get lucky with her.

She stalked into his bedroom to exchange luggage with him before he discovered what was in *her* bag. And found him holding up her lace and silk red-hot panties, a smile on his smug face as he admired them. Her cheeks flushed with heat.

"Wrong bag." She tossed his on his bunk bed, the box of condoms half falling out of it. She jerked her panties out of his hands, shoved them into her bag, and took off with it.

She would have laughed when she saw the twin-sized bunk beds in his room if she hadn't been so embarrassed that he was manhandling her panties. She loved wearing sexy things, even if she had no intention of showing them off to anyone else. Certainly not to a male partner teamed up with her on a mission.

She had to admit that ditching her other partners—who had been Enforcers like her—had been easy. Maybe they had wanted her to lose them while she did all the work on the investigations. David was another story. The situation had changed so drastically—with them now here in the rainforest instead of back home in Texas—that she wasn't certain she did want to do this on her own. The case wasn't supposed to be dangerous, but a trip to the jungle could change that scenario in a heartbeat.

She was still neatly folding her clothes and placing them in a chest of drawers when David knocked on her doorjamb, frowned, and said, "You don't have bunk beds in here? Wanna switch rooms?"

"No, thanks." She slammed the dresser drawer closed, fighting a smile.

He eyed the bed further and shook his head, muttering under his breath, "I should have checked the bed situation out first."

"You mean, you wouldn't have been a gentleman and let me have the big bed?" she asked, loving that she could put him on the spot.

He gave her a quick, heart-thumping smile. "I would have shared it with you." He paused, watching her, letting that sink in. She *wasn't* going for it. He sighed. "Ready for dinner? The dining hall closes soon, and there's no other place to grab a bite unless you want to hunt for it later tonight."

"The dining hall sounds good to me." She didn't mind hunting when she had no other choice. She was wild—used to handling herself as a jaguar in the jungle—but given the option, she preferred eating at a more civilized dining facility.

She peeked into the bathroom on the way down the hall and frowned. "Toilet, sink. Where's the bathtub or shower?"

"Outdoor warm-water showers," David said, looking like *he* was fighting a smile. "Sorry, our bosses didn't splurge on this mission."

She didn't think David was sorry at all. "Your boss got you a first-class seat on the plane."

"Yeah, because the rest of the seats were filled."

"Great." She hoped they'd find the missing teens soon and be out of here before she had to take too many outdoor showers. In this hot, muggy weather, they'd need them.

They left the cabana and headed on the stone walkway to the dining hall, hidden by vegetation as if they were taking a Sunday stroll through the jungle.

"So where are the kids?" she asked.

"From what my boss has gathered, they signed up to do a bunch of the activities near here."

"To be here by themselves, they must be wild too."

"You're right. From what Martin says, they've been coming to Belize with their parents for years. Their parents are general surgeons, so they have the money. The last two years, the boys came down here without their parents."

"Since they were fifteen? Wow." She couldn't imagine. She'd come here with her parents until she was nineteen, and on assignment with the Service after that.

David didn't make any comment, and Tammy wondered if he had been that age when he was running around in the jungle by himself. But he'd probably been with his brother, like these boys were together.

"If Alex and Nate were worried that someone was coming after them because they knew about the missing jaguar, they might have felt safer down here," David said.

"Except that your boss knows where they plan to be. So couldn't anyone figure that out?"

"Possibly. We don't know enough about what's going on with the brothers," David said.

Tammy pondered this as they walked together to the resort's dining hall. Ribbons of pink and orange sky turned darker as the night drew down upon them. *Beautiful.* Parrots talked away to each other, their vibrant plumage of blues and greens standing out against every shade of green foliage imaginable as monkeys called out somewhere in the canopy. Oil lanterns lighted the pathways, though the jaguar shifters didn't need the extra light to see well. The sweet fragrance of orchids wafted through the air, and Tammy felt like she was walking through an exotic garden with a much too hot and sexy shifter.

"So what 'activities' are the boys signed up for exactly?" Tammy asked, bringing her mind back to the mission from the romantic surroundings.

"Zip-lining through the canopy will be first thing tomorrow morning," David said.

She glanced at him. "Okay, not to sound dumb, but what is zip-lining, exactly?"

"It's high-flying excitement when you harness up and whip through the canopy of the rainforest."

She frowned at him.

"Technically, a pulley is connected to a cable strung through the trees. A person is harnessed to the pulley at the top of the cable, and then gravity zips him along the cable to reach a lower point. It's fun. We'll go on the excursion in an attempt to catch up with them."

"You actually want to go zip-lining?" she asked,

not liking where that scenario was headed. At first, she thought they'd just catch the boys when they got to the end of the line. But now she wondered if David meant they were also going to make the trip through the canopy.

"You're not afraid of heights, are you?"

"Of course not. But someone should be on the ground to grab these guys when they get off the platform, right?" She wasn't about to share her fear of heights with him. Not even her brothers knew that about her. "So if you follow them on the zip line, I can meet them when they reach their final destination."

"Shall we toss for it?"

"No," she said a little too abruptly. "I'll meet the teens on the ground when they have finished their ride."

"I don't think that will work. I'll have a better chance grabbing them than you will."

"You said that they'd be more willing to speak to me. I didn't know we had to physically *arrest* them," she said, eyeing him with suspicion.

"If they won't cooperate… Besides, if I'm not with you, they might be more willing to talk to you *before* you get on the zip line. If that doesn't work, I'll be waiting on the other end. Once they can't run away, you can convince them to tell us about the jaguar. I suspect they're afraid they're going to be in trouble concerning the cat. So we'll just have to ensure they know they won't be. As long as the cat is safe and we can retrieve her."

What he said about her appearing to be less of a threat to the boys when they had difficulty with male authority figures and meeting them alone made sense. Still, envisioning the kids bound to chairs, she frowned at David. "So how are you going to grab them?"

"Do you always plan your moves to the very last detail?" David asked.

"Do *you* always wing it?" she asked as he opened the door to the dining room for her.

"Some of those turn out to be my best moves."

"In other words, you don't have a real plan in mind." David only chuckled.

———※———

Partly hidden by giant ferns, banana trees, palms, and a cypress, the large dining room was lit by numerous candles and lanterns, offering a certain ambience that could be considered romantic if this had been a romantic liaison and not strictly a mission. Chatter filled the place, coming from tourists of every shape and size sitting at seven long tables. David sat with Tammy at one that was half empty. The stone tile floors, thatched roof, large ceiling fans, and windows with only screens made him feel as if he was eating outdoors as the rainforest surrounded them with its fragrant smells and unique jungle sounds.

They both ordered the shrimp creole on coconut rice, while David had beer and Tammy, a pineapple rum drink. He quickly ate his meal and shoved the plate aside. "I don't know how long we're going to be here, but if you want, I can pay to upgrade our accommodations."

"Oh?" She sipped from her tall, cool drink, her strawberry curls framing her face, and he thought how pretty she was—with no resemblance to her brothers. David had to thank Martin for giving him this assignment.

He noticed she was studying his bare fingers, which he thought was odd. Most cats didn't wear jewelry, even wedding rings. Too much of a problem if they had to shift quickly. For one thing, they wouldn't want to lose their expensive rings or watches if they left them behind after shifting. No cat would have piercings or tattoos, either. If the shifter was caught by humans, how would someone explain a jaguar with a tattoo or a belly button ring?

"Not married," he finally said, amused.

She glanced up from eyeing his fingers to meet his gaze. "What?"

He held up his hand. "No ring. No tanned area around a white band on the skin to indicate I've been wearing one, either."

Her mouth curved up a bit, but she didn't appease his curiosity.

He waited. She sipped some more of her drink.

He figured the explanation had to be a simple one, but when she didn't explain, he was all the more curious. By nature, cats were. Being a jaguar shifter, inquisitiveness was an inevitable hazard.

"So…do they meet with your expectations?" he asked.

"What?" She frowned a little, appearing not to understand what he was referring to.

"My hands."

She started laughing.

Now *that* reaction he hadn't expected. "Want to clue me in?" He smiled, her amusement infectious.

"No," she said, still chuckling.

He'd learn what she was up to one of these days. He finished off his beer. "So with an upgrade on the rental unit, we'd have an indoor shower. Air-conditioning. Just nicer housing."

"We should be done by tomorrow, if all goes as

planned. Right? We grab the teens at the zip-line place, find out what they know about the cat, and take them home. Let the agency foot the bill like it's supposed to."

"It's your call. But I don't mind you upgrading if you want to." He wouldn't be doing it *all* for her benefit, though he didn't care anything about having or not having air-conditioning, and the outdoor shower was fine with him. He didn't mind footing the bill himself if he could move her into the only place that was still available—a jungle bungalow with only one queen-sized bed. *No* bunk beds.

She put her empty drink glass down and tilted her head to the side, considering him. He swore she could see clean through him.

When she didn't say anything, he said, "Yes?"

He felt like he'd been caught fingering her silky red panties again. He shouldn't have lifted them out of her suitcase. The red silk had been just too tempting. Being a man, he had to imagine what she'd look like wearing the panties. And what she would look like not wearing them.

"Exactly what would the sleeping arrangements be?" she asked.

A middle-aged couple sitting at the end of the table glanced their way.

"One queen-sized bed," David said.

"But there's a couch, right?" she asked.

The man at the end of the table chuckled.

"Tiny couch." David was not upgrading their accommodations to a place with an indoor shower so he could lose his bunk bed to sleep on an even shorter couch. "Are you done with your meal?" He rose from his chair, wanting to end this discussion in a hurry. He figured he was stuck with the bunk bed for the duration of their stay. "We need to get an early start tomorrow. I want to be at the zip-line place first thing before anyone gets there and scope out the area a bit. Just in case the kids arrive early to hang around."

Tammy headed outside the dining hall with him and glanced around at the jungle. "As jaguars?"

"Yeah. Early. Sniff around a bit. The terminal platform is not far from here. The other is about twenty-three hundred feet due west from that." He walked with her down the stone path back to the cabana hidden in the green foliage. "But I also want to explore the whole area around here tonight."

"To see if the kids are staying close by," she said. "They'd have to be, wouldn't they?"

"Unless they have transportation. A car storage facility is near the airport. One of our men used to keep a car there, and the business offers free rides to and from the airport. As much as the boys' parents and the teens themselves visit Belize, they might just have a car stored there. We'll check out the surrounding area for any sign of them. I know their scent, so if they're anywhere in the area, I can track them."

"Wait," she said, stopping David on the path, her hand on his arm, his skin too hot, electrifying, his scent turning intrigued. She quickly released him. "How come your boss knows what excursions the kids have paid for but doesn't know where they're staying?"

"They used a credit card for the adventures, but not for lodging."

"Doesn't that seem a bit odd?"

"Maybe they maxed out the one card and used

another for the hotel. Martin hasn't been able to track another one yet. Either that or they paid cash. But the adventures are all located about a half hour from here, so I imagine they are staying in the vicinity. Maybe even here, if we're real lucky. I didn't smell their scent in the dining room, though, and nowhere out here, either."

When they reached their cabana, David unlocked the door and let Tammy walk in first.

As soon as they entered the living room, she smelled the scent of male jaguars, but no sign that anyone had been on the front porch except for past human tourists and her and David. Inside, the scent of three males now wafted in the air—David's and two others.

Chapter 5

TAMMY HEADED FOR HER BEDROOM, BUT DAVID SEIZED her arm, bringing her to an abrupt halt. She cast him a growly look, warning him to release her at once.

"It's them," he whispered.

"The kids?" she asked, her voice hushed and surprised. The teens appeared to have pursued her and David instead of the other way around.

"Wait here," David said.

Though agents in the Enforcer branch, like Tammy, were trained to use force when warranted, the agents in David's Special Ops branch were more used to employing lethal take-down methods.

Concerned David might react more violently than she would, Tammy shook her head. "You said they'd respond better to a woman."

"Fine," David grunted, but from the tone of his voice, his macho ego said otherwise.

David followed Tammy down the hall as she listened for any sounds other than the jungle noises outside the cabana. Nothing. If the boys were still here, they were not moving about.

She and David peeked into his room first. No one was in it, but his dresser drawers were all standing open. Her annoyance grew as she assumed the boys had rifled through her clothes as well.

They stalked into her room and discovered the same

thing—drawers open, culprits gone. Her chest of drawers stood open, and her neatly folded panties were all in a jumble now. Furious, she ground her teeth.

"They must have gotten word somehow that we were coming here, saw us go to dinner, and broke in," she said. "But I can't see how they'd know we were coming after them. Or what they could have been looking for in my underwear drawer."

"Agreed. I'm not sure, either. It's like they've been monitoring our moves ever since I was thrown in jail."

"Or before that? What if they knew you were tailing them to see if they broke any rules?"

"It's possible. So did they know I was listening in to their talk about the jaguar? Even specifically mentioned her so I would follow them here?" David let out his breath. "See if anything of yours in missing."

Everything appeared to be there, but Tammy smelled the three male jaguars' scents on her undergarments. She growled under her breath.

She returned to David's bedroom and peeked in. "Nothing of mine is missing. Anything of yours?"

"About a half-dozen condoms," David said, peering into the box.

She closed her gaping mouth. Finally finding her wits, she said, "Do you normally keep count?"

That earned her a cocky smile. He was too charming for his own good. "The box was brand-new and hadn't been opened yet." He gave her a sly wink. "You sure there's nothing missing from your room?"

"Nothing. So what is this all about? They wanted us to know that they're on to us?" She'd had the misconception that as an Enforcer, she and her top-gun JAG agent would easily have the upper hand with the teens. Clearly she was wrong.

"They're clever. I'll give them that. They didn't vandalize anything. Just let us know they know we're here." David tucked his box of condoms back in his chest of drawers.

"And stealing your condoms?"

"Shows they're into safe sex."

She rolled her eyes. "Won't that cramp your style, being a half dozen short?" she said sardonically.

He grinned at her, cleared his throat, and said, "I'm never short."

Her whole body flushed hot. She should be used to her brothers' double entendres by now, but she couldn't help reacting to that kind of comment coming from a man she barely knew and to whom she was more than a little attracted.

David stood there, waiting for her comeback.

She was changing the subject. "Okay, so what do we do about tomorrow? They know we're on to them, so they won't do the zip-line adventure, don't you think?"

"Maybe. We need to look for them now. See if we can sense them. The jungle surrounds the whole cabana, and it's dark enough since the sun sets so early—what, 6:30 or so—that we can shift outside and head out."

"What if they're watching?" As jaguar shifters, the teens could see them in the dark if they were observing them.

"They could be."

"Great. I'll shift inside. When I growl, let me out."

Jaguars didn't run in packs. Tammy wasn't used to shifting in front of others, except with her family when she was younger, and she didn't plan to change that scenario anytime soon. David didn't go outside like she expected him to, though. He stood at the front door watching her.

"What are you waiting for?" she asked, frustrated.

"I was going to ask you the same thing. As soon as you shift, I'll open the front door for you."

In disbelief, she stared at him. Men could be so thick-headed sometimes. She didn't want to strip naked in front of the teens *or* him.

Growling, she headed back to her bedroom and slammed the door. She heard him chuckle as his heavy footsteps approached the door.

"Or not. No one told me you were shy," he said, standing outside her room.

She quickly slipped out of her clothes, tossing them on her bed and ignoring him. Heck, did all the women he had worked with strip naked in front of him if they had to shift, no qualms about it?

In a fluid movement too quick for human eyes to comprehend, she shifted from human to jaguar, a beautiful blurring of forms. She felt wilder, more lithe, able to move stealthier and faster through the jungle than as a human. She batted the door with her paw to tell David to open it.

"I take that to mean you want out?" he asked.

She roared.

He laughed and opened the bedroom door. "I didn't want to open the door prematurely." She loped down the hall. "Beautiful." He headed for the front door where she already stood, waiting for him to open it, eager to find the boys.

"Don't run off without me," he said.

They'd already delayed way too long.

As soon as he opened the door, she dashed off. If the kids were watching, she was going to find them before they knew what hit them.

———

David cursed when Tammy disappeared into the jungle as he rushed to strip out of his clothes on the cabana's tile patio. He'd considered stripping to bare skin when he opened the door, but he was trying hard to make her feel comfortable around him.

He wasn't used to a female agent who was shy about stripping and shifting in front of him. He also hadn't had any romantic notions about any of them. Tammy was another story.

Was it Tammy's reluctance that intrigued him? Everyone giving him a hard time about her? He wasn't sure why, but he was fascinated with everything about her.

The more he got to know her, the less he understood her. He had really expected her to wait for him. After the incident in the police-station parking lot, he *should* have known better.

Agents had each other to watch their backs. Tammy was highly trained in combat as an Enforcer, and this was supposed to be a no-fighting mission. She had deadly claws and teeth in any case, but she was still a smaller female jaguar. If she had to fight a male jaguar, David thought she would be in a world of trouble.

He raced through mud from the recent rains, his jaguar paws sliding a little as he headed in the direction she had vanished. A few minutes later, he heard a jaguar roar—female, calling with news, not in distress—thank God. He switched course, diving through giant ferns until he found her. Her golden coat glowed in the filtered moonlight, her chin and belly white, and distinctive black rosettes patterning her coat—unique from any other jaguar. Now that he'd seen her as one, he would recognize her anytime, even if he wasn't close enough or the breeze wasn't blowing the right way for him to smell her delightful scent.

He looked up to a tree branch about five feet off the ground to see what she was observing and saw the oddest sight. One of his condoms filled with water was tied securely to a branch. A vine stretched from that branch to another tree branch several yards away. Another water-filled condom hung in the center of the vine. And one last makeshift balloon was attached to the second tree.

Tammy looked questioningly at him with her vivid blue jaguar eyes. Amused at the boys' shenanigans, he couldn't help giving her a big, toothy jaguar grin. She grunted and scrutinized the condom in the center, and then she began sniffing the ground to learn where the teens had taken off to.

David headed for the other tree and saw something red and glossy on the trunk. Peering closer, he spotted a tiny heart drawn on the pale gray bark. He sniffed at the substance. Lipstick. Watermelon. Tammy's.

It instantly made him think of her lip-glossed mouth and how kissable it had looked earlier when she was sipping her sweet rum drink, her lips sucking seductively on the straw.

He didn't want to show her the lipstick mark because

he was certain she hadn't realized she was missing the tube and she'd be further riled, but she needed to know. He took a deep breath and roared for her. Hidden by the foliage nearby, she dashed back in a flash, her spotted, golden tail swishing. He pointed his nose at the small red heart, accidentally touching it, and got a little on the tip of his nose.

She growled low, then looked at the red that must have been on his nose. Her pink tongue curled out, and before he knew what she was going to do, she took a lick. He was certain her sandpaper tongue washed the lipstick mark right off, but licking him was tantamount to a jaguar kiss, and hell, he wanted more.

Unfortunately for him, she took off running again, and he sprinted after her. They continued to search the whole area and found fresh tire track imprints in the mud, but the boys' trail had grown cold.

Despite planning to do this early tomorrow, David led Tammy to where the zip-line adventure would be to see if the boys had done anything there. Sure enough, after a long trek through the jungle, they found a condom filled with water tied to the platform where the zipper would start out. Another rubber was tied on the cable nearby, and the other at the end of the line. They finally found a lipstick heart drawn on the bottom wooden step from the platform where the zip line ended. Again, Tammy growled.

David was more than a little amused at the boys' mischief. He and his brother had never come up with anything quite as humorous or creative as this.

He and Tammy returned to their cabana, their legs, bellies, throats, and chins splattered with mud. When

they reached the back patio, Tammy batted at the faucet
for the shower, either trying to turn it on herself or telling him she wanted him to do it for her. Happy to oblige,
he shifted and twisted the nozzles on the shower until
the water was warm. When she nudged at him to get out
so she could wash in her jaguar form, he laughed.

"You *are* shy." He smiled, sighed, and headed back
into the cabana. He loved how human she really was.

When he returned, she was too busy enjoying the
shower to notice that he was *still naked* as she bit at the
stream of water. He chuckled, amused at her playfulness. He stepped into the shower and poured jasmine-
scented shampoo on her back. She turned her head and
growled a little, but it was more of an annoyance—a
"leave me alone" rather than "I'm ready to bite" growl.

He ignored her and began lathering her up, knowing she wouldn't like it if she tracked mud all through
the cabana and had to clean it up. Once she shifted into
human form, she'd have to wash the rest of the dirt off
her legs and feet in the bathroom sink, no easy feat.

"You'll thank me in the morning," he said.

Chapter 6

OH MY GOD, TAMMY THOUGHT FOR ABOUT THE TWELFTH time. She *really* tried not to see how hung David was as he leaned over her to wash her head, her back, and even her tail.

She could see the way he had become quite aroused even though she was in her jaguar form.

He crouched to wash her legs. She was muddy all over, so she was glad he was using soap on her. But this was way too personal, even if he was human and she was a cat. She could smell the water, the jungle, and one sexy, aroused male jaguar shifter.

David towered over her in the shower, reaching underneath to wash her belly. He probably couldn't really see what he was doing that easily, she thought. Just to make the chore less of an effort for him and quicker to accomplish, she lay down and rolled over on her back like a very big, satisfied cat. Only so he could ensure she didn't have splotches of mud on her belly.

He grinned, knowing that baring her throat and belly was the ultimate show of trust. She had to admit that she did feel like she could trust him, despite his wickedly hot grin.

Once he'd washed her chest, belly, and throat, she rolled over and got to her feet. She left the shower and shook off.

To her surprise and appreciation, he grabbed one of

the towels and began to dry her, careful to go only in the direction in which the hairs of her coat lay. No cat liked being rubbed the wrong way, jaguar shifters included.

"I'm warning you now. This towel's yours because you wouldn't shift and you got it all hairy. Don't complain if we get charged for having a pet in the place," David said.

If she could, she would have laughed. She licked his leg as a friendly thank-you. She recalled just how aroused he was. Good thing he couldn't tell she was blushing under her jaguar coat. She raced for the door, then looked back at him.

"The things I do for you." He hurried to join her and opened the door.

She yawned, her jaguar jaws opening wide, her tongue curling, and she realized just how tired she was. Once she was inside, he closed the door behind her and returned to the shower while she raced for the bedroom. She paused at his room and considered the size of the twin bunk beds. His feet would be hanging off the railing at the foot of the bed. Did he deserve it? She didn't think so now.

But she didn't want to give up the big bed, either. She sighed and retired to her bedroom. Shifting back to human form, she slipped into a pale blue tank top and a pair of blue bikini panties, the only sleepwear she'd brought, thinking her JAG partner would never see what she wore at night. Taking her toiletry bag to the bathroom, she fished out her hair dryer and blew her curls dry. She yawned again and headed back to the bedroom.

When David entered the cabana and shut the front door, she knew they needed to discuss what was going on with the boys, but she was too tired to sit up and talk with him in the living room. She envisioned keeling over on the couch and falling asleep in the middle of their discussion.

Her mind made up, she turned and called out from the hallway, "I'll share my bed with you. If you don't snore. No tossing and turning, either."

When he reached the hallway, he smiled at her standing in the doorway of her bedroom.

"I'll be quiet as a jaguar." He appeared eager to please, heading into his room with a quick stride, a towel slung low on his lean hips, his arousal tenting the terry-cloth fabric.

Tammy wasn't sure what she was getting into and hoped she wasn't making a big mistake. She climbed into bed and pulled the spread nearly to her shoulders. She thought about David's appearance as a jaguar. His coat was a distinctive tan, not as golden or orange as other jaguars, and he had less white on his belly and under his chin than she had. Beautiful. Just as beautiful as the way he looked in his human form. All hard body, muscular, tanned, lickable.

A few minutes later, he climbed into bed wearing only a pair of white boxers. She swore the queen-sized bed had shrunk to half its size because he took up so much of it.

"What do you think they're trying to tell us?" she asked, turning on her side to discuss what they'd found.

"It's definitely about the zip-line adventure. I don't have any doubt they know we know they were going to be there."

She shook her head. "They probably won't be there tomorrow. And we won't be able to catch them."

"I suspect you're right," David said, arms folded behind his head as he stared up at the canopy over the bed.

"So why the games?"

He glanced at her. "They're smart? They're bored? They're teens? How would I know?"

She let out her breath. "You said you were like them once."

"Okay, yeah. To an extent. But Wade and I bungee-jumped from bridges, borrowed boats to go out into deep waters to fish, went caving where we shouldn't have gone. Dangerous stuff like that. We didn't mess with JAG or Enforcer agents."

"What if it's as you say? You stood up for them at the shifter club. Got yourself taken to jail over it. Maybe they overheard something about the stolen jaguar and were looking into it, but you and I went after them. Maybe they're trying to show us the way."

"More like a wild-goose chase," David said.

She pondered that, wondering again how the boys would have known she and David had come after them. "Why wouldn't they just come out and tell us what they know?"

"That's what we have to find out. Once we catch and question them, we'll turn them over to Martin."

Tammy's parents had kept her brothers and her in line when they were that age. She couldn't understand why these kids were running loose without any supervision. "Why is it that their parents aren't watching over them?"

"Their parents are off in England at a medical conference this summer. They probably figure the boys are old enough to watch out for themselves."

"Yeah, right." She wondered what the kids' parents would think of the boys' actions. Would they have discounted them as typical teen pranks? Been angry with them?

Kids needed some guidance growing up. That made her wonder about David and his brother, and how come they had gotten into so much mischief that the Service wanted to take them in hand.

"And you? How come you and your brother got yourselves into so many dangerous situations as kids?"

"When our mother died, our dad was so devastated that he forgot about providing some…positive reinforcement and direction. Wade and I were on our own."

Tammy chewed on her bottom lip, wondering what to say. Now she felt guilty because she'd assumed he and his brother hadn't had a good reason to be out of control, other than having parents who ignored them, like these teens. She couldn't imagine not being as close to her mom as she was. Her dad, however…

She reached out and patted David's bare chest. His hot, hard bare chest. It just seemed a natural thing to do, but when she noted his heated gaze on her, she quickly withdrew her hand before he thought she was looking for some kitty-cat loving.

"I'm sorry, David. I didn't know." She wanted to know how his mother died, but she didn't want to ask if he didn't feel like sharing. "Were…your parents close?"

"Yeah. They were devoted to each other. Before we lost my mom, we shared a lot of family outings—camping, visits to the Amazon and Belize… Never a dull moment."

She hesitated to ask her next question, but she really

wanted to know the answer before she revealed anything to him about her own parents' situation.

"Your parents never…had any affairs?"

Ever since she'd discovered her father's infidelity, she'd wanted to talk to someone, but she hadn't known whom she could confide in. She didn't know if her mom knew about it, or what she would do if Tammy broke the news to her. Her brothers didn't know, and she was afraid of how they would react. She couldn't tell her cousins Maya and Connor. She'd only met them once and didn't know them well enough. Not that she knew David well, either. But since he was more or less a stranger, maybe he could be more objective. Unless he didn't think cheating on one's spouse was that big a deal.

When David closed his eyes and didn't answer her, she thought he'd fallen asleep.

"David?"

"No, I don't believe either of my parents ever cheated on the other. It's kind of hard for shifters to have an affair. For one thing, we can smell someone else's scent on someone."

She nearly snorted at that. She was the perfect case of being cheated on in a shifter relationship. "Unless the cheating party is away on trips and washes his clothes and himself before he returns home."

Again, David was quiet for a while. He shook his head. "Nah, don't think so." Then he looked at her with concern. "Yours?"

She felt her stomach fall as if she was in a hot air balloon that had suddenly lost a lot of air and was ready to crash. She shouldn't have brought it up. She wasn't ready to talk about it.

"How close are you to your brother?" she asked, unable to answer him just yet. If Tammy discussed this with David, she wanted to know if he would tell Wade. Then Wade would tell Maya, and Maya would tell Connor. Tammy didn't want her cousins to know. They hadn't even met her father and mother yet, and she didn't want to negatively influence them. What if the word got back to her brothers about the affair and they confronted their father?

David studied her. "Wade and I are close. Really close. We've always been. What about you and your brothers?"

She sighed. "As close as we can get."

"But I imagine they treat you like one of the guys."

"In the beginning. But now, not so much. They've become overprotective brothers."

"Yeah, I know," David said, his tone amused.

That didn't bode well. "What do you mean?"

"They called me. Each of them. Before we got together for this mission."

She stared at David, not believing her brothers would do that. Then again, all of them were in the JAG with David and, as such, were nearly like brothers. "*What* did they say?"

"Huntley warned me you only dated humans."

She growled.

"Everett told me you've ditched several partners. Even my own brother called and said I had to keep my hands off you or else."

She couldn't believe it! She barely knew Wade. "I'll kill them."

David laughed. "Does that mean you're interested in dating a JAG agent? You're not going to try to dump me on this mission? And I don't have to keep my hands to myself?"

"I *have* already tried to ditch you," Tammy reminded him, sidestepping his other two points. And now she was in bed with him, showing how well her efforts to ditch him were going.

He was too cute for his own good. She couldn't believe her brothers, and even David's, had warned him about her. As soon as she was done with this assignment—or sooner, if she could get hold of them—she'd have words with them over their interference. The nerve.

"But I've decided I might need you for this mission."

He waited.

She wasn't agreeing to anything else.

"*Okay*, so that means I still have to work harder to get you to agree to the other two conditions?"

She laughed, but he looked earnest! And she was thinking she needed to put on the brakes really quickly before she did something she'd regret—like giving any thought to dating him after the mission was over. After the disaster with the previous guy? The last thing she needed was to date another JAG agent anytime soon.

Chapter 7

DAVID LIKED THAT TAMMY HAD A SENSE OF HUMOR when it came to him. He wasn't all teasing, but he was glad she took his joking in stride. If a woman *couldn't* laugh with him or at him, she was a lost cause. He'd never had to toil this rigorously to get a woman to consider him date-worthy. He liked that Tammy set boundaries. Made her more of a challenge. Working for acceptance would make the reward all the more worthwhile.

He sighed dramatically. "I take that as a yes, I'll have to work harder at it."

Tammy shook her head but was smiling when she did it. That gave him hope.

What bothered him was that he assumed she needed to talk to him about one of her parents having an illicit affair. He wanted her to feel she could get whatever was bothering her off her chest. Had she not confided in her brothers?

When his own brother was upset about something, David had always been a great sounding board. Or so Wade seemed to believe. David liked to think he could be that for him or anyone else.

"Thanks for washing me," she said, startling him from his thoughts.

"Anytime." *Every time*. If he could have his hands on her when she was in any form, he would be a happy cat.

"Maybe we can get that bungalow tomorrow. After

what's happened today, I suspect we're not going to catch up to those two really quickly."

David didn't say anything, mulling over the possibilities and wondering why she'd suddenly changed her mind.

"We're already sharing the bed. I know that. But I'd really like to take a regular shower—indoors, without everyone watching. *If* anyone's watching."

"Sure." He was kind of surprised. But he'd suspected the shower situation bothered her when she hadn't shifted into human form to wash up.

"Do you think they were watching?" she asked.

He fought smiling because she looked so sincere. "If I were still a teenage boy…" David trailed off suggestively.

"Yeah, that's what I thought. And why I want a private shower. We get too muddy and sweaty in this muggy heat not to take showers, and I don't want to put on a show for the teens. I might corrupt their *innocence*."

David chuckled at that. "Yeah, you got it."

"What do you think the staff will think when they see the condoms hanging at the zip-lining place in the morning?"

"Kids' prank. Though they've probably never seen anything quite like it."

"Too bad you couldn't have salvaged them," she teased.

At least he *thought* she was kidding. "I *never* reuse used condoms—even if they haven't been used for the purpose intended."

"Good to know."

He heard a hint of a smile in her voice.

"You'll be watching for us to reach the platform you're on, but how will you see them before they get close enough for you to know it's them and not others on the tour?" she asked.

"I brought a pair of binoculars with me, great for hunting or bird-watching with a 420-feet field of view at a thousand yards."

"Okay, I think that will work well. We'll eat breakfast, and then we'll go to the zip-lining place."

He studied her, wondering if she truly was all right with zip-lining. "I really think you meeting up with them first would work the best. But…"

"What?" she asked.

"Are you sure you don't mind doing it?"

"Yeah. I agree I might have a better chance talking with the kids. Besides, I managed the seventy-five-foot Slide for Life at the Enforcer camp water-survival course—one little handlebar to hold on to, no safety net over the lake, no safety harness. The concept sounds similar to zip-lining, though they didn't call it that back then. The thirty-five-foot water drop was the same thing—shimmied out on a rope and dropped into the lake. I'm fine with it. At least here they have safety hookups. Right?"

"Yeah, they do." He knew she wasn't fine with it. He had smelled her nervousness when she told him earlier tonight that she wanted to be the one at the termination point and not flying through the canopy on a cable. She hadn't wanted to toss for it. She hadn't wanted to do it *period*. He admired her now for giving it a go just to see if they could make a connection with the teens.

"That's what we'll do, then." She was frowning, though.

"What are you thinking?"

"I'm still worried about the missing zoo cat. I hope we can catch the boys quickly, and I hope that they actually know something that will lead us to it."

"I'm going out on a limb here because I don't really know the kids that well," David said, "but I suspect if they believed the cat was in imminent danger, they would already have warned somebody of authority."

"Yeah, but you know how teens can be. Unreliable."

"I agree. But the way they were talking in the club, how they mentioned she was safe… I got the impression they knew it for sure."

"All right. I keep going back to the scenario of how you were following the kids. Here we are trying to chase them down, and they're the ones making all the calls. I still want to know how they knew where we were. How your boss knew so easily where they were scheduled to be, all except their lodging. I know Martin's got the manpower and the resources, but it seems too convenient to me."

"You're back to believing that this is a setup, you mean."

"Yes," she said. "That's exactly what I was thinking. That they somehow let your boss know where they were going to be."

"It's possible," David acknowledged.

"I don't believe this all has to do with fun and games," Tammy continued. "The boys seem too smart for that. Yes, they're playing with us, but I think they're also afraid of a real one-on-one confrontation. They don't know if they can trust us."

"But I protected them from the bouncer at the shifter club."

"Right. But you've been following them, and you were suddenly teamed with me to track the zoo cat I've been looking for."

"So without knowing why we were teamed up, maybe

they thought I was called in to deal with them more harshly if they had committed a more serious crime than underage drinking, like stealing the zoo cat."

"Maybe."

"What if they *did* steal her from the Oregon Zoo?"

She didn't say anything for a few minutes, mulling it over. "Why would they? I checked out the exhibit where she was being housed. Plenty of space to run in. Nicely treed. Running water in a man-made creek in the enclosure. If they did, it wasn't out of vigilante justice for an ill-treated jaguar."

"I don't know. I've let Martin know what we've found so far," David said.

She smiled a little. "Did you tell him about the condoms?"

He just grinned at her.

She yawned. "All right. I'm exhausted. Let's call it a night."

"Good night." David closed his eyes, but he couldn't stop taking in deep breaths of her jasmine soap and she-cat scent mixed into one delightful fragrance. He couldn't ignore the beat of her heart—or his—that told him he was way too turned on, and that she was feeling the same way. He couldn't help feeling the heat of her body and wanting to ratchet it up a few degrees, starting with a kiss.

A kiss. Hell, he'd never gone to bed with a woman when it meant total hands off. But lips…they didn't count, did they?

She'd closed her eyes, but she wasn't sleeping. She hadn't pulled away from him, giving him her back. That meant something. Didn't it?

He could ask. And she could say no.

He could kiss her, and when she got ready to slap him, he'd tell her it was a good-night kiss. And it would be. Unless she wanted more.

He could get lucky and she'd kiss him back.

Somehow it didn't seem right to go to bed with a woman and not at least kiss her good night.

She opened her eyes to see him looking down at her—well, he was judging her lips, but when they curved up a bit, he lifted his gaze to meet her eyes and saw she was watching him.

"What?" she asked.

He couldn't say it. David Patterson, who had no trouble interesting women in kisses and so much more, couldn't say it.

"Don't…tell…me. You want a good-night kiss," she said, but he wasn't certain whether she was offering or…not.

Not about to lose the opportunity, he placed his hand under her chin, lifted her face, and waited only the briefest period for her to pull away if she wasn't in the mood for this. When she didn't, he leaned down and kissed her mouth.

Soft, sweet, tasting of pineapple rum, nectar from the jaguar goddess herself.

He meant to go lightly, cautiously, sweetly. First kiss, first date—if he counted eating dinner with her at the romantically lit dining hall and running as jaguars in the jungle, and her licking his nose and later his leg as a jaguar as their first date. But she curled her fingers in his hair, pressed her hot little body against his, and kissed him back as if they had been dating for a good long while! As if she wanted him like he wanted her.

Now *this* was more like it. He moved his hand to her back and caressed her as their tongues mated. She nibbled on his lower lip, swept her warm, soft mouth across his cheek, and tugged tenderly on his earlobe with her teeth. He was burning up with desire.

He was ready to race back to his bedroom and grab one of his condoms when she kissed his forehead, pushed him gently away, and said, "'Night, tiger." She turned her back to him.

His motor was rumbling like a big cat in heaven. "Hot damn, woman," he said softly, still in the throes of passion, needing to douse the flame that was burning brightly. He throbbed with need.

She chuckled.

He lay on the bed, his arms folded beneath his head, and stared up at the canopy over the mattress. He smiled. If this was only the beginning, they definitely needed the air-conditioned bungalow for however long they were going to be here. A ceiling fan *wasn't* going to do it.

Chapter 8

TAMMY KNEW SHE SHOULDN'T HAVE ENCOURAGED David by kissing him back.

But she was furious that her brothers and his would warn him about her! Sure, she dated human types. That's because most of the jaguar shifters she'd met were either Enforcers or JAG agents, and they thought they were hot stuff. She liked dating humans—for a short while, nothing long-term—who weren't as arrogant.

As for other jaguar shifters? The ones she met outside of the job were usually trouble. The type she had to haul in for causing problems for their kind. Perps were definitely not dating material.

She had to admit she really liked David, despite him being a JAG agent. He was different from the others she knew. Maybe because he seemed genuinely interested in helping the teens and the missing cat. He'd understood her need for privacy earlier and given it to her. He had been protective when she'd run off into the jungle and caring enough to wash her.

She appreciated his concern about her going on the zip line when he had to suspect she wasn't fond of heights. And even that he'd upgrade their place using his own money. That he believed she would make more headway with the teens than he would. *That* showed he thought she was a valuable member of the team.

And she loved how they could discuss the situation

with each other, a meeting of the minds, and brainstorm a bit, unlike working with partners on some of her former missions who either didn't share with her or dictated and expected her to follow along. She couldn't say enough about how much David's approach meant to her.

Still, she felt reluctant to tell him about her father's affair. She loved her parents, but knowing this about her father and having nobody to share her secret with was eating her inside out.

The ceiling fan whirred as it whirled around and around. But she couldn't get cool. Not after that kiss. Not with David's sculpted body radiating so much heat. Not with the mosquito mesh surrounding the bed.

She threw off the bedcover, realizing she must have jerked it off David, too. She glanced at him. He smiled knowingly at her.

Moving to the bungalow was going to be the right move.

She thought again about the lipstick on the tree. She hadn't realized the teens had taken it. Was anything else missing from her toiletry bag? When she'd looked to see what was gone, she'd only glanced at her clothes in the drawers. And when she dried her hair, she still hadn't thought anything about it.

She let out her breath in annoyance and got out of bed.

"What's wrong?" David asked immediately.

"Nothing that important. I'm checking to see if the kids took anything else of mine besides the lipstick. I hadn't examined the bag that it was in."

The mattress creaked as he left the bed. She glanced over her shoulder at him. "You don't have to come with me."

"I never checked my razor kit, either."

She noted the sexy shadow of stubble just beginning to appear along his angular jaw. "Surely they wouldn't steal your razor. They probably aren't shaving much yet. Then again, who would think they would steal my lipstick?"

"I doubt they would have taken my razor," he said as he followed her into the bathroom. "But I won't be able to sleep if I'm wondering whether they absconded with anything else." He unzipped his shaving kit and poked around inside it.

"Missing anything?" she asked. "Doesn't look like anything else of mine is gone." She was relieved about that.

"My bottle of aftershave lotion. Wild Earth Essence— the fragrance of Indonesian sandalwood combined with patchouli."

She had to admit she would like smelling the aftershave on him, though only if he applied a hint of it— much more, and her sensitive sense of smell couldn't handle it. "The hippies wore patchouli—the odor of pot, sex, and forest. It's from the mint family," she said, recalling having read that somewhere.

"I never thought of it that way, but you're right."

She frowned at him, not meaning to, but still… "So you wear it to attract human women?" Here she was defending herself against her brother's claim that she only dated humans. Did David?

"I haven't dated a human since last year. Bad mistake."

"What happened?"

"I learned not to date a woman who had a former boyfriend who wasn't ready to let her go."

She waited for him to elaborate, but he didn't, though

she was dying to know what had happened. Not that it should matter, but it piqued her curiosity. Would Maya know? Maybe David's brother had told Maya and Tammy could ask her. "I don't remember you wearing it earlier before you took your shower." She zipped up her toiletry bag.

"I didn't need to. I wasn't planning on being with any human woman," he reiterated and smiled a little as if he thought she might care. "In truth, the fragrance also attracts jaguars and other kinds of big cats."

"Get out of here." She didn't believe it, yet he looked so sincere.

"Yeah, really. Zoos spray the fragrance in the big cats' enclosures. The cats need to smell new odors, like they do when they're in the wild. The fresh scents enrich their lives. Some of the perfumes and colognes are a real turn-on for the big cats. Researchers have used the fragrances at camera traps in the Maya Biosphere Reserve in Guatemala to gather a more precise estimate of how many jaguars actually live there. The cats love it and rub their cheeks against it. Sometimes they even wrap their forelegs around a tree, rubbing up and down it, collecting the scent, and leaving their own."

"Huh. How did I miss that bit of information?" Sounded like something she should have read. Sometimes her brothers joked about how she knew so much about the most trivial things. She slipped past David to return to bed. "Why would the boys take your aftershave?"

"Looking to hook up with some hot human girls? Or maybe some female jaguar shifters."

"They better watch out or they might end up with jaguars in estrus that don't shift," Tammy said.

David laughed. The sound was too deep, and the way the tips of his ears reddened, she wondered if he had experienced such a thing.

"Has it happened to you?"

He laughed again, but he wasn't telling.

She couldn't imagine facing a full-grown, all-jaguar male that wanted to mate with her. "Too bad the boys already wasted the half-dozen condoms they took from your box. If they do hook up with some girls, they goofed."

"Maybe I miscounted. Maybe they took more than that."

"How many were in the box?" She climbed into bed, never having imagined she'd be having this discussion with her JAG partner on a mission. Or that she'd be sharing a bed with him. Or that she'd kiss him good night.

"One hundred." He closed the mesh curtain around them and settled in next to her. "I admit I guessed at how many were gone."

She mulled that over, not believing he would get such a big box. That had to mean he had sex a lot, was bragging if anyone should see his jumbo box, or was the kind of guy who bought in large quantities, like her dad did. Even so, why did David bring the *whole* box of condoms instead of packing just a few? To keep them pristine? Or because he thought he'd get *really* lucky?

"Do you…always buy goods in bulk?"

He didn't say anything for a moment, the suspense killing her. He smiled at her as if he knew just what she was trying to learn. "Always. Saves money."

She closed her eyes and sighed. Maybe David *was* just like her dad. Her mother said she tried to leave Dad home when she went grocery shopping because he always bought the largest quantity he could. He explained that they'd saved money and trips to the store that way.

Her mother would grumble about the items going beyond their expiration date well before they were used up. When her brothers were still living at home, it wasn't so bad. But now that she and her brothers were living on their own, her mother was about to have a conniption because Dad kept buying in the same huge volume.

"The problem with getting items in bulk is that they expire before you can use them."

David cleared his throat. "They're brand-new. They have a couple of years or more before they expire."

She felt her whole body burning up. She wasn't talking about *his condoms*!

"Okay, the truth is that when you tore off and left me at the jailhouse, I was in a hell of a hurry to get back to my apartment and throw some stuff together. I didn't have time to tear open the new box and grab just a few," he said.

She smiled at the reference to her leaving him behind, just imagining him in a rush like that. In a hurry, and if she bought things in large quantities herself, she probably would have done the same thing—if she had been a guy. She had to give him high marks for practicing safe sex, but most of all, she appreciated the fact that he hadn't acted all macho and pretended he was just oversexed.

Thunder boomed nearby, and flashes of lightning lit up the window and the bedroom. The muggy heat made her want to strip to bare skin, if not for the hot and sexy half-naked man lying next to her. The circulating fan wasn't penetrating the mesh curtains sufficiently to cool her down.

Maybe she shouldn't have invited him into her bed. She sighed. Maybe she should move to the bunk bed and get naked.

She didn't know which was worse—being way too cold or being way too hot. She'd never get to sleep at this rate. She let out her breath.

"What?" David asked.

"I'm hot."

He chuckled. "You sure are."

—◇◇◇—

Waking early the next morning, David was instantly aware of two things: Tammy was gone, and the shower was running outside. First thought that popped into his head—she couldn't be in jaguar form or the door would be wide open. Unless she shifted outside. And he didn't think she would have. Not when she was worried about getting naked if the kids were watching. Hell, she wouldn't even shift in front of him. Second thought was that she was in human form, *totally nude*.

That brought a nice visual to mind. He wanted to ensure that the person showering outside really was Tammy. At least that's what he told himself.

He climbed out of bed, peeked out the glass door, and his jaw dropped.

Facing the jungle, her back to him, she was wearing a barely there string bikini. *Turn around*, he silently pleaded with her. He wanted to see the whole tamale. Although the backside was giving him heart palpitations. Toned ass, tanned, long legged, sweet. Actually, anything *but* sweet. A hot-pink metallic number that made his mouth water. Forget breakfast.

He was tempted to keep watching when she turned off the water, but he didn't want her to think he might be as bad as the boys.

Hell, he was looking out for her welfare. Just like any good fellow agent who was serving as her partner on a mission. He folded his arms and waited, observing. Besides, she was wearing a bathing suit. Not exactly fully clothed for the general public, as far as he was concerned, but she wasn't naked.

With her back still to him, she wrapped the towel around her bikini-clad body. He groaned with regret. When she turned around, she saw him peering out the glass door with a full-blown arousal pressing against his boxers. She had the nerve to smile.

Tammy had thought that if she took a shower before David woke, he wouldn't catch her at it. Glad she hadn't given David a full show, she figured it served him right to be observing her while she showered.

"Tongue's hanging out," she said as he opened the door for her and she moved past him.

"Hope you used all the warm water. Cold's about all I can handle for now," he said as he headed outside to wash.

After he showered, they went to the lodge, and he made arrangements at the front desk to rent the bungalow instead of the cabana. She hated to admit that she'd been worried it might already be rented. She was ready to enjoy air-conditioning at night after they spent their days in the jungle.

She must have looked concerned. He smiled down at her as they left the lodge and headed to the dining room. "No worries. It's ours for a week, if we need it for that long. They're cleaning it and said we could move in later this afternoon after the zip-line expedition."

"Good." She didn't want to shower in her swimsuit the whole time they were here.

As they entered the dining hall, his phone rang, the ringtone playing "What's New, Pussycat" by Tom Jones and making Tammy smile. When she had the chance, she had to get a cute ringtone for her phone like that.

"It's the boss." He answered it. "Yeah, we're working well as a team. I think we might have to make this more permanent."

They took a seat at a table as she cast David a look that said this was *not* going to be anything more than a temporary arrangement.

He winked at her and looked down at the menu as she ordered from hers. He motioned to the waitress that he wanted the same meal that Tammy was getting. The waitress left to put in their orders.

"Yeah, boss." David filled Martin in on the condom exhibition, looked up, and smiled at Tammy.

She felt her cheeks warm.

"Zip-lining right after we grab breakfast." David looked at her again, his green eyes twinkling. "I'll tell her. Talk to you when we have any news on our end. Out here."

"Well?" she asked.

"Martin said he can't wait to have the boys working for him. It'll be a real treat."

"Yeah, until they steal *his* condoms."

David chuckled. "Okay, so the news is that the boys aren't working alone."

"Great. There are more of them down here?"

"Not sure. But Martin had a couple of agents watching two other twin male teens, Peter and Hans Fenton. They're jaguar shifters, same age as the twins, and they have a similar home life. Dad is an engineer; mom works as a nurse. Neither is home to watch the boys. One of Martin's men overheard a phone conversation that one of the teens was having at the mall, mentioning something about a jaguar stolen from a zoo.

"Since the Oregon Zoo seems to be the only one missing a big cat, it's got to be the same case. The kids must be acquainted with each other, and they all know something about the cat. Before Martin could give the go-ahead to take the boys into custody to question them, they disappeared."

"Huh, great. And they're where now?"

"No idea."

"So kind of like where we are with the two teens we're looking into."

"Seems like it. Bright kids. Willful and creative."

"And the cat?" She still worried about the safety of the jaguar.

"I still think she's safe, or the boys wouldn't be leading us on like they are."

She sighed, never thinking that finding the missing zoo cat would be this difficult. Her phone rang, and she glanced at the caller ID. *Henry Thompson*.

Recalling that he was the man from the Oregon Zoo who had been trying to chase down his missing jaguar, and that she'd given him her number in case he had any further word about the cat, she answered the call. "Hi, this is Tammy Anderson. How can I help you?"

"Have…have you learned anything about the cat?"

"We're working on some leads. Nothing substantial yet. Anything on your end?"

"We've got extra security on the wolf exhibits. Never thought we'd have to do the same with the jaguar's enclosure. We've analyzed all the videos posted everywhere and haven't seen anyone who looked particularly suspicious. But it had been wet and misty for several days, so most people were wearing hooded rain jackets or carrying umbrellas. Typical Oregon weather, you know."

"What about…male teens. A group of two to four who were alone at the zoo, no adults with them?"

"I don't recall. I didn't look for anyone like that. I'll review the tapes again. Normally teens don't visit the zoo unless they're with a sponsored group or with their parents. It's not a favorite teen hangout."

"Okay. Well, we don't have anything here yet." She didn't want to get Thompson's hopes up. "I'll let you know as soon as I have some word."

"Yeah, thanks. Same here. I'll go back over those tapes and see if anything else stands out."

From what her cousin Maya had said, Thompson was totally hands-on in tracking down a missing zoo animal. She'd told Tammy that he'd only had trouble with wolves missing from the zoo in the past, so Tammy wondered why he wasn't still in Texas looking for his missing jaguar. Rumor was that Thompson had seen her brothers shift at Maya's garden center, but her brothers refused to confirm or deny it.

Allowing humans to know that jaguar shifters existed wasn't acceptable. Shifters were taught that if a human witnessed them shifting, the shifter had to turn the human. And if that wasn't possible… Tammy sighed.

Maybe Thompson was worried that the zoo's missing jaguar was a shifter and not all cat.

Tammy told David what Thompson had said, and they had a quick breakfast of fresh pineapple, bananas, and cereal before they headed to the zip-line adventure. Tammy's stomach was doing nervous flip-flops, and she wondered belatedly if she should have skipped breakfast. She appreciated how concerned David was that she couldn't manage heights. He didn't say so in so many words, but he did offer twice more to be the one traversing the zip line.

David took the short walk from their resort to the terminal platform and would stay there while she got into a van waiting for her at the lodge along with four others—a couple and their two teenage girls—who were zip-lining today. The boys weren't there.

Before she could ask about them, one of the guides going with them said, "Alex and Nate Taylor said they'd meet you at the starting point."

If so, that was good news, but then she had another thought. "Just meet *me*? Or did they also mention David Patterson?"

"Just you, *señorita*."

They had to have guessed that David would attempt to catch them at the other end. The kids were smart, she had to give them that. Would they even be at the zip-line platform? If not, she would just go through with this. Play the game a little while longer.

The van jostled and bounced along a winding, rutted, muddy road to the starting point.

Trying to get her nervousness under control, she rethought her choice of doing this instead of letting

David be the zipper. He would have looked forward to it. She was considering the whole idea with trepidation. *Scaredy-cat*, she thought to herself. She could do anything she put her mind to do.

When they arrived, she saw a guide waiting for them but no sign of the boys. "Did the Taylor boys already get here and ride the zip line?" she asked the man.

He shook his head.

She planned to let the family of four go first, to wait and see if the boys turned up late.

The family began arguing about who among them would go first, with one daughter adamant that she would go last because she was taking videos. The dad tried to be alpha and take charge of his family. Mom made the final decision as to who would go next, but they were still dallying with putting on their gear.

The guide, Juan, motioned for Tammy and said, "You're on the schedule to start first."

She frowned. "I was waiting for the Taylor boys."

"We can't wait on them, *señorita*. You can meet them at the other end if they show up."

So much for their well-thought-out plan. Letting out her breath in exasperation, Tammy stepped up to the base of a tall ladder and into a harness with straps around her legs that the guide tightened for a firm fit.

She strapped a smelly, greasy, sweaty helmet to her head, hating that part of her enhanced cat senses, though even as a human she would be able to smell the odor to some extent. She pulled on gloves that smelled just as bad—a combination of sweat, suede, and dirty sneakers—and were reinforced at the palm to hold on to one of the steel cables. The guide hooked her up to

a safety line, then preceded her, and she began the long
climb up the one-hundred-foot ladder to reach the top.

Boy, did she get a workout. After the hot, restless
night she'd had, she would have loved to curl up as a
cat in the branch of a tree and take a nap—not this high
up, though.

The platform was like a tree house high in the canopy
of the rainforest. The trees stretched even farther above
them. A breeze whipped about, and the platform seemed
to sway a little as the trees around her did, which gave
her a queasy feeling.

She was glad David wasn't with her because he
would smell her nervous—make that *terrified*—scent.
She hated that her jaguar half didn't quell the fear she
had of heights.

Juan attached the tether on the harness to the zip
line with a carabiner clip, and the safety line to the
same cable. "Just grab hold of the cable here and remember what we told you. To slow down, squeeze
your hand tight on the lower cable. If you get stuck,
just pull yourself along. Near the end of the ride, don't
start braking before you reach the other platform or
you *will* get stuck. Use your hand to stop yourself at
the end. Have fun. If you're afraid of heights, just
don't look down."

How could he tell? Her sweaty hands were enclosed
in the heavy-duty suede gloves, and she wasn't perspir-
ing anywhere else that he could see. Or maybe that was
a standard line he used with all tourists getting ready to
take the plunge.

She heard the first of the family members coming
up the ladder, the girl's helmeted head just cresting the

wooden platform. She was the one with the camcorder, and it was now or never.

Before Tammy could take a breath and attempt to rid herself of the fluttering in her stomach, she pushed off from the platform.

The ride would be over in about a minute if she didn't slow herself down. She wanted to see if the teen jaguar shifters were in the area, watching her, so she squeezed the cable to decelerate, even though she'd love to get the ride over with.

Despite her trepidation, she enjoyed the exhilaration of flying through the air like a bird, if she didn't look down. Being this high off the ground seemed surreal and unnatural.

Sliding down the cable for the 2,300-foot trip with the trees zipping by, she glanced at the area on either side of her. Though some zip lines were designed for speed, this one was set at an angle that would allow the viewer to see more of the canopy at a relaxed pace, even if she hadn't been slowing herself down further.

Though she couldn't see the terminal platform or David through the thick foliage, she could envision him with binoculars at the ready, looking for the boys. She wasn't certain he could observe them if they were hidden in the dense rainforest unless they were moving around and exposed enough.

A soggy breeze whipped around her face, the sound of the pulley sliding on the steel cable loud and grating like a giant zipper being unzipped, amplified because of her sensitive cat ears. Halfway to the ending point, movement in one of the trees several yards ahead caught her eye. She slowed her pace even further, hoping the family waiting on the platform behind her wouldn't mind. Given the angle at which the cable dipped, she was certain she wouldn't get stuck this far out. Gravity would propel her along once she let go of the cable.

A golden jaguar lazed along a sturdy tree branch, maybe ten feet below her and twenty feet away, his blue eyes studying her, his tongue hanging out. He was nearly a full-grown cat. His tail jerked up and down like a whip. That's what had caught her eye. As soon as their gazes met, he grinned—jaguar-style—showing off wicked teeth.

The breeze was blowing in the wrong direction so she couldn't smell his scent, but she was certain the big cat was one of the boys because no jaguar in his right mind would sit in a tree near where humans were zip-lining and remain there watching her. She tightened her hold on the cable, slowing herself to a stop. She could feel the pull of gravity wanting to move her forward, and she had to hold on tight to remain where she was for a few more seconds.

"Alex? Nate?" she called out. "We need to get the jaguar back to her home at the zoo. We need to talk."

The cat was looking just as alert, standing now, concerned.

Then the top cable that the pulley had been gliding on made a strange creaking noise. She felt it weaken, then heard the strain and the sudden crack as the steel cable snapped.

Chapter 9

TAMMY SCREAMED. THANK GOD, SHE'D TIGHTENED HER hold on the lower cable with her left hand just in time. The upper cable that the pulley and her safety line were attached to had snapped in half just ahead of her. The two pieces of steel yanked back from each other like lovers separated. The one threaded through her pulley jerked away like a steel bird with wings and fell to the jungle floor.

The safety carabiner that had held her to the cable dangled from the tether attached to her harness, swinging like a pendulum counting the seconds until her fall. She gripped the lower cable tighter with her left hand, hanging on for dear life and praying to God this one didn't break, too.

She swung her right hand up to grasp the cable, grabbed hold, and took a deep breath. She was probably still about fifty feet in the air. A drop from this height would kill her.

Cold sweat gathered on her skin. Her heart was beating as if she were running in a marathon. Her arm muscles were stretched from bearing her weight, adrenaline pumping through her blood.

Birds chirped, the bugs played their noisy tunes, and frogs croaked as if nothing was the matter. Life for them went on as usual, but all of that seemed to fade into the background as *her* life hung in the balance.

She was breathing too fast. Terrified. *Breathe in. Breathe out.*

The jaguar stared at her, his eyes wide. His every muscle filled with tension, he whipped his tail back and forth. His whole body said he was ready to come to her rescue, but she knew he couldn't do anything for her.

The landing platform ahead of her was visible now, but nearly twelve hundred feet away, merely a small point in the distance.

She was glad she'd worn a long-sleeved shirt and camo pants to shield her from the sun and bugs, but now her hiking boots felt heavy, the weight pulling on her arms even more. The extra weight of the pulley, safety line, carabiners, and the harness added useless pounds. She could do without the extra weight, and if she could, she'd kick it all free.

She realized she didn't have much of a choice. She could wait for someone to come rescue her, and worry that another body weighing down this cable would snap it in two, or that the vibration would shake her loose and she'd fall. Or she could rescue herself, which could be just as dangerous.

Her arms were tiring more with each passing second, and she was mobilized into action by the fear that she couldn't hold on forever and that this cable could break at any moment. Praying she wouldn't fall, she had to reposition her hands. When the pulley had dropped off the cable and she'd fallen, her left hand still held the second cable and was in the correct position. But as she'd swung up to grasp the cable with her free hand, she was facing toward the cat, her right hand in the same position as her left. She needed to release the cable with

her right hand, hope she didn't fall, and turn her hand
inward toward her body.

Armed with binoculars, David watched in horror as the
steel cable above Tammy snapped in two and fell away.
Tammy fell from the hookup, dangling from the remaining cable by only one hand. His whole body turned to
ice. He shouted orders as the guide called someone on
a radio.

"Tammy! Hold on!" God, if only he had been the one
on the zip line instead of her. His heart was drumming
so hard he could barely think straight.

Someone would have to come from above to rescue
her, but he could envision the guide zipping down the
cable and accidentally shaking her loose. He'd seen a
guide slam into a zipper once to send the woman on
her way when she got stuck in the middle of a cable
and couldn't move. In Tammy's case, since she wasn't
attached to the cable any longer, the guide would have to
approach her slowly and lock his legs around her waist.
He could hook her up to a safety line at the very least. If
he could get hold of her pulley, he might be able to hook
her up again to the zip line.

David watched as she finally managed to grab the
cable with her free hand. But she couldn't hold on forever.

"*Sí, sí,*" the guide next to him said to the other person
on the line.

David knew enough Spanish to get the gist of the
conversation, but he figured the man was being careful
about what he said. They were afraid an additional body
on the line would snap the cable, not because anything

was wrong with it. After the other snapped, this one had become suspect also. From what David and Tammy were told when they signed up, the weight limit for the cable with a man and woman on it would exceed the maximum amount.

Tammy was on her own.

———~~~———

A fresh shot of adrenaline flooded Tammy's blood as a good dose of fear invaded her thoughts. She squeezed her eyes shut for a moment. Praying her left hand wouldn't lose its grip on the cable when she let go with her right, she released. And swung precariously. The carabiners and pulley swayed with her, threatening to make her lose her grip. She quickly reached up to grab the cable the correct way.

Thanking the heavens above, she felt the hard steel gripped in her tight-gloved grasp. *Done*. Her arms were shaking with weariness. She had to swing her leg up and over the cable without losing her grip.

The longer she waited, the wearier she became. She tightened her hold and kicked up, missing catching the heel of her boot on the cable by mere inches. Another round of gooseflesh erupted as she swung back on the cable. She waited. Caught her breath. Tried again.

This time she got a leg up and was able to rest her arms for a minute. She swung her other leg, giving her momentum to lift her body on top of the cable. Now she was on top, left hand ahead of her, right foot hooked over the cable, left leg hanging loose just like she had learned at survival training. Only she never thought she'd be traversing a steel cable in the canopy of the rainforest in Belize, fifty feet above the ground, when this was meant to be something fun—and not dangerous.

Of course that brought to mind signing the form saying the company wasn't responsible for death and injury.

Someone was yelling from the platform behind her. And from the one ahead of her. They were too far away and she couldn't make out their words. The jaguar roared in a jaguar's huffing sort of way.

Did they want her to stop what she was doing? No one was coming to get her from the platform behind her, maybe afraid like she was that the remaining cable might also break with additional weight and stress put on it. But she couldn't just hang on to the cable all day. She began to pull herself toward the terminal platform, inching along on top of the cable.

All around her, the jungle teemed with wildlife, parrots resettling in trees, their bright blue feathers catching her eye, the fragrance of orchids surrounding her. The woody vines of lianas were wrapped around the trees, some hanging loose, some as thick as her arms, but all well out of reach. If she could have grabbed one, she could have swung to a tree branch or slid to the rainforest floor. She craved feeling the earth beneath her feet again.

She looked below her at the muddy ground so far away. Her stomach somersaulting, she broke out in a cold sweat. She should have taken the guide's advice and not looked down.

Then she had the thought she could swing the pulley up and connect it to the cable she was straddling. She could glide into home base in seconds. She'd watched the way the guide had fastened it. Heart thundering, she held on with her left hand with a fierce grip and began to reach down with her right, trying to feel for the tethers. She found one. She wished she could just swing it up on top of the cable, but from her precarious position, she was afraid she'd knock herself off. She began to painstakingly draw it up, letting her fingers slip down the tether until she felt the pulley at her fingertips.

To attach it to the cable, she'd have to unhook one of the carabiners and attach the pulley with the free carabiner. That meant she needed two hands to do it. If she lost her balance, she would fall.

The jaguar standing on the trunk branch roared again. Tammy wondered what the guides for the zip-line excursion were thinking. A wild jaguar was out to get her? Waiting for her to fall so he could have a ready meal?

She locked her legs around the cable and prayed her cat balance would help to keep her stable enough. She got the first carabiner hooked onto the cable, but as she unhooked the other carabiner to seat the pulley in place, she lost her balance. She swung underneath the cable, her heart nearly stopping. Feeling every muscle stretched to the limit, she let go with her left leg. She swung it and gave herself momentum, so she could clamber back on top before she became too tired.

Success!

Back on top, she took several deep, refreshing breaths to calm her racing heart. She tried unhooking the carabiner again. This time she managed to reattach it so that the pulley was in place on top of the cable. *Yes!*

Hooked up, she only had to climb off the cable now and release her hold. She hoped to God she had hooked everything up right, and that the cable was still sturdy enough to hold her for the remainder of the ride.

Praying this would work, she moved her leg off the cable, dropped to where she was still holding on to it as if she was ready to do a pull-up, and…released.

———∞———

Eyes glued to the binoculars, David swore he was going to have a heart seizure. And yet, from the moment the upper cable had snapped in two, he had felt his admiration for Tammy increase a hundredfold, not only for her courage, resourcefulness, and strength, but for not giving up.

She swung in her harness seat before the pulley carried her onward, and she flew toward him. No brakes applied this time. He still couldn't feel any relief as she zipped along the cable like nothing had been the matter only seconds earlier. Until she was on the platform, he wouldn't feel she was safe.

He pulled the binoculars away as she grew closer and slowed down at the last second just as she landed on the deck. Before the guide could unhook her, David pulled her into his arms and held her tight against him, not wanting to let go. "Damn, woman, you nearly gave me a heart attack."

She actually smiled at him, and it was the most beautiful sight in the world.

He quickly stepped back as the guide hurried to unhook her. David helped her out of her harness before the guide could. She was shaking hard, the adrenaline still rushing through her blood. His was, too, and he fumbled a little with her buckles.

The guide apologized several times as David embraced Tammy again. When they reached ground ten feet below the landing, they were met with applause from several other tourists standing around the ladder.

Someone offered medical assistance. David thought *he* could use some. But Tammy waved the man away.

"Are you okay, Tammy?" David asked, so shaken his darn voice crackled. He was supposed to be the pillar of strength. Strong, tough Golden Claw Special Forces agent.

"Yes, let's go," she said, her voice wavering a little.

Someone offered them a ride to their resort, but it was not that far a walk and Tammy shook her head. "I want to walk. Thank you."

The family that had been behind Tammy rushed up to see them. They must have gone back down the ladder from the starting platform after the line snapped and been given a ride here, Tammy thought with relief. The husband and wife expressed their gratitude that Tammy had made it back all right. The teen with the camcorder said, "That was too cool. I caught it all! If you want a copy, we can send you the video."

"I don't think so," Tammy said, shaking her head.

"Here, send it to me," David said and gave the girl his email address. "For your kids' sakes when you have them," he explained to Tammy. "They'd want to know how their mother handled a situation in a crisis."

She groaned, but David thanked the girl, wrapped his arm around Tammy's waist, and walked her through the jungle to their cabana. He still didn't want to let her go, whether or not she was feeling more secure now that she had her feet firmly planted on the ground.

As much as he hated to admit it, he was feeling insecure. He hadn't felt that helpless since he was about five and lost his way in the dark after he and Wade had a fight on vacation. They'd gone off in different directions in the jungle. Boy, did he and Wade get holy hell for it, too, since they were supposed to be asleep in their hut while Mom and Dad were off hunting.

"When we get home, I mean, *really* get home, I'm taking you out to any kind of dinner you'd prefer," he said. He wanted to do more for her, anything. He was just so grateful she was alive and well.

"Steak and the theater."

He couldn't believe she had agreed so quickly! He thought he'd have to convince her first. "You got it."

She glanced at him. "I'm talking theater as in a play, not a movie."

"What? You don't think I have any culture?"

She chuckled, and from the impish expression on her face, she didn't seem to believe he was as enthusiastic about seeing the play as he was about escorting her to it.

Chapter 10

"IF THERE EVER IS A NEXT TIME TO TAKE THE ZIP-LINE adventure, you can go," Tammy said. "I'll wait for you at the other end."

"Hey, I don't blame you there." He would have switched places with her in a heartbeat. "Are you really okay, Tammy?"

"Yeah, I am."

When they reached their cabana, she headed down another path into the jungle.

"Where are you going?" he asked, concerned.

"Didn't you hear the jaguar roar?"

"Yeah, was it one of the boys?"

"I'm sure of it. He was watching me, looking like he wanted to rescue me from my little zip-line disaster. Maybe now they'll be more receptive to meeting with us. Otherwise, maybe we can find their trail."

"So was the jaguar you saw very visible or being re-clusive? I never saw him in the dense foliage, even with the binoculars."

"He was sitting in a tree in plain view of the cable, watching for me, or for you, possibly, thinking that you would be the one to go on the zip line, even though they had left a message with the guide that they would meet me at the platform. Had one of those family members gone first and seen him, he would have given them a real surprise. Did the guide at your end hear him roaring?"

Tammy asked, heading in the direction where the jaguar had been when she'd seen him in the tree. When they were far enough from any sign of people, she stopped and began stripping.

David raised his eyebrows—she wasn't being shy now—but he didn't say anything about it.

"We did. The guide wondered what was up. I assumed it was one of the boys in jaguar form, alerting his brother or even me of the trouble you were in. I suspect they aren't quite ready to approach us yet, or they might have met us at the platform," David warned as he hurried to take off his T-shirt. "What if one of the boys steals our clothes?"

"I don't think they will. The one I saw looked like he wanted to help me when I was stuck. If they do steal our clothes, *they'll* be in the worst sort of trouble." She didn't even want to think about that, though she and David could return to the cabana at nightfall in their jaguar forms, since their lodging wasn't too far away and it was surrounded by foliage. Thinking further, she realized that wouldn't work. They needed to move to the bungalow when they returned, so they couldn't wait until dark. They didn't have time to go back to the cabana and change and then come all the way back here.

"Do you believe the cable was tampered with, or that it just broke by accident?"

"No telling. A competitor running a zip-line operation could have been responsible. Or it could just be an overused or defective cable. Safety personnel aren't monitoring a lot of these places that closely," David said. No matter who was to blame, David was ready to take a jaguar-sized bite out of them.

"Yeah. That's what I thought. Have you ever heard of actual cases of cables snapping like that when someone was on them at these adventure sites? One of the cables for the Slide for Life snapped during survival training when an instructor was demonstrating the technique to new Enforcer recruits six months before I had to take the course. He fell to his death from seventy-five feet, but I thought the resorts would be a little more careful, afraid of being sued."

"A few are. Considering the number of people using zip lines, the number of cable failures is small."

"Survival rate?"

"None."

A shiver stole through her as she thought of dangling one-handed from the cable. "Good thing my reaction time is quicker and my hearing is better than a regular human's. I heard the steel *ripping* and tightened my hold on the lower cable before the top one snapped in two."

"I'll say. My heart is still drumming faster."

"I thought it was just because you were so glad to see me."

He laughed and shucked the rest of his clothes. "Hell, that, too."

She finished undressing, shifted, and bolted toward the ceiba tree where she'd spied the jaguar, keeping the remaining zip-line cable in sight so she'd know she was headed in the right direction.

Even if investigators were checking the broken cable, which would have snapped back toward the platforms, she and David should be well out of their sight. She could maneuver much more easily through the jungle as a jaguar than as a human, but even so, it was taking her precious time to get there. She felt David move beside her, the heat of his body, a brush of his fur against hers.

He seemed as shaken up as she had been over the whole incident and was sticking closer to her than she thought necessary. She had to admit she liked the way he'd been so concerned and even offered to take her to dinner. And he'd agreed to the theater, too.

She smelled his delightful, spicy male jaguar scent. David didn't need any of that human-produced Wild Earth Essence fragrance to get her attention.

Going after the teen jaguar was her mission now, but she really needed this—the run on solid ground, muddy as it was, smelling the earth and vegetation around her—to feel connected with all of it. The run helped smooth her raw, jagged nerves.

She truly was glad David was with her on this mission, the first time she really liked having a partner. The other two JAG agents she'd worked with would have told her to stay behind while they investigated the *dangerous* situation. Not because they would have worried about her, but because they thought she would get in their way.

She'd thought David would react the same way after her life-threatening ordeal, and she really appreciated that he hadn't. They finally reached the tree where she had seen the jaguar standing on the branch and smelled the same scent that she had picked up in their cabana, confirming it had been one of the teens. She wondered if the boy had intended to draw her and David into the jungle after they were at the zip line today.

Jumping onto a branch, she looked up, knowing she'd have to go a lot higher in the tree to reach the branch where the teen had been. She didn't mind going up as a cat, though about twenty feet high was usually the limit for her. She normally didn't need to go much higher than that.

Coming down, she was all right as long as she concentrated on the next branch she'd jump to and not the ground. Her cat's balance lessened her fear of heights.

So when David jumped onto the branch next to her, grunted, and looked up, indicating—she thought—that he would go instead of her, she shook her head. She could do this. She wanted to do this. She needed to.

She leaped onto another branch, and another, then one more until she was where the male had been resting while David waited below for her. He'd jumped down and was searching the forest floor for where the teen had raced off to. A few orange jaguar hairs clung to the branch, but what really caught her attention were a pineapple and a bunch of bananas set up in the crook of the tree, almost like a peace offering. She didn't remember seeing them there when she was hanging from the cable.

She couldn't figure the two boys out. As jaguars, she and David had no way to carry the fruit back to their rental unit except with their teeth, just like the boys must have done to bring it up here. But why?

She could envision one of the kids taking pictures of an Enforcer and a JAG agent in jaguar form hauling a pineapple and a bunch of bananas back to their clothes, then posting the images on Facebook or something. She could imagine that cocky Quinn Singleterry snickering about what they were doing down here in Belize.

She jumped down from the tree and joined David. Hearing men off in the distance talking about the cable, she knew they'd have to wait until later to inspect the break. They followed the trail the boy had left when he climbed down the tree. They explored for some time, but when they lost the teen's tracks at a river, Tammy stared across the dark water. They'd never found the other boy's trail, if he'd even been there. The teens *were* bright. If the JAG branch could train them, she thought they'd make good Golden Claw agents.

After exchanging glances of agreement with David, they headed back. Tammy prayed her clothes and David's were still where they had left them. When they arrived at the spot and saw their jeans, boots, and shirts still piled where they had shucked them, she let out her breath with relief.

After scanning the vegetation and observing no sign of any jaguars, she turned to see what David was doing. He'd already shifted, dressed, and was patiently waiting for her. Her brothers would have chided her for being so slow and pushed at her to hurry it up.

"If you want, I can carry your clothes and you can shift back at the cabana," he offered, as if understanding her hesitation.

She hated to be this indecisive. She shook her head, and gentleman he was—except for this morning when he'd watched her shower in her bikini—he turned away. She shifted and threw on her clothes as quickly as she could.

"What's up with these kids?" she asked as they headed back to their cabana.

"They're looking for attention."

"They've certainly got ours. Did you see the fruit?" She glanced at David.

"No, where?"

"A pineapple and a bunch of green bananas were arranged in the crook of the tree branch. Do you figure the fruit was a peace offering of sorts?"

"To appease the jaguar god and goddess," he joked. "Were they there when you first saw the jaguar?"

"I don't know. When I first saw him, I was concentrating on him, trying to smell his scent, but the breeze was blowing the wrong way. I…I just can't remember." She shook her head. "What did they sign up to do tomorrow?"

"Waterfall rappelling and swimming in the natural pool below it. One-hundred-foot drop to the pool. If you want to stay topside and watch for the teens, you can."

After the zip-lining disaster, she seriously thought of agreeing. But she didn't want to let on to anyone—the boys included—that she couldn't handle it after what she'd been through.

"And miss swimming in the water after trekking through the hot, steamy jungle? Not on your life."

He smiled at her comment, his expression one of admiration. She liked that she seemed to have earned his respect.

"I've gone rappelling off a one-hundred-foot tower, and as long as we're not going face-first like in Australian rappelling, I'm good with it," she said. "Well, unless I was in a firefight. Then I'd need my weapon trained on the ground as I rappelled."

"You'd definitely be fearsome. *I'd* think twice about tackling you," he said.

She smiled.

"So tomorrow, we'll have to wear long pants, bug spray, and hiking boots, and take a change of clothes or wear a bathing suit underneath."

"Do you have a bathing suit?"

"Yeah, I have one. Just regular old swim trunks, though. Nothing like what you were wearing this morning." He glanced at her, a hint of a smile curving his mouth. "Speaking of which, have you got something else to wear?"

"Why?

"The water might be a little rough. I'd hate to see you lose your suit."

"I'm surprised you'd say so."

He laughed. "Okay, if we're being honest, I'd hate for anyone *else* to see you lose your suit."

She chuckled. "I like it when you're being honest."

As soon as they reached their cabana, David said, "I'll run off and get the key to the bungalow. It should be ready by now."

"Okay. I'll start packing."

She couldn't wait to move to the bungalow and shower inside, but all those thoughts fled when she entered the cabana and found the teens' fresh scents in the place, meaning they had been here recently. Her heartbeat ratcheted up a notch. She stormed into the bedroom and found David's and her bags were missing. She swore under her breath as she checked the drawers. All were empty.

David walked into the cabana, and before he could say a word, she spoke first. "They've taken our luggage and all our clothes. I will kill both of them."

"I would agree, but I just can't believe they'd steal our luggage," David said, looking in the bathroom. "Our stuff in here is also gone."

"Believe it! Their scents are fresh in here and our bags have vanished."

"Maybe the clerk at the lodging desk had them removed and placed in the bungalow because they needed the cabana vacated to ready it for other guests."

"That doesn't explain the teens' fresh scent in the cabana." And after the one boy seemed concerned for her welfare and offering them the fruit, she really couldn't understand their behavior.

Instead of going to the main lodge, she headed in the direction of the bungalow to see if by some miracle the kids had deposited their stuff there.

"If I'm right about the teens—that they didn't steal our stuff…" He trailed off as he closed the door to the cabana and quickly caught up to her.

"If you're right, what?"

"Maybe you'll believe the boys aren't all that bad."

"I'll believe it when I see it. Besides, not only did they take our bags, they *packed* them."

David didn't appear to think that was such a bad thing. She frowned at him. "I don't like having every one of the male persuasion handling my *personal items*."

Light dawning, he nodded. "I agree," he said.

She suspected he agreed about the boys not handling her personal items, but not necessarily himself.

Despite her ire, when they drew nearer their rental unit, she felt her whole outlook brighten.

A lovely terra-cotta tile porch wrapped around the bungalow. Colorful hammocks hung from the porch roof, and a chaise lounge for sunning begged for attention. The building looked new.

"I *thought* you might like this place better." David unlocked the door and they headed for the bedroom, though she already smelled the teens' scents in the place. In the bedroom, his and her bags were sitting on either side of the bed.

She closed her gaping mouth.

"Looks like they're trying to get on our good side," David said.

Since the black bags looked identical, she grabbed the ID tag on the one on the right side of the bed.

"This is mine over here." Her skin prickling with unease, she glanced at David. "Just like where I slept last night in the bed in the cabana. They couldn't have sneaked into the cabana last night and seen us sleeping, could they have?"

"No. They would have smelled which side of the bed we each slept on."

"So now they're our luggage valets?" She was more confused about the boys' intentions now than ever. "I don't understand them."

"I don't know. It seems to me they're trying to make amends or something."

"Sure seems an odd way to go about it." Though she did appreciate the fact that the teens seemed to be trying hard to win their favor, even if not in an acceptable manner. After the run through the jungle and being stuck in the harness on the zip line for what seemed like forever, she added, "I'm taking a shower before we have lunch."

David opened the door on the opposite side of the bedroom. "Here's the shower."

"What? I thought this bungalow had an indoor shower." She hurried to peer outside.

This one was lovely, surrounded by high stucco walls with a tall, cypress locking gate on one side and featuring more of the terra-cotta tile floors. Potted plants hung on the walls, and at the far side, a chrome showerhead arched overhead. Jungle trees stretched toward the heavens, but they were too far from the walled-in outdoor shower for anyone to see in—if any jaguar happened to be lounging in a tree overhead.

Now this, she could handle. She loved it.

"There's another inside also," he said. "But this one is plenty private, too. You can have the indoor one. I'll take this one."

"Super." She went back inside to check out the other bathroom. This one was just as lovely with its tiled-in shower and marble sink, great for at night, but...the larger outdoor shower appealed for this afternoon. She grabbed a towel and walked into the bedroom where David was unpacking his suitcase. She fished around in her bag, seized her shampoo, and headed for the outdoor shower.

He paused to look at Tammy, her towel draped over her arm, soap in hand. She was sure she'd rendered him speechless as she continued on her way outside and closed the bedroom door.

She set her towel on a wooden bench near the shower and turned the water on. As soon as she began to strip out of her clothes—boots, jeans, shirt—the door opened. Not turning to look, she ditched her black bikini and bra.

With her back still to David, she said, "You can use the other shower."

"I specifically got this place so you could have the indoor one," he said, his voice growing closer, huskier, interested.

In a hurry, she ducked under the water and soaped herself up. "You'll have to wait your turn."

"You don't want to share? We're sharing the bed already. You liked the way I washed you. And we need to hurry if we're going to make it in time for lunch."

She glanced over her shoulder at him, the warm water sluicing down her skin. "If you share a shower with me, you might forget what we need to do next, and we wouldn't make it in time for lunch anyway."

He began to strip off his clothes. "I'd never be *that* distracted."

"Oh yeah?" She didn't believe it for a minute. If she hadn't been dying to eat, she might even be tempted to prove it to him.

But she could take a really quick shower, too. Before he could join her, she moved out of the warm spray of water, grabbed her towel, and covered herself, smiling.

His mouth curved up in a devilish way. "Hell, we aren't in *that* much of a hurry. You had to have missed cleaning a lot of places."

"Got to dry my hair." She gave him a quick once-over—he was a god in the flesh, all tanned, glistening muscle, and way too sexy for her own good—grabbed her clothes, and headed inside.

But not before she heard him say, "Tease."

Chapter 11

AS SOON AS TAMMY WALKED INTO THE BEDROOM, David's cell began ringing. She hurried to get it, dumping her clothes on the bed before she grabbed his phone off the bedside table. *Martin*, David's boss.

She answered it right away. "David's in the shower. What's up?"

"Oh, Tammy. Your boss relayed to me that he couldn't get hold of you."

Probably when she was running as a cat. She was glad he hadn't tried to get hold of her when she was in the middle of her zip-line adventure.

"I was trying to reach David. We still haven't located the other two boys, but we found out that they are close friends with the two you're after, the Taylors, and they all live in Texas," Martin said over the phone.

Tammy's hair was dripping wet, the towel wrapped securely around her. Her skin prickled with chill bumps, courtesy of the air conditioner running full blast. With the phone to her ear, she hurried through the bungalow, looking for the controller for the air conditioner. "Okay, so did the teens steal the missing zoo cat?"

"We've checked a variety of sources, but it looks like all four teens have alibis at the time that the zoo cat went missing."

"Okay." She'd need to let Henry Thompson from the

Oregon Zoo know that looking through the video footage wouldn't help.

"The boys wouldn't have had an easy time of getting to Oregon and stealing a cat from a zoo without someone noticing they were missing from home and leaving a trail to that location. What I can't figure out is if they just wanted to steal a cat, why not from one of the local zoos in Texas instead?"

"There must be something special about *this* cat," she said.

"That's what we're figuring. We're trying to determine if any of the boys have any connection to someone in Portland. So far, we haven't found any."

Tammy found the AC controller and turned it off. David walked into the sitting area dressed, his hair wet.

"Your boss," she said to David.

He nodded, but he didn't make a move to take the phone from her. She explained to Martin what had happened to them today—the boys not showing up for the zip-line excursion, the accident, seeing the jaguar in the tree and how he acted like he wanted to help Tammy, and the boys giving them a peace offering of fruit and moving their luggage to the bungalow. At first she was worried Martin would overreact to the zip-line fiasco, but all he said was, "Wait, go back to the zip-line incident."

She let out a breath and started over again. The first time she'd washed over the details, just giving the mere facts—the cable broke, but she made it to the other side safely.

Martin hesitated way too long to respond, and she was certain he was going to have some investigators of his own look into the matter. "Sounds to me like you're making inroads with the boys. Good work."

"What about the other kids?" Tammy asked.

"Vanished. They didn't go home. But we couldn't find any record that they've flown to Belize to join the Taylor boys, either. We're still looking for them."

"Okay, so is that what you called about, or…?" she asked, not wanting to give up the phone to David and have to hear other news secondhand.

David smiled at her, appearing to know just what she was thinking. His gaze drifted over her towel, the terry cloth clinging to her wet curves. She might have the phone, but she couldn't get dressed until she gave it up, and that meant David was making the most of her undressed state in an appreciative way.

"No, that's it for now," Martin said.

"Thanks. I'll let you talk to David." She turned off speakerphone, handed the cell to him, and returned to the bedroom to dress.

—⁓—

"Yeah, boss?" David said, watching Tammy enter the bedroom with the towel wrapped around her provocative, wet body. She shut the door.

"Watch out for her, all right?" Martin said over the phone.

"You got that."

"Something's really wrong here. The kids haven't done anything quite like this before. Something's up. And the zip-line incident? It might be just a faulty cable like Tammy said, but you know me—I don't like that one of our people could have been killed. I'll send some men to check it out further."

"I agree. We'll keep you informed if we learn anything more."

He ended the call and turned to see Tammy leaving the bedroom. "Are you ready for lunch?" she asked, her gaze shifting from him to her phone as she busily tapped in something on the cell.

"Yeah." He eyed the sundress covered in purple flowers and green leaves—nice and short, displaying her long, tan legs—and her sparkly sandals. The dress had spaghetti-thin straps, and no bra that he could detect. Somehow, he'd envisioned she'd be wearing more camo pants, heavy boots for hiking in the jungle, and a long-sleeved shirt, like she'd been wearing when she went on the zip line. Not looking like she was a spring flower ready to be plucked.

That made him realize how much she was distracting him. She sure had his attention.

He pocketed his phone and glanced at the couple of bruises on her arms, reminding him she could have been killed when the cable snapped. He took a deep, settling breath and escorted her to the dining hall. "Are you texting your boss about all that's happened?"

"Yeah, I told my boss. He must have called when we were exploring in our cat forms." She frowned, so busy concentrating on reading that David took her arm to guide her so she didn't stumble over anything on the uneven stone path.

"Something wrong?" he asked.

"Yeah. Something's wrong. I had an idea while you were talking to your boss. I wondered if the boys had shared anything on Facebook. Sure enough, the brothers and the other two boys, Hans and Peter, posted a cryptic message on Hans's Facebook page saying that the jaguar was going to catch and eat the dirty, little mole burrowing into the Yard. I think they're trying to tell someone something." She handed him her phone so that David could read it for himself. "Since 'Yard' is capitalized, like Scotland Yard, don't you think that could refer to our policing force?"

"Hell."

"Agreed. What if 'dirty mole' refers to a corrupt agent, possibly leaking particulars about the jaguar investigation to whoever else is involved? What if in the beginning, the boys were looking for evidence that either of us was the bad guy. Then believing we weren't, they tried to make up to us in their misguided way. Breaking into our cabana was not the way to go about it."

"I agree. So they made this cryptic enough to protect themselves in the event that anyone who might be involved reads their pages. Damn it to hell. We've got to call our bosses and let them know about this new development. They'll need to investigate this now to learn if one or more agents could be taking bribes from other jaguar shifters or humans who are involved in criminal activities. No one likes to think that our own policing force would have some bad cats, but it does happen sometimes."

"I think that's why the teens aren't coming forth and speaking with us. Maybe they're even afraid that if we are okay, others could be watching us."

"All right." He handed her phone back to her and pulled out his own. They stepped into a little alcove surrounded by vegetation with a stone bench sitting on one edge of the circular stone pavement and a water fountain in the center, the water running out of a bronze girl's pitcher.

Tammy paced as she spoke to her boss, while she vaguely heard David talking to Martin farther away, his brow furrowed, his stance tense.

"We think the boys believe there's a mole in our organization," she explained to Sylvan.

"Hold on." Sylvan was off the line for a minute or so and then said, "Okay, got it."

"Have we had anything like this in our branch?" she asked her boss.

"We've had a few in each of the branches over the years. When we catch them, it's kept hush-hush. The fewer who know, the better."

She was certain Sylvan wouldn't know, but she had to ask. "Any idea who the corrupt agent or agents might be?"

"None offhand. We have agents on assignment all over the place at any given time. Just a minute."

She knew her boss was having an analyst search records in a hurry.

"Tammy, none of them seemed to be in Oregon at the time the cat went missing. It could mean one of our agents coordinated the theft of the big cat with someone else who isn't an agent in one of our branches." He paused. "Anything else?"

"That's all I have for now."

"These kids could be playing with fire. If what they say is what we think it is, we're talking maybe one guy who's rotten in one of the branches, probably more. They're making significant money on the side, or they wouldn't be risking their necks. They're not going to like getting caught. And they'll take down anyone who can expose them."

She didn't want to think what would happen to the rogue shifters when the JAG caught up to them. She didn't believe the JAG would give the traitors a second chance if what they were involved in had cost shifter lives, and she hoped for the boys' sakes that they weren't involved.

"All right. I'll have men on it at once."

"Yes, sir." She pocketed her phone and saw that David had already ended his call. He was frowning. "Something more is the matter?" she asked.

"Martin's worried that this could get a lot more treacherous than he first suspected. And who knows what that zip-line business was all about."

"I already suspected there was more trouble than we first thought because of the way the boys didn't want to just meet with us and tell us what's going on. As for the snapped cable, that likely has nothing to do with us or the boys."

"Did you also deduce that, due to the circumstances changing, it bothers me that you're here?" he asked, a brow raised.

Tammy actually smiled at David. And not in a heart-warming fashion. More wickedly evil. He wasn't sure what that meant.

He wrapped his arm around her shoulders as they headed out of the alcove and was glad she didn't resist the intimacy. "What?"

"This is a real change for me, I have to admit. *I* usually ditch *my* partners."

"I'm serious about this," he said, but he wasn't really. Sure, he didn't want her in further danger, but if he had to have a partner to rely on, he wanted it to be her. It was her case and he believed that she was making progress in winning the boys' trust.

David opened the door to the dining hall. The aroma of marinated beef kabobs saturated the air as tourists filled the seats nearly to capacity.

"So, what else did your boss say?"

"He said you'll have better luck with the kids. So you're staying and I have to be extra protective."

"I like your boss. He thinks the way I do." She gave David another sexy smile, and he was glad they'd have air-conditioning tonight.

"But," he added, "if we learn someone sabotaged the cable, we might have to rethink this whole business."

"Right. It might be too dangerous for you to be here. After all, *you* might have been on the zip line instead of me."

"You know that's not what I meant," David said.

"Since neither of us is going anywhere for the time being, how do you want to proceed this afternoon?" Tammy asked, sounding serious now. "I think we should still try to find the boys and learn what they know about the missing zoo cat *and* this mole in the agency."

"My thoughts exactly. Well, almost exactly," David said, having a really far-out notion. It might not work, and he hated to offer the suggestion, which might seem degrading since she was a highly trained Enforcer.

"What?" Tammy asked.

"Okay." He took a deep breath.

She frowned at him. "I'm not going to like this plan of yours, am I? What? I have to stay home while you do something dangerous? I've been through that with the other JAG agents I worked with. I thought you and I had a partnership of sorts."

"Uh, yeah, we do. But we haven't been able to catch up to the kids, so what if we do something to get their attention? If they sit still enough, I can chase them down. Maybe talk to them."

She folded her arms. "And what am I supposed to do?"

"I don't want you to get the wrong idea about how I regard you on the mission."

"For heaven's sake, David. Just say it."

"What if you had a tanning session in your string bikini?"

Her mouthed gaped. "What?"

"Hell, Tammy, unless the teenagers aren't in the area, I doubt they could resist taking a gander. I might be able to catch them gawking and speak with them."

"Can't we come up with something better than that?"

"We can chase after them all we want, but I was thinking maybe we could draw them to us somehow. Not sure what else we could do."

"Okay, so you could prowl around the jungle, looking for them in the event they're in the area."

"Sure. I'll help you with the suntan lotion first."

"No, that'll be part of the show," Tammy said, catching on to the idea. "I'll lather it on *slowly* while you're out looking for them. Maybe they'll get careless and you can catch up to one of them and explain we only have their best interests in mind."

Inexplicably, David felt jealousy flare up inside him. Maybe this wasn't such a great plan after all. He was still fairly sure it would work—but he didn't want anyone to see her in that bikini but *him*.

"On second thought, I don't know if I like leaving you alone."

"I think the kids are in more danger than I am—since they seem to know something about the cat and a bad agent—or they *will* be, if the bad agent learns we're trying to catch the kids and find out what they know."

"I have to agree, but I still don't like leaving you alone."

"I'll be okay, David, as long as I'm not sliding along any more cables."

After they finished lunch, they headed back to the bungalow. She couldn't help thinking that if they weren't on assignment, she'd totally enjoy being with David like this. Nice meals and some medium-energy tropical adventures, if she didn't count the zip-line fiasco. She had high-energy adventures when she was running as a jaguar with him, and she liked those too. Even the sleeping arrangement wasn't altogether bad now that they had air-conditioning.

As they got ready for their new plan, Tammy slipped into her bikini and grabbed a bottle of suntan lotion, sunglasses, and a hat.

David paused to get an eyeful of Tammy's front.

"Hot damn, the teens don't know what they're missing if they aren't watching the bungalow's porch this afternoon."

"Just you remember what *you're* supposed to be looking for."

"Some jobs are a hell of a lot tougher than others. I'll go out the back way through the outdoor shower room if you want to lock up after me."

"Gotcha."

She followed him out but nearly ran into his back as he abruptly stopped. "We had visitors," he said.

She moved around him to see what made him say that. The pineapple and bananas were sitting on the table by the shower. Her skin chilled. She was certain the kids were trying to reach out to them, but she was creeped out by the way they were sneaking in without her or David's permission. They *really* needed some adult guidance.

"Gate's locked," David said, examining it. "One of them had to have leaped on top of the wall as a jaguar, jumped down, shifted, and unlocked the gate for the other one."

"I think they like us. So this is a good sign," she said, despite her misgivings about the way they were going about this.

She grabbed the bananas and pineapple, meaning to carry them inside where it was cool, but something that had been tucked behind the fruit fell off the table. She peered down at the small plastic tiger, which was like the kind for sale at zoo gift shops.

"What is it?" David asked, crossing the patio to see.

"A tiger," she said.

"A clue."

"Most likely. But what's it telling us? Our missing jaguar's at a different zoo? Why a tiger? The toy was the closest representation of a big cat to a jaguar that they could find at the gift shop?"

"Hell if I know. Or maybe it's at a zoo where they have tigers. I'll call it in. Lock the gate after me."

"Yeah, like that really keeps anyone out. If the bad guys are agents in one of our shifter branches, they can do what the teens did." With her hands full of fruit, Tammy couldn't grab the toy tiger, too. "Can you tuck the tiger under my arm?"

"I'll do better than that."

She thought he was going to offer to carry something in for her. Instead, he scooped up the small tiger and slipped it under her bikini's top strap. He grinned at her as he called Martin.

After she returned to the patio, David said, "Couldn't get hold of him." He looked her over again. "I don't know about the boys, but if I saw you rubbing lotion all over that body, I wouldn't be sitting in a tree watching. I'd be here in a flash, offering to cover every inch of you."

"Maybe another time."

"You mean it? Like another scheduled date? Not just going out to dinner and the theater?" He didn't wait for her to say no, just pumped his fist in victory and headed outside so she could lock the gate.

She laughed, his cockiness and sense of humor growing on her. With sunscreen in hand, she went out through the front door and began covering herself with the lotion at the slowest pace she could in case the boys were watching and David could get the jump on them. She topped the lotion with insect repellent, and she was all set.

She hoped she wasn't just putting on a show for a couple of toucans sitting in a nearby tree, their bright green, orange, red, and blue-colored bills making them stand out against the green foliage.

Settling down on the chaise lounge on her stomach, she hoped that if either of the boys was watching her, they weren't in human form with a camera in hand. And if they did take pictures, she hoped they wouldn't post them on the Internet.

She could imagine the ribbing she would get from fellow agents if any of them saw the pictures. "Thought you were on a job." "Hell of an assignment, Anderson." "This is what you call working a case?"

A howler monkey screeched in the canopy, making her heart skip a couple of beats. She kept thinking about the toy tiger the boys had left them…

The teens had packed David's and her bags. Had they left any clues inside their luggage?

Chapter 12

IF DAVID *COULD* LOCATE THE TEENS, HE *HAD* TO SPEAK with them, so he searched for them in his human form. Moving as a jaguar, he could be stealthier and much quicker—he could chase one of the boys down if they were in their cat form—but they wouldn't feel as safe as they would if he approached them as a more vulnerable human. Unless they believed he was armed.

He made a lot of racket in human form as he followed their scent trail, wanting to prove that he had no intention of sneaking up on them. He wanted to allow them the option to retreat, if they'd rather, or stand their ground if they felt safe enough around him. Smelling their scents, he knew they'd been spending a lot of time in the area, watching the resort, him, and Tammy. Hell, and their scent was combined with *his* aftershave!

When he finally saw a golden jaguar lying on a branch of a mahogany tree observing him from above, tail still, blue eyes meeting his gaze, he stopped. Instantly, he was relieved to see the boy. Maybe this was their chance. He was certain from the cats' recent scents that his brother was close by, eyeing David, ready to protect his brother if David made a threatening move. Like pulling out a gun.

David climbed into an adjacent tree, the process slow and tedious compared to jumping into it when he was in cat form. He made his way up the branches until he reached a high enough one where he could see the bungalow…and Tammy stretched out on her back in all her glory. Tiny scraps of metallic pink fabric covered only part of her breasts, and the bikini bottom was just as enticing.

He wished only *he* was observing her. Once he was settled on his branch, he kept his focus on Tammy as a way of being less intimidating than if he stared at the jaguar. Cats often perceived eye contact as a threat or challenge, and David didn't want to get off on the wrong foot before he even started. Well, that was only part of the reason. The view of her was too damned enticing not to watch her. And he *was* keeping an eye on her for her safety—since he *was* her partner.

"First," David said to the jaguar, "are you Alex?"

The cat nodded.

"Okay, great, Alex. We're the good guys. I understand you know something about the missing zoo cat, and all we want to do is return it. A Mr. Thompson, affiliated with the Oregon Zoo, told Maya Anderson, my brother's wife, all about the case. She asked her cousin, Tammy Anderson—the she-cat lying out on the chaise lounge—to see if she could find the missing cat.

"I was following you and your brother because my boss is interested in having you work with the agency." David figured he might as well spell it all out so the boys knew just where he was coming from.

For all David knew, the teen had already vacated the tree and hadn't heard a word he had said. That would be just his luck. Making a big speech to an empty tree. David glanced in the jaguar's direction. He was there, but he wasn't watching David. He had his eyes glued on Tammy. He couldn't blame the boy one bit.

"My boss also said there could be an agent on the take. He thought you and your brother might have been trying to tip the agency off about it indirectly—and that you might be worried Tammy or I was crooked."

The jaguar grunted.

David smiled. "My boss wants to work with you and your brother. Just like he worked with me and my brother, Wade, when we were your age." David told the teen about his mother dying and his dad going off the deep end and some of the stuff they had pulled when they were the teens' age. "Martin took us in and now we get to go on all kinds of dangerous missions and high-risk adventures, but we're helping our kind out, instead of risking our necks for no good reason. And…getting paid for it. Can't beat that."

He looked back down at Tammy and sighed. "On some missions, the perks are well worth the risk."

The jaguar growled.

David nodded as if he could read the boy's thoughts. "Yeah, I know. I told her she should return home. I don't want her here if it gets too dangerous. She's trained more as a police officer than as a Special Forces agent like me." He glanced at the jaguar. "Like you could be. The training's rigorous as hell, but it's worth it in the end."

David refocused on Tammy, her skin glistening in the sun. "My boss sees the good in the two of you—and that's saying a lot. What do you say to that? Are you willing to talk to us?" He again looked at the boy, but the jaguar was standing, his tail flicking back and forth, his ears alert, hair ruffled, his gaze focused on Tammy—anxious. He growled low.

David twisted his head around to see what was

wrong. The towel wrapped around her nearly naked body, Tammy was talking to two men, a dark-haired one and a blond. What the hell?

David immediately started to scramble down the tree as fast as he could, attempting not to break his neck in the process. Once his booted feet hit the ground, he took off running through the dense rainforest for the bungalow.

———⁓———

Tammy heard the wooden steps leading to the deck creak, and though she couldn't smell who it was from the way the breeze was blowing, she didn't think it was David, or he would have warned her he was coming. Was it one of the boys? Maybe while David was looking for them, they had come to see her instead. Like David had remarked—to be the ones to spread the lotion on her.

She didn't want to startle the boys if that's who had joined her. On the other hand, her Enforcer instincts urged her to get up and face the threat, if there was one.

She opened her eyes and turned her head. And stared at the two men, shocked to see them here. Weaver—his hair black and eyes amber, an interested smile on his smug face, and Krustan, blond-haired and blue-eyed, wearing the same stupid smile.

She quickly stood, grabbed her towel, and secured it around her bikini-clad body. "What are the two of you doing here?" She hadn't meant to sound so annoyed, like she felt guilty about what she had been doing or that she was embarrassed that they'd nearly seen her naked. She normally only wore the bathing suit to lie out on her back deck at home in total privacy.

"We had a mission a couple of hours away. Sylvan

called and said you might need our assistance. We can't
stick around, but we're not too far away," Weaver said.
He was the one who always took the lead when the two
of them worked together.

"Sylvan did?" She was surprised that their boss had
sent anyone to check on her without telling her first.

She really didn't like that the two agents had seen her
spread out on the chaise lounge, looking as though she
was having fun at the branch's expense.

"Yeah," Krustan said. "Looks like you're hard
at work." He glanced in the direction of the jungle.
"Having any luck?"

That was odd. To him, it should have looked like she
was only tanning. Why would he ask if she was having
luck with that? She did wonder if he had guessed what
she was attempting to do with regard to the kids. Even
if Sylvan told them about the mission *she* was working
on, how would Weaver and Krustan know David was
looking for the missing teens?

Instead of answering him, she asked, "What are *you*
working on?"

That got Krustan's attention. He gave her an odd
smile. She'd dumped both of the men early on the assignments she'd worked with them. Krustan had obviously seen her more as a potential date than a fellow
agent who could actually help solve a case. That's why
she'd ditched him and found the missing jaguar-shifter
toddler they'd been tasked to find on her own.

Weaver's idea of trying to locate a missing shifter
teen was to frequent shifter clubs. She wasn't sure why
he loved them so much. He didn't drink heavily or dance
that she'd ever seen. But the missing teen never went to

the clubs, so Tammy had followed leads on Facebook where he'd corresponded with friends in a covert way and discovered where he was staying with a friend. With Enforcer intervention, he was reunited with his family.

As far as she was concerned, neither agent could help her with this case or any other.

Krustan finally said, "We're looking for a couple of runaway teens."

"Down here?" She prayed to God they weren't the Taylor twins' friends trying to meet up with them in Belize. The more of the kids there were in the same place, the greater the chance that whoever might wish them harm could locate them.

"Yeah, they're wild. The boys come down here with their parents all the time, so they know the area well," Krustan said.

Alex and Nate? Her boss wouldn't have sent Weaver and Krustan to look for the same two brothers. Not that Sylvan had sent her to chase down the teens, either. Her assignment was to locate the missing zoo cat. Of course, that meant using whatever means she could, and if that necessitated bringing in a couple of wayward teens the JAG could take under its wing at the same time, so be it.

She recalled what Martin had said. He had a couple of JAG agents looking for the other boys. Had Sylvan also sent two Enforcer agents? It wouldn't be the first time that one branch was clueless about what the other was doing.

Feeling a little paranoid, she wondered if *these* two agents might be corrupt. "What are the boys' names?"

Weaver smiled—a little evilly, she thought. "You know, Anderson, you got us both into hot water on the cases we worked with you because you solved them and didn't inform us."

Which served them right.

"You just went right into Sylvan's office and told him how you had taken care of the missing kids' cases. So you think we trust you? You have your own assignment to take care of, and the next thing we know, you might be itching to solve our case, too, and attempt to show us up again."

She smiled just as evilly back. "Well, I don't know how you're going to solve your case if you don't have a shifter club to check out, Weaver. But I'd watch out for Krustan. He couldn't keep focused on business with me around."

Krustan's smile broadened. "Hell, Anderson, you think I could get one lick of work done with you parading around in a string bikini? I still want to know…" He paused and looked around at the jungle again. "Where's your partner? Did you ditch that JAG agent already?"

"He's working."

"She *has* dumped him," Weaver said, laughing, but he glanced in the direction of the thick jungle foliage as if he was afraid David might be out there watching them.

She hoped he was.

"Here are our cell numbers," Krustan said, handing her a piece of paper with both numbers written on it. "If you need our help, just call. We might be out of pocket, running around as jaguars from time to time, you know, but keep trying, and we'll drop everything and be on our way."

"Oh, so you want to help me with my mission but don't want my help with yours? Typical," she said. But something was off. He sounded earnest, she thought. Like they were really worried about her. Not just here to hassle her or because their boss made them come to check on her.

"Why were you at the jail?" she asked again.

Krustan looked at Weaver, as if waiting for him to give the green light.

Weaver folded his arms and looked down at her. "My TV was stolen. Had to fill out a police report, if you have to know the truth."

"Yours…too?"

"Yeah, yeah. Don't let it get around."

She almost smiled. Weaver had bragged about having one of the best security systems on the planet, poking fun at her when her own TV had been stolen. No one would ever break into his place without paying for it, he'd said. She was so tempted to ask if they caught the burglar.

As if he knew just what she was thinking, Weaver frowned at her. "After what you pulled with us, you don't deserve anything from us. You know that, right?"

"Yeah, but…"

"Still think you can do it all on your own?" Weaver asked. "Not this time, Anderson. We know how you are with kids. You like them. You don't think any of them would lead you astray. But these kids…" He shook his head. "All I've got to say is don't trust them. They could get you killed." He turned to his partner. "Come on, Krustan. Let's let Anderson get back to her job. She looks like she really needs to concentrate on it so she can solve her case."

"Hell," Krustan said, "you sure you can do your mission on your own, Weaver? Seeing as her partner is conspicuously absent, it sure looks like Anderson could use a good man to watch her back."

"And front," Weaver said, slapping Krustan on the back. "Come on. We've got work to do." They both sniffed the air and headed off the porch. "Later. Oh, and that shimmery pink swimsuit looks real good on you."

"I'll say," Krustan added, giving her another long look as if he could see it beneath her towel.

As soon as the men disappeared into the jungle, Tammy took a deep breath. She didn't trust them one iota. Something wasn't right about them being down here. She was certain of it.

If the men speaking to Tammy meant her any harm, David would never reach her in time. He had to remind himself that she knew hand-to-hand combat. But he didn't even want to think of how she'd manage that in that teeny-weeny bikini.

He was nearly out of breath when he reached the edge of the jungle and the bungalow. Tammy was nowhere in sight, and his heart was thumping his ribs at breakneck speed. Out of the corner of his eye, he saw two jaguars. Both the boys were hiding among the trees, having moved much more swiftly than he had in his human form, ready to come to his aid if he'd needed backup. Fearless and intelligent, they'd make damn good agents someday if they were willing to take some training and listen to the boss. And it looked like they were willing to trust Tammy and him a little.

He raced up the steps and sniffed the air, smelling two male jaguars—not the boys' scents. But the two men had to be shifters. He grabbed the doorknob to the bungalow and twisted. Locked.

Fumbling in his pants pocket for the key, he found it, jammed it into the lock, and opened the door.

"Tammy?" he shouted, panicked as he rushed for the bedroom.

As soon as David heard the shower running in the bathroom, his racing heartbeat slowed a little, and he turned and stalked in that direction. Reaching the door, he knocked. "Tammy?"

"David? I'll be right out."

Relief filled him instantly. To let the boys know she was all right, he left the bungalow and observed the jungle surrounding them. He didn't see either of them, but he called out, "She's okay. Just taking a shower." Not that they needed to learn all the details, but he wanted them to know she was safe. He suspected they were within earshot, waiting. He added, "You're welcome to come see us anytime, day or night. If you're in any kind of trouble, we're here to help you and will watch your backs if you let us."

When he received no acknowledgment, he wasn't sure if they had stuck around. He went back inside and decided to take a shower on the patio, as hot and sweaty as he was.

He was in the middle of soaping up when he heard the back door open. He turned and saw Tammy wearing a different smocked sundress—this one bright blue, short, and strapless. How did he ever get so lucky on a mission?

"Sorry…I didn't mean to barge in on you." She turned to leave.

"No, stay. Doesn't bother me. We need to talk. I was worried about you."

"I had company."

"Yeah, I saw. Nearly gave me a heart attack. Almost killed myself trying to get back here in time to rescue you. It's not easy getting down from a tree in human form that fast."

She smiled and sat down on a bench near the bedroom door. "Thanks for worrying about me. I nearly had a seizure when I smelled their scents on the patio, opened my eyes, and saw them coming up the stairs. They're Enforcers. Martin must have told my boss he was concerned about my safety. They said Sylvan sent them to get into contact with me."

David frowned at her as he continued to soap himself up, amused she was half watching him, as if she were getting used to him. "Do you know them well?"

"Weaver and Krustan are their names. I've worked with each of them on assignments before. I ditched them both each time."

He was glad she'd dumped them and not him, but he was also curious. "So why send them to check on you if you didn't care to work with them?"

"They're the only two Enforcers in the area, they said. They've got another mission, so they can't stay here. They just wanted to let me know they're working an assignment about two hours from here and that I could call if I needed them."

"Do you trust them?"

"No, not in the least. They said they were looking for two shifter teens. I'm worried they're the Taylor twins or their other two friends. I didn't think my boss would send them to track down the same boys that your boss tasked you to find, though. I tried calling Sylvan to see if he had told them what I was actually doing here. No reception."

Tammy glanced back at the bungalow and her face went from worry to wide-eyed recollection. "Oh, I forgot! Be right back." She ducked inside.

Chapter 13

WHEN TAMMY DIDN'T RETURN QUICKLY ENOUGH FOR David's peace of mind, he rinsed, turned the water off, and secured a towel around his waist. He had just opened the back door to the bedroom when she nearly ran into him with something in her hand.

"Lion," she said.

"Another toy. Where did you find it?" He was really surprised, thinking both of the teens had been with him in the jungle—watching her.

"Suitcase. Mine."

"Oh, from when they packed our bags before they moved them from the cabana. Gotcha. Okay, so we've got another big cat. Big-cat sanctuary?"

"Or zoo," she said, sitting on the bed, watching him.

Suddenly, he recalled how people at the shifter club had been dressed and smelled of different kinds of animals, as if they worked with them. He snapped his fingers. "The circus is in town."

Her lips parted. "The man that bumped into me going into the jail—he was wearing a handlebar mustache and smelled like a lion."

"Yeah. I would have thought he was a zookeeper, but I saw a bunch of them at the club when I confronted the bouncer."

"Circus," she said. "Okay, we'll have to call that in. Did you locate the boys?"

"Hell, yeah. Even a human could have smelled them."

She raised a brow in question.

"They were wearing my aftershave. And *way* too much of it."

She laughed. "I take it that they were in jaguar form."

"They were. I had quite a talk with them. Well, at least one of them. Mostly one-sided. A grunt and a growl from one of the teens—Alex. I imagine Nate must have been in another tree, hidden from view. If not, he sure as hell missed out on a steamy swimsuit viewing."

She smiled at the compliment. "So, did we make any headway?"

"They both came with me in their jaguar skins to rescue you from your unknown assailants. So I'd say that was a definite yes."

"Good. Maybe they'll come see us."

"I hope so. I gave them an open invitation anytime, day or night." He finished throwing on a pair of shorts and a T-shirt. "If you don't mind my asking, why did you ditch those two Enforcers?"

She raked David with her gaze, rose from the bed, and patted his T-shirt-covered chest. "They were always removing their clothes in front of me, as if I wanted to see their naked bodies."

She headed out of the room.

He jammed his feet in his sandals and hurried after her. "Hell, did they pull anything with you?" He was ready to kill a couple of Enforcers.

"You mean, like, kiss me? In a big bed? No. They wouldn't have lived long."

"Good. Your boss would have had two fewer Enforcers."

She cast him a warm smile. "So what's next on the agenda?"

"The teens have been staying in this area. The JAG in me says to keep trying to locate them and get them to reveal what they know. But I feel they're reaching out, so for now, I'll give them a little more free rein. Maybe they'll approach us soon."

"I agree. What if we did something that they don't have scheduled? Think they might follow us?" she asked.

"What did you have in mind?"

"Kayaking—white-water trip."

"Sounds good to me. Let's see if we can get scheduled."

"I already booked it after I came in to take a shower. I thought if the boys came to see us, we'd skip it. But since it's still iffy about them contacting us in person, we might as well go now and see what happens."

With water to drink, sunscreen, dry clothes in a waterproof bag, bathing suits under their shorts and T-shirts, and river shoes, Tammy and David joined a group taking a bus to the river.

When they reached the river, David pulled off his shorts. He wore a pair of blue swim trunks splashed with pink skies and green palm trees, his tanned legs and toned torso just too hot for her not to take another look. Of course, he had to catch her at it and gave her an amused smile. Not that he wasn't admiring her shimmering, green one-piece bathing suit, too.

The water was a blissful seventy degrees, green, and crystal clear. Tammy ended up with a hot pink kayak and David got a lime green one. Eight other guests had signed up. No sign of the teens, but Tammy was still hopeful they might show.

Vibrant blue, lime green, hot pink, canary yellow, and bright orange sit-on-top kayaks for white-water rafting bobbed in the clear water. Everyone wore either red or yellow vests and red, yellow, or blue helmets, making Tammy think the collective group of kayakers looked as colorful as the plumage on the parrots in the trees.

After a lesson in the basics of maneuvering a kayak, they got on their way. They splashed through several easy rapids, Class I and Class II, and paddled through large, calm pools of water after each drop. Tammy was having too much fun to remember her mission, learning to surf the waves, carving smooth arcing turns, and jumping up on some of the higher drops.

She was drenched, laughing, and having the time of her life—watching a speedy kingfisher darting into the river for a fish and parakeets flying overhead—when she saw movement in the trees on the bank. A splash of orange in the filtered sunlight. Black spots moving like leaves in the shadows. *Jaguar*.

Tammy had been so busy maneuvering the kayak the right way that she'd lost sight of David. Glancing around, she nearly flipped her kayak on the next rapid. Was David ahead of her or behind her? Had he seen the jaguar?

It had to be a shifter. A nonshifting jaguar wouldn't be out at this time of day, not this close to the river with humans about. She wanted to beach the kayak, shift into her big cat, and search for the jaguar. The hunting instinct was in her jaguar blood. But she couldn't leave the tour group without arousing suspicion.

The group of kayakers ended up in the final pool where a bus would take them back to their resort.

She glanced around for David and saw his stern face. Something was wrong.

"Did you see the jaguar?" he asked her quietly as he removed his soaking-wet life jacket.

"Yeah, one of the boys, right? Or do you think it could have been a regular jaguar?" she asked.

"I doubt it. And I don't think it was one of the boys, either. I saw both of them."

Tammy's stomach fell. "One of our dirty agents?"

"That's what I'm afraid of. The jaguar wasn't Weaver or Krustan, was it?"

"I couldn't tell," Tammy said. "The jaguar moved too fast. I only got a glimpse of him in the shadowy rainforest, and I was having trouble staying afloat. If it wasn't one of the boys, why come after us?"

"Either believing the kids are following us and he hopes to intercept them, or he thinks we'll lead him to the boys."

"That's just great. We need to let the boys know if they don't already. Maybe they can leave, and we can stay here and try to catch whoever this man is and learn what he wants."

"We can do that, but given what we've seen so far, I doubt they'll tuck tail and run. And whoever is after the boys, once they're gone, he will be also."

They turned in their gear, changed into dry clothes, and climbed onto the bus with the rest of the group.

When they arrived at their resort, they both got cleaned up at the bungalow and walked to the dining hall for dinner. They'd just sat down when David smiled at her. "Hot damn, they're here."

She turned to look at the entrance to the dining room

and saw two boys as tall as David, though not as filled out, one with sandy hair and blue eyes, the other's hair darker, his eyes just as blue. They nodded in greeting and appeared somewhat like kids who were in trouble, hands shoved in the pockets of their Bermuda shorts, heads bent slightly. "Tammy, I want you to meet Alex and Nate Taylor," David said, rising and shaking one boy's hand, then the other.

Alex, the blond, looked like a surfer dude, his hair streaked by the sun's rays. Nate looked like he spent as much time outdoors—lighter tan—as he did indoors. She immediately smelled David's Wild Earth Essence aftershave on the two of them, and he was right. They'd used way too much.

"Ma'am," the boys said in unison, trying to sound polite.

"Will you sit with us?" Tammy asked, motioning to the chairs next to her and David.

They sat on either side of David as if they'd prefer being in his place, seeing her rather than sitting beside her. Maybe they were shy. She shook her head at that. They didn't look shy in the least as both smiled at her, and she wondered if that had to do with seeing her in the string bikini earlier.

The waitress took their drink and beef fajita orders, and when she left, David got down to business and asked the boys, "Okay, so what's going on?"

Alex snorted. "You tell us. We're down here minding our own business—not getting into any trouble—and two agents are trying to track us down. Now we've got three more on our case." He had the good grace to be fighting a smile.

"You're not all innocence," David quickly said, as

if he believed Tammy might be snookered into believing the teen. "You know something about the missing jaguar, for one. But what do you mean there are three more? Are you referring to the two agents who talked to Tammy? And now there's a third?"

"Yeah, something like that," Nate said. "We were following your progress down the river today as you went kayaking, watching your backs."

David couldn't help but appreciate the kids for believing they were protecting him and Tammy.

"You were running as jaguars?" Tammy asked.

They shook their heads. The waitress deposited their drinks and dinners on the table. When she left, Tammy said, "You couldn't have been kayaking, unless the two of you were in another group behind ours and we didn't see you."

"We were," Nate said. "Did you see the jaguar in the trees?"

"We did," David said. "I knew it wasn't either of you."

"We figure the jaguar was following the two of you in an effort to catch us." Nate turned to Tammy. "Do you know if it was one of the Enforcers who spoke with you on the porch?"

Tammy shook her head. "I didn't see enough of the cat to recognize him."

"I don't know either of the men," David said. "So it still could have been one of them."

"How did you know they were Enforcers?" Tammy asked, suspicious. Neither she nor David had said which branch the men worked in.

"They're chasing after our friends."

Tammy's mouth gaped.

David frowned. "You've been in touch with the other two boys?"

"Yeah, sure, they're leading them on a wild cat chase," Nate said and grinned. "They'll never find them. Those two are great at leaving false trails."

"Krustan and Weaver said they were after two boys. I was afraid they were trying to track the two of you down," Tammy said, recalling how they warned her not to trust the kids. Was that because the kids knew something about them being bad agents?

"We're glad you were assigned to go after us," Nate said.

"Yeah, real glad," Alex added.

She bet they were after they had seen her showering in her bikini and lying out in the sun later. She wondered what had happened to Martin's men who had been following the boys' friends.

"Thanks for wanting to help me when the cable snapped," she said to the boys, not sure which to really thank.

Alex frowned. "Wished I could've done something. You were really cool out there. But what if it wasn't an accident?"

"What could anyone have hoped to gain by sabotaging the cable?" Tammy asked. "What if one of the members of the family with me had gone first instead?"

"Maybe it was a warning to leave the case alone," Alex said. "Both of you were signed up to go on the expedition. So were we. We learned the family didn't sign up until this morning. If someone sabotaged the cable, it was most likely done last night after everyone had left for the day, and after they knew who all had signed up."

"All right, so for the sake of argument, I still ask why? You say a warning. If one of us had died, how would that help whoever had done it? It would just make us all the more resolved to learn who's behind this."

Nate finished his soda. "If Alex or I had been killed, it could have convinced the remaining one of us to hand over the cat and quit trying to get someone to investigate the mole in the Service. If it was one of you, it might have been an attempt to get you out of the picture until they could get to us. Win-win scenario."

She still didn't believe it would have worked if someone had tampered with the cable.

"Why did you go first, Tammy?" David asked, his brow furrowed.

"The family of four was arguing about who would go first. The guide said I would—to get us on our way." She frowned. "Actually, I thought something else was odd. He said I was scheduled first. I just figured he said that because he needed someone to go before we ended up staying there all day. But his saying that there was a schedule gave me pause. I would figure whoever wanted to go first would."

"Hell," David said, fishing out his phone and making a call. "Martin, we need you to check into something else. We need to have the guide who hooked Tammy up investigated."

"The man's name was Juan," she said.

David repeated what she said to his boss. He looked at Tammy. "Yeah. Just in case he was paid to have her go on the zip line first. All right. Out here."

The waitress gave everyone refills on their drinks and then left again.

Tammy wondered why David didn't tell his boss that the kids were here talking to them. Maybe to keep from spooking them.

"You know we weren't drinking alcoholic beverages at the club that night. We knew you were following us," Alex said to David, a twinkle in his eye.

"And you also know just being in the club meant you were breaking the law," David said. "You didn't have to drink anything alcoholic to be in the wrong."

The boys exchanged glances.

"But you didn't stop us," Nate said.

"That's another reason we let you in on the secret," Alex said.

"Yeah, and we wanted you to know we knew about the jaguar because we thought you might be an honest agent. Not for sure, though." Nate drank his soda.

David nodded. "We figured as much."

No one said anything for a moment, and then Tammy said, "We couldn't check out the cable earlier because inspectors were examining it. After nightfall, we can return and see if anyone cut into it."

"Yeah, if someone had cut it, he would have been tethered to the other cable, free to saw at the cable that broke," David said.

"Okay, so we do that later tonight." Tammy asked the boys, "What about the zoo cat?"

"We don't know anything about how it was stolen from the zoo," Alex said evasively.

"Yeah," Nate said. "But you've got to find out who the mole is in your organization."

"All right, let's talk about that," David said. "How do you know there's a mole in one of the branches?"

"It all had to do with the missing zoo jaguar," Nate said.

"You have the cat?" Tammy was glad the boys were safe enough for now, and they needed to learn about the mole, but she had to know about the jaguar. "She's being taken care of?"

"Yes," Alex said.

"We'll keep in touch with you, but you've got to catch the bad guys in your organization before we agree to come in or turn over the cat to you," Nate said.

"Why the toy lion and tiger?" she asked, not liking that the boys were still being so cagey concerning the whereabouts of the cat, as if they still didn't trust them. She and David were fairly certain now it had to do with the Oregon Zoo. She'd get back to questioning him about the mole after that.

Alex shuffled in his seat and nodded once to his brother.

Nate produced a toy elephant and set it down on the table. "So, what do you think?"

Tammy almost laughed. They were still playing a game of Clue.

David wanted to get on with the big reveal and wasn't interested in playing games any further, but Tammy looked willing, smiling and appreciating the boys, and he could tell she was really winning them over big-time. "Okay, lion, tiger, and elephants at a zoo." She raised her brows.

They were smiling, but neither said yea or nay.

"Or a circus," Tammy and David said at the same time, both suspecting that was really it.

The boys' smiles broadened.

David admired Tammy for having more patience with the teens than he did. He was glad she was along on the assignment as far as dealing with the boys was concerned.

"Wait a minute," David said. "So you're saying someone from a circus stole the zoo cat?"

"And if that's the case, how would the cat be safe?" Tammy asked in a worried tone. "Some circuses have cruel animal trainers. The cat might be horribly abused."

"Totally agree. We saw the news about the stolen jaguar, and Alex and I did some searches online. We came up with the circus angle since it was being held near the Oregon Zoo and the cat was missing the day that the Wilde & Woolly Maximus Three-Ring Circus left Portland," Nate said.

"Yeah, all we had to do was check online to see their schedule. Next stop was Dallas, and they were hiring one hundred and fifty temporary workers. More than five hundred people showed up to apply. Despite the odds, we got jobs with the circus. When we toured the temporary facilities, we searched for the jaguar, figuring we'd quit our jobs if she wasn't there.

"We were hired to do custodial maintenance mainly, so we could go places that the other temporary hired help—ushers, ticket takers, and ticket sellers—couldn't go as easily. They were kind of stuck in one place. We had a lot more maneuverability. Each of us had viewed the picture of the missing jaguar on the news, saw another picture uploaded on a blog site about a family's trip to the Oregon Zoo, and figured we'd know the jaguar by her spots if we saw her. We assumed they wouldn't have her in one of the circus shows yet because training her would take time," Alex added.

"Yeah," Nate said. "Two days after we started working there, we finally found her hidden in a cordoned-off area. She was in a small cage, separated from any of the other big cats—three tigers and a lion. You wouldn't believe how hard it was to steal her away with security watching the place at night, lights everywhere, and tons of performers staying on site. Over a hundred and fifty performers and permanent circus personnel actually live at the site, unlike the rest of us that went home nights."

"So why didn't you contact someone with one of the branches and get her sent back to the zoo?" Tammy asked.

"We did," Nate said, his face darkening. "We called the Guardian branch. The operator transferred us to another branch. I didn't catch which one because Alex was asking me something just as the man began speaking on the phone. He said he'd meet us and take care of the cat right away. He wanted to know who we were, but we weren't willing to say, afraid someone might believe we stole the cat from the zoo originally and that she had never been with the circus."

"Yeah," Alex said. "We could just see ourselves getting a bad rap for trying to do the right thing. We set up a rendezvous point, but we weren't able to see the dude because of a big commotion nearby—drug bust, cops everywhere—but the pickup was made. For two days, we all watched for news stating that the Oregon Zoo jaguar had been recovered."

"Nothing," Nate said, sounding angry. "We called the zoo and said we'd heard the jaguar was found. The man we talked to said it was still missing. Why would it still be missing? That had to mean the agent we dealt with was working his own deal and the cat was never turned over to the zoo."

David ground his teeth. "Hell. Did he give a name?"

"Yeah," Alex said. "Yours."

Chapter 14

THE CLINKING OF SILVERWARE IN THE DINING ROOM sounded in the background as David tried to curb his anger. He couldn't believe anyone would use his name in the act of committing a JAG crime. Who the hell had set him up?

Nate cleared his throat. "Looking back on the situation, we weren't sure. He hesitated when he said his name, which made me suspicious. We used a phone he couldn't trace. But at the time, we didn't think anything of it, until the cat wasn't returned to the zoo. We risked our necks rescuing her and now where was she? Well, we only had one place to look that we knew of."

"Not the circus again," Tammy said.

"We really didn't believe she'd be there. Who in their right mind would return her there? On the other hand, we knew if she was, we'd have even a worse time trying to free her this time. We all still had our jobs there, so the four of us—two of our closest friends, Alex, and me—went to the circus the next day to perform our regular jobs and, of course, the cat's cage was now being closely video-monitored and roped off so we couldn't see if she was even there.

"Only certain staff members could get near the area where she was being kept. So we were certain she had been returned to her cage. We worried someone might try to kill her and get rid of the evidence since we knew about the missing jaguar. Even though they didn't know who we were."

"Or they set her up as a trap to catch you," Tammy said.

"Yeah, that's just what I was thinking," David said.

Nate nodded. "We figured the same, so we were really careful."

David wasn't surprised. He had to admit they had done the right thing by calling the Service—if only they'd gotten hold of someone who hadn't been involved in stealing or covering up the jaguar's theft. He wondered who the hell would use his name in the commission of a crime and which branch that agent had been with.

"You said the jaguar is safe." Tammy was frowning again.

"Yes, we created our own diversion. We let a lion loose from his cage, though we fed him first and he was still in an enclosed area. We didn't want any people or the lion hurt, either. But we had to do something drastic enough so that we could slip in and steal the jaguar again. We knocked out the cameras. When we reached the cage, we discovered she was there and found her heavily tranquilized. We got a wheelbarrow that clowns had used for one of the shows, covered her with some wild-looking clown fabric, and carted her to our car. We didn't have a cage this time and had to take her in the backseat of our car. We didn't want to put her in the trunk, because we were afraid she'd get sick from exhaust fumes. She slept the whole time, so no problem."

"Yeah, because Nate was driving and Peter and Hans were sitting up front, which meant I had to sit in back with the cat," Alex said. "The plan was I'd shift if she came to, and hopefully, she would like me and not try to rip me to shreds."

David couldn't believe it. Not that he and his brother hadn't saved lives a couple of times before the Service took them in, but the commission of a crime had been taking place and they had to do something. He really admired the boys for working so hard to rescue the jaguar.

"But where is she now? You didn't call the zoo?" Tammy asked.

Nate shook his head. "We didn't want the zoo officials to believe we had anything to do with her being stolen. Or our parents to know what we were up to. They don't care what we do as long as we don't get into any trouble."

David and Tammy shared glances.

"Also, we were worried that someone working at the zoo had something to do with stealing her in the first place. How else would anyone be able to take her from there so easily without anyone noticing? And we didn't trust anyone in any of the branches anymore. We didn't know who all was involved. So we just hid her," Alex said.

"Who's taking care of her now?" Tammy asked.

"Let's just say she's being cared for in the best manner possible. But we can't say where because we really don't know. That way if the crooked agent or agents catch up to us, we can honestly say we have no idea."

"But you do have an idea, or you wouldn't know she's being taken care of satisfactorily," David said.

"Yeah, we do." Nate finished his meal.

"You still don't trust us?" Tammy asked.

"We trust *you*. Just not either of the organizations that you work for," Alex said, "or we wouldn't have even agreed to talk with you. We want whoever it is to pay for the crime against the jaguar. We have to confide in someone, and we knew you were trying to get her home. As for David, we weren't sure. He was following us, and we worried he might have realized we were the ones who stole the jaguar from the circus. But everything he told us panned out."

"You thought the Enforcers Tammy talked with were the corrupt agents because they were searching for your friends, knowing Hans and Peter were involved in this with the two of you?" David asked. "But if they were assigned to look after them, like I was with you, and overheard the reference to the zoo cat, they could be trying to find the cat and bring all of you in to work with the JAG."

"How many agents do they need assigned to our case?" Nate asked.

"Four of us, I would assume. The two who are looking for your friends and the two of us," David said.

Alex snorted. "That's what we figured. So why are the two who were closing in on Peter and Hans in Dallas not the same as the two looking for them here? Our friends lost the two Enforcer agents in Belize good. But if the JAG wanted them, why wouldn't they send JAG agents like they did in Dallas? Why send Enforcer agents to Belize?"

Not liking that scenario, David wondered the same as the boys. He pulled out his cell phone. "I can check on that." He glanced at his cell and shook his head. "Damn, no reception again."

Nate rose from his chair and Alex followed suit.

"But what if whoever's after you followed you here?"

Tammy asked, standing, as if she was ready to take the boys into protective custody.

"Whoever it was…they did follow us here, we're certain." Alex grinned. "He might be an agent, but we've been playing games like this since we were little. Oh, and by the way, thanks for the rescue at the club. We owe you one, David."

"Yeah, we were afraid we'd have to really get rough with the bouncer and might have hurt him," Nate said.

"Joe Storm? Are you kidding? He has killer fists," Tammy said. "No way should you ever confront him."

David stood. "Agreed. How about the two of you go on a hunt with us, Alex, Nate? We can call it your first official initiation into the Golden Claws. I think you're ready."

The boys grinned and nodded their assent.

"I love to hunt," Tammy said, her voice verging on a growl. "Let's go."

When they arrived at the bungalow, both David and Tammy tried to get hold of their bosses to confirm who was down here—or who should be down here—looking into the situation with the teens before they went on the hunt. But they had no success.

The boys had stripped and shifted in the outdoor shower area. They waited until she and David shifted and could watch their backs. She wished the twins had had JAG training before the *initiation*, but the boys seemed so keen on it and she thought it would be good for them to get a feel for being part of a team. She also believed that if the boys were allowed to participate with her and David, they would be more inclined to join the JAG when they felt it was safe to do so.

With four of them watching out for one agent in

jaguar form, it would be no contest. Unless more agents were down here causing trouble.

Keeping the gate to the outdoor shower area locked, the four of them, one after another, jumped to the top of the wall and over, and then headed into the jungle. They first went together to check out the snapped cable. Tammy didn't know where the two pieces would have ended up falling, but as they reached the first of the platforms closest to the resort, they couldn't find the cable at all. It was no longer attached to the tower.

Sure, the investigators had to take it and study it in a lab, probably. Damn. They all stared up at the point where it had been connected, as though that would shed light on where it was now. They headed to the terminal tower 2,300 feet away to see if that half of the cable had been removed also. Most likely yes, but they still had to verify it.

When they reached the other tower, they discovered the same scenario. They would have to let their bosses deal with the issue and learn what they could about the cable when the investigators were through examining it.

They split into pairs, Tammy following Alex while David took off after Nate, now hunting the mystery jaguar they had seen when they were kayaking. They ran through the rainforest as four big cats, heading straight for the river where they had white-water kayaked to locate the scent of the jaguar they had seen in the trees. All the while, they searched for any signs the jaguar had been in any of the areas near where she and David were staying, but came up empty.

She thought that was odd. Surely whoever knew about the boys being here—and her and David also— the agent or agents would be hanging around near their bungalow, trying to get hold of the boys if they showed themselves. He wouldn't even have to chase after the boys. He could just wait for them when they appeared near the bungalow.

She sniffed the air a little more. Then again, she had smelled Weaver's and Krustan's scents near the bungalow because they had visited her on the deck and left through the jungle.

Alex reached the river first and ran downstream, diving in and out of the trees, up one, and down again, repeating the exercise several more times while David and Nate went upriver.

Tammy concentrated on watching the area around them, ensuring no one was following them and letting Alex search for whoever the jaguar shifter was.

She concentrated on the smells in the air and on the ground—tapir, birds, monkeys, the sweet scent of pineapple, and orchids. The fishy odor of the river scented the air. But she still hadn't found any sign of another jaguar. Just a whiff of David's, Nate's, and Alex's scents from time to time.

They finally reached where the kayaks had been loaded into the water. From there, they continued searching for the big cat.

They had gone maybe another quarter mile when she paused to smell the base of a mahogany tree. And recognized a jaguar's scent. A JAG agent's scent. Quinn Singleterry. Her heart skittered. It couldn't be a coincidence that he had tried to charm her into working with him instead of David and then showed up here in Belize.

She couldn't wait to discuss it with David at the bungalow, but most of all, she wanted to notify Sylvan of this new twist in the situation. Still, they had no evidence to prove Quinn was involved in any of this. She'd always been thorough, not only in solving crimes, but ensuring the bad guys were truly responsible for the crimes committed. As much as she wanted to take Quinn down if he was the bad agent, they had to proceed with caution. They couldn't risk the zoo jaguar's safety or the kids', either.

When they couldn't find any other clues, they returned to the place where they'd put the kayaks in the water. Alex grunted at her, and she took that to mean he was leaving her to return to his own rental unit, wherever that was. He roared for his brother, who responded in kind.

David called for her, and she moved in his direction, unable to see him yet in the dense foliage. She roared back, letting him know she was joining him. The twin brothers melted into the dark jungle, the night fully upon them, and vanished.

Before she reached David, something struck her, giving her a near heart attack. A large body, jaguar, male, muscled. He knocked her hard into the river.

She went under the rough water. When she surfaced, she coughed up warm water as the river carried her downstream.

The cat was nowhere in sight. At least that she could see as she tried to catch her breath. He'd been downwind of her or she would have smelled him before he hit her.

He'd lunged, slammed her into the river, and vanished. If he'd wanted to drown her, he hadn't done a very good job of it. Not that she was complaining.

She fought the current pulling her toward the next waterfall. She struggled to keep her head above the foaming water and reach the shore as the roar of the waterfall grew louder the closer she got.

Chapter 15

SHOTS FIRED. ONE POP! TWO! HELL AND DAMNATION. Where was Tammy? They should have met each other by now.

In a near panic, David roared for her as he raced in her direction, but she didn't respond. He roared again. Still no response. Fearing she'd been shot, he continued to search for her until he found the last scent of her at the river's edge. And Quinn Singleterry's scent, too. What the hell was going on?

David circled around and checked the trees, but she hadn't moved anywhere around here. He couldn't find Quinn's scent either. Had he gone into the river?

David turned to look at the swiftly flowing river. She had to have fallen into the water.

He roared again and took off running downriver, diving through underbrush, trying to spy any sign of a jaguar bobbing up and down in the turbulent water as the full moon shown on the white caps. No sign of her. He called to her again. He hurried off in search of her, hoping the boys might have heard his calls and help with the search, but they hadn't responded, either.

He prayed they were just out of his range and that no harm had come to them. Frustrated with his lack of speed on the shoreline, he feared she was moving more swiftly downriver because of the pull of the water. He squinted his eyes and thought he saw something way up ahead in the water nearing the waterfall, and he roared. He lunged forward again. If what he saw was Tammy, he had to reach her before she went over the falls and hit the rocks below.

Tammy barely could keep her head above water, choking on it, getting a snootful of it and having to sneeze, which forced her muzzle into the water again for another bout. She was a strong swimmer, like all jaguars, but the water going down the wrong way was hindering her. She needed to get out of the water, run back upstream to where she'd been when she was knocked into the river, and let David know what had happened to her.

He was sure to be frantic when he didn't come across her on the riverbank like he should have. Over the roar of the water, she heard David calling out to her. She tried to roar back but she swallowed another mouthful of water. *Damn it.*

Coughing, choking, and sneezing, she got another nose full of water. She felt like she was drowning as she persisted in swimming toward the shore. Her cat paw pads finally touched the slippery moss-covered stones beneath the water. She scrambled for purchase and dragged herself onto the rocky bank. Trying to catch her breath, she sneezed again and again, and coughed up more water. When she felt she could breathe in and breathe out normally, she roared to let David know where she was and that she was safe.

David answered her, growing closer as he ran in her direction. Feeling relieved, she shook off some of the excess water, coughed and sneezed again, and then

raced to join him. She climbed the steeper rocky areas
with a leap and a bound, until she smelled him on the
breeze coming off the water and swirling downstream.

His scent grew stronger until she was practically on
top of him, his eyes glowing green in the moonlight.
God, she loved seeing him. He looked so endearing—
his overprotective he-cat expression mixed with a look
of unguarded anxiety.

They greeted each other nose to nose at first, whiskers brushing gently, caressing. Assuring each other
they were okay. But he quickly nudged at her wet neck,
a question in his action, wondering why she'd decided to
go for a swim, no doubt. She licked his muzzle and was
ready to return to the bungalow, but he wasn't leaving.
Instead, he checked her over from head to tail, making
sure she hadn't been injured. When he seemed content
that she was all right, he nudged at her to return.

Appreciating his concern, she ran back with him, still
trying to detect any smells that would indicate who else
might be out here. The cat who had knocked her into the
river had been big and had to have been male, since he'd
been much bulkier and heavier than her, but she hadn't
had time to smell his scent before she plunged under the
water and had to come up for air. His scent on her had
washed away in the water. Had it been Quinn?

She couldn't believe the guy was in on all this. She
had always assumed that he thought all jaguar-shifter
females were put on this earth to swoon at his feet with
adoration, nothing really criminal.

When they reached the backside of their bungalow,
she leaped on top of the wall surrounding the shower
and jumped down. Her fur had long since dried. David

landed beside her and again nuzzled her in a way that told her he'd worried about her. Had he seen what had happened to her?

Before she had the chance, he shifted and unlocked the door to their bedroom using the key hidden inside one of the potted plants. "What the hell happened out there?" he asked.

She ran inside and shifted. "Did you smell Quinn Singleterry's scent where you were?"

"Hell, yeah."

From the feral look on David's face, she assumed he thought Quinn had knocked her into the river.

She pulled on a T-shirt and panties. She was worn-out and past ready to go to bed. "I'm all right."

"Hell, Tammy," David said and approached her, still looking a bit shell-shocked. He pulled her into his heated—very naked—embrace. She wondered if he always acted this way when he learned a fellow agent had become a rogue. "I thought I'd lost you."

Frowning, she looked up at him. "If you smelled Quinn where I'd been knocked into the river, it must have been him."

"What?"

David hadn't known? What had he thought happened?

"A male cat slammed into me, shoving me into the river. I didn't catch his scent at the time, but I had earlier."

"I heard two gunshots fired."

Now it was her turn to look shocked. "Are you serious?" She knew he was, but she just couldn't believe it.

"Yeah. When I reached where you had been, I couldn't find your scent trail and was certain you fell into the water—*after* you'd been shot. Twice. I roared and roared, trying to get you to respond as I headed downriver. You didn't call back."

"I…I didn't hear anything at first. I was underwater for a few minutes, trying to get to my feet and paddle. Coughing, choking, and sneezing after that."

"Did Quinn end up in the river with you?"

"Not that I saw. He might have. I was concentrating on returning to shore. I assumed whoever did it shoved me in and took off. I'm not sure what his purpose was. He couldn't have drowned me unless I ended up going over the waterfall and slammed into some rocks down below and knocked myself out. I didn't have a lot of time to look around to see if anyone else was in the water with me."

"I don't know what to believe. Had he tried to save your life by protecting you from the gunman?"

"Maybe. We should call this in."

David cupped her face and took a deep breath. "I thought I'd lost you. Twice now. Your brothers and mine would kill me." Without any warning, he kissed her.

He wasn't working up from sweet to something hotter, just kissing her—lips to lips, tongues entwined, hands in her hair—and holding her close, lost in the moment.

She loved the way he was so tender and passionate at the same time, wanting so much more. Not that she should even entertain such a notion.

She kissed him with just as much exuberance, enjoying the feel of his warm, sexy mouth against hers, the caress of his hands on her cheeks, as she stroked his bare back with as much tenderness. She knew she should pull away and remind him they needed to let their bosses know what was going on.

After one more kiss.

David had nearly had a seizure when he'd heard gunshots fired. He knew Tammy had been in that vicinity, and he couldn't get to her fast enough.

Two thoughts had run through his mind. The shooter was a jaguar shifter and could see in the dark. Or he was a human wearing night-vision goggles. Had he meant to shoot her? Or just any big cat he might get a bead on? The cable-snapping incident and now this were too much of a coincidence.

David pulled her close and hugged her tight. He reminded himself that he was solely on a mission, that Tammy was a fellow agent and his brother's wife's cousin. Which meant his goal in holding her close was to reassure her—and himself—that everything was all right.

She smelled so heavenly, felt so soft in his arms, and kissed like an angel and a siren in one. Maybe once they were done with this mission, she really would consider dating him, despite what her brother said about her preferring humans. She'd already agreed to going with him to dinner and the theater. Maybe a trip to a pool, beach, lake, or something where he could enjoy the sun with the she-cat, too.

All he wanted to do right now was kiss her and hold her tight. His cell phone rang. Damn!

She quickly pulled free. "We've got reception. See if it's Martin. I'll grab my phone and see if I can get through to my boss."

Whoever it was, David wanted to kill him for the interruption. He got his phone and saw it was his brother, which more than surprised him, though he still couldn't tamp down his irritation. "Wade?"

"Martin called me and said that things might get a little hot for you. Any leads on who the bad agents are? We've been trying to come up with possibilities."

"Tammy smelled Quinn Singleterry in the area."

"What did Martin say? Did he send him down there to sniff around and help out?"

"Not that Martin said. You know he's pretty thorough. We just got back from searching the area." David explained about the gunshots fired and the jaguar pushing Tammy into the river.

Silence.

"You still there, Wade?"

"Damn it. What the hell's going on?"

"We don't know. The kids said they stole the jaguar from the Wilde & Woolly Maximus Three-Ring Circus that had stolen the cat from the Oregon Zoo. When the boys tried to hand the cat over to an agent, he turned out dirty and returned the jaguar to the circus. Not only that, but the agent used my name."

"Hell. Has to be someone we know, then. I'd come to help you both out in a heartbeat, but Martin's got me on another case. And Tammy's brothers are on an operation right now in Costa Rica."

"I know. We're okay." At least David hoped so. "We're not certain the shooter was aiming for Tammy. He might have been a hunter."

Tammy motioned to David that she had news. "Got to go, Wade. Will let you know what else we discover when I can."

"Keep her safe."

"I'm doing my damnedest. Out here." David said to Tammy, "What have you got?"

"I got hold of my boss. Sylvan says neither Weaver nor Krustan are down here on an assignment. They're supposed to be on R and R. Martin told him two JAG agents are trying to track down the teens, Peter and Hans Fenton, the friends of the Taylor boys. Sylvan will attempt to call Weaver and Krustan and question them concerning the matter."

"Damn. All right. Let me call Martin and see what he has to say about Quinn." As soon as David got hold of Martin, he explained the situation with the kids, the circus, Quinn, the shooting, and the two Enforcers.

Martin was silent for a long time, mulling the situation over. "Okay, so was the shooter a hunter or something else?"

"We don't know for certain. I planned to explore some tonight to see if I could find shell casings or discharged firearm cartridges once I returned Tammy to the bungalow and made sure she was okay."

Tammy gave David a look that meant she wasn't happy with the notion.

"The kids won't say where the cat is until you prove who the rogue agents are, right?" Martin asked.

"Yes, sir."

"I'll have some agents check into the circus. I don't like this situation with Enforcer agents lying about why they're down there, or that someone was shooting at Tammy. Especially after the zip-line *accident* earlier."

"I'm with you on that."

"I'll make some inquiries into the situation with Quinn. He's on leave for a couple of weeks. I know he's had some financial issues, but I wouldn't think he's involved in any of this," Martin said.

David wasn't as sure about Quinn as his boss seemed to be. Why the hell was Quinn down here in this particular place at this particular time?

Then again, Martin had recruited him and had worked with him more closely than David had. Martin and Quinn were big fly-fishing enthusiasts, and if anyone ever got them on the subject, they'd talk an ear off. David liked fishing and eating fish as much as the next jaguar, but he preferred catching his prey in a lot faster way—with jaguar fishing hooks.

"Watch your backs," Martin said.

"Will do."

Tammy stretched like an elegant feline. "Okay, we have to go as jaguars. It's the only way we can travel that well at night and reach the area. We look for shell casings or spent cartridges, the rounds also, and the shooter's scent. We can take a small bag in case we find any evidence. You can shift, place the evidence in the bag, and shift back."

"You know I don't want you in harm's way, right?"

"Yeah, and I really appreciate it. Since I'm allowing you to help with my case, are we in agreement?" She cast him an elusive smile. "I brought some small plastic bags that we can use."

"All right, but you stick close to me," David said.

She snorted. "I was going to say the same to you."

She couldn't be serious. "Who's carrying the plastic bag?" he asked.

"I will. That way you can be all ferocious and growly while we're running through the jungle. Just in case we run into anyone dangerous."

He chuckled. "Works for me."

When they walked out on the shower patio, he saw a new bottle of suntan lotion. He read the attached note out loud: "'If you ever need help with putting on the lotion, we'll be there. AN.' Looks like the teens bought you a special brand of suntan lotion. You sure got their attention."

"You *were* focused on them when you were trying to chase them down, right?

"Most of the time, yeah."

She shook her head. "Did you have any doubts the swimsuit would work?"

"Yeah, I did. I wasn't sure they'd be around when you acted as bait."

"You know, I'd really like this assignment if there were no flying bullets or snapping cables involved. I don't think I've ever had as much fun as I did during the white-water kayaking," she said.

"I have to admit I'm enjoying it almost as much as a vacation, if we could just stick to the fun adventures and I'd get to oil you up next time."

"Maybe some other time."

"I'm taking you up on it, you know."

They shared a look that said he had every intention of following through, and he thought from the hint of a smile in her expression that she was willing. But first things first.

They shifted on the shower patio, and Tammy took the bag in her teeth before they leaped over the wall and headed into the jungle. It was around eleven, so David hoped whoever had shot at Tammy was holed up in his rental unit now and sound asleep.

An hour or so later, they found the site where Tammy

had gone into the water. David sniffed the air and
ground like she was doing. And smelled the cat who
had to have knocked her into the water. It definitely was
Quinn Singleterry's scent.

She looked at David, and he saw the question in her
blue eyes. He wondered if Quinn had attempted to save
her by slamming his jaguar body into hers just as the
rifle was fired. When Quinn had first met them at the
jailhouse, David could have sworn he didn't have any
real clues about the missing jaguar. Now David wasn't
so certain.

How had Quinn known a shooter was getting ready to
fire a rifle? How was he involved in all this?

Except for the noisy cicadas droning on and crickets
chirping, they didn't hear any human voices or jaguars
calling to each other. The water splashed over rocks here,
rapids churning, the smell of fish and fresh water, but
no odor of gunfire in the vicinity. Maybe the shots came
from across the river? Or from a high-powered rifle?

David glanced at Tammy. She was looking across
the water like he had been. She had to be thinking the
same thing. The shooter had been on the other side, in a
tree most likely. Though the cliffs on the opposite bank
would also give someone an advantage.

She turned and headed away from the river, smelling
the ground, looking for the two spent rounds of ammu-
nition. He sniffed at nearby trees at the same height as
Tammy stood to see if he could find either of the rounds
embedded in the trunks.

Before he located them, he heard Tammy scratching
the bark of a tree nearby, growling softly.

He hurried to join her, smelled the base of the tree

trunk, and saw the metal rim of a round buried in the bark and sapwood. He poked at it with his nose but smelled no scent on it. The shooter had to have been wearing gloves when he loaded his rifle. Swearing to himself, David shifted into his human form and crouched down, trying to pull out the round with his fingers, but it was buried too deep.

Tammy scratched at it again with her long, wicked jaguar claws, but she couldn't get it out that way, either.

"I'll have to return here with my camping knife," David said with regret and shifted back into his jaguar form. He looked around the area some more, searching for the other round but not finding it. He'd hoped he could locate it in the mud and they'd have at least one of the rounds for evidence.

Tammy finally stopped scratching at the tree to also look for the other round. When he sensed she wasn't nearby, David's heartbeat accelerated. He glanced around and saw her at the river's edge, staring across the swirling water. He joined her and nudged at her to come with him. At this location, they wouldn't be able to get out of the water on the other side because the cliffs were too high and the flow of the river was strong.

He led her upriver until they found a better place to cross.

Before they entered the water, he nuzzled her nose. She licked his. He smiled and waded into the water.

He glanced back to see Tammy leap in and swim toward him.

When they reached the other side, he waited for her to climb onto the bank and they raced toward the cliff. Though the chances were slim that the shooter was still in the area, he couldn't help the nagging concern that plagued him.

Sniffing the whole place, David caught a scent. Damn. He couldn't believe it. What the hell would Joe Storm be doing out here? And why the hell would the bouncer be in Belize hunting a jaguar? He was a jaguar shifter himself!

David recalled Tammy's discussion with the boys and her earlier remark to him. She seemed to have known Joe. At least she'd mentioned he had killer fists. How had she known him? Just visits to the club, or something else? He wondered if she had worked with Joe on assignment in some special capacity while he had still been with the JAG branch. Had she ditched him as a partner? And this was payback? But why now?

Having been a marine, Joe was knowledgeable enough to know to remove the discharged cartridges, except he hadn't removed the round in the tree yet. David suspected he hadn't forgotten. He just hadn't been there yet. That didn't bode well. If Joe came back when David returned with a knife, he could have trouble.

At least now they both had the shooter's scent. They knew who he was and could report back to the boss with the information. He glanced at Tammy.

She was still looking for cartridges. He grunted at her to come with him, and she hurried to join him.

Now for the tedious part of this business. They had to return to the bungalow so he could get his knife, and then he'd have to make his way back to retrieve the cartridge.

A soft pattering of rain started to fall. He and Tammy returned to the river and swam across. He was feeling more and more drained of energy, and as slowly as Tammy swam this time, being pulled farther downriver than before, he was certain she also was struggling with weariness.

After they climbed out on the rocky bank, they headed straight back to their bungalow. An hour later, they stood in the outdoor shower room, the rain coming down in a deluge now. He shifted and opened the door for Tammy. She shook off under the eaves and ran inside.

"I've got to return to where we found that round embedded in the tree and dig it out," David said as he rummaged through his bag for his knife.

Tammy emitted the jaguar version of a groan. She hadn't shifted, but was sitting on the floor in front of the door, watching him and waiting for him.

"You don't have to go with me this time. Now that I know where the round is, I should be able to find my way there quickly and return."

She shook her head.

He appreciated that she felt she had to watch his back, but he was sure no one would be out there at this time of night. The rain was coming down in sheets. They hadn't discovered Joe thus far. David felt he would be safe enough. "I'll be fine and back before you know it."

Again, she shook her head.

"All right. Don't say I didn't offer. You could be snuggled in bed, rain pouring overhead, dreaming about chasing butterflies or something."

She gave him a toothy grin.

"Or chasing me, even better." He smiled at her, found his knife, and let her back out into the pouring rain.

He shifted, and then they were off again.

Between being tired and having trouble searching for the scents in the heavy downpour, they looked forever before finding the right location. The river was overflowing its banks already, the water even more of a rush now. When they reached the tree that wore Tammy's claw marks, he stared at the place where the round had been.

All that was left was a hole with a few gouges around the edge.

Chapter 16

FURIOUS THAT THE SHOOTER HAD RETURNED AND RE-moved the round in the tree after all they'd been through to locate it, Tammy wanted to strangle him. What the hell was Joe Storm up to?

She couldn't believe she'd ever dated the jerk. But he was always on his best behavior with women. *More* than best behavior.

Beyond wanting to strangle Joe, she was ready to collapse in bed and sleep the remaining night away as well as half the next day. But she figured David would want to know how she knew Joe, now that they had discovered he was the shooter.

Did Joe hold a grudge against her? Maybe. But she really didn't want to talk to David about this. Martin might know something about it, and he could tell David.

After returning to the bungalow and cleaning up, she dried her hair and then headed for the bedroom. David was sitting on a chair, wearing a pair of blue boxers, his cell phone to his ear. He shook his head at her, indicating he couldn't get through.

Not that she expected a signal with the torrential rain.

She pulled the covers aside to find fragrant purple orchid petals and a silver foil-wrapped chocolate sitting on top of her pillow. Now that was definitely the bright spot in her day.

She glanced at David to see if he had seen them. He

was frowning at the gifts. She smiled and took a deep breath to smell the fragrant flower, the heavenly aroma of chocolate, and a hint of the teens, one on the candy wrapper, the other on the petals.

"From the boys, I presume, when they delivered our bags yesterday morning," she said, unwrapping the chocolate. "I think all the gifts and messages prove they truly do trust us. They're good kids."

David grunted. "They're obviously trying to butter you up."

"I'm not easily 'buttered up,'" she said, though she loved that they were making the attempt.

She popped the chocolate into her mouth and moaned with delight, not realizing how much she had missed it while she had been here.

"Could have fooled me. Does chocolate make everything all better?" he asked.

"You bet. Though they could have left even more." She smiled and climbed into bed, noting that David had turned the air conditioner on full blast again and her skin was already freckled with goose bumps. "Are you hot?"

He only gave her that sexy smile.

She rolled her eyes. She'd fallen into that one.

Yeah, he was hot and sexy and anything a girl could want in the short-term, she supposed, not that she was biting. She'd thought her parents had a great deal going for them, but after discovering that her father had been fooling around on the side, she wasn't ready to commit to anyone. She'd already been burned once with a JAG agent her brothers had highly recommended, a friend of theirs who had turned out to be the highest order of rat. *Joe Storm.*

She had gone out with a human guy after that, but he'd left her wanting something wilder—like David.

"Are you cold?" David asked.

"How could you tell? Are my lips turning blue? Do you see my chill bumps?" She was only half teasing.

"We need to talk about what's going on. If you're too cold, I can set the air conditioner so that it's not as frigid. Or we can…share some body heat. I'll definitely think better if we snuggle. Otherwise, I'll keep thinking about it. It's torture being with you but not really being with you."

She had to admit David was cute. If one of the other men had said that to her when she was on assignment with him, she would have expressly said, "No thanks." David was another story. Still, she wasn't just giving in.

Working with some of the single agents, Enforcers and JAG alike, she had never felt they appreciated her abilities to get a job done. How could she want a deeper relationship with an agent who couldn't also value her for her vocation? Not that David had been anything like that—so far. Yet she kept waiting for him to show his *true* spots. To prove he was just like all the rest.

Humans were fine for dating, but not for the long run. How could she explain to a human that she had big teeth, big eyes, and big spotted ears—the jaguar's version of the hungry wolf—if he ever riled her too badly? Or that she liked to take moonlight runs as a jaguar from time to time?

"If we cuddle, it could lead to a lot less thinking," she said pragmatically.

David smiled, and his expression was downright wolfish. She realized he took her comment for agreement.

After all, she hadn't said no. He pulled her into his arms, and she went willingly—enjoying the solid, warm feel of him as the air conditioner cooled the rest of her down. She was certain his thoughts were not on the case, the kids, the missing zoo cat, or the missing rounds.

Being the good little Enforcer that she was, she was thinking about the mission for the two of them. As much as she told herself they shouldn't be doing this and needed to keep their relationship on a totally professional level, she loved curling up against his warm body.

"Okay, so the shooter returned to the scene of the crime and learned we knew the round was lodged in the tree. Had he been watching us the whole time?" She hated that he might have been and they hadn't caught him in the act.

"Maybe. If he didn't have his rifle with him, that would account for him not shooting at either of us this time." David's hand caressed her arm gently.

"His scent wasn't anywhere near the tree, which meant he hadn't crossed the river to find it earlier."

"Agreed."

"He had to have crossed the river carrying the rifle in a waterproof bag, unless a bridge exists above or below where we were, but I don't recall seeing any."

"Also agree," David said. "I don't believe there are any developments on the other side of the river for miles."

She'd been avoiding the obvious question she was certain David wanted to ask. And David, being David, was giving her a chance to come clean, she thought. "Okay, yeah, I know Joe Storm."

David continued to caress her arm, not saying anything, just watching her.

She let out her breath in a heavy sigh. "Okay, okay. I dated him."

David's eyes widened fractionally.

"My brothers knew him and thought I might like dating him. Joe was fun, took me to some nice restaurants. I really thought I was falling for him."

David's hand stilled on her skin.

She shrugged. "When I'm in a relationship with a man, I don't share. I found out by mistake that he was dating another girl. He'd gotten his date nights mixed up. That's the problem when you're working a job and juggling multiple girlfriends. He thought we were supposed to be going out on a Saturday night, and I was all for it. He acted really strange, mumbled something concerning another *appointment* he'd forgotten. I told him no problem, though I was disappointed. I'd been gone on a job for two weeks and wanted to spend some time with him before the next assignment."

She ground her teeth, still irritated about it.

"He canceled on your date so he could go out with another woman?" David asked, sounding incredulous, like he couldn't believe anyone would do that to her.

She valued David's comment more than he could know.

"Nope. We had already arrived at the club when the call came in. He shrugged and said it was no big deal. Of course, I didn't know what the call was about. He said it was JAG business. I had no reason not to believe him. He didn't bother phoning the person back to say he couldn't make it. So I figured it was one of those situations where he could show up or not, no RSVP needed.

"This woman arrived at the club just as we were taking our seats, asking him where he'd been because she'd been waiting for him to pick her up at her apartment for more than half an hour. She said she thought maybe she had it wrong and was supposed to meet him there. I wasn't sure if she was telling the truth or was suspicious that he was seeing another woman. She started screaming at me as if *I* was the one stealing her boyfriend. So that's how I learned he was a two-timer. But she and I weren't the only ones seeing him."

"There were more than just the two of you?" David sounded shocked.

Tammy gave a sarcastic little laugh. "Yeah. I guess he mostly dated humans. He'd make sure he didn't have the smells of any other woman clinging to him, but he didn't have to worry so much with the human women. Unless one of them wore perfume, the others would never know the difference. With me, he had to be a little more careful."

"I never knew."

"Yeah, well, the woman started telling me how he had broken up with two different fiancées, and I got suspicious and began investigating him on the sly after I broke up with him. I discovered he had two *current* fiancées, neither of whom he had broken off relations with. Once the word got to his boss, Martin felt that someone with so little integrity wouldn't make a good JAG agent. So he fired him."

David was caressing her skin again but slower now, as if he was pondering the ramifications.

"And that's how I know Joe," she said.

"That's why he was let go? We thought it was because he coldcocked one of the other agents. Though we were surprised that had been enough to get him fired. I had no idea he was dating so many women at one time."

"Welcome to the club."

"We're not all like that, Tammy," David finally said, his voice thoughtful, as if she thought all agents were like Joe.

"No. I met your brother and he seems like a nice-enough guy."

David's mouth twitched into a hint of a smile.

"My brothers are okay when they want to be," Tammy said.

"I've never strung a woman along or dated more than one at a time," David said.

She wasn't sure if he was mentioning it as a way of sticking up for the male race in general, or if it was more of a personal declaration.

Not sure what to say, she patted David's chest. "Good to know."

That earned a dark chuckle from him. He let out his breath. "Did Joe feel any animosity toward you? Believe you had anything to do with him getting fired?"

"I didn't tell Martin about Joe's situation with women, if you think that could be a reason he shot at me."

"Yeah, it could be a darned good motive. Did he believe you told on him?"

"Maybe. I don't know. I didn't have anything further to do with him after I learned what I could."

"Hell, what if Joe's been working with dirty agents since he was terminated from employment with the JAG branch? He has a possible grudge against both you and the JAG branch. How long ago were the two of you dating?"

"Six months ago. We'd only been dating for a couple of months. Some of that time I was gone on missions. Or he was. If he thought I had something to do with him getting fired and was angry with me, why didn't he do something about it when he got canned? He could have killed me anytime."

"The jungle is a great place to get rid of someone you have a grudge against without anyone being the wiser. He might have just snapped recently. Maybe he knew you were looking for the missing jaguar, and he's involved in the theft, in addition to believing you had something to do with his firing. That could have put him over the edge."

"Wait, how would he have known exactly where I would be when he fired the shot? I was traveling all over the jungle. Just like you and the teens were."

"Hmm, not sure. You told the teens he had killer fists. He never hurt you, did he?"

"Emotionally, sure. I was upset when I learned he'd been seeing other women behind my back, pretending he was away on missions and that he loved me so sincerely. But physically, no."

"I had another thought. I think Quinn must have saved you by pushing you into the river. I don't believe he was involved in the shooting."

She had thought the same thing. "How did he know about the shooter? Do you think he was in cahoots with Joe but didn't want him to hurt me?"

"Martin seems to believe Quinn's still a good guy. I'd have to agree that he tried to help. What I want to know is if he was really looking into the stolen cat issue or if that was a ploy to work with you. Or like you said, he is involved but didn't want you shot."

"You probably know him better than I do."

"We've served on five missions together. Boss said he's had some financial difficulties."

"Not good."

"No. Other than that, he has a sister he adores, and believe me, if anyone came on to her like *he* does women, he'd bite the guy's head off. His dad was always catting around and took off when he was a teen. His mother teaches English at a local community college. His sister is a college freshman, no major yet. He had an older sister who committed suicide. I think he feels somewhat responsible for her death, though he would never say why. But it makes him even more protective of his younger sister. He loves hamburgers, hates onions—says they aren't helpful in a man-woman relationship—and I doubt he'll ever settle down."

"Any negatives?"

David looked down at her.

"Besides that he's in debt and is a womanizer?"

He snorted. "Sounds like enough negatives to me."

She chuckled. "I mean, any reason he would be involved in any of this?"

"Financial. But he's really hard-core about the Service. So it's difficult to see that he would jeopardize his career to be one of the bad guys."

"He wouldn't be the first guy who appears to have everything going for him but turns to criminal activities for money."

"True. I wonder, too, who would have used my name when the boys called to turn the jaguar over to the agent."

"Someone who thought you wouldn't get wind of it, maybe. Or someone who believed you'd try to work with the teens and wanted them to doubt your integrity. So why would Quinn be out here if he's not working on this case?"

"Maybe he has his own agenda. Maybe he's really interested in you."

Tammy snorted. "A guy like that could have any woman he wants. He certainly wouldn't bother with someone who isn't interested. Can you think of any reason why he would be looking into this case?"

"What if he knows who the corrupt agent is?"

Tammy took a deep breath. "So why not just come clean about it?"

"Maybe Quinn doesn't have proof. He's thorough when he does a job, and I can't see him hurting anyone's good name on just a supposition that the agent is crooked."

"Okay, I can believe that," she said, snuggling even more against David's hard, warm body. Wanting more from him. She was sure he'd go along with it if she suggested doing something more…but she was still a little wary of making too much of…*them*.

David stroked her hair in a tender caress, while her hand rested on his bare belly. He leaned down and kissed the top of her head.

"Thanks for coming to my rescue," she said softly, feeling dreamy and comfortable with him, like they belonged together like this, like they'd been together for a while. Facing danger did that to shifters—brought them closer. Not quite like this, usually. But with him, she felt…differently.

Her fingers slid over his belly with a gentle sweep.

He lifted her chin and looked into her eyes. "Tammy…"

She swore he looked a little misty-eyed. Or was that just lust?

She didn't care. All she wanted was him, now, this

very minute. She'd been in life-threatening situations before. And she'd needed time to decompress. What a way to do it. She'd never been with a partner that she'd felt anything for other than camaraderie if they worked well together, or disdain if they had not. With David, she really wanted…*more*.

Still, she was afraid to be hurt again. "No strings," she said, as if that would make the situation more tenable if he dumped her after a few dates. She kissed his lips—his warm, firm masculine lips.

He broke off the kiss and said in a caring way, not annoyed but like this really meant something to him and he wanted her to know how much, "I don't do one-night stands, Tammy. Not my style."

She sighed, sounding exasperated, but she was secretly pleased at his declaration. "I'm…the same way, only things haven't worked out."

"I understand." He continued to stroke her hair with one hand, his other arm wrapped around her, holding her to him and showing possessiveness in an affectionate way.

She studied him for a moment and saw the sincerity in his expression, then sighed again. "Fine. Then we're dating now. All right?"

He gave her the warmest smile. "You've got it." He didn't even try to couch his enthusiasm.

She loved his impulsiveness and zeal. She might be a wild cat—as in able to live in the jungle—but when it came to sex, she didn't really see herself as the aggressive kind.

Until David started kissing her. *Ohmigod*. What had made her want no strings attached?

He started nuzzling with his mouth against hers, his hands sliding up her tank top, leaving trails of heat everywhere he touched her skin. She was half burying him with her body, straddling one of his muscular legs, rubbing her sex against him like a cat affectionately rubbed against someone. Only she was leaving her scent on him, claiming him.

He drew his leg up a bit, making her groan as his thigh increased the contact between them. She was ready to come, never having experienced the rush this quickly. She felt like a tigress, licking and kissing his lips, pressing for entrance, making him smile.

His hands were busy at work, first sliding up beneath her top, but then he quickly seized the ends and tugged it up to remove it, forcing her to quit kissing him for a second.

Then he was kissing her again, with only her nipples rubbing against the light hair on his chest, and she thought she would die of pleasure.

For a moment, he ran his hands down her back, caressing, stroking, but as hard as he was and as much as she could smell his musky desire, she figured that wouldn't last. Sure enough, he slipped his hands under the waistband of her panties and cupped her buttocks, squeezing gently. Only she wasn't going for gentle. She wanted it all.

She began to rub his cock through his boxers, and that made *him* groan. She smiled, feeling wickedly in charge, when he flipped her on her back, pulled off her panties and tossed them, and then jerked off his boxers.

Now he straddled her leg, rubbing against her and leaving his sexy scent on her. With the same maneuver he'd made with her, she meant to raise her leg a little to increase the contact between his cock and her, but he slid his hand down to stroke her between the legs. The kissing had turned to suckling as he moved his mouth to a breast, his tongue toying with her nipple and teasing her into a higher state of ecstasy. Her hands were in his hair, her fingers tangling in the strands, while she was barely able to breathe. The climax hit so quickly that she cried out with awe and joy, her whole body awash in sexual gratification.

He was quickly off her, and she felt the loss of heat at once and the disappointment that they wouldn't finish this together. He grabbed a handful of condoms and stuck them on his bedside table—making her smile—and then quickly sheathed himself before he again joined her on the bed.

She welcomed him with open arms, her legs parted, ready.

Tammy was hot, sexier than the devil, and David had to add *wildly unpredictable* to her list of traits. He loved her for it.

He nestled between her legs this time, rubbing his cock against her sweet sex. He cupped her face and began kissing her mouth, her cheeks, her eyes. He was ready for anything. As soon as she began to kiss him back, her lips brushing, pressuring, nipping at his, her arousal fed his own. Their bodies moved against each other, their fueled cat scents turning them on all the more.

He felt he was on fire despite the air-conditioned bungalow, the she-cat making his blood sizzle. The jungle sounds faded into the background, and all he could hear were their breathing and heartbeats drumming hard. Her hands skimmed his back and buttocks as he tried to rub against her, taking pleasure in kissing her breasts, suckling on her nipples, and smelling her arousal. He kissed her mouth again, and she parted her lips. As soon as he inserted his tongue inside, she sucked on it, making his erection throb with eagerness. Her breathing was as ragged as his. He wanted to be deep inside her so badly that he could barely stand it.

Her nipples were tight and rubbed his chest as she moved in his arms. The intensity of the heat built inside him. She groaned deep in her belly like a feral cat. The erotic sound nearly undid him.

She ground against his erection, making him groan out loud. She smiled. The vixen.

Her luscious body was flushed, her nipples taut and blushing. She wrapped her legs around his hips, and he couldn't hold off any longer. He penetrated her. Slowly. Until he was inside her to the hilt. She was gloriously anchored to him, and she began to move with him. Sweet heaven, she was desire personified.

Her teeth grazed his neck and then his shoulder. He pumped into her like a man possessed. Her teeth and tongue and mouth were making a sensual assault on his neck and throat, and then she worked her way to his jaw. As much as he wanted to make this last, he couldn't. His hands tightened on her buttocks as he drove into her. He felt as though he was ready to explode.

White-hot heat filled him. He let go, bursting with the release. He held on to her, loving that they were still joined, feeling one with her, wanting to hold on to the pleasure and the moment and her.

"I'm ready to sleep now," Tammy finally said in a softly sensual but sleepy voice. "What about you?"

"Hell, yeah." But that meant snuggling all night with the she-cat, and he hoped they woke up to another bout of this…soon.

Chapter 17

LATE THE NEXT MORNING WHILE TAMMY AND DAVID were slowly waking up in bed, Tammy said, "Today we were supposed to go waterfall rappelling. I'm thinking the boys probably won't be there, or we could watch over them. Since we've already talked to them, and if it was Joe Storm targeting me, he might be planning to take one of us out at the waterfalls.

"So what if we get something to eat, then run as jaguars, search the area surrounding the waterfall, and see if we can locate him readying an ambush? We'd have to keep out of everyone's sight, but we could move faster and, with our noses to the ground, could find Joe's trail much quicker if he's been in the area."

"He could be in place now," David said, agreeing with her. He kissed her head, his hot, hard body wrapped around her in a loving embrace.

She really could get used to waking up like this in the morning. The other guys she had dated seriously had slept on their own side of the bed, and she'd thought that was the way all guys preferred to sleep. But this was really, really nice.

"Yeah. Maybe we can take him down. I'd certainly be willing to chance it. You want to do it?" she asked.

He sighed. "You like to live dangerously, don't you?"

She smiled up at him. "Isn't that a prerequisite to joining the Service?"

"Yeah, for me, not for you. Your job isn't supposed to be this treacherous."

"Ha! Says you." She shook her head and untangled herself from his sexy body. "Why is it that most JAG agents think their jobs are more dangerous than an Enforcer's?"

His mouth curved up.

"Don't answer that." She meant to mention that he had been watching two teens at a club, and how dangerous was that? Except that David *had* risked getting killed by stepping in and protecting the boys from Joe Storm's fury. And her brothers had been in numerous life-threatening situations, many more than she had in her job.

"All right. Let's go," David said, slipping out of bed naked.

She admired him for a second. *So* hot. "Do we run as jaguars from the bungalow in broad daylight? Or shift in the jungle? My preference would be to…" She hesitated. Her choice would be to shift in the bungalow. But practically, there was probably more of a chance for a human to see them running from the bungalow as jaguars, though each of the places was surrounded by vegetation. She took a deep breath. "…shift in the jungle."

"As much as I'd prefer to turn here and not have to leave our clothes out there, it would be safer to shift out there," David said, pulling on a pair of camo boxers. He smiled at her eyeing his boxers. "They blend with the foliage better."

"As long as you don't misplace them."

He chuckled.

She slipped into her camo pants. "Good thing we have an enhanced sense of smell, or we'd be in real trouble."

"We'd never find our clothes upon our return otherwise," he agreed.

She pulled out a small camo backpack. "We can tuck our clothes into this."

They had finished dressing when Tammy's boss called. "Anderson," she said.

"Tammy, one of our agents discovered that Joe Storm had a flight home late last night to Las Vegas. And Quinn took a flight to Los Angeles an hour after that."

To some extent, she was surprised to hear it. "And, they are both exactly where now?"

"We weren't able to track either of their current locations, but we're still working on it. The airline confirmed the two men were on their flights. You won't be able to get a flight out until tomorrow afternoon, but I've had our people book you both for a return passage. We need you here looking into the circus situation."

"All right. We'll take the time to search the area for any other clues concerning Joe and Quinn in the meantime. Joe might have figured the boys aren't planning on going on any of the excursions they'd signed up for. Now that we know he's involved and by protocol we would inform our superiors, he's probably rethinking his strategy."

"I agree. We'll let you know if we pinpoint either of the men's locations in the meantime."

"What about Weaver and Krustan?"

Her boss let out his breath. "No getting hold of them, either. But we haven't found that they've taken any flights out. Though they could make their way back via other means."

"All right. Thanks." She pocketed her phone.

David was leaning against the dresser, arms folded across his chest. "Joe and Quinn have left, I take it."

"Yes, back to the States." She explained the rest to him. "Since we have the free time on our hands, I still think we should search the area around the waterfall to see what we can learn. I'm curious whether he had a hunting stand set up somewhere in view of the waterfall."

"Let's go."

They grabbed a quick bite to eat, then headed out to the jungle, shimmering light filtering through the rainforest.

The trek through the jungle was hot and muggy as David and Tammy kept an eye out for any movement along the way. When they found a place to strip, they did it in a hurry and stuffed their things in the camo bag. David tucked it among the dense ferns. Tammy shifted and watched for any signs of anyone, listening to the sounds of the jungle, but except for a few voices drifting from the resort, there was no other indication of humans in the area.

David shifted and they took off running in the direction of the waterfall.

They searched for any hint of Joe or Quinn having been in the area—and Weaver and Krustan, while they were at it. They also checked for the boys in the area. David was just as alert, tense, listening, watching, but nothing seemed out of the ordinary.

Now that Joe and Quinn were gone, Tammy didn't believe anyone else would take a shot at them when they were traveling to the waterfall rappelling site. Even if Joe had still been in the area and planned to attack her or David or the boys, she figured he wouldn't be looking for them, but would be ready in a tree somewhere with the perfect view of the waterfall.

She saw something flick out from a tree. She studied the branch. A seven-foot boa coiled around it—the snake's dark brown- and gray-banded skin so indistinct that it nearly blended in with the bark, the flick of its tongue the only thing that gave the reptile away.

When they reached the site, she wanted to split forces, but she thought better of it and figured David wouldn't go along with it, either. Tammy took in a deep breath, smelling the air drenched with the fresh, watery fragrance of the rapids flowing over the cliff and the waterfall splashing into a turbulent pool below.

The burgeoning sunlight collided with the waterfall, creating a multicolored arch, the red, green, yellow, and purple forming a soft, misty rainbow. The climb was steep, at an angle, the rocks moss-covered and slippery.

They kept watching for any sign of the boys or her fellow Enforcer agents, but nada. No jaguars, none of them in human form. Had they missed spotting them if any of them were in the area? In the dense vegetation, it would be easy to hide.

Birds flitted about, leaves fluttered, insects flew around them, all distractions that caught their cat eyes. Cats could detect the slightest movement, so she was constantly looking, seeing something, but not the right something.

Then she smelled a whiff of Joe. David had, too. His whole body was rigid, ready to take action, his ears perked, nose sniffing, tail twitching, just like she was reacting. She dashed off in the direction of the smell.

Joe's scent trail led them down a steep incline that would be easy to traverse without ropes if they were in human form and was even more easily navigated in their jaguar forms.

They found his scent where he'd climbed a tree, and David hurried up it while she searched for Joe's trail leading away from there. She was so intent on her surroundings and the trail that she had gone quite a distance before she realized David wasn't with her. She waited, twitching her tail hard, anxious to keep going.

David dove out of the brush to join her, looking a little anxious that he'd lost her for a moment, and then they continued on the path she'd found. Not that there was an actual human kind of path. Just the scent trail the cat had left.

They found a site where Joe appeared to have pitched a one-man tent, the vegetation flattened in one area, fern fronds broken. It was close to the river, a mile and a half south of the waterfall. He hadn't needed to maintain a campfire because he could just hunt as a jaguar and eat his meal raw.

It looked as though he'd packed up his gear and gone, no sign of anything left behind.

She was ready to give up the search when David nudged at her to follow him. Wondering what he thought was wrong when she smelled no sign of Joe, any other cats, or humans in this direction, she loped behind him. She was contemplating what they would do until they left. She hoped the boys would see them again before she and David took off on their drive to the airport in Belize City and flew out tomorrow.

She and David had traveled maybe eight miles, and she was really wondering what in the world was leading him in this direction, when they came to another waterfall. He began to make his way down the steep rocks to the bank surrounding the pool beneath the tumbling water. She kept sniffing the air, smelling David instead, loving his sexy scent but trying to catch any sign of what he was investigating as she followed him down the rocks that would have been treacherous for a human without rappelling equipment.

After David reached the narrow, rocky bank below, he swam into the center of the pool. She paused on the moss-covered rocks edging the pool, the water crystal clear blue, as she watched him, waiting for him to do something. He shifted. She looked up at the steep cliffs all around them covered in thick vegetation, and then back at David. He was observing her, looking expectantly.

"The water's great. We have tons of time to kill. Want to join me?"

She gave him a jaguar grin. After surveying the cliffs one more time and seeing no sign of anyone, she jumped in and shifted into her human form. She stood on the rocky ground, the delightfully warm water like a lovely bath, caressing her shoulders. She swam to him. "What did you find in the tree?"

Business first, David mused. He'd have time to have some fun with the she-cat before they had to leave their jungle paradise. He was certain his mouth curved into a hungry smile right before he took her into his arms and held her sweet, very naked body tight. "Joe had been in the tree and had a perfect sighting for shooting his rifle. No evidence left behind."

"So we're done with investigating for the moment?"

"Yeah, I'd say we enjoy the water a bit. What do you think?"

He was glad she was of like mind as she reached up and locked her arms behind his head and started to kiss him. Only her kisses were molten hot—no slow build-up—tongue tangling with his in a jungle dance, her body moving against his, rubbing against his already rigid erection.

"Hot damn," he groaned against her mouth, his hands fisted around locks of her silky, strawberry blond hair. Her eyes closed as she gyrated against him, grinding her soft flesh against his.

His hands slid down her back until he molded them around her soft ass and pressed her tighter against him. She bit his lower lip gently, combed her fingers through his hair, and turned his blood into a raging inferno.

When he'd seen the other pool, he'd hoped they could find another one farther downriver, just for this, and that she'd be as interested as he was.

Her eyes a bit glazed, she started kissing him all over again.

Worked for him. He was still in the kissing part of the seduction, enjoying the sweetness of her mouth, the tactile delight of stroking tongues, the way her finger-nails glided over his back in a delicate caress that made him think of a cat's claws mostly retracted. He swore she was purring even before he slid his hands down her buttocks and squeezed.

She reached under the water and began to stroke him, and he groaned. He'd never last. Not with the press of her breasts against his chest or her hand on his cock, driving him to madness. He wanted inside her now, but maybe she wasn't quite ready. He leaned down and took a nipple in his mouth and suckled. That made her stop stroking him. Good. He wanted to pleasure her first.

He molded his hand to her other breast, felt her nipple

poking into his palm, licked and gently tugged on her nipple with his lips and then his teeth. She was leaning back, making soft moaning sounds. He slipped his hand from her breast and under the water, stroking her nub, already as hard as his erection was. She locked an ankle around the back of his thigh, her hands around his waist, her eyes closed, concentrating on the strokes as he was concentrating on the way she seemed to feel pleasure in them. Tension filled her expression as he slipped two fingers deep inside her and she moaned.

He felt the exquisite rumbling of her release, muscles quivering. He loved that he could do that to her.

"Mmm," she said, sounding relaxed and ready to slip under the water.

The water lapped at the top of her breasts.

He sank into the water in front of her and began kissing her again, rubbing against her, waiting for her to let him know she was ready. She settled a leg around his hip, and that was his green light. He grasped her other calf and lifted her, centering himself between her legs, and eased in.

She began riding him—hot, wet, and beautiful in the rainforest in Belize in the middle of a waterfall pool on a sunny summer day. Nothing could be better or more special than this, he thought, loving every bit of being with her. And wanting so much more.

Omigod. David filled her to the brink and more. Tammy had never done anything quite this wild in her life. Ever. And wouldn't have ever considered doing such a thing if it hadn't been for David. With him, it seemed right. More than right. *This* was wonderful.

She was riding him as she kissed and licked and

gently bit his neck. He'd have a few light bruises to show she'd claimed him. Every time she did it, he had a more feral-cat look about him and growled more, his ravenous eyes shining in the sunlight peering between the building clouds. And she loved it.

He pumped into her, the waterfall spilling into the pool, drowning out the sound of their groans and sighs of pleasure, their bodies washed in the splashing water. She felt him tense just before release.

He hugged her tight to his hard body, letting the warm water swirl around them, soaking in the sounds of the rainforest, and they both laughed when it began to rain. She'd always remember their last day in Belize as the most fun sexual experience she'd ever had. And romantic. And…wild.

She clung to him, enjoying just being with him in this way, pushing out all the worries of the world, because as soon as they left Belize and this peaceful little place of paradise, they were bound for more trouble.

Chapter 18

DAVID DIDN'T WANT TO RELEASE TAMMY IN THE WA-
terfall pool. She felt so good in his arms and in this
place, as if it was a jaguar-shifter haven for mating.
He'd never been with a woman with whom he wanted
to cherish the moment for as long as he could after they
made love. Previous girlfriends would roll over and go
to sleep after they made love in bed, needing their space.
He treasured how Tammy loved to cuddle, sharing the
intimacy of the moment longer.

Yet he needed to release her so they could return to the
resort, eat, and retire to the bungalow to pack. After that,
he planned a lot more bed sport—if she was agreeable.

Instead, he held on to the naked she-cat in his arms
and soaked up the feel of them, their bodies still joined.
Even thinking of them like this was making him harden.

She lifted her head from his chest and smiled. "I
think…you've got a tiger in your tank."

He chuckled, but he didn't make a move to disen-
gage them.

"Maybe we should get back to the resort," she said,
her finger caressing his nipple as if she really wasn't all
that interested in returning.

"Agreed." He still didn't let her go.

Her smile broadened.

He leaned down and kissed her on the mouth, one
last long, searing, hungry kiss. "This doesn't end here."

"Mmm. I don't want you to get the wrong idea about anything, but all I've got to say is wow."

"Which means this doesn't end here," he reiterated. He wanted to remind her that he didn't believe in one-night stands—in tropical settings or anywhere else. When he had sex with a woman, it was only the beginning of a blossoming relationship.

Still, since he was getting worked up and she wasn't quitting with her strokes and she'd resumed kissing, the notion of doing this a little longer appealed.

He loved how attuned they were to each other. When they were finished for a second time, they shifted into their jaguar forms and paddled toward the shore, her tail waving in front of his nose. He wanted to grab it in playful fun.

And he almost managed to snag the tip, right before she climbed out of the water and shook all over him. She gave him an impish, toothy jaguar grin and then began to lick the water off her body, but the light rain wasn't helping. He wanted to suggest they switch, and he lick her body while she licked his.

She leaped up the rocks to the cliffs above and they headed back to the resort. The sun had disappeared behind the clouds and would begin to fade as it did at this time in summer. By 6:30, the sun would have set. With the sun-blocking trees and a storm overhead, that meant it would be dark even earlier. They skirted way around the area where the waterfall rappelling site was, assuming the guide and tourists would have been there and headed back to the resort by now, but David and Tammy needed to be careful.

They were getting much closer to the resort, only about ten minutes away, when they heard a jaguar roar.

Tammy and David looked at each other. They both dove into the jungle in the direction they'd heard the cat roaring, and David prayed that if it was one of the boys, neither was in any danger.

―――∕∖∕∖∕∖―――

The rain ceased, and after an hour of searching for the jaguar, Tammy and David reached a bungalow where the kids seemed to be staying, since their scents were strongest there. Why would the boys lead them to the rental unit this time?

Inside, the place had been trashed—the teens' scents and David's aftershave fragrance were here, but so were Weaver's and Krustan's scents, and Joe Storm's. Tammy felt nauseous with worry as she rushed through the one-bedroom unit, searching for clues that either of the boys was still here.

None. If they'd had luggage, it was gone now, too. And if they'd parked a car nearby, it was no longer here.

David nudged at Tammy to leave with him, and then they returned to where they'd left their backpack. It was gone.

Feeling panicked for the boys' safety and now their own if they couldn't find their clothes, she and David backtracked, circled the area, and sniffed the ground. She recognized the teens' scents around here. Right here. Where they'd left their clothes. The boys had to have taken them. What the hell was going on?

She looked at David. He was staring off into the jungle, whiskers moving, ears twitching, sensing smells, movement, anything to clue them in that the boys were nearby.

What if not only the boys' place had been trashed? What if theirs had been also?

Men tromped through the brush in the distance, calling out, "Tammy Anderson! David Patterson!"

Crap! What the hell had happened? Now, neither she nor David had any clothes, so they couldn't change forms. They needed to get back to their bungalow, shift, dress, and let the staff know they were fine.

They ran until Tammy found a big tree to climb into. She grunted at David and leaped into one of the lower branches.

He joined her, nuzzled her face, and sat down. They listened for the men combing the rainforest, calling for them, looking for them. She hated that they worried, but for the moment, she and David couldn't do anything about it.

When the men's voices faded into the jungle, she and David jumped down and loped back to their bungalow. Men's voices speaking in Spanish near their rental unit made Tammy and David halt in their steps. *Great.* They couldn't even sneak into their place to get some clothes.

In the distance, they found a tree to climb with a view of their place. She smelled Nate's scent here. So the teen had watched their bungalow from this vantage point. Luckily, it was far enough from their rental unit that the teen couldn't see beyond the wall of the outdoor shower.

They watched four men in uniform leave the bungalow, one remaining behind, sitting down on the wooden chair on their deck. *Super.* He was going to wait for their return, in case they showed up?

Not that she wouldn't have done the same if she was them, worried about the missing tourists.

She and David watched the man for more than an hour, but he wasn't dozing and he wasn't leaving.

Someone moved out of the jungle toward the man and said in Spanish, "No sign of them. They just vanished."

"They haven't come back here yet, either."

"Okay, I had to take a break and see if they had returned." The man stalked off to the dining hall.

The officer folded his arms and stared into the jungle.

Tammy nudged David, telling him she was leaving the tree to sneak into their place if she had to. They had to let the men know they were okay, though she couldn't figure out why anyone would be searching for them.

David shook his head, letting her know he didn't want her to go anywhere. Fine, she'd be the lookout and come to save him if he got himself into trouble.

He jumped down from the tree and ran off. She lost sight of him in the thick foliage, and then saw the man returning from the dining hall.

"Anything yet?"

"No," the officer said.

"I will be back." He headed into the jungle.

Her heart nearly gave out as she worried David and the searcher would run into each other, but David in his big-cat form ran around the back side of the shower wall. With a soaring leap, he landed on the top of the wall, and before the guard could look, David jumped down inside.

She wondered what David would say after he shifted and dressed when he spoke with the officer. How would he explain that he'd suddenly shown up without the guy seeing him arrive? How would he explain where Tammy was? Not good. What if the officer thought David and his girlfriend had a fight, and he had gotten rid of her in the rainforest?

She stood, ready to jump down and join him, but saw David leap onto the top of the shower wall, still as a jaguar, and jump down into the bushes. What was he doing?

He raced into the jungle and within minutes was climbing back into the tree to rest on the branch with her. She waited for him to tell her something, totally clueless about what was going on.

He shifted. "Hell," he said. "Someone trashed the place like they did the boys', and our clothes, suitcases, everything is gone. Maybe that's why the police and others are searching for us. Believing we met with foul play."

She wanted to groan out loud and managed a low, angry growl instead.

Chapter 19

TAMMY WAS SHOCKED THAT ALL THEIR STUFF WAS gone—passports, cell phones, and clothes, so they couldn't even shift. She just stared at David, unable for a moment to think of what they had to do next.

He wrapped his arm around her neck and let out his breath as he sat naked in the tree and she curled up next to him on the branch as a big cat. "We'll figure something out."

Like what? Break into another bungalow, steal someone else's clothes, tell the staff they were all right but needed a ride to the nearest U.S. Embassy for passports and a way to call home?

What a disaster!

"Joe had been in our bungalow."

What? He was supposed to have been long gone. A chill went up her spine.

"Of course the kids' scents were there. And I smelled Quinn and Weaver and Krustan. So it seems like we had a party at our place, only the host and hostess weren't there."

So they were all in on this together. Quinn, too? He was supposed to have taken a flight out. And so was Joe. Damn it!

"I've got to wait until the people staying in the cabana farthest from our place have gone to the dining facility—the one out of the policeman's view. Most of the guests are sauntering over there now. I can't wait too long, or everyone will be retiring to bed. I'll grab some clothes for us, and we can return them once we're able."

She nodded and shifted into her human form, and he pulled her into his arms. "I worried that when they saw you, they might try to arrest you for getting rid of me in the rainforest," she said.

He smiled and kissed her cheek. "I did have that thought, too. But when I saw that nothing of ours was there, that was the least of our worries."

"We can't even call anyone to let them know what a mess we're in."

"Yeah. We'll have to get dressed, and hell, I don't know. Make up some story."

"Was it trashed really bad?"

"No, just the drawers pulled out as if they were looking for stuff. Mattress shoved aside. I was worried someone might have planted drugs to make it look like we were selling or something and get us into more trouble. But nothing. The living room appeared fine. It looked like they were just searching for something."

"And our intel had it wrong that both Quinn and Joe had flown out already."

"They must have paid someone else to take their places and given them false IDs." He glanced in the direction of a cabana hidden in the foliage. "Okay, this is as good a time as any. I've got to go."

"I'm going with you."

He studied her expression for a moment, kissed her mouth, and rested his forehead against hers, his hands cupping her face. "All right. We do this together."

They shifted, leaped down from the tree, and moved through the darkening rainforest like two shadowy predators. Off in the distance, she heard men still calling for them and felt terrible that they were going through all the effort for nothing.

She wanted to strangle whoever stole their clothes and the rest of their personal items, stranding them in such a dangerous way.

She was following David toward the cabana he had targeted when he suddenly veered off. She wondered where he was going, worried that maybe he'd heard the people returning to their cabana while she had missed hearing the warning sounds.

Then she realized he was following a scent trail— Alex's and Nate's.

The boys had been all over this area, so why follow a trail they'd left now? She saw a rubber—XXL, unused, lying on the ground.

She sniffed it. Alex had held it. So he must have dropped it at some time when he went this way.

Several yards away, she saw another one. Every few feet they found another. Like Hansel and Gretel leaving bread crumbs to find their way back home.

She and David moved deeper into the rainforest until she realized they were headed for the pool at the base of the waterfall rappelling site.

David reached the edge of the cliff and peered down. He grunted. She hurried to join him. Down at the base of the cliff and next to the pool of water now shimmering in the moonlight sat both their bags.

She looked at him to see his take on it, and David gave her a jaguar-sized and very toothy grin.

David quickly found a path he and Tammy could take. They made their way down the rocks, glad that jaguars were good climbers, and finally reached the solid-rock ground. He watched Tammy for a moment, saw she was doing fine, then loped over to quickly inspect their bags. The boys' scent was all he found on them. He shifted and unzipped his and found only a dozen or so condoms left, though everything else appeared to be there, when he saw movement out of the corner of his eye and turned.

Tammy joined him and shifted, then checked out her own bag. "Nothing missing in mine."

He lifted his nearly empty box of condoms and she smiled a little.

Then lightning speared the night sky and they both glanced up before the rains started again. Hell. More rain suddenly burst from the clouds.

Hurriedly dressing, David said, "Let's see if we can find another, safer way out of here."

Tammy dressed just as fast. And then they finally found an easier slope, buried in trees and shrubs and vines, and made their way up to the top.

Tammy looked totally worn-out. He pulled her into a hard embrace and kissed her wet lips. "Let's go."

The rain continued pouring down on them as they rolled the bags through the jungle, stumbling over plants and buttress roots in their path.

"The condoms are all gone," Tammy said as she looked around the path for them.

"Good Boy Scouts. Leave no trace behind." Not that he thought the boys had been in the Boy Scouts. Most of their kind didn't participate in human-run organizations like that. He could just imagine a boy shifting on a camping trip, wanting to be one with nature and his jaguar half.

"Do you think the boys have been watching us the whole time?" Tammy asked.

"Maybe, until we picked up our suitcases and they made sure no one else had discovered them."

David wrapped his arm around her shoulders and gave her a squeeze.

"Okay, we've got to talk about a couple of things. Weaver's and Krustan's scents were in our place and the boys' bungalow also. What do you know about them?" David asked.

"Weaver is a club addict. He's there all the time. He dates some, pays his bills, and never is in any trouble, except when I solved the case without him and Sylvan was pretty hot under the collar about it."

"So he could have a vendetta against you."

"Maybe. He's kind of a mystery otherwise. Sticks to himself. Reads James Bond novels. Big on security, but had his place broken into anyway. That's hush-hush, by the way."

David smiled at her.

"Weaver loves chocolate cheesecake. When they serve it at the branch's dining hall, he's the first one in line to get a couple of slices."

"Anybody who likes chocolate cheesecake can't be all bad."

She laughed.

"What about Krustan?" David asked.

"He loves women. Like Joe and Quinn. He likes

being with someone. Not a loner. He's on the Enforcers' volleyball team."

"What about you?"

"The guys are way too rough. I actually tried out. Had the big, hulking guys landing all over me. Left their sneaker tread marks on my shins. Decided I needed a different sport. Like…running."

He smiled. "I love running, playing chase…especially if you're in front of me. Anything else?"

"Krustan's got a cute little shih tzu that he adores. He's brought him to work a couple of times, once when the condo he was living in caught on fire, and he said his dog won't eat if he kennels him. And another time when it was the day for agents to bring their kids to work and tell them about what they do, Krustan brought his dog. I think he uses him to catch the women's eyes, too. Do you think someone who loves such a cute little fur ball would be a bad guy?"

David smiled at her, shaking his head. "But you ditched him on assignment and he could still be sour about that."

"Yeah, I agree. So I don't know. All four of them in on this? Joe, Quinn, Krustan, Weaver?"

"Could be."

When they finally reached the lodge, they looked half-drowned and muddy. They'd come up with a story, though. They dragged their luggage onto the lodge's deck and rolled into the dimly lit place.

While most of the accommodations were separate bungalows and cabanas, ten rooms could be rented here for those who didn't want to be as surrounded by the jungle and wanted cheaper accommodations.

Card tables were set up for guests who enjoyed playing games at night. The guests were all tucked in their beds. Everything was quiet. Except in one of the rooms upstairs. David heard the soft moaning and groaning of a couple making love. That was one problem with his enhanced cat hearing.

Both he and Tammy were dripping water all over the tile floor. He glanced down at his bedraggled partner, and she smiled knowingly up at him. He smiled back and she blushed.

He rolled his bag to the counter and tapped on a bell. No one came to the front desk. He rang it again.

A dark-haired man, Carlos, the manager, came out, his eyes half-lidded, but they instantly widened in recognition. He sputtered in Spanish. Remembering his English, he said, "The police have been looking for you everywhere." He pulled out a phone to call someone.

"We went on a hike, and we saw a couple of men taking off with our luggage and realized they must have broken into our bungalow and stolen it. We chased after them through the jungle. It took hours to catch up to them. We had our passports, cell phones, everything in the luggage and couldn't afford to lose them," David quickly said, the same speech he had rehearsed a few times before they arrived at the lodge.

It was a flimsy story, but the lodge manager seemed so relieved to have them back that he didn't question it. He relayed the message to the police in Spanish.

"We finally just got back here and wanted to report that we're okay and got our luggage back."

"Anything stolen?" Carlos asked.

David said, "No. We chased them off."

"Description?"

David made up a couple of fake descriptions—two scrawny, tall, blond males, middle-aged, wearing black ninja-type clothes—figuring no one would find anyone to question who fit that account.

"The men had broken into your room and made a mess of it. We've straightened the place up. Here's the new key. You...you stay longer?" Carlos asked, sounding concerned that his place might get a bad review over this.

"We're leaving tomorrow," David said. "We're tired. We need to get to the bungalow and clean up and go to bed."

Carlos spoke to the police again. "*Sí.*" Then he said to David, "The police want to talk to you in the morning."

"All right. We'll see them in the morning."

He headed outside with Tammy into the pouring rain. They rolled their suitcases along the stone path until they finally reached their secluded bungalow. He had to walk slowly because Tammy was dragging, she was so tired.

When they got inside, he said, "Take a shower and I'll wheel our bags into the bedroom."

She nodded and headed for the bathroom.

They would sleep and then discuss tomorrow's plans in the morning. Since the boys' place had also been broken into, he suspected they wouldn't be staying there tomorrow. He hoped the kids were okay and that they'd get in touch soon. But for tonight, he and Tammy needed rest.

He headed outside to the patio shower to wash off the mud and found a pineapple and a bunch of bananas sitting on the bench. He cleaned up and grabbed the fruit. When he lifted them, he saw a note that had been written in indelible waterproof ink. Otherwise, it would have been impossible to read, as wet as it was. RTN HM. CT? AN

Return home? David carried the note and fruit into the bungalow and noted Tammy was still showering in the bathroom. He set the fruit down on the dresser, opened her bag, and found a skintight tank top and her red silk panties that he'd admired when they had first arrived.

She walked into the bedroom, towel wrapped around her body, and looked at the selection he'd made for her to wear. She shook her head. "The way you keep this place like the polar ice caps, I need to wear flannel pj's."

He laughed and grabbed a pair of boxers. She eyed the fruit and the note.

"What do you make of it?" he asked.

"Return home? Connecticut? Alex and Nate." She slipped on her panties.

"Yeah, that's what I figured. Except on the CT, I suspect it might be cat."

"Do they mean they're going home?" She pulled the tank top over her breasts, and he smiled at the sight of the fabric stretched across them, her pointed nipples visible.

"Uh, yeah," he said. "I think so."

"Question mark on the cat. Asking us if we want to know where it is?"

"Or the cat is missing."

Tammy's expression darkened.

"We don't know for sure about anything. I suspect after their place got broken into, they left the area. Maybe after they picked up the condoms, they drove to Belize City for the next flight out tomorrow. They might even be on our flight."

She climbed into bed with David, and he pulled her into his arms and yanked the covers over them. "Yeah. It's time to check out the circus," she said.

"Yeah, it is." He held her close, loving the smell of tangerine on her. "You hungry?"

She shook her head. "Just tired."

He should have eaten a couple of bananas. He was starving, having missed eating dinner and then exercising so much today. But he wanted Tammy snuggled against him all night. He breathed in her sexy smell, listening to her heart beating and absorbing the warmth of her skin.

"Why did you pick this for me to wear?" she asked sleepily.

"Ever since I saw those panties, I wanted to see them on you. I had an awful time visualizing you wearing them."

She chuckled.

"When we were eating dinner here the first night, you were staring at my hands. Want to clue me in on why?" he asked.

She laughed. He smiled. She explained to him what she'd read. Then *he* laughed. "So did I meet or exceed the survey result?"

"You have to ask?"

He caressed her arm. "Here I thought you were checking out whether I was married or not. You sure aren't anything like what I expected."

"Good or bad?"

"You have to ask? We need to finish this assignment, pronto."

"So we can get the cat home."

"And so we can date like normal people would." He was not letting her get away. Maybe they'd have what it took to make the relationship work for the long-term.

"We are not like normal people of the human variety," she reminded him and kissed his chest.

How well he knew.

———∿∿∿———

The morning came too early as the police knocked on their door and David explained to them all that had happened, repeating what he'd said last night. The story sounded crazy, except the break-in had corroborated that someone had entered their place, made a mess, and their bags had disappeared. With promises that they'd apprehend the men, the police left. David didn't believe they would make much of an effort, though, since he and Tammy had "thwarted" the would-be bandits and had all their stuff back.

Despite eating a couple of bananas before they headed to the dining lodge for breakfast, David was still starving. Even so, he rushed Tammy through breakfast, their bags already packed in the rental car, and then they took off. He had important business to attend to before they caught their flight.

———∿∿∿———

When David said they had to leave extra early to reach Belize City for something important that he had to get his boss, Tammy wasn't sure what to expect. Something pertaining to the mission, she thought. So when David stopped at a stand where a woman was selling candy, Tammy raised her brows at him in silent question.

"Wangla," he explained. "It's sugar, oil, and water, like peanut brittle only made with thousands of sesame seeds. Boss loves it. If we come home without a bag of it from Belize, Martin will not be happy. I swear he sends one of us on a mission down here every so often just to pick up his sweet treat for him."

Smiling, Tammy shook her head.

"Don't tell me your boss doesn't expect his agents to bring him home anything if you're on assignment in different places."

"Sylvan?" she asked, her voice arching with surprise. "All I know is that he loves two long-horned cows that he babies on his ranch. I can't imagine bringing him anything that would make his cows happy that they don't already get on his pastureland."

"Not into sweet treats?"

"The cows?"

David laughed.

The traveling was long and tedious on the return home to Dallas. After all the craziness yesterday and all the physical exercise they'd had, they were both exhausted, but neither was able to snooze much on the plane. This time, Tammy did rest her head against David's shoulder— and noticed she'd pleased him by doing so—though she never got quite comfortable enough.

As soon as they headed for their cars in the Dallas airport parking lot, David seemed quieter than usual. Contemplating things, she thought. Just like she was. Or he was just plain tired.

The weather was hot and humid here, almost as much as the jungle had been, but without thick foliage to stop it, a stiff breeze blew around them.

"At least now we have really good reception and can get hold of everyone for answers when we need them," she said to David.

"Yeah." He didn't say anything more than that, so she quit talking.

They finally reached the parking tower and she said, "My car is parked on the third floor."

"Mine's on the first."

"Okay, so you want to meet up tomorrow and go to the circus? I need to clean up, wash clothes, get some rest, et cetera."

He looked down at her, his green eyes studying her gaze. "I'm not sure you should be alone until this investigation is done."

So *that's* what his silence was all about. He was worried about her and probably suspected she wouldn't buy into his protectiveness. Which she wouldn't. Not when she was safe at home. She needed to get this business back on a professional basis. Meet with partner, search for clues, go to own homes at night. They could work in the dating—*later*. When they were in Belize, it was different. They hadn't had much of choice about sticking close. And it was safer that way. She supposed she should have told him that up front. She had just assumed he'd be thinking along the same vein.

"Hey, I'll be fine. No zip-line adventures, no running through the jungle. I'll be home, security system armed, just doing girlie things—like maybe painting my toenails or taking a bubble bath and reading a hot romance."

He smiled a little at that, but the worry crease still wrinkled his brow.

"I'll call you and we can have bedtime talk—later.

I'll tell you I'm tucked into bed and everything's fine. We'll both sleep in our separate beds. In the morning, we'll be refreshed and ready to go. I'll start the laundry. Fix myself a meal. Unwind a bit and get started on the investigation tomorrow."

"I could bring a movie over, pick up something for us to eat…"

"Babysit me? No way. Tomorrow we'll get together. Early." She patted him on the chest. "We'll be together all day. On the case."

Now that they were home, she really had to get focused. She'd never wanted to mix pleasure with business when she'd worked with other partners before. She knew *David* was the only reason she was having trouble keeping the two notions separate. Even if they had agreed to dating.

"Okay. You don't want me to walk you to your car?" he asked.

She laughed. "You'll want to drive it and…" She shook her head.

He was smiling a little. Yeah, when the guys got close to her car, they forgot about the girl who owned it.

She didn't want to share a long kiss good-bye—well, truthfully she did—but that might show she was changing her mind about his coming home with her. Once she tilted her head up to kiss him and he leaned down to respond, and her arms went around his neck, and his tongue slipped into her mouth… Well, hell, she was having a really, really hard time sticking to her plans.

She was certain the hot and sexy way he kissed her meant he was trying to change her mind, too. She groaned a little as his hands slid down over her backside and he pressed her against his growing arousal. Luckily, there was no one anywhere nearby to see their public display of affection. She suspected tonight might be the only night that she could resist having him come home with her if they always kissed like this after they wrapped up business for the day.

"Uh, tomorrow," she said, still wrapped around him, and he wasn't letting go, either. Then she pulled away and smiled.

"Are you certain?" He could smell that she wanted to take this further.

"Yeah, look forward to tomorrow." Then she turned and headed for the elevator before she took him home with her.

He didn't move. She would have heard him rolling his bag along the concrete floor to wherever he'd parked his car. He was watching her. Making sure she made it to the elevator by herself. Or maybe he just wanted to wave good-bye or something. She was way overthinking this.

When she reached the elevator and got on, she turned to see him observing her, somber as could be. Trying to lighten the mood, she smiled, waved, and shut the door just as she smelled Quinn Singleterry's scent in the elevator.

Chapter 20

DAVID LET OUT HIS BREATH IN EXASPERATION. WHAT was wrong with him? Tammy was applying the brakes big-time, and he knew when that happened he had to step back and let her have her space. But he desperately wanted to close the gap between them and feel the heat of her body, to listen to her soft sighs and the beat of her heart. He wanted to share the time they could together, just enjoying a night off, but even so, he knew they'd mull over the case, maybe even come up with some ideas. Two heads were definitely better than one.

Hell. He had to get on with business. He pulled out his phone and started hauling his bag to his car parked in the back forty, while calling his boss. "Arrived at the airport. We're picking up the investigation tomorrow."

He'd filled Martin in on the stuff that happened yesterday while they were waiting to board the plane in Belize City, at the same time Tammy had updated her boss. Martin was the kind of guy who listened carefully before he made any judgment or response. He'd really been silent while David had told him about being stuck in jaguar form, the police searching for them, and their missing bags. David also mentioned that Quinn and Joe had been at their bungalow *after* they purportedly flew into the States.

"I have to admit, though we suspect Joe Storm is involved in all of this, I'm really surprised that Quinn would be. I presume he's doing some off-the-books undercover work. I can speculate all day long on this. We'll just have to bring him in for questioning." Then his boss reiterated, "I'm going to have a little talk with Alex and Nate about stranding agents without their clothes so that they have no safe way to shift."

"I agree," David said. "At least it all worked out. Truthfully, I think the boys had some misguided notion of protecting us from whoever ransacked our place. I can see where the kids will be an asset to the branch. They just need some guidance." Much as he and his brother had at that age. "We just need to make sure they know they're valued."

"I agree."

"You'll have fun training them." David was glad he didn't have the job. He could just imagine the kids pulling pranks on their JAG instructors—all in good fun—just like he and Wade had done some years back. "We're going to the circus tomorrow. Do you have any word about it?"

"The owner, Cyrus Wilde, says that someone stole the jaguar from the circus last year."

Processing the information, David didn't say anything for a moment. "The jaguar had been at the Oregon Zoo for a year."

"Yeah. So what if the owner is right? What if the jaguar was in the circus's possession to begin with, and it was stolen and handed over to the zoo?" Martin said. "And all they did was take it back?"

"Why would the circus have stolen it? Why not tell the zoo it was theirs and prove ownership? Also, if the jaguar had been the circus's, the cat should be able

to perform some acts. How long had they had her?"
David asked.

"A month, Cyrus said."

"Had the jaguar learned any tricks when they had it
the first time?"

"I didn't ask."

"Okay, so the zoo cat, if it's not really the circus's
cat, wouldn't have had time to learn a lot of tricks during
the short time the circus had her this time," David said.

"Right. That's the only lead we've got. He reported
the cat stolen a year ago, but no one took them seriously,
Cyrus said. And you're right about them stealing the
cat. Unless they can prove she was theirs, which means
they have official paperwork showing legitimate ownership, they're not getting her back. He explained that a
former manager had made a mess of their records, and
he couldn't find the paperwork to prove she was theirs
on short notice."

David thought it all sounded fishy. "What if they
falsify records to use for their cover story?"

"We'll check it out with the authorities and ensure
it's all authentic."

"Any word on whether any of the boys came home?"
David finally found his car.

"No. They seem to be lying low."

"What about the Enforcer agents, Quinn, or Joe Storm?"

"Haven't been able to contact or locate any of them,"
Martin said. "Sylvan's had no luck with his men, either.
I do have some other news. Juan, the guide that hooked
Tammy up to the cable at the zip-line adventure, went
missing. He was bragging about some tourist paying
him extra money on the side if he had the customers go

in a certain order. Tammy was the only one who showed up from the group originally scheduled that included you, Alex, Nate, and Tammy. One of the boys, Alex or Nate, was supposed to go first. You after that. Tammy was scheduled for last. Instead, Tammy arrives with the family of four. Juan most likely figured since she was the only one named on the list, she would go first. This friend of Juan's said Juan went to get paid afterward and hasn't been heard from since. The other guide said that he was busy helping with the family, so he didn't see the way Juan hooked her up to the cable."

David didn't like where this was going.

"Juan wasn't paid just to have the four of you go in a certain order, we don't believe. The pulley shouldn't have come off the second cable when the first broke. It should have remained in place. We've viewed the teen's video you sent us several times and sent a copy to investigators in Belize to help with their analysis. In reviewing the video, we could see that the guide hooked up the pulley to the top cable properly, but with the second one, he made the motions like he was connecting the carabiner to the lower cable, but he didn't.

"I checked for accidents that have occurred at other resorts to see if this could have happened accidentally. In two cases, similar incidents had been reported. One woman held on for dear life as the pulley was only partway hooked on and wasn't seated on the cable. She was badly skinned up and bruised when she came in to the terminal platform. The other had to be rescued. So what I'm saying is that it happens sometimes. The guide is distracted and doesn't hook up the zipper correctly."

"Was he distracted?" David asked, popping open his trunk.

"From what we could tell from the video, Juan glanced nervously at the kid filming him as he hooked Tammy up. That could have been what distracted him."

"But?" David knew his boss had come to a different conclusion and had good reason.

"His disappearance and his bragging about receiving money lead me to suspect he was paid to sabotage the excursion. We suspect the guide didn't know that the other cable had been cut."

"Wait, you know for sure it was cut?" David set his bag inside the trunk and slammed it closed.

"I had Tammy's brothers go to Belize as soon as they finished their assignment in Costa Rica to speak with investigators checking into the zip-line cable breaking. It had been cut."

"And?" David asked.

"Quinn's scent was on the cable."

David swore under his breath.

"He might not have had anything to do with the cutting of the cable. He could have just been there ahead of us, checking into it."

"And incriminated himself intentionally?" David asked, not sure why his boss would still be defending Quinn.

"Possibly. This other business of him sending someone in his place on the plane trip home... He did do that once during an investigation to throw a perp off. The perp got careless, believing Quinn had left the area. Quinn nabbed him then. I haven't been able to get hold of him, but he's always ignored calls from the branch when he's on vacation. If he's doing some undercover work on the side, that's not so unusual, either. He's done it before. So no red flag there."

"So you believe he might have been in Belize, trying to get Joe to give up names of those who are dirty in the organization?"

"Maybe."

"Okay, so what else about this Juan, the guide?" David opened his car door, got in, started the car, and rolled down the windows. He turned on the air to cool the vehicle before he left the parking tower.

"We figured Juan would have thought nothing would happen to the rider because the top cable would have allowed her to continue on her way unharmed. At least that's what we suspect. Everyone said Juan would be willing to earn some extra money on the side, but he wouldn't have done so if it meant someone would die. At least that's what his friends and relatives said. Investigators learned that he hadn't ever been convicted of any major crimes. Petty stuff—traffic violations, stole a watch once, nothing that would endanger someone's life," Martin said.

"And we have no way of knowing who was paying him."

"That was the interesting part." Martin gave a dramatic pause.

David knew it couldn't be good.

"The guy told one of the other guides that the man who was paying him said if any of them wanted to earn extra cash, just to get in touch with him."

"You're kidding. So who the hell did he say he was?"

"He said the man's name was David Patterson."

David swore under his breath. Who the hell was trying to set him up?

"David, I want you to stick close to Tammy at all times. Even if whoever tampered with the cable hadn't meant for her to be injured, after learning Joe fired the weapon at her, discovering she'd dated him and thrown him over, and with the possibility he's involved in the missing jaguar case, I want you to stay with her always. Both of you, watch your backs."

David was damn glad that Tammy hadn't been targeted for the zip-line accident, but he wasn't happy the line had been sabotaged. "Gotcha. I'll let you know when I have anything new."

They ended the conversation. He'd make a couple more calls to update his brother on what was going on and call his dad to let him know he was safely home. David knew his father worried about them ever since he and Wade had joined the Service.

"Wade says you're working with a woman this time," David's dad said when he called.

"Yeah, Dad."

David knew where this conversation was going. Every time he worked with a woman on assignment, his dad would ask if she was single and the one. His dad had been certain they had been every time. David hadn't. Not those times. This time, he wasn't about to speculate. Well, maybe a little. He could see settling down with Tammy. She was fun, sexy, impulsive, and he loved that she was able to handle his sense of humor. Not everyone could. And he loved working with her. Between coming up with ideas for solving the case and doing a helluva job going after the facts, she couldn't be a better teammate. He didn't know what the other agents' problem had been. They were idiots.

"Wade says you're getting along well with her."

"Yeah, Dad." *Really well.*

His dad was a romantic. He had loved their mom and had never remarried after her death. He felt both Wade and David would be happiest if they had a she-cat to love.

His dad had been thrilled when Wade married Maya. He had welcomed her into the family as if she were his own daughter. He was all set to be a grandfather. He had already bought a playpen and crib, and childproofed his home as much as possible. He would make a great granddad—when Maya became pregnant.

His dad cleared his throat. "When do I get to meet her?"

David chuckled. "We're just…dating."

"Hot damn, you're dating already? You'll be married to her before you know it."

"How do you come to *that* conclusion? Quinn's sister dumped me for that Joe Storm. Hillary didn't like my work life."

"Olivia was nuts. You said yourself you weren't sure about her because she was so guarded about what she was doing. Olivia was cheating on you, and Hillary didn't like that you were secretive about your work. This is different. Tammy does the same kind of work you do; you get along with her brothers; you like her cousins; and you asked for this assignment with her. Your brother is married to her cousin. It's like one big, happy family. You're a shoo-in. Do you want me to talk to her?"

"No."

His father laughed. "Well, if you do, I'll put in a good word for you."

"Thanks, but I don't think that would help."

"You know your mom did the same thing to me," his dad said.

David had never heard this story. "*No*," he said, elongating the word. He thought it was love at first sight, and within three months, they were married.

"We'd been going out every night, playing card games with friends, movies, dinners out, and she finally said she needed a break. Wanted to wash her hair, paint her toenails…"

David was reminded of Tammy's comment. He didn't know his mother ever painted her toenails.

"Well, she just said she had to take a break."

"And you let her. Right, Dad?"

"Hell, no."

David grinned.

"I tried. I went out with a friend of mine who said he knew a woman who needed a date that night. He was seeing another woman at the time. I wasn't interested in getting to know any other woman. I just wanted to go out. I was living in a small apartment, young, single, itching to have fun."

"You went out with another woman while you were dating Mom?"

"We *weren't* married. And I wasn't seeing anyone else. Anyway, what happened was, the 'blind date' was about eight-months pregnant."

David laughed.

"I could have killed my friend. I walked out and went to see your mom. She had her hair up in curlers, bright red toenails, and wouldn't let me in her apartment. Not until I told her what her not going out with me meant. She laughed so hard when I told her about the blind date that she let me in. Told me it served me right for going out without her. 'Course I asked her: What was I supposed to do? I didn't need to doozy up my hair and paint my nails."

"Dad."

He chuckled. "Loved your mom. I chased her around the dining table a few times before she finally let me catch her, and we watched a movie. Tammy Anderson might say she needs a break, but when you show up, it'll be a whole other story."

David laughed, shaking his head. "If you say so. Love you, Dad. Got to run."

"Okay, Son. Thanks for letting me know you're home safe and sound."

Hoping his dad wouldn't get Tammy's phone number and call her with good intentions anyway, David headed home. He would wait for Tammy to get settled at her place. After that, he'd let her know the good news. The boss had ordered him to stick to her like honey on white bread.

But first he had to stop at his place, wash up, and be perfectly presentable—like he was on a date—not just an agent on assignment.

The hair on the nape of Tammy's neck rose as she smelled Quinn's scent in the airport parking-tower elevator. Fairly recent. He had to have come home on a different flight before theirs. The kids must have returned home. So Quinn had? Which meant he was after them? Why else would he have been in the jungle and returned when they left? What about Joe? Had he truly returned also? And Weaver and Krustan?

Okay, Quinn had undoubtedly left the parking area

by now. A long time ago. He wouldn't be lurking here, waiting to pounce on her.

He wouldn't know when she was returning home. And he had to be a good guy if he'd saved her from Joe shooting at her. Right?

Since she had been in such a rush to catch the flight to Belize without running into David, she hadn't paid as much attention to where she'd parked as she normally would.

Every sound of tires rolling, of brakes being applied, of cars honking as people made sure they'd locked them, of footfalls off in the distance, even her own bag's wheels rolling on the floor caught her attention. Unfortunately, she didn't have a fancy key fob for her older model Jaguar, so she had no way of pushing a button and making her car honk for her.

She had to rely on her sense of smell. Forget her faulty memory.

Rubber tires, men's aftershaves and women's perfumes, oil, old chewed-to-death and run-over globs of bubble gum, concrete, and gas fumes all assaulted her, but she was too far from her car because she couldn't smell it. Not its new paint job or new canvas car top. Quinn had disappeared in a different direction than she was going now, which gave her some consolation. Unless her car was parked in the direction he had gone. The parking tower was breezeless, shaded from the hot sun but still warm. A fine sweat broke out all over her skin.

Then she smelled jaguars, males, two, neither of whom she recognized. She followed their scent, not being very unobtrusive as her sandals clicked on the concrete and the wheels of her bag rolled along.

She heard a trunk lid pop open and hurried toward the

sound. Two boys—about the age of the Taylor twins, one a redhead and freckled, green-eyed, the other more blond, his eyes just as green—glanced in her direction. They both stared at her for a minute, resting their luggage in the trunk, mouths agape, eyes wide.

"You're *her*," the redhead said. "Aren't you?"

"If you mean Tammy Anderson, yeah."

They both looked around the lot as if they were expecting David to be with her.

"Are you Peter and Hans Fenton?"

They looked at each other as if they weren't sure if they should say.

She smiled. "It's okay. I guess everyone's come home. Um, you wouldn't mind telling me where the cat is, would you?"

The boys finished loading their bags, and then the redhead shut the lid. "Where's your partner?"

"Are you Peter or Hans?"

"Peter."

"He's getting his car on the first floor. We're headed home." She didn't ask where the boys were going, figuring they wouldn't want to tell her, and it was probably safer that way. "Did your friends get back all right?"

Hans smiled. "Yeah."

What did *that* mean?

"You know Martin Sullivan also wants to work with both of you, right?" Tammy asked.

"Yeah, and it might not be too bad a deal if we get agents assigned to us who look like *you* do," Peter said.

She smiled. She wondered if Alex and Nate had told these boys about her sunning on the chaise lounge.

"Did you need something?" Peter asked.

The cat. But they weren't sharing. As much as she hated mentioning it, she thought the boys would see her as being totally fallible if she did. "Um, yeah, my car."

Both boys smiled.

They looked like they thought she lost her car all the time. "We were in a rush to make our flight. I normally always know where my car is."

They both grinned like "Yeah, right." They glanced at the keys in her hand. Looking to verify why she hadn't used them to find her car? Wondering if she was telling the truth? The kids were as clever as the other two.

"No key fob," she explained.

"Oh, some old car," Hans said with a slightly arrogant air. Like she couldn't afford anything newer on her Enforcer salary. "What does it look like?"

"Yellow, convertible roadster. Jaguar."

———※———

Tammy shouldn't have given Hans and Peter Fenton a ride in her car. Not until they told her something she needed to know. Like where the cat was. But like when David had protected the other twins from Joe Storm in the shifter club, she thought she had won these over to an extent. Maybe they'd still come around.

Since she could take only one of the boys with her at a time in the car, Hans had ridden with her out of the Dallas airport. She had to pull over and let Peter switch cars with Hans so he could have a ride. She had been so amused when the boys saw her car. They were in awe. She figured if a she-cat teen had walked by, no matter how hot she was, the boys wouldn't have given her a second glance.

"Can't wait to tell Alex and Nate," Peter said and thanked her.

"You sure you don't want to tell me about the cat?"

"She's safe," Peter said. "You need to find who's rotten in one of the branches or more."

"The cat really means something to each of you. More than just a mission to rescue her and send her back to where she belongs. You wouldn't have even met her before you saw the news announcing she had been stolen from the zoo. Yet, it seems more personal. Why?"

He just stared out the window and didn't say.

"Peter, had you seen her before? At the Oregon Zoo?"

"I gotta go."

She suspected the boys had seen the cat in person before she was stolen, not just on the news. But when and where?

Once she arrived home, Tammy's first order of business was to call her boss before she settled in for the night.

"We're back in Dallas. Any word concerning what Weaver and Krustan were doing in Belize?" she asked Sylvan.

"I haven't been able to get hold of them. Either they're not answering their cells or they're out of range."

"Okay. Well, I'm at home, and we'll be going to the circus tomorrow as soon as it's close to opening time."

"All right. I'll let you know if I get word from either Weaver or Krustan."

"Thanks." She set her cell on the bathroom counter and looked longingly at the whirlpool tub, but duty called.

She started the wash first. Before throwing her jeans into the machine, she checked the pockets and felt a crinkly piece of paper. She pulled it out, wondering what it was. Krustan's and Weaver's phone numbers.

What if they just weren't answering their boss? What if she phoned them and they thought she had an emergency and would pick up when they saw it was her on the caller ID?

She returned to the bathroom and grabbed her cell phone and glanced at the numbers. The first was Krustan's. She hesitated. Which should she call?

Both, she decided.

She punched in Krustan's number, and after a few rings, someone picked up the phone. *Good.*

"Hello?" a man said, sounding out of breath.

"Krustan?" She barely recognized his voice. Was he in trouble? Running from danger somewhere in Belize?

"Anderson?" He sounded shocked to hear from her.

"Yeah, are you okay?"

"Hell, Anderson. This is not the time to be calling me, unless… You're okay, right? Not in any life-threatening danger. Right?"

"We need to talk." She didn't want to answer him for fear he'd think she was okay and cut her off before she asked him what he had been doing in Belize.

"Not right now. I'm kind of busy," he said, his tone of voice short.

"Who's that?" a woman asked in the background, sounding miffed.

Tammy closed her eyes. That's why he was short of breath. She didn't want to visualize him naked, panting, on top of a woman, when he answered what he must have thought was Tammy's distress call. She did appreciate him for that.

"An agent I work with," Krustan said to his female companion. Then he got back to Tammy. "Call me in the morning. Unless this is an emergency."

"Someone cut the zip line I was traversing in Belize. And Joe Storm—you know him? He fired two rounds at me." She waited.

"Honey?" the woman said.

Krustan swore softly. "I thought that JAG agent was supposed to be protecting you."

"You said I could ask for your help if I needed it. You said Sylvan asked for you to check on me. He said he didn't know you were down there. That you were on leave. What is this all about? What do you and Weaver know that you're not telling me?"

"Ask David Patterson about Olivia Farmer. He dated her for a year."

Tammy felt like the floor had disappeared beneath her.

"What has she got to do with any of this?"

"She may have everything to do with the case you're working on. Ask David." Krustan hung up on her.

She stood frozen in place, stunned. Not knowing what to think.

She called Weaver. No answer. She tried again. This time he answered. She heard jungle noises in the background and lots of laughter and talking. The club. So she and the boys returned home and so did Weaver and Krustan? What was going on?

"What's wrong?" Weaver asked.

"You're at the club," she said.

"Yeah. Did you want to join me?"

"What were you doing in Belize?"

Silence.

"I know the truth about you being on leave. Why were you in Belize?"

"Krustan already told you to talk to David Patterson."

Pacing, she frowned at the tile floor in her bathroom. That meant Krustan must have called Weaver right away and given him a heads-up. "All right, I will. But why were you in Belize?"

"Tammy, call us back if you're in trouble." He hung up on her.

Damn the both of them.

She would have called Sylvan back and told him where Weaver was, but she figured she'd already gotten Weaver into trouble once. If he truly did mean to help her out if she needed him, she wasn't going to ruin that chance.

She thought to call David, but she was afraid that if she did, he'd want to talk in person. She needed a night off. Tomorrow would be soon enough to learn what he knew about Olivia and how she might pertain to the case. She told herself it didn't matter that David had been dating Olivia. They must have ended their relationship because Olivia had started dating Joe, and he'd asked her to marry him.

Tammy sighed and walked into the bathroom. She considered all her bubble bath powders and oils sitting on the little glass shelf below her bathroom window: Blackberry Sweetness, Coconut Comfort, Mint Melody, Luscious Honeysuckle, and Sexy Vanilla. A bubble bath would feel wonderful.

Within minutes, Tammy was curled up in a warm, sudsy vanilla-scented bath, trying to forget about anything pertaining to the case. She needed to unwind and recharge her batteries for the next day. The silky water caressed her skin as she breathed in the sweet smell, reminding her of baking chocolate-chip cookies with her mother during the holidays. Yet another, more recent, more pressing memory came to the forefront—making love to one sexy jaguar in the warm pool beneath the waterfall.

She swore if he wasn't such a hot cat, he'd have looked like a sad little puppy dog when she'd left him standing there in the airport parking tower. But she knew this was the right thing to do. Tomorrow, they'd get back to business. How could either of them keep their minds on the case if they gave in to their jaguar hormones all the time?

Yeah, so why did she wish he was in her big whirlpool bathtub, sharing her bubble bath with her now?

The doorbell rang. Her heart skipped a beat. Her skin prickled. She frowned. The person standing on her front porch *better* not be the nosy neighbor across the street. She stopped by every time Tammy got home from a trip to tell her everything that had gone on in the neighborhood while Tammy was away. Gertie Jessup was great as a neighborhood watch of one, but usually she waited until the next day to apprise Tammy of everything that had gone on.

Tammy didn't want to hear all the neighborhood news. Not right now. She wanted to relax after her wild adventure in the rainforest. She'd make time for Gertie later—the widow was just lonely because her grown kids lived two states away with their own kids.

If she ignored her, Gertie would go away.

Tammy ground her teeth. She knew she was fooling herself. Gertie would keep trying until she got her attention.

The doorbell rang again, and then her phone played

its new ringtone: "Rock and Roar (J-A-G-U-A-R)." The big cat roaring in between lyrics made her smile, despite the annoying interruption to her bath.

But then Tammy remembered that her neighbor didn't know her cell phone number. Letting out her breath in a huff, she got out of the water, grabbed a towel, and hastily dried off. Concerned it might be her boss with an update since she'd called him earlier, she seized her phone off the marble bathroom counter and looked at the caller ID.

David Patterson?

It better *not* be him at the front door.

Chapter 21

WHEN TAMMY ANSWERED THE PHONE BUT DIDN'T SAY anything, David worried something was wrong. An open phone line didn't bode well. "Tammy?" he said, his voice dark with concern. He was ready to break down her door.

"You'd better not be standing on my front porch," she said, her voice just as dark, but instead of being concerned, she was highly annoyed.

Relieved she was okay, he smiled. He should have known. "Boss's orders."

Silence.

"Martin said I had to watch your back at all times." And front and whatever else David could watch, he thought. She didn't say anything. He lost the smile. "Were you busy?"

"Come back later. Tomorrow. Like we planned." She ended the call.

She...hung...up...on...him.

He glanced around at the red brick homes, upper-middle price range. Older development with established trees in a woodland environment. *Nice.*

He noticed a woman peeking at him through the curtains across the street, her hair white and curly, blue glasses perched on her nose. He smiled, hoping to dispel any of the woman's worries that he was bad news.

She let the curtains drop. Either she thought he was okay, or she was calling the cops.

Time to bring out the big guns. He called Tammy's boss next, watching the house across the street while he punched in Sylvan's number. The curtains parted again and the woman studied him through a pair of binoculars. He wanted to pull his own pair out of his bag and scrutinize her, just to see what she would do.

But he didn't.

"David Patterson," Sylvan said on his cell. "Anything wrong?"

"Yes, sir. My boss wants me to keep an eye on Tammy for her own protection, considering what's happened to her."

"What's happened to her?" Sylvan asked, his voice hardening.

"Nothing new since we returned home. But she told you about the zip-line cable snapping, right? The line was precut and the lower pulley rigged so someone could have fallen to their death. I'll send you the video of the whole thing. We also know Joe Storm, former JAG agent, fired two shots at her. My boss is worried that she needs someone to stay with her 24-7 until we resolve this case. But she doesn't want that arrangement. I'm standing on her front porch, but she's not budging about letting me in."

"Hell and damnation. She didn't tell me a thing about the shooting. The zip-line incident—she mentioned that, but without proof it was anything other than an accident… Are the two of you not working well together? I can assign someone else."

"No," David said way too vehemently. "I mean, we're working great together. She just wanted a night off. But it isn't safe for her—at least we don't think so."

"I'll call her."

"Okay, thanks." David ended the call. He glanced at the house across the street. The woman was still eagle-eyeing him through the binoculars. He waved at her in a friendly way and sat down on the front porch swing. He swung back and forth, nice and easy, making him wish he was sitting there with Tammy, rocking gently with her tucked under his arm.

A butterfly flitted about on a red rosebush next to the porch as he swung some more.

He expected Sylvan to lay down the law with Tammy, and she'd automatically capitulate. When David didn't get a call back and she didn't come to the door, he envisioned her arguing with her boss.

He sighed and glanced at the house across the street. The woman had lowered her binoculars, but she was still watching him. Probably the most excitement she'd had in a while.

Ten snail-paced minutes passed. He called her boss, no response, sighed.

Swung some more.

His phone jingled and he saw it was Sylvan. Not good if Tammy wasn't coming to the door. Or maybe she wasn't quite presentable.

"Yeah, Patterson here."

"Okay, listen, David. She said you and she are working great together—I just had to confirm that bit of information—but she said she needed a night off."

"And you told her she can't be alone, right?" David had a bad feeling about this.

"She said, and I quote, 'He can house-sit. Watch the house. And I'll see him in the morning,'" Sylvan told David.

"All…right," David said slowly.

"Are you okay with that, or do you want me to send another agent to watch the house for her, and you can take a break, too?"

"No, I'll live with it." David wasn't about to let some other yahoo watch out for her. Not when they didn't know who was dirty in any of the branches and could be involved in this. "Thanks. I'll let you know if anything happens."

"Do that. Thanks for watching out for her."

"No problem." David ended the call and phoned his favorite pizza-delivery place, and then sat back down on the swing.

The woman watching him had disappeared from the window. He kept expecting the police to arrive at any moment. Half dozing on the swing, he heard a vehicle pull into the drive twenty minutes later. The pizza delivery. He paid for the large pepperoni pizza and two bottled waters, and then set them on the round glass table next to the swing. Pizza slice in hand, David got comfortable again on the swing. Not such a bad deal as house-sitting went.

The neighbor was at the window again. He motioned to her with the pizza box, offering for her to join him. She vanished.

He chuckled. He was certain he'd thoroughly rattled her. Her door opened. She was holding a covered plate. Wearing a flowery housecoat of bright purple and yellow and a pair of sneakers, she shut her door and walked across the street to join him.

Now this got interesting. He was usually good with pets and kids. He hadn't thought he could add nosy neighbors to the list.

"Hi, I'm Gertie Jessup," she said, climbing onto the porch, her gray eyes gazing up at him. "Tammy's neighbor. I watch out for her. Not that we have much trouble around here, but when she's gone, I watch her place."

"Ah, she's lucky to have you for a friend," David said. "I'm David Patterson. You want me to take that from you?"

She handed him the platter, and he looked at the plastic-covered sugar cookies.

"For…Tammy?"

"*No*," Gertie said, elongating the word as if she thought he was being foolish for asking.

"Have a seat," he said, motioning to the rocker. "You want some pizza? The other bottle of water?"

"What kind of pizza?" she asked, eyeing the box.

"Pepperoni."

"Okay," she said begrudgingly.

That appeared to be the start of a long-lasting friendship. She began telling him all about the happenings in the neighborhood, including how Fritz, the miniature schnauzer down the street, caught Mitzie, the miniature poodle, and they'd have Schnoodles before they knew it.

"And two men came to see Tammy," she said.

That got his interest.

"One of them rang the doorbell and then knocked. 'Course I knew she had left, but I didn't know when she'd be back. They peered in the front picture window, but she had the blinds closed so they couldn't see anything. Maybe they were listening for someone. They went around the side but found the gate locked."

"What did they look like?"

"Hunters. Or…army guys. They had those

camouflage fatigues on and boots, and baseball caps in the same camouflage material. My husband served in Vietnam, and that's what he wore. One had black hair and the other blond. They looked in good shape."

"Vehicle?"

"Blue sedan of some kind. Don't know the make. But I did get their license plate number just in case they were planning on breaking into her house." She pulled a piece of paper out of her pocket and read it off. He made a note of it on his phone.

"Thanks, I'll have someone check into this and make sure they're okay."

"Oh, good," Gertie said with obvious relief, sighing heavily. "I was so worried no one would take me seriously. You know the old saying, 'Cry wolf.' I was afraid if I made a big fuss over it, nothing would come of it. Then if something bad *did* happen, no one would listen to me."

"With the kind of work we do, you never know. I really appreciate you telling me. I'll let my boss know and Tammy also."

"Good, good. You're such a nice boy." Gertie went on to tell him about the noisy kids racing bicycles down the street.

He tried to ignore the passing time, though he had to admit the lady was entertaining, and he figured she enjoyed talking to someone and sharing a meal, even if it was fast food. He disclosed a little about going with Tammy to Belize on a hush-hush mission and how her boss needed him to watch her back for a while, just so Gertie realized he was one of the good guys.

As it got dark, Gertie finally rose from the rocker

and said, "Well, I don't know what's wrong with that girl, letting a nice boy like you sit out here all by your lonesome when she needs your protection. She's always very sweet. I was going to tell her all the news, but when you get to see her, you can tell her for me. If you need to use the bathroom, just come on over. I'll watch her place in the meantime."

He stood. "Thanks. I didn't want you to worry that I'm trouble. We've got to be out in the morning, looking into this case some more. But otherwise, I'll be sitting right here." He patted the swing.

Gertie leaned close to say, "She's been peeking out the blinds every once in a while. Probably wishing you were talking to her instead of me. That's why I stayed as long as I did. I wanted to make her wait to be with you when she was giving you such a hard time. Figure as soon as I leave, she'll be begging you to come in." She winked at him and headed back across the street.

He grinned at the woman and thought how much she reminded him of his maternal grandmother before she passed away.

As soon as Gertie walked inside her house and shut the door, Tammy's front door opened. "Grab your stuff and get in here," Tammy said, her face red with irritation. "*Now.*"

David had the damnedest time hiding a smile.

Chapter 22

TAMMY WAS FURIOUS. FIRST, DAVID SHOULDN'T HAVE been here. When she wouldn't let him in, he had the gall to call her boss! And that led to her boss chewing her out for not telling him about the shooting incident, when they didn't know if Joe Storm had meant to shoot her or not. She explained to Sylvan how Joe wouldn't have known she was going to be at that spot at that time. Hell, she didn't even know it. So she really didn't believe he had it in for her. Sylvan was also angry she hadn't told him anything *further* about the zip-line situation. She was shocked to hear it was not a faulty cable, and she hadn't even known!

Sylvan had tried some psychological babble on her—she swore he thought he was an amateur psychologist—saying if she didn't want to work with David, he understood and he'd have someone else assigned to the case. She *wanted* to work with David. *Tomorrow*. *Not* tonight. She was taking the night *off*! Why couldn't anyone understand that?

No way did she want someone else working with her on the mission. Not after she and David had made some headway with the teens. And she honestly enjoyed working with him.

To top it all off, David had made friends with Gertie. And had even told her about their trip to Belize. Oh my God, the news would be all over the neighborhood within a matter of days. No one had known what Tammy did for a living. Not that he'd told Gertie exactly what she was doing. He'd made Tammy sound like a super undercover operative. Gertie had been eating it up.

She couldn't believe Gertie actually ate pizza with him, either. She'd turned up her nose when Tammy had invited her over for pizza a few months ago when Joe had stood her up for a job-related assignment. Afterward, Tammy figured he'd lied about it. But she couldn't believe Gertie would turn her down and take David up on it! Pizza was not on her neighbor's list of healthy food choices. She'd been a dietician before she retired.

And Gertie had baked cookies and given them to David. She *never* baked Tammy cookies. Not that she'd wanted any, but it was just the idea. *He* wasn't Gertie's neighbor.

Talk about buttering someone up. And damn if David hadn't been loving all that attention. She was so fuming mad that she couldn't even finish her bath after her boss called.

She knew she'd get an earful from Gertie if she made David sit outside all night. Besides, Tammy wouldn't be able to sleep if he continued to sit on her porch and *all* the neighbors saw him there. She could imagine someone calling the police and making a super mess of the whole situation.

"What do you think you're doing here?" she asked as David retrieved his black bag from his car and hauled it inside her house. And what did he think he was doing by talking to her boss and sweet-talking Gertie on the front porch? Before Tammy could close the door, she saw Gertie smiling out her picture window and waving.

Tammy forced a smile, waved, and slammed the door—and then turned her ire on David. Or planned to. He wasn't there. Just his black bag sitting next to the recliner.

She heard him in the kitchen, opening cabinets.

"What are you doing?" she asked, joining him in there.

He looked up. "Uh, garbage can?"

"Under the sink."

He dumped his empty water bottle and raised the pizza box. "Some more pizza in there."

"No thanks. I had a healthy chicken salad."

David stuck the remaining pizza in the fridge as if he lived here.

She glanced at the plate of cookies.

"They're good. You want one?"

"I can't believe she baked you cookies." She sampled one, and the sugary sweetness melted in her mouth.

"Smells like *you* were baking cookies." He glanced around the kitchen.

"Vanilla bubble bath."

"Hmm, sweet," he said, looking at her anew.

"Yeah, well, my bath was interrupted. Twice. Once by you, and once by my boss."

He smiled, not looking like he regretted either interruption. "Want some milk?"

She shook her head. He started looking in the cupboard. "What are you looking for now?"

"Cups."

"Move right in, why don't you?"

"I'm here to serve and protect."

She snorted.

"Sure you don't want some milk to go with the cookie?"

"Cupboard up above, next to the dishwasher." She let out her breath in an annoyed huff. "Get me a glass, too." She paused. "Please."

He got them two glasses of milk, and she carried the

cookies into the living room. "Here you were, fussing about the boys bringing *me* gifts." He set the glasses of milk on the table and she placed the plate of cookies beside them.

"She made the cookies for *both* of us."

Tammy didn't believe that for a moment.

"The boys only gave *you* one piece of chocolate. Not enough to go around, unless you'd shared it with me."

"I could have used more."

"And you probably wouldn't have shared."

He had that right.

"She wanted to make sure I was a good guy." David pulled out his phone, called his boss, and told Martin what Gertie had said about the two men coming to see Tammy. "Not sure who they were, but if you could run the plate, maybe we'll have a clue."

Tammy couldn't believe that Gertie had actually given David some worthwhile neighborhood news. And that she had gotten their license plate number. But Tammy worried who it had been. Weaver and Krustan maybe?

When David got off the phone, he sat down with her on the couch. She should have sat in the recliner. His gaze took in the table where her flat-screen TV used to sit. "Television in the shop?"

"Stolen. I haven't had time to replace it."

"Did Gertie see anything?"

"No. Wouldn't you know she was visiting her daughter in Kansas City to see her grandson's second-grade graduation."

"I take it they haven't caught the culprit."

"Nope."

"Human?"

"Yeah."

David told her what Martin had said about the cut zip line and how Juan had disappeared after sabotaging the second pulley on the lower cable.

"Why would he have done that to the second pulley? Even if he had orders on who should go first, okay, no real red flags there. But you'd think he'd wonder why anyone would want to not seat the pulley properly on the second cable."

"Enough money exchanged hands maybe, so he didn't bother putting much thought into it. We may never know the truth. As to other matters, you said you were going to have a bath—"

"Which was interrupted," she reminded him. She wasn't letting him forget that. She had been enjoying it, but she couldn't let go of her annoyance. Not only that, but she'd been watching periodically to see if David was going to leave and let someone else take his place "protecting" her.

"And you had dinner. So what else did you have on your laundry list? Besides doing laundry."

"*You* are supposed to be serving and protecting. So you said." Which she didn't believe. He was enjoying this too much, and looking ridiculously sexy while doing it.

And yet? He had apparently won Gertie over with that sweet and innocent look while he sat so wistfully swinging on the front porch.

"I can't believe you engineered this whole situation so that you could stay the night," she said.

"I feel better knowing you're safe, Tammy." David sounded so sincere that she realized he was being honest with her.

She patted the velour couch. "I only have this small couch for you to sleep on."

He smiled at her, and the look was part big-cat hunter and part amused. "Much better than the swing out front. What made you change your mind?"

"My neighbors."

He laughed.

She loved the sexy, deep sound of it. She couldn't help but like him, the more she saw of him and how he'd been so nice to her neighbor, the teens, and even her, despite her trying to put some space between them.

She eyed his clothes—nice dress pants, shoes, button-down-collared shirt. Had he dressed up to impress her? Anything he wore, or didn't wear, made an impression on her. He didn't even have to try. It wasn't all about looks.

"Looks like you're dressed for a business dinner. Not a 'serve and protect' mission."

"Undercover. Appearances can be deceiving." He unbuttoned the top three buttons of his shirt and the ones on his cuffs, and rolled his sleeves up. "The dressier look was to impress your neighbors."

She laughed. "Which at least with regard to Gertie, you excelled at."

He smiled. "This is my more casual bodyguard look."

"I have to admit you dress up nice. Kind of a trial run for the theater. You know, I was trying to…well, get this back on more of a professional basis."

"Sure," he said, but his smile said otherwise.

She folded her arms. "I didn't want to talk about this tonight, no business, but…since you're here, what do you know about Olivia Farmer?"

"What?" His eyes couldn't have gotten any rounder. *Not good.*

"I got hold of Krustan tonight to try and learn why he and Weaver were in Belize. He said you dated Olivia, and she could be key to this whole investigation."

"She's dead. Committed suicide two months ago."

"What? Oh, David. I'm so sorry." She hadn't known *that* part of the equation. She wished Krustan had told her.

"We broke up last year. She had started seeing Joe."

"Joe Storm." Tammy felt sick to her stomach, already hating where this was going.

"Yeah. The guy gets around. Olivia and I were going along great—dating stuff—movies, clubs, trips. She started missing dates, saying she had headaches…"

"She was seeing Joe at the same time?" Tammy couldn't believe it. Well, she could as far as Joe went. But what kind of woman would do that to David? He was just too sweet.

"Yeah. At first I believed her. And then I thought maybe she was just tired of our relationship. I tried to add some zing to it and asked if she wanted to visit an island."

"Don't tell me she turned you down."

"She didn't have a chance to. I kind of suspected she was seeing someone else, so I went unannounced to see her. Joe answered the door wearing just his boxers."

"You must have been pissed off."

"You could say that."

"Why didn't you tell me when I mentioned I'd dated Joe? You must have hated that I'd been seeing him, too." Yet David had never let on. He had been angry, but she'd thought it was just because he believed the guy had hurt her.

"I didn't believe it was important. It was in the past.

I moved on a long time ago. At the time, I figured she did me a favor."

"Yet I bet you didn't feel too bad when you knocked him out at the club."

His smile was a little sinister, but then he frowned. "Hell, Tammy, after he shot at you, I would do a lot worse if I ever get my hands on the guy. Even if he hadn't meant to shoot you."

"So why would Krustan believe Olivia would have anything to do with our case?"

"I haven't any idea. Except that it all seems to involve Joe."

She let out a sigh. "I guess it's time for bed. But… if you think I'm going to change my mind about the bed…" She eyed him with suspicion.

"The couch is fine. Really. I'll curl up in a little ball like I used to do as a kid."

She laughed. She was halfway thinking of letting him do it, too. Then again, she could envision him trying to get comfortable and having a miserable night of it.

They had a lot of ground to cover tomorrow. She'd keep thinking of him tossing and turning on the couch and never get any sleep herself. When it came to him, she was way too much of a pushover.

She stood, and when he rose from the couch, she took hold of his belt loop and tugged at him. "Come on. It's getting late, I'm tired, and we have a lot of work to do tomorrow."

He grabbed his bag and headed with her to the bedroom, wisely not saying anything about her changing her mind. She could imagine him grinning from ear to ear like a jaguar version of the Cheshire Cat.

Chapter 23

DESPITE HOW TENDERHEARTED TAMMY HAD BEEN THE last time David faced sleeping on a bunk bed that was too short, he really believed she would leave him with the option of retiring on the couch, which was even shorter than the bunk beds. He figured he'd just strip naked and shift. Lying down anywhere as a jaguar would work for him. He was surprised she hadn't thought of that.

He was really going to try to give her some space this time, not touch her air-conditioner setting, and behave himself. Not that he wanted to. He wanted to kiss her and so much more. What better way to wind down after the long road trip and plane ride today?

Before they reached her bedroom, he noticed a room made into a study and a closed door that he suspected led to a third bedroom.

She glanced in the direction he looked and smiled. "You don't want to see what's in there."

"Sort of a storage room?"

"Yeah. Stuff I need to sort through and get rid of."

Her bedroom was all blues and greens, reminding him of water and the jungle. And Tammy with him in the waterfall pool.

"My side is the right side of the bed," she said, just like it had been in Belize. "Guest bath down the hall is yours for showers and the like. I'll be right back."

That meant his side was the left, and it sure sounded

like something more permanent to him, even if she hadn't meant it that way.

In the guest bathroom, he quickly stripped off all but his boxers—before she changed her mind—brushed his teeth, returned to the bedroom, and climbed into bed. No sheer mesh curtains here to keep the bugs out. No noisy jungle sounds. The sheets smelled of the she-cat and fragrant vanilla with a hint of springtime freshness. And the sheets were satiny soft, just like she was.

She pulled the covers aside, glanced at his bare chest, and climbed into bed. She was wearing a large, navy-blue T-shirt this time, but even so, it reached high thigh and was sexy on her. The shirt didn't hide her curves and only fed his imagination.

He wasn't going to kiss her, he told himself. She wanted to keep their relationship strictly business until after the mission, now that they were home. He could understand that. To some extent.

"You appreciate why I needed to keep some distance from you, don't you?" she finally asked, glancing up at him and looking so damned sexy that he nearly forgot the part about how he wasn't going to kiss her.

"Yeah, you were afraid you'd lose focus on the assignment," he said.

She snorted.

"You can't be worried that *I'd* lose focus."

She laughed. "Yeah, I am."

Intending to prove he could deal with it, he said, "Here I was going to discuss the case with you, talk over what we could do tomorrow, and—"

"You mean like plan our next move?"

"Yeah, I can plan things, too," he said.

"Sometimes, it's better *not* to plan." With that, she slid up his body until she reached his mouth. And kissed him.

She didn't give him just a sweet little peck on the cheek or mouth that meant good night, sleep tight, and don't let the bedbugs bite. This was a hell of a lot like the kiss they had shared in the bungalow bed. He was trying not to let his imagination run wild—if that wasn't where it was headed—but he was all for it if it was.

He half expected her to pull away like when they'd been in bed together the first time, a sumptuous slip of a taste of fantasy and then it was gone. Well, not quite gone, because he'd thought about it forever.

Her hot little body was rubbing against his thoroughly rock-hard erection, her tongue slipping into his mouth as she pressed her T-shirt-clad breasts against his bare chest.

He slid his hands up her shirt and felt her soft skin and thought of the vanilla bath she'd taken. "I love how you smell, like cookies fresh from the oven," he said.

She threw back the covers, took his hand, and tugged. "Come on."

Great. He'd said the wrong thing and was being relegated to the couch.

He climbed out of bed and grabbed his pillow—at least while he stayed here, he was claiming it.

She glanced at the pillow in his hand. "What's that for?"

"The couch."

She gave him the wickedest smile. "You can leave it."

He didn't want to ask where they were going and spoil the fun—at least he hoped it was something fun. Otherwise, he wanted to be back in bed making more hot and sexy moves with the she-cat. "I thought you were tired." He didn't know what to think.

She took him into a bathroom that had a nice-sized whirlpool bath for two. She started filling the tub with warm water.

"You're taking another bath?" He couldn't help sounding so surprised.

"I don't need to remind you about what happened to the other. Since you were the cause of the interruption—twice—I figure I can take it and finish it this time while you're serving and protecting me."

He smiled, really getting into his new role. "I'll wash your back. Have a soft sponge?"

"I hope you'll do more than that."

"Hell, yeah." He still wasn't sure what she had in mind. He glanced at the bath oils and bubble baths sitting on a shelf.

"Preference?" she asked.

"Sexy Vanilla," he said. "Men don't take bubble baths, and I don't want any of the guys to smell honeysuckle or some of those other fragrances on me if we run into them during the investigation."

She laughed. "Some other time."

Well, if she was into making another date of it, how could he turn down that kind of an offer?

"You're in for a real treat," she said, pouring in some of the bath powder.

"I believe that." In his wildest dreams, he'd never thought he'd be making love to a wild she-cat in a tub filled with bubble bath. Then again, he never imagined he'd make love to her in a tropical pool at the base of a waterfall, either. Jaguars loved the water, and this definitely appealed to the cat side of him. She made sex fun and interesting, though he'd be just as happy making love to her in the bed. *Later*.

The vanilla-scented bubbles rose to the surface of the water as she turned on the jets. He stripped off his boxers, and before she could remove her nightwear, he pulled off her panties. He slid his fingers into her warm, wet sheath, and then hurried to remove her shirt so they could get down to business. He kissed her mouth as the water continued to fill the tub, his cock bumping against her stomach as she kissed him back. Her fingers combed through his hair, and her teeth nipped at his lips.

He was breathing hard, feeling the heat sizzle between them, the cat's hunger roaring to be appeased. Her tight nipples grazed his chest, her soft belly rubbing against his stiff cock, stirring the fire into a blaze.

He moved with her, rubbing his chest against hers, his erection teasing her belly. He heard her ragged breathing, saw the arousal in her blue eyes, felt her hands gliding over his arms, squeezing the taut muscles. Every touch, every sound was an erotic caress on his heightened cat senses.

"Water," she whispered against his throat, as if she was afraid to speak above a whisper for fear she would break the lust-filled spell they were under.

He reached over to turn off the water before the tub was filled too full, while she climbed in and settled down into the bubbles. She looked intriguing, the bubbles clinging to her breasts and dangling off her taut nipples, the rest of her hidden from view, like a tempting pearl waiting to be discovered. He couldn't decide which was more enticing—observing her like this, half hidden from view, or seeing her in the waterfall pool, the water clear and revealing everything about her. He decided he loved both.

This would be like a treasure hunt. He climbed into the water and settled in front of her. He pulled her onto his lap, her legs straddling him so he could kiss her and touch her where he wanted.

He slid his hands over her silky skin, the soapy water making it even more so. He felt like they were in a milk bath as he kissed her parted lips, which were inviting him in. He ran his hands up her thighs, enjoying the tactile exploration when he couldn't see what he was doing. He'd been concentrating on what she felt like, the way she was kissing his mouth, exploring his with her tongue, and fingering his hair, so he hadn't realized she'd moved her hands below the water, searching for his cock, until her fingertips brushed it. She smiled wickedly and took hold. He bit out a groan and the vixen smiled again.

He stroked her between her legs, the feel of her nub hard as she moved against his fingers, encouraging him to go faster. The bubbles caressed her taut nipples, and with his free hand, he ran his fingers over a breast, soft, firm, and the perfect size for his large hand.

She let go of his erection and gripped his shoulders as if she was so caught up in what he was doing to her that she couldn't do anything but cover his mouth with hers and kiss. Her tongue teased his and licked his lips. She barely breathed, her actions frantic as she tried to find release. He stroked her feminine nub as she tensed, nearly there.

Her heart and his were beating hard. The smell of her sex and his—combined with the sweet fragrance of vanilla and the scent of jaguars in lust—filled his senses. He moved his lips over her cheek, down her jaw, and then to her neck and gently sucked on her. He marked her as she had marked him. His fingers continued to stroke her sensitive nub. She cried out with pleasure, and he smiled to think he had brought her to fruition with the same technique.

He was ready to join with her in the worst way, to feel her inner muscles throbbing around him. He lifted her and slid inside her and then thrust, splashing water over the sides of the tub.

He wanted to apologize for making a mess, but she brought his face down to hers and began kissing him all over again, telling him without words that the spilled water didn't matter.

All there was between them were heat and softness, desire and pursuit, and a big cat's unfulfilled hunger.

They were kissing again, their hands sliding over shoulders, arms, and backs, caressing, stroking, loving. He was desperate to reach that climax, to feel the ultimate sexual high.

He couldn't stop the inevitable if he'd tried. She was arching against him, rising and then coming down hard, pleading with him to finish her off again, when he came and she followed. His hot seed spilled into her.

"You're such a hot and sexy distraction that I can't help myself when I'm with you." He kissed her again, thrusting the last couple of times until she'd milked him dry. He rested with her in the warm water, looking into her glazed blue eyes. Two satisfied cats.

They were still joined, and he liked that feeling. That connection. He wasn't in any hurry to separate from Tammy.

"I like bubble baths," he said, leaning over to kiss her cheek.

"I just bet you do."

Only if he could enjoy them with the she-cat like this. She seemed like a contented kitten, and they enjoyed the closeness until the water grew too cold.

They helped each other dry off. Together, they mopped up the soapy, wet floor.

"I hope that made up for my interrupting your bath earlier," he said as they climbed into bed. He pulled her into his arms to cuddle some more.

She caressed his chest with the tips of her fingers. "You're addictive. I just wanted to get *that*"—she motioned in the direction of the bathroom—"out of the way so we could remain focused on the job."

"Addictive, eh? Ditto for me. Anytime you want to get *it* out of the way to focus on the assignment, I'm all for it."

He sighed deeply and so did she. Two happy jaguar shifters ready to sleep.

His phone rang. She laughed when it played the pussycat jingle. He reached over to the side table, glad he'd thought to set his phone there, and answered it. "Yeah, Martin?"

Tammy rolled over onto her side, her back to David.

"The car tags belonged to a vehicle that must have been borrowed while the owner was away on vacation. He said he never knew it had been gone. No sign of forced entry, nothing left behind in it. He would have sworn it was there the whole time," Martin told David.

"Maybe Tammy's neighbor didn't get the right license tag number after all."

"Possibly. She might have transposed the numbers. I'm having a man check the car out tomorrow just in case. See if it has any jaguar scents in it."

"Okay, sounds good."

"Did she finally let you inside the house?"

David looked at Tammy's naked back, the covers pulled up over her hip, and thought about their romp in the bubble bath. "Yeah." He could envision his boss smiling at the news.

"Good show. Safer that way."

"It sure is." Safer and a hell of a lot nicer. He and Martin said good night.

David spooned Tammy with his body. He swore she purred as she nestled closer to him, seating her ass next to his crotch. He was almost embarrassed when his cock stirred to life.

She chuckled.

Chapter 24

AT THREE IN THE MORNING, DAVID HEARD A SCRATCH-
ing noise at the bedroom window. Tammy didn't
twitch a muscle. She was sound asleep. Unwrapping
her sweet body from his as he tried not to disturb her,
he finally managed to untangle their legs and slipped
out of bed. He stalked to the window and peered out
the curtains to see Alex and Nate in their jaguar forms
standing on her dark brick patio, tails swishing in the
hot breeze.

So they had come home. But what in the world were
the two of them doing here? And in cat form? Unless
they'd had trouble. And needed a place to hole up.

Great. About now, he wanted privacy with Tammy.

He waved at them, signaling he was coming out to
meet with them. He snagged a pair of jeans, threw them
on, grabbed a couple of T-shirts and shorts out of his
bag for the kids to wear, and headed for the back door.

When he got outside, Alex shifted, accepted the
clothes, and then yanked them on. Nate remained in his
cat form and sat down on the patio, watching David.

"Okay, so you're home. Well, not home, but you're
back here. What's up? I thought the two of you were
going to lie low somewhere," David said.

"They've stolen the jaguar," Alex said. He sounded
choked up, and David could see the boy was fighting tears.

"Okay, son," David said and gave him a fatherly pat

on the shoulder. "We'll get her back. I swear it. Where did you have her?"

"At an old farm out in the country. Some friends were taking care of her. Giving her fresh meat, water, keeping her locked up in a long cement run where the farmer used to care for a couple of wolves. The jaguar had part of a barn to hide in when she wanted seclusion. I'm sure she didn't like the wolf smell, but it was the best we could do on short notice."

David thought about his aftershave and how the cat might have liked that if she hadn't turned up missing.

"No one knew of the place. Someone must have learned of it, watched for our friends to come and go, and stolen her. The padlock on the gate had been cut off, so whoever it was had been prepared," Alex continued.

"Where are the two of you staying?"

"With friends. We didn't realize you'd be here."

So they'd come to see Tammy alone? "I'm here protecting Tammy, considering someone shot at her in Belize."

"Oh, yeah, sure," Alex said, not sounding like he believed that was the *only* reason David could be here. Then he frowned. "Someone shot at her?"

"Yeah." David explained what had happened after the boys had left them. "Will the two of you be all right? Safe where you're staying?"

"Yeah, as long as whoever the mole is doesn't come for us. We don't know who he is or where the cat is. We figure for now he'll leave us alone. We'll let the two of you grab the cat this time."

David hated asking the kids after what Martin had told him last night, but he had to know the truth. "The owner of the circus said the cat was theirs. That some-one stole the jaguar from them a year ago and donated her to the zoo."

His face expressionless, Alex didn't say anything, his gaze steady on David's. David didn't like the conclusions he was drawing from the scenario one bit.

"Okay, tell me the truth. *Did* you steal the circus cat and give her—"

The patio door opened and Tammy stood in the doorway in her T-shirt and jeans, shoeless like he was. "Come in, why don't the two of you?" she asked.

Alex's startled expression turned into a big smile. "Sure." He grabbed the extra T-shirt and shorts from David and hurried inside with Nate following behind.

David shook his head at Tammy. She smiled back at him and headed inside. Nate snagged the T-shirt and shorts from his brother with his teeth and disappeared into the guest bathroom.

David closed the back door and locked it. Nate rejoined them, and David said, "Okay, like I asked before, did the two of you steal the cat from the circus and turn her over to the zoo?" He would understand why if they'd learned the cat was being abused, not that it made it right to steal her.

"No," Nate said as he and his brother took a seat on the couch.

David didn't believe it. Why didn't Alex say so right after David mentioned what the circus owner had told them? "You personally didn't steal the jaguar a year ago," David said, believing the teens were getting technical with him, so he tried to pin them down.

"No," Alex said.

"Do you boys want some cookies and milk?" Tammy asked, ruining David's attempt at interrogation. She was definitely the good cop in the good cop/bad cop scenario.

"Sure," both of them said, their expressions brightening.

David wanted to shake his head but caught himself before he did.

Tammy gave him a small smile as if she knew just what he was thinking, patted him on the shoulder reassuringly, and disappeared into the kitchen.

"Wow," Alex said, his voice low. "You are sooo lucky."

Yeah, David was. He was already hoping things would work out for Tammy and him for the long run. For now, he was one lucky cat.

"Yeah," Nate whispered. "If I could work with an agent like her, I'd join up without a second's hesitation. And *protect* her like you're doing."

"Yeah, even if you've still got bad guys in the branch. We'd help weed them out."

"What if the female agent was the bad guy?" David asked.

"Well, if I got hooked up with her, I'd make the most of it while I was checking her out," Alex said, grinning.

Nate vigorously nodded. "My plan of action, too."

David laughed, thinking the boys were too much like he and Wade were at their age. "Yeah, and that would be your big mistake."

Tammy returned with a tray of cookies and glasses of milk.

While David looked on, the boys devoured the cookies and milk as if they'd been starved for eons. He was a little disappointed that Tammy had given all Gertie's cookies to the twins, and he had lost the chance to sample any more of them.

"Okay, if you didn't steal the cat from the circus, who did?" David asked, getting back to business.

"Who said anyone stole the cat from the circus and gave it to the zoo? The crooked owner?" Alex said. "And you believe *him*? We only rescued the cat from the circus a few days ago. Did they report it was stolen?"

"Not that I know of," David said.

Alex nodded sagely. "See? They didn't tell the authorities. Why not? If something gets stolen, the owner informs the police. Did they really report the stolen jaguar a year ago?"

"I'll have to check into it in the morning," David said. He was certain Martin would have verified the owner's claims, but David didn't want to say so and be wrong. "On another subject, why did you steal our clothes in the jungle? Obviously, that was why Nate roared for us. To get us to find you. We figured you wanted to lead us to your place to show us that someone had ransacked it. But why steal our clothes?"

"We always packed our bags in Mom and Dad's car and parked it different places so whoever was looking for us wouldn't find our bags while we were running as jaguars in the rainforest. We discovered someone was searching our place when we returned," Nate said.

"We worried the men would grab your stuff and search it. We didn't know if you had anything in your luggage that might reveal something about us. Though we'd looked," Alex said.

So that *was* why the boys had rummaged through their belongings earlier.

"Why take our backpack that had our clothes in it?" Tammy asked.

Alex cast a glance at Nate.

Nate cleared his throat and said, "We didn't want you to accidentally run into the men in your human form if you caught them in your place. You didn't have any weapons on you. If as jaguars you had caught them, you could have taken care of them."

"Yeah, and we were also afraid they might find your backpack and get rid of it. So we just grabbed it all and hid it," Alex said.

"We didn't want to return your stuff to the bungalow after the break-in, afraid someone might still be watching. Alex had the idea to use the condoms to give you a trail to follow, since you'd probably figure out what it meant. We had to do something to lead you to your bags."

"And you hung around the waterfall," Tammy said.

"We had to make sure only you got your bags. We didn't want anyone else to find them. We would have stripped down and shifted and made sure if anyone had it in mind to grab them, they'd change their minds. Fast," Nate said.

"And we had to clean up the mess we made. We picked up the others, too, before the zip line was open. We only meant for you to see them to get a clue where we'd be." Alex finished the last of the cookies.

So they hadn't left the other condoms for the staff to find. David was glad about that.

"Oh, and just so you know," Nate said, "we paid your fine for helping us out with Joe Storm."

"My boss would have paid it," David said.

"Yeah, but the JAG branch shouldn't have to. So we paid it," Alex said.

"Thanks," David said.

The boys shared looks, and then Nate said, "We wondered if you could teach us how to knock someone out the way you did Joe, in case we ever have trouble with a dude like him in the future."

Before David could answer, Tammy said, "No. Messing with someone like that would likely get you killed."

They looked at David as if waiting for his opinion. The boys couldn't genuinely believe he'd go against what Tammy had said. Not when he knew she was right and he wanted to return to bed with her and hold her close the rest of the night.

"She's right, guys. Do you have anything else you want to discuss with us that will help with finding the cat or learning who took her from you the first time?"

The boys shook their heads.

"Let's call it a night," David said. "You sure you're going to be safe leaving here on your own?"

"Yeah," both said at the same time. They went outside and gave the T-shirts and shorts back to David, then shifted and took off. Their car had to be parked nearby. Sure enough, a few minutes later, he heard the car engine roar and the vehicle retreating down the street.

David returned to the house and locked the door.

"So what did you gather from that little exchange?" Tammy asked, setting the empty cookie plate and glasses on the tray.

"More is going on than meets the eye. I don't think they're telling us everything." He eyed the empty cookie dish. "Did you *have* to give them the rest of the cookies?" he asked as he helped Tammy carry the dirty dishes to the kitchen and put them in the dishwasher.

"They're growing boys." She patted David's stomach. "*You* have to watch that you don't end up looking like Santa Claus."

He grabbed her up and tossed her over his shoulder.

She squealed in surprise and laughed. "What are you doing?"

"Getting some exercise while I take my bag of Christmas toys to bed. I can't tell you how much I'm going to enjoy unwrapping them to make sure the presents are all still there."

Chapter 25

THE NEXT MORNING, DAVID CALLED HIS BOSS FIRST thing to inform him that the jaguar had been stolen from the boys. He glanced up to see Tammy examining his keys on his key ring as she joined him. He hadn't realized he'd left them on the dining table.

Not a happy director, Martin growled, "If they had turned the cat over to the Service, she would be safe now and back at the zoo."

"The last time the boys turned the cat over to the Service, she ended back at the circus."

"Hell, yeah," Martin said. "Don't remind me."

David was certain whoever was involved would pay big-time. After he and Martin finished talking, Tammy and David planned to head over to the circus grounds.

"Why do you have so many keys?" she asked, handing them over to David. "I have my house key to the front and back doors, car keys to my car doors and trunk, and that's it."

"Looks like I have a few I should have gotten rid of a while back."

She raised her brows as she climbed into his car.

"They don't belong to anything any longer." Hell, he hadn't even realized he still had the extra keys. Just never thought about it until he saw Tammy puzzling over them. One was to his old girlfriend's place. Two belonged to Quinn's sister, Olivia.

He eyed the keys. One was to her house and another to her car. Then he noted the one to his safety-deposit box, recalling she had signed the signature card so she could access it if she wanted to. He had never put anything in it. Had she?

Tammy had grown quiet and was leaning on the door, her head resting against the window.

In the time that they had been working together, he'd noted she was definitely a morning person. Very talkative. *Until now*. This morning, she had barely said anything to him even after she had a cup of hot green tea and a bagel, only giving her boss a brief call to inform him of the missing cat, until she'd asked David about the keys. Then she had zoned out again.

"Rough night, huh?" he asked.

She cast him a wicked smile. She was just as much to blame for their making love half the night as he was. He smiled back. He wanted a repeat performance tonight, but they'd have to take a catnap—separately—if they were going to manage it.

They arrived at the circus grounds a half hour before a free preshow time when circus-goers could get autographs from performers on the arena floor. But they couldn't get in until the circus actually opened its gates. Without a warrant to look around, they had to use finesse in learning what they could.

As soon as they gained entrance, the smells of food—roasted peanuts, cotton candy, turkey legs—and animals—lions, tigers, elephants, a bear, and dogs— swirled around them on the hot Texas breeze.

Three huge yellow-, red-, and blue-striped circus tents dominated the grassy field. Beyond that, what looked like a trailer park had been set up to accommodate the performers.

Somewhere back there, they would also have the animals that they used in the performances in cages or tied up.

"This way, folks." A couple of what David thought looked like the bouncers in the jaguar shifter club motioned to him and Tammy to enter one of the tents.

"We've come to see the owner about a missing jaguar. We're trying to track it down for him. Is Cyrus Wilde available to talk to us?" David asked.

"Mr. Wilde had family business to attend to. He's in Madison, Wisconsin," the man said. He was wearing a black T-shirt with a circus tent and the name of the circus screen-printed across the front, and he had wild, curly red hair.

"What about the manager?" Tammy asked.

The man jerked his thumb toward a trailer mostly hidden by the tent, a sign displayed on top saying, OFFICE. "He's in there. Didn't hear anything about a missing cat. I'm sure Randy would have told us to be on the lookout for you."

"We only just tracked down that the cat had been stolen from here. Thanks." David touched Tammy's back with a silent message to move before the guy changed his mind and said they couldn't bother the manager.

She quickly stepped out. The two crossed the grassy area and were promptly stopped by a clown with a red rubber nose, white face paint, enormous red-painted lips, and a bright orange curly wig. "This area is for performers and staff only."

"Out of my way," Tammy said to the clown with a

stern voice and an even sterner expression. "You don't want to be a casualty. Do you?"

The guy looked at David as if confirming she spoke the truth. He smiled and shrugged. "Bad clown experience," he guessed.

David hurried to join her as she continued on her way to the manager's trailer.

"So you had a bad experience with a clown?" David asked Tammy.

"When I was about ten, my parents took us to a carnival. A clown whipped flowers out of a hat too close to me and gave me a bloody nose."

"Hell, I would have killed him."

She smiled. "You wouldn't have needed to. I hit him between the legs of his baggy clown pants—just an automatic reaction. He cried real tears. But I didn't feel bad. I had a bloody nose that hurt like the devil, and my mother was ready to shift and bite the guy. Both my brothers stomped on the clown's oversized shoes before he fell to the ground in pain."

"If I ever go to a Halloween party with you, I'll know what *not* to wear," David said.

She chuckled. "You can go as Tarzan." She smiled as she looked down at his body as if just imagining him wearing a loincloth. Damn, if her gaze didn't stir things up.

He took her arm and walked faster before he got into some significant trouble.

When he knocked on the manager's door, a gruff-sounding man shouted, "Come in!"

David exchanged looks with Tammy.

"Sounds like he's having a bad day," she whispered.

David nodded and opened the door.

The dark-haired man looked up at them and stopped shuffling through papers at his desk. "Who the hell are you?"

"We're here to speak to Cyrus Wilde."

"He's had family issues. He's not here right now."

"Okay, well, we've been told a jaguar is missing from your circus. We've been trying to track it down for Cyrus."

"He said nothing about this to me. When was this supposed to be? I've only been the manager here for a month."

David thought that odd. Wouldn't everybody know about the missing jaguar? Even if the man hadn't been there but a month. Especially if the circus had stolen it back from the boys recently. And even odder, Martin had talked to Cyrus just a couple of days ago, and he never mentioned that he wasn't at the circus. "It was originally stolen a year ago," David said.

Randy let out his breath and waved at the grounds. "You can ask some of the staff if you want. But we have a lot of turnover with the employees. Not sure who all was here back then. A couple of clowns, I think."

David gave Tammy a look. If anyone had to question a clown, he'd do the talking.

"And the owner, of course, was here." Randy motioned to a picture of a man standing next to the lion's cage—the same man who had bumped into Tammy as he was headed into the police station. He'd smelled like a lion and was wearing a handlebar mustache. He must have liked the big cats. Maybe worked with them some.

"He was at the police station a few days ago," David said. "Did that have to do with the stolen cat?"

The manager shook his head. "Brand-new popcorn machine. Someone stole it."

David wasn't about to give up on the manager yet, even if he hadn't been here when the owner claimed the cat was first stolen. The circus had to have some documentation showing the cat had been here at one time. "Have you got any pictures of the jaguar performing? Dated pictures?"

Randy eyed his messy office with papers scattered everywhere—floor, table, desk, an old musty-smelling tweed couch, and shelves. "This is the mess I got when I first started working here. With having to manage the show, I don't have time to sort through this disaster area."

David glanced at posters of the current show that hung on corkboard. Four metal file cabinets stood against one wall. "Maybe something in one of the filing cabinets."

"I don't know what the previous manager's filing system was, but there aren't any labels on anything. Nothing filed alphabetically, numerically, nothing." He went to one of the cabinets, opened a drawer, fumbled through some file folders, closed the drawer, and proceeded to do the same with the others.

Files were meant to organize things, David thought. Why have them otherwise?

"Well, hell, I can't find anything. *If* there are any documents concerning the cat, my guess is they'd be in one of these cabinets," the manager finally said.

"Do you mind if we look?" David asked.

"We wouldn't even mind straightening the files up for you if it would help," Tammy quickly offered.

The manager stared at the cabinets and then shook his head. "The owner would have to okay it."

"You think that pictures of the cat might have been misplaced or stolen?" David asked.

"Misplaced? Sure. Stolen, I wouldn't think so. Thrown out? Maybe. If it happened last year, that's a long time ago," Randy said.

Missing pictures, posters, or anything related to the jaguar seemed a little too convenient. If he and Tammy could have looked at a photo of the cat, they could compare the rosette pattern with the cat's pictures from the zoo and try to get a match. The only other way to confirm the owner's story was to get the cat to perform. But for that, they needed the jaguar.

"Feel free to speak with anyone who isn't working on getting ready for the next show."

"Thanks," David said, pausing at the door. "Was the other manager let go? Or did he quit?"

"Fired. After some sloppy business dealings, fraternizing with some of the female entertainers on the job and the like, Cyrus fired him. He wanted to make sure I kept my hands off the women. Or the men. I'm a happily married man, so no issues with me there."

"So Cyrus canned him."

"Yeah. You don't work, you get fired. He told me he should have gotten rid of him earlier than that. The guy thought he was a real Casanova. Had the women all scrapping over him. Bunch of damn cat fights going on constantly. That's what Cyrus said. He only mentioned it to me because he wanted to make it clear to me that he wouldn't tolerate that crap from me or anyone else he hired for this position in the future."

"The former manager's name?"

"Joe Storm."

David and Tammy exchanged looks. Why did Joe's name keep coming up in the conversation?

"Thanks," David said. "We'll ask around."

As soon as they were far enough away from the manager's trailer, David called Martin. "The manager claims he doesn't know anything about a stolen jaguar. He's only been working here a month. Can you have one of our people check and see if there were any police reports showing the owner had reported a stolen jaguar?"

"Yeah, sure."

"We're going to see if we can find anyone on staff who was here last year and ask around. But also, new news. Joe Storm was acting manager, probably between the time he lost his JAG job and got hired as the bouncer for the shifter club."

"Why was he fired from that job?"

"He was playing Casanova."

"Typical. I'll let you know what I learn about the police report. Out here."

The sweet smell of cotton candy and cinnamon-scented churros filled David's nostrils. An elephant trumpeted in the background; people were laughing, talking, and shouting; and carnival music playing overhead as he noticed Tammy speaking to a woman in leotards and a tutu who looked like she might be part of the permanent staff with the circus. He hurried to join her.

"Yeah, Joe was cute. But nothing with him was permanent. He was with one woman and then another. He had a real reputation. I don't think he was doing his job much, so he got fired." She motioned to a guy in tights. "That's one of our aerial acrobats. He had a run-in with Joe."

"Yeah, what's up?" the guy asked, joining them.

"They want to know about Joe Storm."

"I was dating the tightrope walker and aerialist, Mindy, and he started hitting on her. It didn't matter to him if some other guy was seeing the lady. He didn't bother the married ones, though. But he sure pissed off some of the guys."

"Do either of you know anything about a jaguar in one of the shows?" Tammy asked.

"I don't know anything about them. I mean, yeah, I've seen the elephants and the dog lady with her prancing mutts. Got an allergy to cats, so I stay away from them," the guy said.

The girl shrugged. "The animals smell. On a hot day, they make my eyes water. I don't go anywhere near their cages. My show is first, so I'm gone before the animals make a mess of things. Sure the clowns run around scooping up the poop, but still…" She shuddered dramatically.

"Thanks," Tammy said, sounding exasperated.

She and David waved down another woman, who smiled at them. "You want my autograph?"

"Uh, well, yeah, sure. What do you do at the circus?" Tammy asked, fishing the circus brochure out of her pocket.

"Trampoline and bars gymnast," the girl said, signing her name across the front of the brochure.

"How cool," Tammy said, and David was thinking of Tammy being an aerialist on the cable in Belize, except she hadn't had any safety line.

"Actually we're looking into a case of a missing jaguar and wondered if you knew Joe Storm?" Tammy asked.

"Joe," the girl said, suddenly all dreamy-eyed. "If he could've stuck with me, I would have settled down with him. Real sweet temperament. But he's just not the settling-down type. I've got to run, but..." She cast an interested glance in David's direction. "Did *you* need my autograph?" She smiled so sweetly that he suspected she would like to give him her telephone number, too.

"Uh, yeah, sure." He noted the annoyed look Tammy gave him. But what could he do? They had to keep up appearances.

The girl signed his brochure.

"What about the jaguar?" Tammy asked.

"I don't remember anything about a jaguar. They have tigers. Really got to go." She smiled again at David, and it was a lot friendlier than the smile she gave Tammy. And she'd taken longer to sign his brochure than Tammy's.

Tammy yanked it out of his hand before he could read it. "With all my heart. Love, Zelda Younger," Tammy said in a really sweetly annoyed way and then in a darker, "she-cat is pissed" tone of voice, "*and* she left a phone number."

"Maybe she gave it to me in case I wanted to call her to discuss Joe or the jaguar."

"Right." Tammy tossed the two brochures in the trash.

He chuckled.

Tammy didn't know what to think. Why was it that everywhere they went, Joe Storm was involved? And why couldn't they confirm any sightings of the jaguar? She gave David another irritated look. "You didn't have to smile so much at her. No wonder she gave you her phone number. I'm surprised she didn't give you her address."

She wasn't sure why David's response was irritating her so much. Maybe all this talk of Joe was just riling her up.

David was about to respond when an athletic blond woman dashed across the field. Without warning, she jumped on David, wrapping her legs around his lean hips, hands on his shoulders, looking up at him with adoration. "Oh my God, David, is that you?"

Shocked at the woman's action, Tammy stared at her and David, forcing herself not to fold her arms and trying to keep from growling. So the woman just jumped any man's bones and after the fact asked if he was the right man?

David's hands were planted under the woman's jean-covered ass, which meant she was seated against his crotch.

Tammy reminded herself that his relationship with the other woman had nothing to do with her, and that he had to be over and done with it if he was now dating Tammy. So why was she fighting the feral need to shift and draw blood? Both the human woman's and David's?

When David didn't put the woman down, Tammy was about to suggest in a totally catty way that they meet up later so he could visit with his old girlfriend. But when she opened her mouth to propose it, the woman said to David, "It's me. Merilee Beckett."

"Yeah. How could I forget? Where's your boyfriend?"

Tammy narrowed her eyes a little at David. How could he forget? A throaty growl slipped out, though she'd meant to curb her jaguar urges better than that.

David didn't look her way, but he smiled just a little. He'd definitely heard Tammy's growl. *Damn it.* She didn't want him thinking she was jealous. She was *not* envious of his relationship with this woman or any other.

"Howard? In the slammer. We broke up again and he learned I was dating some other dude, and he killed him," Merilee said.

"You didn't go back to Howard this time?" David asked.

"Hell, no. He's got life." She smiled. "So I'm working a gig at the circus. Ticket taker. But I'm free until two. Want to get some lunch?"

"Why don't you?" Tammy told David, as if she was part of the conversation, trying to sound totally business-like, professional, and not like a jealous jaguar who was ready for a catfight with another female over a male.

"Sure," David said, glancing at her, looking as though he'd forgotten they might be working a mission together. She was his partner. Remember? She could have roared in annoyance. "I'll meet you…?"

She *so* wanted to say that he was on his own. Don't worry about meeting her anywhere. He could concentrate on finding the bad agents in the branches, and she'd locate the missing cat like she was first tasked to do. She was in Texas again, no need to have another agent teaming up with her to protect her like when she was in the jungle. End of story.

He was waiting for her to decide, his mouth curving up a bit. She was scowling. But that was because he was still holding on to Merilee.

"At two, where the kiddie pony rides are set up," Tammy said, way too belatedly.

David finally released Merilee, and Tammy turned and stalked off before he saw just how furious she was. She shouldn't have been. He was just getting together with an old girlfriend and probably intended to learn if she had any inside information about the circus.

Although if Merilee had just started working for them, she probably knew nothing.

But if she could escort him around the place, David was sure to get more out of Merilee if Tammy wasn't hanging around.

Tammy heard a lion roar and headed in that direction, thinking where one cat was located, the others would also be. Just as she made her way around a blue house trailer, a man stepped in front of her—sexy, built, and wearing a darkly interested smile. "Only performers and permanent staff are allowed back here," he said in a thick Russian accent.

She looked him over—he wore tights, no shirt, and leather bands around his wrists. With his hard abs and pecs, he was really hot for a human. "What do you do?" If she'd still had her brochure, she could have asked for *his* signature, and she would have told him to sign it: *With all my love, whatever his name was* and add his telephone number.

"Duo balancing with Luke," he said.

Another man headed toward them, but *he* wasn't smiling. "She's not a new hire, is she?" he asked, his tone abrupt, same accent as the other man's.

"No, Luke. At least I don't think so."

"She's not allowed back here." Luke was dressed in the same manner, the same hot body, but he was fairer in coloration, his jawline stronger.

"Thanks, but the manager okayed my being back here to talk to a couple of people about the missing jaguar. I'm trying to locate it for the owner. Do either of you know anything about the big cat?"

"We joined the circus three months ago, so we don't

know anything about it. Must have been before our time here," Luke said.

"Okay. Well, thanks. I just thought my friend was working back here, and we were supposed to meet for lunch and—wait. There he is," Tammy said, pointing in the direction of the trailers, pretending she saw a friend.

Before the duo-balancing guys tried to stop her, she stalked off toward one of the clowns—the same clown she'd given the evil eye to—who was talking to a woman walking a couple of dogs. Tammy was intent on seeing where the lion was caged up, hoping she'd smell some sign that the jaguar had been here and maybe even still was.

The dogs were yipping, excited, and Tammy smelled elephant droppings in that direction.

The animals had to be contained beyond the trailers.

She started heading that way when she thought she saw the Enforcer agent, Weaver, slipping behind one of the trailers. She quickly changed her plan, deciding to follow him instead. Suddenly a man called out to her, "What the hell are you doing here?"

She turned and saw Quinn Singleterry coming out of the blue trailer as he quickly secured his hair in a tail. What was *he* doing here?

Chapter 26

TAMMY WATCHED AS A WOMAN PEERED OUT OF THE trailer that Quinn had exited, her brown hair all in shambles, looking as though she'd had a thorough romp with him. The woman frowned at Tammy as if she might be interested in doing the same with Quinn.

"See you later," Quinn said to the woman. He kissed her cheek in more of a sisterly way—as if he was trying to put on a show for Tammy—and hurried to join her. He took her arm and led her away from the trailers. "What do you think you're doing here?"

She immediately yanked her arm out of his grasp. "Investigating a missing zoo cat. What else?" She was annoyed with herself that she had given him a reason, though he already knew that's what she'd been working on. "Besides, what business is it of yours where I am?"

"This is a restricted area of the circus for safety and insurance reasons."

"Like you have some kind of special pass? The manager approved my being back here. What are *you* doing here?" As if she had to ask.

"I assumed you could figure that one out for yourself," he said, smirking.

"Were you also investigating the missing zoo cat, which is why you were here and…following up leads in a trailer?"

His smile broadened.

"How did you learn that Joe Storm knew where I was going to be when he tried to shoot me? *I* didn't even know where I was going to be."

"He was shooting at me."

Her jaw dropped. She quickly closed her mouth.

"Only you suddenly appeared and I had to get you out of harm's way fast."

"He was shooting at *you*?" That thought had never occurred to her. She had been running, so she could see how she suddenly appeared in the shooter's path, and she could have been hit accidentally. And it sure would explain why Quinn had been there at the right time and the right place to save her.

"Yeah. I suspected he had something to do with the missing cat, but it was a lot more than that—one or two agents in the organization are bad. He's working with them, I'm certain. So I asked him to meet with me."

"Alone? In the rainforest? Kind of dangerous, wasn't it? Didn't you figure that he would try to kill you, rather than give up his contacts?"

"It goes deeper than any of that, Tammy. Would you like to get some lunch and we can talk?"

"Sure."

About a dozen long picnic tables were situated in a grassy area with people milling around, crunching on candied apples, slurping pink or blue snow cones, munching on vinegar fries, licking ice cream, and devouring funnel cakes. With so many people, including a group of clowns on stilts who blocked her view of the tables, she couldn't see David or Merilee, no matter how much she tried to look around those in her way.

Circus-goers were standing in long lines at the various

concession stands, and she and Quinn were finally able to order. There were too many choices. She hadn't been to a carnival or circus in years. She picked out a hot dog, purple cotton candy, and roasted peanuts, all served in a clown hat. Though she tried to look for David and Merilee again after she ordered her food and while the man prepared it for her, she still didn't see any sign of them. Had they left the circus grounds to eat somewhere else?

She was trying *really* hard not to care.

She scooped up her clown hat and thanked Quinn for getting lunch for her, recalling she didn't have any money on her—too late.

"How can you eat all that?" Quinn asked, after getting a turkey leg and a soda as he looked down at her figure. He led her to one of the tables.

"I burn the calories off while I'm working."

"And playing?" he asked, brows raised.

She ignored him and took a bite of her dog.

"I see you ditched your partner."

She wasn't about to let him know that David was here with her now. Maybe if Quinn thought she was working alone, he would feel freer to talk to her about what she needed to know.

Before she could ask him any questions, Quinn looked beyond her and smiled.

Tammy twisted around to see what he was smiling at—David talking to Merilee at a table in the distance. Tammy let out her breath in annoyance. She had thought maybe Merilee sneaked away with David to one of the trailers, but she didn't believe the woman would have access to one if she was just a ticket taker. So much for Tammy pretending she'd ditched her partner.

"She's David's old girlfriend. They had some catching up to do," she explained, hating that she sounded like she was defending him.

"She's been seeing Joe Storm," Quinn said, sounding irritated.

Tammy's lips parted slightly in surprise. Hell, the guy sure got around, not that she was really surprised. "Who *hasn't* been seeing him?" she blurted out, and then wished she hadn't and licked some of the ketchup off her hot dog. Just like she shouldn't have added, "Just like you." She supposed she said so because she'd dated Joe and didn't want Quinn thinking he was any better than the guy as far as being with women went.

Quinn smiled a little at that. "I didn't know you were keeping count."

"The two of you are cut from the same spotted cloth. I don't keep track. I can just imagine."

"Not exactly. See, he makes false commitments to women he's dating. Asks them to marry him. The women I date know I don't plan on marrying them. Not only that, but he's into illegal stuff. I'm certain he's working with someone in one of the branches, and they're getting kickbacks on the crimes committed. Only somehow my boss got the notion I might be involved. Any idea how that might have happened?" Quinn asked.

"So Martin got hold of you?"

"Yeah."

She shook her head. Quinn thought *she* was responsible for his getting in trouble? "Okay, you were on an unscheduled trip to Belize, just happened to be stalking the boys, and were there when the shooting occurred.

Kind of makes one speculate. Then you pretended to take a flight home?"

Quinn lifted his head a little, smiled at someone behind her, and waved. She didn't look this time. "I wondered when David would notice you were eating lunch with me. He shouldn't have taken up with Merilee and left you alone. You are still his partner after all, right? He looks like one pissed-off cat. Funny how he was having a fine time eating lunch with her until he saw you sharing lunch with me. The storm clouds moved right in and rained on his little picnic."

"He probably doesn't trust you. You have to admit you were being sneaky in Belize. If you'd wanted to let us know you were there and working the same case—"

"I wasn't. Working the same case as you, that is. If you'd said you wanted to work with me in the beginning, I would have turned you down. I was just giving David a hard time. Nothing personal. Except you're a woman. After Joe nearly shot you…" He shrugged. "I would have been justified in worrying about you."

"Why did he want to kill you?"

"He was seeing my sister. He promised to marry her. She had everything planned. I hadn't ever seen her happier. I discovered he was a total fraud. Had a string of girlfriends and another fiancée planning a wedding for a month after my sister's. My sister was so distraught that she killed herself."

"Oh, Quinn, I'm so sorry."

"Yeah, well, I felt responsible because I had told her the truth about the other women."

Tammy couldn't believe he'd feel that way. "Joe was responsible for breaking her heart. And she would have learned the truth eventually anyway. It wasn't your fault."

"You were one of the women he was seeing at the time."

Astonished, she stared at Quinn. Did he condemn her, too? "Wait. I investigated the women, including the two fiancées, he had been seeing. Olivia Farmer and Evelyn Higgenbottom. No Singleterry."

"Olivia had been married once before."

Tammy shook her head. "I'm so sorry. I had no idea. I was broken up over the whole thing myself when I learned Joe was seeing other women and had been hiding it from me."

"I know. She'd been seeing David before that. He would have been good for her."

Tammy snapped her gaping mouth shut. Olivia was Quinn's sister, the same woman David had been dating. And he'd caught her with Joe. Not to mention that all three men had worked together in the JAG. Crap.

"I told Martin about Joe's lifestyle. I couldn't bring my sister back or smooth over my mother's grief at losing her oldest daughter. But I could get the bastard fired. Joe loved being a Golden Claw just as much as he loved being with a woman. It wasn't until later that I learned he was working with bad agents. I wanted to meet with him to learn who was dirty in one or more of the branches. I swore to him he'd be free of prosecution. That we'd strictly go after the rotten eggs in the organization. He gave me a date, time, and location to meet him in the rainforest."

"And he tried to kill you. Why didn't you realize he might try to do that?"

Quinn finished his turkey leg and sct the bone down on the paper plate, but didn't say.

"Why would he trust you? Why would he want to give up the men and cut off his money source?"

"Because I know he's dirty. And he knows I know. If he doesn't come clean, we'll take him out, but it would be better if we learn who the bad agents are first. I guess he wanted to get me back for having him fired. Maybe he thought if he killed me, the evidence I have that links him with dirty dealings would never come to light."

"Maybe he's worried that you might still tie him into the criminal activities, despite what you said. That you would turn him over to the authorities along with the bad agents." She still didn't trust everything Quinn was saying without further proof to back up his every word. "What about the missing zoo cat?"

"Is that why you're here? Thinking it was at the circus? They've never had one here."

Now *that*, she didn't believe. "How would *you* know?"

"I checked."

"You said you had a couple of leads about the zoo cat, but they didn't pan out. You said you weren't working the case."

"Just something I'd overheard. Probably the same thing you heard. That the zoo cat was here at the circus. But you know how leads are. Most don't go anywhere. Still, if I could have easily solved the case, I would have done so."

"Okay, so why would the owner say it had been reported stolen?"

"Was it? Reported stolen? Have you checked and found they filed a police report?"

She didn't say anything. They'd have to check into it. But it did bother her that the manager said he couldn't find the paperwork on it. She wondered if Joe Storm, the one who must have reported it, had not done so at all.

"The owner must have lied about having a jaguar. Or something," Quinn said.

"Why would he do that? Besides, the boys said they saw it here." She wasn't going to let Quinn think she was completely taking him at his word. She wasn't going to mention the part about how the teens said they'd stolen it from the circus, either. Did Quinn already know? "Were they lying, too?"

"Teens can be teens. Those two have been in enough trouble that the Service wants them under their wing, right? So what makes you think they've been perfectly honest with you?"

Quinn had her there. She'd wanted to believe in them, for one thing. But that didn't mean she should. She remembered Weaver's comment that she shouldn't trust the kids.

"Why were you following them?" she asked.

"I wasn't. I was trying to reach Joe."

"What do you know about Krustan and Weaver?" she asked.

Quinn sat up a little taller. "I worked on a job with Krustan once. He's really got an eye for the ladies."

"Competition for you."

Quinn smiled.

"Did you know the two of them were in Belize looking for the friends of the two boys we were trying to get in touch with?" She was certain Quinn had to have come across their scent trails at the very least.

"I smelled Krustan in the jungle and another male jaguar that I didn't know. Must have been Weaver. I really don't know anything about them being down there or what their business was. I never ran across them. I didn't even learn why you were there with David, knowing you were looking for the missing cat and it couldn't possibly be in Belize. Until I heard the kids he was supposed to be watching had some information about the cat and had disappeared in the rainforest down there. I did run across two other male jaguar scents. Heavy aftershave lotion. Don't know who it belonged to. Couldn't have been the boys unless they're doing some heavy-duty shaving."

"What I don't understand is why Martin would send two men to look for the other two boys, and then Peter and Hans skip to Belize. But instead of the JAG agents who were looking for them following them down there, Weaver and Krustan were after them. And they were supposed to be on vacation."

Quinn shook his head. "I don't know. Seems you or your boss would know the men better than I would. Are you certain the other two boys were actually in Belize?"

Tammy finished her cotton candy as she considered Quinn's comment. She'd never smelled the other male jaguar scents. But Alex and Nate had said their friends were good at evading pursuers. They probably hadn't been close to where Alex and Nate were, or they would have made for an easier target. And they had been at the airport. It didn't mean they'd come in from Belize.

"I don't know for certain if the two boys were in Belize. We'll have to check into it further."

She recalled having smelled several shifters' scents at their bungalow and the boys'. She narrowed her eyes at

Quinn. "Why were you in our bungalow? You, Quinn, Weaver, and Krustan?"

"I didn't see any of them. I had heard about a couple of tourists that went missing. The two of you— specifically. I checked out your place to see if I could learn anything. No foul play at the time. Just you were gone. Your luggage was gone. I smelled the two jaguars' heavy aftershave scent and that was it. I heard you had returned later that night, and I couldn't find Joe, so I came home to try some other angle concerning the crooked Service members."

Plausible, but she wasn't sure she trusted him. "We believe the cat thief and dirty agent has got to be someone with financial issues." She watched Quinn closely to see his reaction.

He smiled a little as if he knew just why she'd brought it up. "I think Merilee's getting angry now. But David's not making a move to come rescue you from me," Quinn said, changing the subject.

"He knows I don't need a rescue. What do you know about the zip-line accident?"

Quinn faced her. "I don't know anything about it, except that it was posted on YouTube and Martin sent a note to all Golden Claws that he wanted us to watch the video as part of a training exercise."

"A *training* video? And *YouTube*?" *Great*. Tammy felt her whole face heat.

"Got to admit you did a hell of a job rescuing yourself, Tammy. Where was David when all this was happening?"

She wasn't about to defend David's actions concerning that, either. He couldn't have helped her. Had David sent the video to his boss? She frowned.

"The video didn't say why you had to rescue yourself. What happened?"

She shook her head. She wasn't going to explain what they suspected if Quinn didn't know anything about it. "So you were going to talk to Joe, and then he tried to kill you? You're here now, and he's still there? Or is he here now, too?"

"I have no idea where he is. After he tried to kill me, I figured we were beyond talking. But I couldn't track him down."

"So you're here still on a break? Or on a mission?"

"Seeing an old girlfriend. And yes, I'm on a break."

"Why didn't you want me here? At the circus?"

"Would you believe that I didn't like that you had seen me here with a woman?" he asked.

"You're kidding. Right? I wouldn't think you'd care what I, or any other woman, would think."

He ignored the comment. "I'm surprised you're still with David on this assignment. You have quite a reputation to uphold."

She raised her brows in question.

"For getting rid of partners on a mission," he said. "You had a great start when you left David at the police station. Talk about a cat eating crow. It was killing me not to comment to him on it, and it was killing him that I didn't say a word."

She could just imagine. "You never know how long a partner will last. Some longer than others." After David's little exhibition with Merilee, Tammy was thinking he'd outlasted his partnership with her. She wondered how long and well he had known Merilee.

The notion irritated her, and she was annoyed with herself for letting it.

"They're leaving," Quinn said.

She refused to look to see where David and Merilee were off to.

"Wonder where they're going," Quinn said, baiting her.

She still wouldn't bite.

"You don't know about their history, do you?" Quinn asked.

Chapter 27

DAVID THOUGHT HE'D GET LUCKY AND GET TO VISIT with Merilee behind the scenes, so he could learn one way or another if the jaguar cat was here. He thought Tammy would realize what he was doing—strictly business, even if he had to play along a little with Merilee's enthusiasm to see him. After the insanity of dating her, no way was he ever going to take up with the woman again.

"So is she your new girlfriend?" Merilee asked, dragging David toward the trailers.

"Partner. We're working a mission together. We're searching for a missing jaguar the circus had. Do you know anything about it?"

Merilee smiled, and he was afraid that smile came with a price.

"What do you know about it?" he rephrased.

"*Well*," she said dramatically, "I've been dating this guy, and he mentioned something about a jaguar that's been more trouble than she's worth."

"Really. Name?"

"Tiger."

"What?" he asked.

"That's the name he called the jaguar. You know. Like a joke. The cat's a jaguar named Tiger. Circus thing, I guess."

"Uh, yeah. The guy's name?"

"You won't get jealous, will you?"

"No." David tried his damnedest to not sound exasperated.

"Okay, well, a lot of guys don't like him. And when women hear that I'm going with him, they get jealous."

"Joe Storm," David guessed.

Merilee gaped up at him. "Wow, you could be a mind reader."

"What did he say about the cat?"

"Nothing. That was it. He'd been really exasperated. Said he'd worked hard to get her and then she was gone again. I don't know anything about it other than that."

"Did you see her?"

"I'm not supposed to say."

"I won't tell anybody." He hated lying to her, but they had to find the cat.

"Yeah. He had to feed her, and I wanted to see her. She was pretty. We went back to his place, and she was stolen."

"Did he bring her back?"

"If he did, he hasn't said anything to me about it. David, I just want to say I'm sorry about what happened to you when we were seeing each other before."

Still angered over the situation, David had to know the truth. "Why did you cover for Howard?"

"He said he'd kill me if I didn't come back to him. He said he'd kill my family—my little sister, my mother and dad." She took a deep breath and let it out. "I didn't have any choice. I'm sorry about you losing Olivia to Joe, too. I can't imagine how you felt when she committed suicide. First Olivia, you are all shook up, then you meet me, and I nearly get you killed." She cleared her throat. "Now I'm dating Joe. I was afraid you'd be mad."

"Thanks, Merilee. No. I've moved on." David really didn't want to get into it any further with her. "So where was the cat when he took you with him to feed her?"

"In the grassy area, far, far away from the camp. I was wearing cute little sandals. What a mistake. Got bitten by fire ants galore. Couldn't see the mounds in the dark."

"Can you show me?"

Merilee waved at her sandals.

"Can you motion in the direction it was?"

"Well, it was dark, but off that way, I think."

"Okay, listen, I'll check it out and then I've to get back to my partner and work." He handed her a card. "If…if you hear anything about the jaguar, give me a call. Okay?"

"Sure." She reached up and kissed him on the lips.

He gave her a very brief kiss, pulled away, and said, "Later." He stalked off in the direction she had motioned.

If it hadn't been for his keen sense of smell, he wouldn't have located the area where the cat had been. But he smelled that she had been near the border of the circus grounds. Joe had probably put her there temporarily, moving her closer once he had surveillance set up.

He had to get back to Tammy, not liking that Quinn was eating lunch with her. He could just imagine what he might say about David's involvement with Merilee, and possibly Olivia.

Tammy wanted to learn about David and Merilee's relationship, but she didn't want Quinn to know she was interested. She shrugged.

"He met her at a shifter club in Pensacola."

So they *did* have a history back in Florida.

"She'd broken up with a boyfriend, and David had broken up with a woman he'd been dating for a while, so he asked Merilee out. They were an item for about a week before the former boyfriend wanted Merilee back."

"Wait. Not the one who killed another of her boyfriends?" How could David have anything further to do with her?

"Yeah, that one. He shot David. Nearly killed him. It was touch and go for a few days."

She stared at Quinn in disbelief. Why hadn't anyone told her? Though she supposed it wasn't the thing to talk about over breakfast, and there had never been any reason to bring it up. Because shifters healed so fast and well that they didn't have scars from injuries. Otherwise, she would have seen his scar and asked him about it before this.

"I've never seen Wade so upset. He was sure he was going to lose his brother. Their dad was at David's hospital bed for nearly the whole time, too. I don't think David's dated a human since then. I'm kind of surprised to see him speaking to Merilee now."

"She went back to the bastard who shot David?" Tammy couldn't believe this. She was ready to punch the woman out, and she didn't think of herself as a violent person.

"Yeah. Said she didn't see what had happened. No witnesses. David's word against Howard's."

"The gun? Bullets?"

"Bullet went clean through David. From the significant loss of blood he had, he passed out. The bullet vanished along with any other evidence. Howard had an airtight alibi."

"Let me guess. He was with Merilee at home the whole time."

"Yeah, but even better. He was home nursing his mother who had the flu. *And* Merilee was with the two of them the whole time."

Tammy frowned. "So why is David talking to her now?"

Quinn smiled. "Like you said. Gathering information."

Somewhere private and personal, she suspected, and she didn't like it one damn bit. Even if he gathered a ton of information about their case.

She rose from the table. "Got to find my partner."

Quinn frowned. "You look like you had a lightbulb flicker on. Got any idea what's going on?"

"Yeah, I think Merilee's behind this whole thing." *Not.* "Thanks a lot for lunch, Quinn." She would have told him she'd buy next time, but she didn't want to offer and give him the wrong idea.

"Tammy…"

She watched him as he rose from the table.

"Just be careful. All right?"

"You, too. If Joe's out to get you, he could be a dangerous threat."

"Yeah, how well I know."

"Wait. You said Joe had been dating Merilee?"

"Yeah. Here and in Florida."

"Did David know she was also seeing Joe?"

"You'd have to ask him. David may not have been seeing her at the same time that Joe was."

How many of the same girls had Joe and David both dated?

—m—

"Tammy." David waved her down, looking perturbed with her as she headed for the pony rides.

So why was he miffed with her? For having lunch with Quinn?

Tammy couldn't help being so annoyed with him. "I can't believe you talked to that Merilee woman after her boyfriend nearly killed you."

"Quinn told you?" David sounded angry.

"Yeah."

"He shouldn't have. What were you doing with him?" David asked, his voice growly when he had no business sounding that way.

Not when she was conducting business. Could he say the same? "Interrogating him like you were interrogating Merilee. Right?"

He snorted.

"What? Is that a no, you didn't ask her about the missing jaguar? Or a no, you don't believe I was questioning Quinn about important issues related to the case?"

"So what did he say?" David asked, trying to lead her to the parking lot.

"Wait." She pulled away from him. "I want to investigate where the cat would have been."

"I already checked."

"Oh." She felt two feet tall. So maybe David had strictly been conducting... She eyed the hint of shimmery pink lipstick on his lips. She folded her arms and scowled. "And? Did you smell the jaguar?"

"Yeah, she was here. Joe was feeding her and had stolen her."

"Quinn says she wasn't ever here."

"Shows what he knows." David glanced in the direction of the trailers. "Okay, so they've stolen her again and now they have her hidden somewhere else. They probably intend to wait to have her join the circus until after they've packed up to leave for their next destination."

"The new destination is?"

"Miami, Florida. I want you to know that my speaking with Merilee had all to do with trying to solve this case, Tammy. Nothing more."

She chewed on her bottom lip. "Sorry. I mean, it really doesn't matter." She needed to pull away from him, to distance herself, to gain her equilibrium. Whenever she was close to him like this, she couldn't think straight. She wanted more with him. Something permanent, but she kept falling back on her father's infidelity, and Joe's also. Had David dated all the same women as Joe? Well, hell, that included Tammy, too, didn't it?

"Yes, it does matter. How you feel matters to me. Believe me, after Merilee stuck up for that bastard when he damn near killed me, I felt only animosity toward her. But she told me he threatened to kill her and her family if she didn't stay with him. When she said she worked here, I figured it would be worth putting my feelings aside to see if I could slip into the off-limit areas of the circus with her. And she gave me a tour."

Of just the off-limit areas of the circus? Not Merilee's normally off-limit areas? If the woman even had any off-limit areas. Tammy couldn't put aside the vision of Merilee jumping David's bones. Or that he was wearing her lipstick! He didn't have to hold on to Merilee's ass as she jumped his bones. He could have put some distance between them. And if they were going to kiss, he didn't have to do it on her lips.

"Okay, listen. I know this goes deeper with you. I haven't asked because I figured you'd tell me when the time was right. That's what I've always done with Wade when he felt the need to get something off his chest but wasn't ready to talk. He knew I'd always be there for him. You asked me if I thought either of my parents ever had affairs. I don't believe so. Did you want to talk to me about your parents?" David asked.

Now? "You'll tell Wade and he'll share with Maya and…"

"No, I won't. This is strictly between the two of us. If you want to talk about it, I'm here for you."

She took a deep breath and reminded herself David wasn't like the other men had been in her life. She was just rattled with all the news about everything. "Sorry, I just…okay, yeah, we'll talk… I'm okay."

She glanced at the concession stand, where she'd seen the churros and wanted to have one in the worst way. "I have to get something first."

"Where are you going?" he said, quickly catching up.

"I haven't been to a carnival or circus for years. I want a churro. I'll even share. But…you have to wipe off Merilee's lipstick first."

His ears turning a little red, he grabbed a napkin off the counter, wiped off the lipstick, and rejoined her while she waited in the long line. He paid for the churro, and when she had the tube-shaped doughnut rolled in cinnamon and sugar in hand, she offered the other end to him.

"Want to take a bite?" She held it out to him, but she wasn't letting go.

He smiled at her, his green eyes twinkling in the sunlight. She smiled just a little.

"Is…this a test?" he asked.

"You bet. Of your willpower. Go ahead. Take a bite."

He reached for it with his hand. She shook her head. He chuckled, the sound dark and intrigued.

He took a bite. She ate a bite off her end.

She offered it again. He took another bite. "This is great," he said.

"They sure are."

When they finally reached the middle, laughing, they finished it off, but they weren't truly done. She licked his cinnamon-coated lips. He went further with her, licking her mouth, pulling her in tight for a hug, and spearing her smiling lips with his tongue until he gained entrance.

"Hmm, really, really nice. I think sharing churros with you has become my favorite thing to do," he said, and she felt his arousal against her, proving he *really* did like the idea.

"We'd better leave before we make too much of a scene," she said.

When they headed for the parking lot, she finally said, "Okay, as to my father, I found love letters he had stored in an old chest in the attic. I was looking for a diary I had written when I was thirteen and came across them. They were written to him, signed EL. I don't know anyone with those initials."

"What was the date? And why would he have kept the evidence?"

"They weren't dated. As to why he'd have them, my dad is a pack rat. Not only does he buy everything in jumbo quantities, but he never throws anything out."

"What if they were written to him when he was in high school? Maybe they were sent to him before he met your mom."

"She mentioned Mom a couple of times. Like she knew her and they were friends. How could this woman have done that? If she was a friend of Mom's, too?"

He pulled Tammy close. "We don't really know all the circumstances. We could be jumping to conclusions about this. Have you spoken with your dad about it?"

"No. I'm afraid of what he'll say. What if he's still seeing her? Instead of writing letters, maybe they're texting each other now. It would be easy for them to do." She let out her breath. "I've tried to hint at it to my dad, attempting to learn the truth. He's not taking the bait."

"And your mom?"

"She doesn't seem to know anything about it. Or she's pretending he didn't do anything wrong."

"Seems to me that it isn't something you have to concern yourself with. If it's over and done with, that's that. As long as your father isn't still seeking another woman's arms and he's learned his lesson…"

"Yeah, but…what if the woman was Maya and Connor's mother?"

David frowned at her. "Do you have any proof she was seeing your father?"

"One of the letters said she was pregnant with a boy and a girl. She shared the date of their births—the same as my cousins'. What if they aren't my cousins? What if they are my half sister and half brother?"

"Did the woman say your dad was the father of the twins?"

"No. She was married to my dad's brother. He left

before the babies were born. Why? Because he learned the babies weren't his? When I mentioned to Mom and Dad about meeting with their niece and nephew, Maya and Connor, Dad made excuses why he didn't have time to see them. That wasn't like him. This was before I was searching in the attic and came across the letters."

"It might have taken place, but they've come to terms with it and it's over and done with. If you're feeling that your dad's and Joe's situations have anything to do with us, they don't."

They got into the car and she let out her breath. "I can't let this go. I have to know if Maya and Connor are my half brother and sister." One way or another.

Chapter 28

BEFORE THEY HEADED BACK TO TAMMY'S PLACE, DAVID drove to his bank, not wanting to bring up something that might be a sore spot with Tammy. "I didn't remember anything about the keys on my key ring until you mentioned it. I hadn't thought anything about them. But you're right. I don't need some of them. They were"—he glanced at her—"keys to old girlfriends' places."

Tammy cast him a hint of a smile. He hadn't expected that. He thought she'd be annoyed. She shook her head. "You and my dad. First the jumbo stuff. Now, the pack-rat stuff, too?"

He was glad she wasn't peeved again with him. "I'll get rid of them. But it reminded me that I have one that goes to a safety-deposit box. It's free because of my savings and checking accounts there. Olivia had a signature card, too, though she wasn't listed on my bank accounts. We were planning to get married until I saw Joe at her house dressed in only his boxers. I just never thought about the safety-deposit box. I never used it. But maybe she did."

"And you're hoping to find what?"

"Why did Weaver say Olivia was important to the case?"

"She was seeing Joe. Joe's involved in the case," Tammy said, sitting taller in the car seat. "What if she knew of his involvement in the crooked dealings? What…what if she didn't commit suicide?"

"Quinn knew her best. He was convinced she had."

"Okay, well, maybe we'll find something there. Also, another thing keeps puzzling me. Both Quinn and Weaver told me I shouldn't trust the teens because they've been in trouble. I get the impression they know something. Is it a way for them to discredit the kids so we don't believe them? Or are the kids really untrustworthy?"

"With regard to the cat?"

"Yeah."

"You suspect something. What?"

"They know the cat."

David pulled into the bank lot and parked. "What do you mean?"

"You know, like she's almost a pet. Like it's personal. I really don't believe they just happened to see the news that the cat was missing from the zoo and they went into superspy mode to discover that the circus was in town at the same time. They were choked up about her being stolen again when they visited my house last night. Like she really means something to them."

David had to admit he agreed with her reasoning. "So you're thinking…"

"What if they had witnessed the cat at the circus last year and knew she had been abused. So they stole her and gave her to the zoo. When they saw that the Oregon Zoo cat had been stolen and found out that the circus had been in town, and that it was headed to Dallas, the boys' neck of the woods, they hatched a plan to steal her again."

"Makes sense. After we check my deposit box, I'll give the kids a call."

"Maybe I should."

He chuckled and walked with her into the bank. "Sure. That'll work. Do you have any more cookies to give them?"

When he got into his safety-deposit box, he was surprised to see it filled with stuff.

"A phone? Why would she have a cell phone in here?" Tammy asked, trying to turn it on to check the address book. "Dead."

"My charger will work on it. It's in the car. Bills of sale for tons of merchandise—laptops, video gaming equipment, televisions, sound systems—some really high-dollar items," David said, rifling through the papers.

"In her name?"

"Quinn's."

"Her brother's?"

David nodded.

"Why would her brother's stuff be in your box?"

"Why would Quinn have all these receipts? And why would she have them?" David asked.

"What if Quinn is the crooked agent? And he was working with Joe when he was in the branch until they had a falling-out over Quinn's sister's death, Quinn got Joe fired, and now Joe wants Quinn dead?" she asked. "Maybe Quinn gave it to Olivia to safeguard. She knew you never used the box, so she felt safe hiding them there."

"Okay, you explained on the way over here about how Quinn said Joe was trying to kill him and not you. That Quinn was trying to convince Joe to give up the agents, but if he is the agent and had been working with Joe, it makes sense that the two of them are on the outs and trying to kill each other," David said.

"What if the sister knew about her brother and Joe being crooked and started hiding some of the evidence in your box? Was she the kind of person who would turn her own brother in if she knew he was conducting illegal business?"

"She was really close to him. Like I am with Wade and you are with your brothers. Would you turn one of your brothers in if you learned he was doing something wrong?"

"No, I'd try to convince him to turn himself in before it was too late. Do you remember ever hearing Quinn and Olivia arguing about anything?"

"A few times. Once about her driving his car without his permission."

"Where had he been?" Tammy asked.

"With Joe at the club."

"So if Joe was seeing Quinn about business dealings, and she started dating Joe, somehow she could have learned that both he and her brother were dirty. She threatened her brother, told him to give it up. If Joe learned of it, he might have killed her," Tammy said.

"Yeah. We'll turn this stuff over to Martin and he can check into it further."

***

Tammy and David arrived at the red brick and glass headquarters for the JAG branch—a small building with a sign that featured a cat paw, golden claws extended, and simply said: Golden Claws, Inc.

As soon as they entered the building, four JAG agents glanced at David and Tammy, and then smiled.

"Last time I got to work with an Enforcer, the agent

didn't look anything like that," the redheaded MacAvoy ribbed his friends.

"Yeah, she looks even better in person than she did when she was risking her neck on the zip line," Ogilvie said, winking at her.

Tammy flushed a nice shade of red and glanced at David, frowning a little.

"Hey, guys, you were supposed to be following Peter and Hans. What happened?" David asked.

"Hell, they gave us the slip. We searched for them in Colombia, never could find them. When we returned here, we heard they might have been in Belize," Ogilvie said.

"The boys are all a bit slippery." David nudged Tammy toward Martin's office before anyone else could comment and embarrass her further. "Sorry about that. The guys have ribbed me every chance they get since they learned what you looked like on the zip line."

"So you shared the video with your boss?"

David just smiled.

Martin ushered them into his plush office, the walls lined with photos of catfish, red snappers, and bass he'd caught, and even a stuffed swordfish that he'd had mounted above them. He motioned to a couple of leather chairs. "What have you got?"

"Bills of sale in Quinn's name. Not sure why he would have documentation for selling this stuff. Maybe it was a way of trying to legitimize it, even if he didn't own the personal property in the first place." Now would Martin believe Quinn was doing something he shouldn't be? "What do you think?" David asked.

Martin snorted as he started looking over the papers. "I think we've got our mole."

"How so?"

"Five of these bills of sale could be for personal property that belonged to some of our agents who reported it stolen. We considered that one of our own people might have been involved. That an agent working for us had cased the places when visiting as a friend. But everyone who had visited their homes had airtight alibis for the time of the robberies. The times of the burglaries were spread out so that it wouldn't make them look so suspicious."

"The actual thieves had been human, right?" David asked.

"Yes," Tammy said. "At least the ones who had stolen my TV had been. But I'd had a party three days before I met you, David. They were mostly Enforcers—but a couple of JAG agents turned up."

"Was Joe there?" David asked, his voice sounding a little too growly.

"No, of course not."

"Quinn?"

"Yeah," Tammy said darkly. "He wasn't invited, but he came as the date of an Enforcer who was. That was first time he spoke to me, saying he had clues about the missing zoo cat."

"Your house got broken into and your TV was gone."

"Yeah," Tammy said.

"So our agents, if they were Quinn and Joe, must have been casing places and hiring people to steal the merchandise. How did you come by these?" Martin asked.

David explained about the safety-deposit box he never used. "Mind if we take Olivia's phone with us to see if we can get any clues? After that, I'll turn it over to you."

"Good deal."

Tammy was glad they were not with a regular human police force where all evidence had to be turned in. Any evidence in a case like this couldn't be used to convict a criminal in a court of law. Not if the perp was a shifter. No going to prison for them. Evidence was strictly for ensuring they got the bad guy.

"I'll have someone check into the rest of these bills of sale. See if they have to do with recent thefts. Hell, if that's the case, Quinn shouldn't have been having any financial difficulties," Martin said.

"Maybe it was all a ruse. The money is in offshore accounts. No one would suspect him because he's in debt up to his eyeballs, paying off a new car, and whatever else he owes on," David said.

"Yeah. Good point," Martin said.

After that, Tammy and David returned to his car, and while David drove, Tammy turned on Olivia's phone, charging it in his vehicle. She knew they needed to learn what they could, but that didn't lessen the eeriness that was slip-sliding through her—with the notion the woman was dead and most likely had safeguarded secrets on her phone.

"Got anything yet?" David asked, glancing at her as Tammy was going through the address book first.

"Your phone number, Joe's, Quinn's, and a whole bunch of others."

"Weaver's? Krustan's?"

She looked through the numbers. "Hmm, no, I don't see either of theirs."

"That's good—for their sake."

"Well, looks like we got a fence in here," she said.

"Oh yeah?"

"Yeah. I remember seeing this guy's name in the papers a while back. He got busted for reselling stolen merchandise." She punched in a number in the address book and turned on the speaker.

David frowned. "Who are you calling?"

"Joe. Martin can't find him. Quinn said he can't. What if he's dead?"

"But now he's got a dead woman calling him—if he's alive."

"Yeah, if he answers—"

"Quinn?" Joe said, startling Tammy. The sound of his angry voice sent shivers up her spine. "You son of a bitch. You said you got rid of all her stuff. Quinn?"

Tammy ended the call pronto. She was breathing hard, her heart pumping fast.

"Proves Joe's alive and still talking to Quinn. And we figured Quinn was involved," David said.

"I think it's more than that. I think...I think they killed Olivia."

"Yeah, I was thinking along the same lines." David pulled into Tammy's driveway, and as they left his car, they waved at Gertie peering out her picture window and headed inside the house.

"What else did you find on Olivia's phone?" David asked as they sat down on her couch together.

"Pictures." She cuddled close to David. "Looks like close to four hundred."

"Of..." He stared at the pictures as she brought each of them up.

"Merchandise. Stolen?"

"Serial numbers on some of it." David pulled out

his phone and called it in to Martin. "Here are some serial numbers you can have someone check into from Olivia's phone. Looks like she knew all about the business and was documenting it either to turn it over to someone, or hoping it would keep her from being murdered. Tammy placed a call from Olivia's phone to Joe, and he answered. So we know he's still alive."

David smiled. "Yeah, I'm sure Joe was either thinking Olivia had come back from the dead, or Quinn was playing a nasty game on him. He indicated that Quinn was supposed to get rid of all the evidence. So they've been working together."

"Oh…my…God," Tammy said. She couldn't believe it.

"Hold on," David said to his boss as he looked at the picture.

"Quinn and Joe killed three men in the woods. She was taking the pictures. She had to be in on it with them. Otherwise, I don't think she could have sneaked up and caught them at it without them noticing. That's why she could take the pictures of the merchandise and serial numbers. She had access to all of it. She was in on it. But something must have gone wrong. Something that caused her to distrust them." Tammy handed the phone to David. "Here, share all that you can with Martin. I'm going to get hold of Weaver. He said Olivia was important to this case. I'm calling him back."

David began sharing the pictures with his boss, as Tammy called Weaver. He picked up right away and she thought he must have expected her to call, or maybe he worried she was in trouble.

"You knew Joe Storm and Quinn Singleterry were dirty."

Weaver snorted. "We have no proof. We can't just go accusing anyone of committing a crime. You know that."

"But you didn't tell Sylvan you were working on this, either, did you?"

"We couldn't tell the boss we were working the bad agent angle on our own. He would have insisted we help you with your jobs. Hell, *you* might have been the bad agent."

Tammy scoffed at that. "Why not trust Sylvan enough to let him in on your plan?"

"If he had known we thought the agent was JAG, he would have turned it over to Martin Sullivan. We wanted to be the ones to solve it."

"You should have stayed with me, and I could have helped you *after* we found the missing kids. So what made you suspect they were committing criminal acts?"

"The missing zoo cat. I saw Joe and Quinn at the shifter club with two women. Joe had too much to drink. He was mouthing off about the jaguar—furious that it had been stolen from the circus after he'd gotten it. He was working as the manager at the circus at the time, not the club's bouncer yet. I didn't think anything about it. What bothered me was that Joe was with another woman when Olivia had thrown David over for Joe, and he had plans to marry her. I didn't know he had another fiancée or that you were seeing him.

"I liked Quinn's sister and I hinted to her that Joe and her brother were coming to the club with other women. I thought she should know. Later, I heard Joe talking about getting the jaguar back, and about that time you were tasked with look for the missing zoo cat. Even though I didn't think the two were connected, it seemed like an odd coincidence.

"I got the impression Joe had secured the jaguar originally via unscrupulous means, and if he did that with one of our distant jaguar *cousins*, what else was he criminally involved in? Quinn too, since he knew all about it. Krustan and I got to talking about it. He'd always wanted to date Olivia. You know how he is. Anyway, he wanted to help me prove they were crooked."

"Did you know Olivia was dating Joe behind David's back?" She probably shouldn't speak ill of the dead—she noted David had quit talking to his boss and was looking at her—but she thought Weaver should know the woman wasn't all sweetness and innocence. And she could have been involved in the whole rotten mess.

"No, I hadn't known that." Weaver paused. "She committed suicide after I told her about Joe's unfaithfulness. It didn't help that Quinn was partying right along with him and keeping it a secret from her. I…I felt I was somewhat responsible for her death."

"Quinn said he told her about how Joe was seeing other women," Tammy said. "He said *he* felt responsible for her death."

Weaver was silent for some time. He said, "No. He didn't tell her. And I don't believe he planned to. Joe and Quinn were having a fine time of it. I called her from the club while I was watching her brother and Joe, and when I told her, she was shocked, outraged. She didn't know. But she had quite a temper. So I could see her tearing into Quinn and Joe when they came home after a night of debauchery. She might have slipped into the club to see for herself that night. I don't know. It was so crowded, I never saw her. But that same night she committed suicide."

"What if she confronted Joe and Quinn when they arrived home and Joe murdered her?"

"I don't think Quinn would have allowed it."

"What if Quinn killed her because she knew all about their illegal business and threatened to expose them? And Joe had to go along with it because they were all too deep in the business."

"Have you got proof?" Weaver asked, interested.

"My partner and I are working on it," Tammy said. "Thanks. You've been a big help. I'll put in a good word for you and Krustan. Oh, wait, one more question. You said that the teens weren't to be trusted. So did Quinn. Do you have anything to back up your statement?"

Weaver laughed. "Why is it that I feel that I'm doing your job for you and I'm not getting any credit for it?"

"I promise I'll let the boss know how much you helped me on the case."

Silence.

"You like those boys," he said.

She waited.

"They kill the messenger," Weaver added.

"I'll kill the messenger if he *doesn't* tell me."

"You're not going to like what I have to say."

"Just spill it, all right?" She barely managed to quash the *damn it* she was about to tack on.

"The kids stole the cat from the circus."

She breathed in a sigh of relief. "I already know that."

"A year ago? The first time she was stolen from the circus? And given to the zoo? I'd overheard rumors that a jaguar was stolen from the circus. I looked into it because no one had reported a thing about it. Joe was a jaguar shifter, had worked for the JAG, and was now working as the manager for the circus. So it made me curious that he hadn't brought it to the attention of the police or someone. Maybe not the Service, because he probably had hard feelings toward anyone there.

"As I was looking into it on my off-duty hours, I discovered four sixteen-year-old shifter teens had stolen the cat and turned her over to the zoo. They'd forged documents to indicate she was from a big-cat shelter and needed a home. They'd contacted the Oregon Zoo because it was on a list, wanting a jaguar to replace theirs that had died. The kids stole the cat and made arrangements for a Mr. Thompson to pick her up. I didn't know why the kids had done it. Didn't really care. She had great accommodations out there and was being well cared for. I suspected she was being abused in the circus and the kids wanted to rescue her. Okay? Now you've got your story."

"Thanks, Weaver," she said, couching her very growly instincts.

"Don't be too hard on them, okay? I really believe their hearts were into saving her. And I salute them."

"Thanks. I will put in a good word for you and Krustan." She ended the call and looked at David, who was studying her.

"What's wrong now?"

"The kids lied to us."

Chapter 29

TAMMY WAS FURIOUS WITH THE BOYS. NOT FOR stealing the jaguar from the circus in the first place, but for not trusting her enough to realize she would have cheered them on for trying to keep the jaguar safe. She explained what she had learned to David and said, "We need to get hold of them, but we don't have their phone numbers."

"How about Facebook?"

"Right! I'll try that. What are you going to do?"

"Join you. I just finished sending Martin Olivia's pictures, her address book information, and texts that seemed important. She had even texted back and forth with the fence herself. She was involved up to the top of her blond head. Martin has issued arrest warrants for Joe and Quinn, and he's made the other branches aware of it. Top priority."

"Good. I wonder if they have any more merchandise stashed away. The cat may be there also. I need to get in touch with the kids and ask them about stealing the jaguar from the circus in the first place. And how they knew about her."

She shook her head and settled down to message Alex: Dear Alex,

"No one writes 'dear' in a Facebook message," David said, reading what she was writing.

"I'm annoyed with them. When I'm irritated, I start

out with a more formal greeting." She frowned at David.
"Quit critiquing my message."

He chuckled. "Okay. Go ahead."

She typed: I was made aware that you and your friends
stole the jaguar from the circus and gave it to the zoo last
year. Why didn't you tell us?

No response.

"They may not be monitoring their messages,"
David said.

She drummed her fingers on the desktop, then typed
in: Alex, we need to know the truth. If she was in danger,
we totally understand. You won't get into trouble for it.

Alex messaged: They were mistreating it.

Relieved that he was monitoring his FB and felt comfortable enough to respond, Tammy typed: How did you
know about the cat? Had you seen her at the circus?

She waited. And waited. She began drumming her
fingers on her desk again. David took her hand, kissed
it, and held on to it.

She shook her head. "Either he's talking to Nate and
trying to come up with another wild story, or he's a really slow typist."

"Or typing a lot," David said.

Alex sent: We knew her before.

"I knew it!" she said to David. "I was sure they had
more of a personal stake in this."

She messaged: Where?

She thought he'd quit responding, afraid to say.
David tugged at her to sit with him again. "You're a
bundle of nerves. Come on. Relax a little."

She sighed, then sat on his lap on her desk chair while
she leaned back against him and tried to relax.

The message from Alex popped up: Old couple running cat reserve. He died. She had to find homes for big cats. Lions, tigers, ocelot, cheetah, and jaguar. Two years volunteered to take care of cats. Guy wanted jaguar. Said he had cat reserve. We followed him to make sure she was taken care of. He took her to circus, handed her over to owner. Owner wanted unique cat. Took us forever to steal her. They had trained her to jump through fire hoop. They shocked her or starved her when she didn't mind. We gave her to zoo. Heard Oregon Zoo cat missing. Checked. Found same circus in area. Put 2 & 2 together. You gotta find her. She can't stay with circus.

Tammy took a deep breath and typed: We'll find her. What was the woman's name who owned cat reserve? We'll talk to her about giving the cat to zoo. We know who bad agents are. Lie low. As soon as we have cat in protective custody, will let you know. Same with men.

Alex: Dora Smith. Alex texted Tammy the phone number. Then added: We want to help.

She smiled and typed: Join the Service and you can.

"All right, you want me to talk to the woman?" David asked.

"Let me. You find out where the jaguar is." She smiled at David.

"Let me have all the stress-free jobs, will ya?"

She laughed. "I figured you needed something really easy to do for a change." She pulled out her phone and left the office while David got on her computer.

David loved Tammy. He decided he'd never had this much fun on a mission, despite how dangerous it was. He heard her talking on the phone and assumed she'd gotten hold of the owner of the cat reserve.

"Great," Tammy said, and the way she said it, she sounded truly pleased. "As soon as we find her, we'll let you know." She poked her head into the office. "Are you ready for dinner?"

"Sure, anything is fine with me. What did the cat lady say?"

"She would never have given the cat to the circus. She's all for sending her to the zoo, and she'll write something up to that effect. The cat was supposed to have gone to another cat reserve. The man lied and had false papers. Are you finding anything?" she asked.

"I'm looking at some of these photos of buildings and trying to locate any addresses. I suggest we check them out."

She peered over his shoulder at the monitor. "To see if we can find any that contain stolen merchandise—"

"And a cat."

―――⁓―――

"So if Joe wasn't working as manager for the circus any longer, why would he try to steal the cat back and give it to them? I mean, he was fired." She'd fixed them a quick bite to eat before they'd left on their scouting mission. This time she drove David's car. He navigated for them as they headed for some of the locations they thought might possibly yield the cat and stolen merchandise.

"Joe would do it for money. As soon as the boys said that Cyrus Wilde wanted a unique cat for the circus and knew the woman was looking for cat reserves that would provide a good home for her big cats, I asked Martin to do some checking on him. He learned Cyrus's mother was already dead—died three years ago. He wasn't visiting his sick mother when we dropped by the circus. He left town because we were asking too many questions. Turn left here, five blocks."

"Okay, so Cyrus paid for the cat. He fires Joe as a rotten manager. But by now the cat is trained to jump through fire hoops and she's stolen. Lots easier stealing her back than trying to start training a new cat."

"Plus they didn't have to buy her from the cat reserve lady," David said. "She just wanted a home for her. Getting hold of a new cat would have been harder for him, more costly than paying Joe, or they wouldn't have come to an agreement."

"Right. So, he pays Joe to get her back, and the cat is stolen again. Joe had to have been pissed," she said, pulling into a parking lot in front of a brick warehouse.

"Yeah, and he doesn't like troublesome teens anyway. So he learns they are in Belize and tries to get rid of them, or at least one of them, on the zip-line adventure. Doesn't work because you go on it instead. Joe finds and searches their bungalow, probably looking to get rid of the boys and learn if they have any evidence about the cat. He and Quinn drop by our place, looking for kids and clues."

Tammy and David headed to the building, sniffing the air and listening for sounds of a big cat. Nothing. Being Sunday, everything in the area was quiet. She didn't smell any sign of Joe or Quinn around the building.

"Hmm. Why did Joe shoot at Quinn?" she asked.

"Had a falling-out maybe? They're both trying to kill each other? If Quinn's sister had been murdered and they both had been involved in it, each might be afraid the other would let the proverbial cat out of the bag. If

Quinn killed Joe or vice versa, the one who outlived the other would be free and clear of the crime. Maybe."

"So who picked up the cat the first time?" she asked.

"Joe. The second time? Looks like they hired humans to help so neither Joe nor Quinn could be connected with the theft of the cat at the farm. Out of respect for Quinn and his family, several of the JAG agents went to the funeral for Olivia," David said. "If Quinn was involved in killing his sister, well, hell, I would never have believed it." They sniffed around another building. "Nothing here. Let's check the next place on our list."

They investigated six more buildings with no luck. "Maybe they moved their stolen merchandise to a new location after Olivia's death in case she told anyone about their criminal actions," Tammy said. She paused and considered how dark it was getting to be. "It's nearly midnight."

"Yeah, we have ten more places to check out. You don't want to stop, do you?"

"No…no. I want to find the cat tonight if we can." She peered around the area and frowned, listening but not hearing anything suspicious. "Do you feel like we're being followed?"

David looked around at the dark buildings. "I've been trying to visualize some of these buildings Olivia has pictured that have no numbers. So I haven't really noticed."

Tammy studied the buildings, and not seeing anything, she shook her head. "Where to next?"

"Over there, I think. See, there's a partial street sign in the picture."

"That metal building right over there."

"Yeah, we'll leave the car where it's at and walk there."

When they reached the door to the building, Tammy glanced at David, wondering if he smelled what she smelled.

"Yeah, the cat's been here. And so have Joe and Quinn." He quickly called it in to his boss. "Juan, the guide who hooked Tammy up to the zip line?" David said to his boss, glancing at Tammy. "Okay, I'll tell her." He hung up. "They found Juan."

"Alive?"

"Yeah, and he gave a description of Joe Storm. Martin sent pictures of both him and Quinn down there, but he positively identified Joe."

"I'm glad Juan's okay."

"I have mixed feelings about it, considering he got paid to make you go first and you could have died."

"Yeah, well, I probably had a better chance at surviving than that family did."

"Agreed. I'm going back to the car to get the bolt cutters. You wait here."

She paced, hoping the cat was truly inside and safe, and that the troops would arrive before anyone bad did. But no matter what, they had to stay here. They had to protect the jaguar if she was here. They couldn't allow anyone to hide her somewhere else or, worse, get rid of her because she was turning out to be too much trouble.

Chapter 30

TAMMY WAS EXCITED ABOUT DISCOVERING THE ZOO cat in the warehouse if she was truly there, but still she worried that the building would be guarded, or someone might be there. No vehicles were parked out front. They'd left David's car on a side street two warehouses down and walked here. Her heart raced as David returned with the bolt cutters. The warehouse looked like any of the others. Maybe 20,000 square feet, three stories high, metal, except inside this one, they heard the whirring of motors.

She glanced at David. "Fans," he confirmed.

He cut the padlock on the metal door with a snap. He shoved the door open with a grinding noise and closed it back up. In the dim glow of the outdoor security lights showing through dusty windows thirty feet above, she and David saw tons of crates stacked high. Huge fans blew inside the building, which wasn't usual for a warehouse that just housed normal merchandise. In the hot Texas weather, if something was alive in here, they'd have to cool the place off a bit.

A television was set up, a couch in front of it, and one popcorn machine, with recently popped popcorn. "My TV!" she exclaimed.

"How much do you want to bet that's the circus's new popcorn machine?" David said.

"Weaver's TV is probably in one of these crates."

She smelled the strong odor of cat urine to the south of them. *Jaguar*. It was fresh, too. "She's probably in there," Tammy said, pointing to the large fenced-off area, the tops of the chain link visible beyond the tower of crates. They couldn't see the cat yet and Tammy hoped she was still there.

"Joe and Quinn have been here," David said as they hurried to maneuver through the narrow aisles between crates and found the cat watching them from the top of a crate inside the fenced-in enclosure.

Tammy was elated. "Yeah, and a handful of other men—all human. I don't recognize anyone else's scent, though." She hoped that Joe and Quinn were the only two in the organization that were bad cats this time around. Tammy smiled as she moved around to observe the cat's flank. "That's her, same spots as in the zoo picture."

Whipping his phone out, David updated his boss to let him know they were at the correct location. "Yeah, Martin. We got her, and this is the right warehouse. The crates might be filled with stolen goods also. No sign of anyone, but Joe Storm and Quinn Singleterry's scents are strong here. Okay, hurry. The place was unguarded, but it doesn't mean we won't have trouble soon. Gotcha. Out here."

David paused, frowned, and glanced at the closed door. "Someone's coming," he warned.

She heard the footfalls also, growing closer to the warehouse door. David seized her hand and they sprinted away from the fenced-in jaguar and ducked behind some wooden crates. She had so hoped Martin's men would get here before anyone else did.

The door groaned open and shut again. Footfalls headed in their direction, one pair.

Maybe it was one of Martin's men. But wouldn't he call out and let them know who he was?

"Come on out, Tammy, David. We know you're in here," Quinn said. "We saw your car parked at the warehouse down the street. We followed your scent all the way here. So I know you're here. What I don't know is how the hell you ever found the warehouse. It was a carefully guarded secret."

Tammy knew he was listening for them, trying to discern where they were exactly. David was carefully removing his clothes, trying not to make a sound. Impossible when it came to his jeans zipper and a cat's enhanced hearing.

Quinn swore under his breath, his head turned in their direction. "You've got Olivia's phone, don't you? I looked everywhere for it." He didn't say anything for a moment. "Ah, hell, don't tell me she documented evidence with that damned phone. How did you find it? Nearly gave Joe a heart attack when he got the call from her cell. Accused me of being a bastard, thinking I was taunting him, that I had her phone and evidence, or some damn thing."

Engines grumbling, three eighteen-wheelers pulled up in the parking lot in front of the warehouse.

"Don't worry. Everything will be gone before any of this can be reported. I'll be gone. Joe, too. The missing circus cat. And you and Tammy. It's all my fault, really. Olivia was happily dating you, David. She got wind of Joe and my off-duty *investments*. She wanted in. But the only way she could join us was if she got rid of you."

Tammy glanced at David. He just shook his head, like he hadn't a clue as he untied his boots. She couldn't help feeling bad that he'd been thrown over for money.

"She was trying to be really obvious that she wanted to end things with you, but I think she had a soft spot still for you. Joe said he could kill the romance. And he did. You arrive at her house to find him there, and voilà: he was into the business and you were out. What she didn't figure was that no matter how much she was part of the business, she wasn't going to be Joe's main squeeze. He just isn't geared that way. Somehow she got suspicious about Joe seeing other women. She blew a gasket and well, end of partnership."

No one moved. She thought she heard a zipper being pulled down in Quinn's direction.

Quinn said, "You probably are wondering if I really wanted to work with you on looking for the cat, Tammy. I truly did. I didn't want David involved. See, if I could have gone with you to Belize instead, we could have had some good times. You would have met with some accident. Kids, too, but they were a lot cleverer than Joe and I thought they would be."

She narrowed her eyes. Bastards.

Quinn let out his breath. "You know that Joe was aiming to shoot David, but he moved out of the way. Joe got a bead on one of the boys, and he disappeared into the trees. Then there you were. I was trying to maneuver so you'd get it, but you moved and I was afraid I'd be hit, so I leaped the only way I could, knocking you into the water, and took off before David came looking for you. Joe was pissed." He paused. "It's time to end this now. The movers won't come in until we give the go-ahead. So let's get this done."

She knew he couldn't see them any more than she and David could see Quinn. Was Joe with him? She didn't hear his footsteps, which meant he could be wearing his jaguar coat and making no sound, plodding alongside Quinn, silent. Unlike dogs' toenails that clicked on cement, cats kept their claws retracted unless they needed them. Then again, if he was here, he had to have come as a human and would need to remove his clothes here and shift.

David had already stripped off his clothes. He was getting ready to shift. Still, he couldn't win against two of them.

She reached for her shirt and started lifting it, but David grabbed her hand and shook his head, speaking in a hushed voice. "He's probably got a gun. You stay back here. I'll take care of this. Call it in."

"But he said 'we.' Joe's most likely here too. You can't take out two of them by yourself."

"As a jaguar I can while they're in human form. Stay here."

Tammy had just opened a line to her boss when a jaguar leaped on top of the crates. Startled, she screamed and dropped her phone. David shifted and jumped away before Quinn could pounce.

They were fighting on top of her phone, maybe even had stepped on it and disconnected the open line to her boss. She saw a glimpse of another jaguar and recognized him right away.

Her former boyfriend. Joe Storm. She started stripping.

He looked like he might even regret what he'd have to do. But she knew too much. At least he was giving her a chance to fight him when he could have just killed her.

The crashing of crates nearby made her heart skip a beat. Cats' claws scrabbled on the floor to get traction.

As much as she wanted to look in David and Quinn's direction and see what was happening, she had to concentrate on the very real threat in front of her. She removed the remainder of her clothes and shifted.

Her heart was racing a hundred miles a minute. She couldn't win. He was too big. Too powerful. All she could think of was his killer fists. And in jaguar form? A jaguar's paw could kill with one strike. Adrenaline coursed through her blood. Mind over matter, she leaped at him.

They tangled, claws extended. They scratched with a vengeance, hissing, wicked canines bared. They swiped with their paws, only he got the best of her because his forearms were longer. He knocked her down against the cement floor. Her cheek was bleeding, the claw marks stinging and burning. He waited for her to scramble to her feet, to come at him again. It was as if they were in a workout, only he meant to allow her to fight him a little before he killed her.

She'd never last at this rate. She growled and jumped again, attempting to swipe him in the head with a powerful paw like he'd done to her, but because her forelegs were shorter than his, she had to get closer to him.

He wouldn't allow it and took another swing at her. Looking like a startled cat, she hissed and jumped straight in the air to avoid his powerful swing. She thought he looked surprised at her maneuver before she landed again on her feet. He leaped this time, as if he was tired of the game. Anticipating his move, she dodged out of his path. He missed her and slammed into a crate with a bang and growled.

She would have felt smug satisfaction if she wasn't

trying to stay alive. She whipped around and bit his flank, hoping to impair his ability to fight. He roared and turned so quickly that she wasn't able to avoid his slashing swipe of a paw. His paw connected with her temple, knocking her down.

Lying against the crates on the cold concrete floor, she saw white sprinkles against blackness and knew she was done for.

David had fought Quinn before as a cat in practice sessions. He knew Quinn's strengths and weaknesses, but *Tammy* was David's weakness. He'd gotten in some hefty claw marks on Quinn's back and neck. When Joe attacked Tammy, David glanced in her direction and left himself open to attack.

He couldn't fight the two cats at once. He had to finish this with Quinn if he was to have any chance at saving Tammy from Joe.

Where the hell were David's fellow agents?

All teeth and claws, he fought Quinn like a jaguar who was demon-possessed, full of rage, human heartfelt emotion, and a feral big cat's need for survival and desire to protect his mate.

Quinn might also have known David's strengths and weaknesses, but he wasn't prepared for David's relentless, mauling attacks. David wouldn't let the cat catch his breath. Quinn tried to get in a swipe with his claws or a powerful swing. He attempted to bite back, but David was ruthless. Quinn had to die—now.

They'd been snarling and hissing and roaring so much that David hadn't heard the other cats' growls. Not until he bit Quinn in the back of the neck, killing him. Quinn dropped to the cement floor in a dead jaguar heap.

David quickly turned to protect Tammy. She was lying on the floor next to a stack of crates, not even twitching her tail. She looked dazed. Nearby, Joe was fighting a losing battle. Tammy had her own force of JAG agents in training taking care of Joe. The four boys—all in jaguar forms—ripped Joe to shreds.

His body hurting like hell, David loped over to Tammy and licked her cheek where she was pressed up against a crate on the cold concrete, her eyes open, watching the boys. Her gaze turned to David, but she wasn't getting up.

Fearing she was mortally wounded, he shifted and ran his hand over her body, looking for injuries. "Tammy?"

She closed her eyes.

"Don't close your eyes. Tell me what's wrong." As if she could when she was in jaguar form. "I'll call for medical assistance." David quickly got dressed and grabbed her cell phone off the floor. "Sylvan." The line was still open. He rejoined Tammy, sat on the floor, and pulled her head into his lap.

She was breathing all right. Her heartbeat sounded okay, but he wondered if she had a concussion.

"David? What the hell happened? We've got men on the way," Sylvan said.

Yeah, a little too late for that, David wanted to say. "Tammy's injured and needs medical attention. Appears to me she has a concussion."

"On it."

"Three eighteen-wheelers are here and the men waiting for word to enter the building. They need to be taken care of. We found the cat. A cleanup crew has to get here ASAP. Not sure how secure this place is. And we need the cat picked up. Someone should call Henry Thompson from the Oregon Zoo to let him know she's safe."

Joe and Quinn were dead and had shifted into their human forms, unable to hold their jaguar forms in death. The boys were panting heavily as they stood nearby, bloodied, tails twitching slightly, watching David.

"Joe Storm's and Quinn Singleterry's bodies have to be collected. I need to call my boss."

"You take care of Tammy until the medical crew gets there. Everyone's already on the way. Martin alerted me that they're on it. But I'll clue him in on what's happened since then."

"Tell him the JAG has four new recruits who have already completed their first bona fide mission. Which means they need to be on the payroll for this."

"You got it."

They ended the call and David noticed Nate had curled up at Tammy's feet. David stroked Tammy's head and smiled a little at Nate.

"I need all of you to shift and dress and wait out of sight until help arrives. You can direct them in here when they get here," David said, wanting Tammy to shift so he could dress her and talk with her before the medical personnel and anyone else arrived.

With backward glances at Tammy, the boys did as they were told. He heard them just beyond the crates hurrying to get dressed, talking to each other about what they could have done differently with better results.

"Nate, next time, duck when I swing. I thought for sure I'd killed you," Alex said.

"Hell, yeah," Nate said. "Me, too."

The other boys snickered.

"Don't claw over a bad cat's back when I'm trying to take a bite out of him, Hans," Peter said. "I almost bit you."

"Yeah," Hans said. "We really need to learn to co-ordinate our teamwork better if we're going to do this right the next time."

If they didn't sound like him and Wade at their age. They had done all right. With no formal training or anything. And against one badass cat like Joe Storm. They'd done a damn good job.

"Tammy, can you shift?" David asked. "I'll help you dress."

She shifted but laid her head back on the concrete floor, her cheek scratched and bleeding, a red knot on the side of her head. Angry, bloody claw marks trailed down her arm and across her waist. She was beginning to heal already, but she would need some tender, loving care for a few days, and *he* would be the one to provide it. He rushed to get her clothes and helped her to sit. She leaned over and held her stomach like she was going to be sick.

"Nauseated?" he asked.

"Yeah."

"Do you need to throw up?" He pulled her shirt over her head and was going to help her onto her knees if she was going to vomit.

"I'll…be okay," she said, her voice way too breathy and her skin ice white.

"Okay, I'm going to help you on with your jeans. Sorry, this is going to hurt." After he zipped up her jeans, he glanced at her sneakers, bra, and panties and heard several vehicles pull up outside. He slipped her bra and panties into his pockets just as the troops arrived.

Men took care of Quinn and Joe. David hated to think what Martin would have to tell Quinn's parents, after having also lost their daughter. Joe didn't have any family that anyone knew of.

Tammy was seeing double and having a mother of a headache as they loaded her into a waiting ambulance. Before David could get in and ride with her to a special clinic reserved for their kind, Alex and Nate approached, the other two boys watching and hanging back a bit. "Can you call our parents and let them know we didn't get into a fight because we were causing trouble?" Nate asked.

David looked over all four boys who were wearing claw marks and bruises like he was. "Hell, yeah. I'll let them know you're officially JAG agents in training and had your first assignment. Hell of a job, boys."

The boys smiled.

"You were following us, weren't you?" David asked.

"Yeah. We figured the two of you would notice. When Tammy Facebooked us, we were sitting down the street from her house, watching, waiting for the two of you to make your next move," Hans said. "We were trying to be really super secretive about it, but we had to know if you'd found the cat."

"We saw you go into the warehouse and we waited, figuring we'd be your rear guard. Joe and Quinn arrived, and we didn't have any choice. We had to enter the warehouse and shift to save Tammy," Peter said. "Good thing we came inside because right after we did, those trucks pulled up."

Alex said, "I know we should feel bad that we had to take Joe Storm down, but…" He looked back at Tammy in the waiting ambulance.

"He would have killed Tammy if you hadn't killed him," David said. "Sometimes we have to do things we would never consider doing otherwise in the name of defending others."

Tammy growled.

The boys chuckled. "You mean, defending those we love," Nate said.

David cleared his throat. "Uh, yeah, that's what I said."

Alex said, "Maybe I should ride with her to the clinic instead."

"Nothing doing." David got into the ambulance. He could handle one she-cat no matter how growly she got.

A car squealed to a stop near the ambulance. Weaver and Krustan hurried out of the vehicle. "Hell," Weaver said. "Is Tammy all right?"

David opened his mouth to speak, but Tammy reached out and touched his arm. "Tell them we already solved the case." He grinned at her and then back at the Enforcers who folded their arms.

"We got hell from your JAG boss because we dropped by Tammy's house and then got hell from our boss when Martin called Sylvan about it. We only stopped at her house to find out where she was going next to search for the missing cat," Weaver said.

Before the EMT closed the door, David told the boys, "We're going to Morrow's Theater last Friday night of the month, seven sharp. It's part of your training. We'll expect you there."

"A play?" Nate asked, sounding alarmed.

"Yeah."

"Is it a murder mystery like *Sweeney Todd*?" Alex asked.

David looked at Tammy, not sure what they were attending. She cast him a small smile. "*Annie*."

"A musical?" he said, his own voice sounding a bit alarmed. He nearly groaned but said to the boys, "Seven."

He wasn't about to tell the boys what they were in for if they hadn't heard. It would be part of the training to see if they could follow directions. "And dress nice," he added, giving the boys a stern look.

The EMT shut the door, and Tammy and he were off to the clinic.

He kissed her forehead and said, "Hang in there, honey."

"I'm all right," she said, her voice thready.

"We'll just have the doctor check you out and make sure. Anyone you want me to call?"

"Thompson, about the jaguar."

"Sylvan's taking care of it. What about your brothers?"

"No," she said, closing her eyes.

He leaned over and kissed her uninjured cheek. "Your parents?"

She shook her head slightly.

"Your cousins?"

She groaned a little at him.

"Okay, no one. Until after you're all checked out." He sighed. "I know this isn't the place or time to do this, but…we're going to have to get married. You know that. Right, Tammy?"

The EMTs chuckled.

Chapter 31

AFTER THREE DAYS OF HOME REST, TAMMY WAS FEELing like her old self. David had moved in to watch over her and make sure she had no more ill effects from the concussion she had suffered. His boss had been nice enough to let him have sick leave, even though there weren't any allowances for taking care of a girlfriend.

David was setting up her TV after getting it back and was planning on fixing her dinner and watching a movie with her tonight.

She was just about to curl up on the couch, loving how attentive David had been, when someone knocked on the door.

"I'll get it," David said, hurrying to get the door. "It's your…dad."

He had met her father at the hospital, but she worried what he would think when he saw David here with her. Though she was glad she was dressed in jeans and a shirt.

"Come on in, sir," David said.

She was surprised to see that her dad was here. He and Mom had just visited her at the hospital. The last time she'd really spoken with him was about him visiting her new cousins. He'd made all kinds of excuses, which was so unlike him and had made her suspicious. "Dad," she said and gave him an inquisitive look.

"We've got to talk," her father said.

David said, "I was just going to fix dinner." He walked off when nobody objected to his leaving them alone.

"What's wrong, Dad?" He looked so grim that she worried something bad had happened to her mother.

"Your mother said you've been asking some…unusual questions regarding your cousins."

Tammy's stomach tightened.

"She thinks maybe you believe I've been unfaithful."

Tammy heartbeat accelerated. This was going to be a lot harder to talk to him about than she'd thought.

"I haven't been, Tammy. Your mother and I have been married for thirty-five years and not once did I stray. So what's this all about?"

Tammy pulled the afghan hanging over the couch back onto her lap. "Maya and Connor Anderson."

Her father didn't say anything. If he hadn't been unfaithful, why didn't he say anything?

"My brother was a wanderer," her dad finally said. "When he met Eva, Maya and Connor's mother, we thought he would settle down."

Eva? EL?

"He'd come home on leave from the army and met her at my parent's home. We were having Christmas dinner," her father continued.

"Wait. Aunt Eva was at my grandparents' house for Christmas? Why?"

"She had an abusive father. She was staying with us."

"Okay. And…?"

"My brother was always the charmer. And she started dating him, but after they married, he couldn't stay."

Something more wasn't being said. She heard the hurt in her father's voice, the weariness in his expression, but also something else. Irritation with his brother? She wondered if her father had really liked Eva before his brother showed up for the family Christmas. Maybe her father had been taking it slow with her, and his charming brother had swept her off her feet and married her.

"But…Maya said her father left as soon as he knew Eva was pregnant. Was he afraid of taking care of a couple of twins?" Tammy asked.

Her father didn't say anything for a long moment. He let out his breath on a heavy sigh. "I am Maya and Connor's father."

She felt as though the couch had melted out from under her.

"I wasn't seeing your mother at the time, Tammy. We met a couple of months later. Eva didn't know she was pregnant until after she married my brother. They had moved away, he left her—he told us he left, but didn't say why, and made no mention that she was pregnant. She disappeared. Never had any contact with us.

"Your mother had known Eva and wanted me to find her and make sure she was okay. I used some resources I had to locate her, and when I did, I learned she had twin toddlers, and she was visibly upset that I'd found her. Which I couldn't understand. We'd been friends. Well, more than friends. Until I realized the babies were mine. She was afraid I'd want to take them from her and raise them as my own.

"I had to take some responsibility for them. She accepted money to help raise them with the condition that I wouldn't see them."

"Dad," Tammy said, not believing this.

"It's different for a mother, Tammy. She bore them,

loved them, nourished them. Sure, they were mine, too, but when she began seeing my brother, I moved on and began dating your mother. I felt a financial responsibility for the kids and would have spent time getting to know them, but she didn't want it."

"She abandoned them when they were sixteen." Tammy felt horrible that Maya and Connor's mother had done that to them after their…well, *her* father had never been there for them, either.

"She said she'd never wanted kids. The birth control pills she was on didn't work, apparently. Or she'd missed taking a couple. But she did stay with them until they were able to manage on their own."

"At sixteen?" Tammy shook her head. "You mean, running the landscaping business?"

"Yeah. I gave them an interest-free loan. I helped set them up. I wanted to give them the money outright, but they would have suspected something wasn't right about the deal. I told them I was a good friend of their mother's, which I had been, and your mother had been also. If they ever needed anything, to just call. They never knew that the man who married their mother was my brother, that I was their father, none of that. And they only called every once in a while to thank me for my generosity and sent me monthly checks, which I never cashed."

"They never said anything about it?"

"Sure, Connor did. Each month, he'd call and say he sent the check but it wasn't cashed. I told him I didn't need the money right away. That he should just earn interest on it, and when I needed it, I'd ask him for it."

"And they didn't think that was suspicious?"

"I'm sure they did. But they didn't ask, and I wasn't

offering. I finally mentioned that their mother was married to my brother, which if he'd been their father, would have made you their cousin and me their uncle."

She let out her breath. "*Dad*," she said in an elongated, annoyed way. "Why didn't you tell us?"

"If I told you, you would have gotten in touch with them." He sighed. "I did finally tell you that you had *cousins*, thinking that they should know they had family. I…I couldn't tell you I was their father. But I don't want you to believe I cheated on your mother."

Tears filled her eyes. She felt choked up all at once. She'd thought the worst of him when he hadn't done anything wrong. "Does Mom know?"

"Yeah, when I located Eva and learned the kids were mine, I told your mother everything. I was upset, not sure what to do. We were raising you kids. She said she would have probably felt the same way as Eva. And when Eva left the kids, your mom was all for my backing their business for them. They've made a great success of it and have been free and clear for years."

Tammy frowned. "We're not cousins. We're half siblings."

"Don't you tell them."

"Dad, Maya nearly didn't marry Wade because she was so worried she'd be like her parents. They need to know. Either you tell them or…" She didn't want to be the one to give that kind of information to her half siblings. "Well, you tell them."

Silence.

"Dad?"

"As a family."

"Do my brothers know?"

"No, just you and your mom."

This was going to be awkward.

"One last question. What does EL stand for?" Tammy asked.

"Eva, Love. That's what I always called her."

Tammy frowned. "Does Mom know that?"

"No. And you're not to tell her, either."

She couldn't believe it! Now every time she heard her father refer to her mother as Mary, Love, she'd want to slap him. Couldn't he have thought of something more original to call her? Maybe it went along with his habits of purchasing in quantities or being a pack rat. Did David have a special term of endearment that he used on *all* his girlfriends, too?

She took a deep breath and let it out.

"Since this seems to be confession time, is there anything you want to tell me about David Patterson?" her father asked, jerking his thumb in the direction of the kitchen.

No, definitely not. "Well, I don't know if anything will come of it, but…" She shrugged, not about to talk about what she and David had been doing of late. "You never know about relationships," she said noncommittally.

"He's here now, and I suspect he's been here since he brought you home from the hospital."

Her whole body flushed with heat. It was one thing to tell her dad that she was dating David, quite another to tell him the JAG agent was spending the night, every night, and more, and had been for some time. She really didn't think that would go over big with her dad.

"I want to talk to him," he said when she didn't answer her father fast enough.

"He's kind of busy with fixing dinner and…"

"Let…me…talk…with…him."

She let out her breath in a huff. "David? You want to come here for a sec? Dad wants to talk to you."

David couldn't have been more thrilled. As long as Tammy's father was of like mind with what David wanted.

Tammy looked like she was ready to die of embarrassment, her cheeks flaming red. She might not be ready for this conversation to take place between David and her dad, but David was. He came in, sat beside Tammy, wrapped his arm around her, and said, "Yes, Mr. Anderson?"

"Are you marrying Tammy?"

Right to the point. David liked that.

"That's up to your daughter."

"So you've asked her to marry you?"

"We haven't gotten to that part yet."

"I'll be perfectly honest with you. I know you've been here, protecting my daughter before this, then watching her after her injuries, so I've gone along with it, or else I would have had you transferred. If you didn't know it, I've donated a lot of funds to the Service over the years, so I have some clout there."

David wondered what Tammy's father's business was that he could afford to give away a lot of money. For a good cause, sure, but still.

"Yes, sir."

"I've talked with both her boss and yours to confirm you were needed there on this assignment."

"Yes, sir." David smiled at Tammy. He liked her father. She looked like she was about to die from worry. He had to admit he was glad *his* father hadn't called to talk to her.

"I've spoken with your brother, Wade, all about you."

Hell, David thought to himself. It was bad enough her father probably dug up some information about the trouble he'd gotten into in his youth, but he sure didn't want his brother telling secrets about him that only he and Wade knew.

Her father continued, "I've had thorough background checks run on you and your brother—all about who you'd been seeing, why you'd been shot by a girlfriend's ex-lover, the missions you've been on that the JAG director could share with me, family ties, and the trouble the two of you got into when you were teens and had lost your mother. I've also looked into your financial state, and I can say I approve."

"But?"

"No buts. I just don't want you taking the situation with my daughter lightly and stringing her along. When my sons told me that Wade was hitting on their 'cousin' Maya, I started the background investigations. I just never thought that his brother—*you*—would get involved with my daughter, Tammy."

"It was just an assignment."

"Yeah, except your boss told me you requested to work with her."

David heard a hint of a smile in her dad's gruff voice. "Yeah, I did."

"Not just because you wanted to find the missing zoo cat."

"My mission was to bring in the boys who knew something about the missing zoo cat," David said truthfully.

"You didn't ask to work with her just because of the missing cat or the boys. Both my sons and my son-in-law requested that you work with her, and you yourself wanted to. To keep her out of danger."

David cleared his throat. "She's very capable, sir."

"I saw the video of her," her father said.

David glanced at Tammy.

She was frowning at him.

"Yes, sir."

"You have my blessing," her father said.

David paused. "Thank you, sir."

"Now, what are you waiting for?"

David chuckled. "The right moment when she's in more of a receptive mood to say yes." He smiled at Tammy. Her eyes widened.

"So ask her."

"Right now?"

"No time like the present."

"I've got to do this right."

"I'd like you to try now," her father said. "But I'll leave you to do it in privacy."

Her father kissed Tammy good-bye, and David walked him to the door and shook his hand. "She's special," her father said.

"She sure as hell is." David smiled, and then they said their good nights and David locked up.

"So…how are you going to do this right?" she asked. Before he could come up with something, she held up her hand. "I'm kidding. Well, not really, but I'm not serious. My father is nuts. I don't want…"

"I don't agree. I think your father is extremely sensible. He's done a background check on me and approved me." David pulled her from the couch. Her sweet cinnamon-scented breath mingled with his—so close their lips hovered, nearly touching. He slid his fingers under her shirt, cupped her lace-covered breasts in his hands, and kissed her. Her mouth pressed his back—hot, needy, wanting. "I love you, Tammy. And hope that you might come to love me."

She smiled up at him. "You don't think this is too impulsive—of both of us?"

He combed his fingers through her hair, his gaze on hers. "No. I've done a number of harebrained impulsive things in my life, but this is not like that at all."

She smiled and kissed him, then pulled away from him.

"So it's not a done deal yet? I need to get your father and mine to convince you what a great choice of mate I'd make? Your brothers? My brother? My boss? Maybe your boss?"

She laughed, pulled on his belt loop, and headed for the kitchen.

"When's the right time, Tammy?"

She smiled up at him. "Aren't you cooking us something?"

He sighed heavily and slipped his hand around hers. "We make a great team." David swept aside her hair and brushed it over her other shoulder. He nuzzled his cheek against her neck and kissed it. His hands slipped underneath her shirt. Finding the fastener in the front of her bra, he unsnapped it.

"David," she said, but as soon as he clamped his large hands over her breasts, she closed her eyes and concentrated on the feel of him touching her.

His hands were slightly rough, abrading her nipples, making them tingle and swell and eager for more of his chafing touch. In a circular motion, he massaged her breasts, which grew heavier with his gentle squeezes. Liquid heat pooled between her legs.

She brushed up against his crotch in a playful and teasing way to get him back—and felt just how hard he had become and smelled his arousal. Hot, sexy cat and David's special all-male scent mixed together like an aphrodisiac meant to entice a she-cat. *This* she-cat.

She rubbed against his stiff erection for good measure twice, and he groaned. She smiled. *Yeah.* He was all ready for her. "Yeah, I can see us going to Costa Rica together, no mission, a waterfall pool and...I never thought I'd be saying this so soon, but...I love you, David."

He slid his hands down her waist, unbuttoned her jeans, and pulled the fastener down with a zip. "Let's take this to bed."

They hadn't made love in the last three days because of the headaches she'd been experiencing. Just hugged and cuddled and kissed. She glanced at the stove. He hadn't started dinner, which was the only reason she'd come into the kitchen. To make sure nothing would burn while they were making love.

"No dinner?"

"I couldn't decide what to make when your dad was talking to you." He lifted her in his arms and carried her back to the bedroom. "So...is it a yes?"

"How does three weeks sound?"

"Hot damn."

She laughed and wrapped her arms around his neck. She loved how cute he could be.

He set her on the floor and quickly dispensed with her clothes and his. She climbed into bed and he moved in next to her, quickly spreading her legs apart as he nuzzled her bare neck with his tantalizing mouth, licking with his wet tongue.

She gave a little cat's rumble of ecstasy as he ran his hands over her thigh, up and down, his thumb grazing her crotch in a tantalizing tease. And then he began to stroke her hard and deep between her legs.

He purred in her ear, "Mmm, Tammy," tickling the shell of her ear with his tongue, his voice like a big cat's motor running at full speed.

She'd needed this, the closeness, the intimacy between them. The tenderness and the passion. She was primed just in anticipation as he stroked her nub, then plunged two fingers into her.

She felt like she was lifting off the bed as she pressed into his fingers, and then the climax hit. She shattered into a million pleasurable fragments. Exquisite tremors pulsed through her, and she cried out in wonderment and relief.

She couldn't believe how hot he made her feel, how quickly he could arouse her, how much she really needed this.

As soon as he felt and smelled Tammy come, David was ready. Her breasts rose and fell with her every breath, her nipples dark and taut with need. For a moment, he allowed his hungry gaze to linger on her. He pushed inside her, deeper and deeper until she was anchored fully to him. She rolled her hips and added to the exquisite sensation.

She was meant for him. He knew just what he wanted. Tammy. Here with him today and tomorrow and the next. Scent-wise, heartbeat-wise, they were in total sync. They could work cases together, be a team always if they could get their bosses to agree to it. If not, maybe one of them could switch branches. He would do it, anything to be with her.

His blood was hot and pounding hard in his veins. He wanted to claim her for now and forever. The way she ground against him, he couldn't hold on. He released his seed deep inside her, pumping as she met his thrusts. He was done, yet not. He wanted more of this—as soon as he could work up to it again.

She was beautiful. And he wanted her to be his mate.

He couldn't deny how much he needed her. The way she teased and played with him proved she wanted him, wanted this as much as he did.

That *he* was important. That *they* were more important.

She stroked his arms and smiled up at him, appearing perfectly content. "How about...*two* weeks?"

Chapter 32

TWO WEEKS LATER, DAVID ARRIVED HOME FROM WORK after an unbelievable day, thinking about the close-to-home assignment he now had after marrying Tammy. He'd thought that they'd have a *little* marriage ceremony, as fast as they had thrown it together. He *wasn't* waiting to marry her. But between her mother, Maya, Kat, and a dozen female Enforcers, they had put on a show to rival the Queen of England's.

Everyone came—her family and his; the JAG members who could attend, saying this was the event of the century as they never thought either he or his brother would marry; her Enforcer friends, including Weaver and Krustan; and Henry Thompson, so thrilled to get his jaguar back. Even Gertie Jessup and several more of Tammy's neighbors helped fill the church pews to capacity and then the Arboretum for the reception.

Glad it was a whirlwind affair and over and done with, he had moved right into Tammy's home, vacating his apartment, pronto. He sighed as he unlocked the front door of the house and walked in, still not believing the assignment Martin had given him.

Her boss and his were trying to keep them together while Tammy and David enjoyed their newlywed days. Which he loved—they were perfect for each other, and getting to know each other meant movies and dinners and lots of kitty-cat loving.

But he hadn't expected that to mean he'd get stuck with the kind of job he did. On top of that? He had to take Tammy to the theater tonight when all he wanted to do was kick off his shoes and the rest of his clothes, undress her, and spend a whole hell of a lot of quality time in bed.

"You won't believe what the boss assigned me to do," David said, pulling Tammy into his arms as she greeted him at the door with a hug and kiss.

"Hmm, I love you." And she kissed him soundly back.

"The feeling is totally mutual, honey." He smelled her heavenly she-cat fragrance and sniffed at the air. His brows rose. "Steaks?"

"Yep."

He kissed her mouth and hugged her tight. "I love you. How did you know I could use a steak when I got home?"

"The boys called me."

He grunted. "Hell, so you already know Martin gave me the mission of training them."

"You'll be good at it."

"Ha! They actually said they wouldn't work with any other instructor. Can you believe that not only would they dictate terms to the JAG director, but that Martin would agree? Not only did I get stuck with training Alex and Nate, but the other twins, too."

She chuckled. "And you love it." She pulled him into the dining room where she'd set out perfumed lilac candles, steaks, baked potatoes, soft rolls, and spinach.

He eyed the huge bouquet of roses and the coupons attached to it as they sat down at the table. "What...?"

"From Henry Thompson. Lifetime passes for the Oregon Zoo. He also sent some to the boys. And he's paying their way to come see Aurelia after their training ends."

"Aurelia?"

"The missing jaguar. Aurelia is Spanish for golden. That's what the boys called her, and Thompson renamed her that for the zoo."

"Huh. I never thought of her as anything more than the missing zoo cat. As to the boys and their training, they're doing their damnedest to make it as *fun* as it can be. I don't know who's learning more, them or me. Anticipating how to deal with their next antics and trying to stay on top and in charge is truly a challenge."

"I'm sure you're doing a great job."

He smiled and then got serious as he buttered his potato. "The worst of it is that everyone in the branch knows what I'm stuck doing. I've had more people drop by to watch the training, as if it was a damn spectator sport."

She smiled a little as if she was amused.

"The thing of it is," he said, cutting into his steak, "the boys don't think I'm giving them training that's challenging enough."

She raised her brows and buttered a roll. "Truly? I would think that you would do a good job of keeping them busy."

"No," he said. "Not according to them."

Her phone played the jaguar song, and she paused to get it.

"Go on. I promise I will only *eye* your steak and not eat it."

She patted him on the shoulder. "Remember, I'm a jaguar, too. You eat my meat and you pay for it."

He laughed. He loved her.

Tammy lifted her phone off the kitchen counter. "My boss." She answered it and noticed David smiling an awful lot, like he knew just why her boss was calling her. Had Sylvan approved her leave so she and David could go to Costa Rica for their honeymoon? But now if David was training the boys, he couldn't go right away. She sighed.

"Tammy, I got a call from David's boss, and Martin asked if I could spare you for an assignment," Sylvan said.

Wait, what happened to her leave?

"He's got four boys David's training, and they asked for you personally to help. I said sure because you knew them and it would be a pleasant break for you, considering the last mission you were on. Plus, with you and David marrying, it would be nice for you to team up for an at-home assignment. After the training is complete, the two of you can go on your leave. I've already approved it. David's boss has signed off on his, contingent on training the boys in the first phase of their instruction."

She swung her gaze to David. *He knew!* He grinned at her.

"Uh, okay," she said, eager to pay one big cat back. She was about to take David's steak away from him, though he'd nearly devoured the whole thing. "Do I get hazard pay?"

Her boss actually laughed. "You'll be reporting for your new duty tomorrow. That's all I had. Talk to you later."

She ended the call. "When were you going to tell me the rest of the news?" she asked David, sitting down to eat her dinner.

"You'll love the job." David grinned. "Just like me. But it means we've really got to watch each other's backs. They give their teachers gifts, too."

"Uh-oh."

"Yeah, for me, a box of condoms to replace those they took. They said they suspected I didn't need them any longer, but that I could give them to someone who might."

She laughed. "Oh, yeah, I could see you asking who could fit them."

"I left them in one of the men's rooms at work. Maybe someone can use them. They also bought me a new bottle of aftershave."

"Which you don't need, either," she said, digging into her spinach.

"Right. I left it at work, too, for the other poor souls who could use a little help attracting a wild cat. Who knows what the boys might end up bringing you so that they can be teacher's pet."

"Maybe a new tube of lipstick."

"Yeah, to replace the one they took from your bag. I just wanted to give you a heads-up. Oh, and I saw your brothers. They acted a little odd toward me. Not sure why."

Tammy shrugged as if she didn't know. David wasn't the *only* one who had a secret tonight.

"Krustan dropped by the training today."

"Oh?" She knew from the smug expression on David's face that he had come out on top of whatever the discussion had been.

"Yeah, he had the notion you should have dated him. But more than that, you shouldn't have hooked up with a JAG agent."

She sipped some of her wine. "Ah, like dating him would have ever happened."

"That's what I told him."

"I bet he loved that." She cut up some of her meat.

"Not only that, but I forgot to mention to you that yesterday, my brother and both of yours cornered me during a training break about a firecracker of a female jaguar shifter who called each of them and chewed them out—"

"I told you I would as soon as the mission was done. They had no business warning you about me. I had to wait until the wedding was over with, though, to make sure we got some nice gifts."

David laughed. "We guys have to stick together, you know."

They could stick together all they wanted, but the women were in charge tonight.

"Now that the case is solved and the boys are under the JAG's jurisdiction, *and* they wanted me to help teach them, I have a few choice words for them," Tammy said.

David was smiling. "About rifling through a woman's things?"

"Yes, even if they were trying to locate anything we might have had on them."

"And stealing our clothes in the jungle?"

"Absolutely, even if they meant to protect us from the bad guys."

"Agreed."

As soon as David cleared the dinner dishes away, he took her hand and said, "Are you sure we have to go..."

She knew he wanted to spend the night in bed with her. Which they would—after the show. "Yes. You promised. And you already ordered the boys to go, so you can't pull out now. If only so you can make sure they attend." Tammy pulled her keys out of her purse and handed the one to the Jaguar to David. His smile couldn't have stretched any further. She shook her head. "You'd think you were ready to make love to her."

He hurried her out to the garage, ran his hand over the car's top, and then took it down. "You're the only woman for me."

But he sure looked like her car could be the second woman in his life. She had to laugh to herself about it. *Men*.

When they reached the theater, she was thrilled to see Wade and Maya parking nearby. David looked dumbfounded.

Tammy slid her arm around David's. "There are Connor and Kat, too. And my brothers."

"Well, I'll be damned," David said. "That's why they were growly with me today. I thought I'd done something wrong. What did you do? Shame them or bribe them into coming?"

She laughed. "If anyone gets wind of you going to a theater production of *Annie* and they want to give you a hard time about it, they'll think again."

Both of them raised their brows to see Sylvan arrive with a date in tow. He was even more dressed up than usual, even though the dress for these events in Texas ranged from formal to practically sloppy. Tammy blinked. "Well, I'll be…"

"Damned," David said, finishing Tammy's comment. They looked around to see if Martin was there as they entered the theater.

Sylvan swung around to talk to them, the woman on his arm a jaguar shifter, but Tammy didn't know her. "Great job, Tammy, David. Great teamwork. I have to say if the JAG director hadn't taken the boys in, I would have recruited them."

"They're great kids. I'm…surprised to see you here," Tammy said.

"Are you kidding? When so many from the Service were coming? Besides your wedding, this is the event of the season. Talk later." He headed down the aisle to their seats.

"Do you see Martin?" Tammy asked David.

He looked around and waved as Martin came through the doorway. Martin wasn't by himself for long. The boys followed him in.

Tammy smiled. "The boys came."

"Yeah, when they saw the boss was here, they probably figured it was a good thing they made it. How in the world did you talk your brothers into coming? I can see Kat and Maya browbeating their husbands into it," David said. "But since your brothers are unattached…"

She chuckled. "I told them that hot she-cats like the theater, so they'd better get used to it. And if they paid attention, they might even find a single one at the show. Works every time."

"Maybe that's why Martin showed up. Maybe they could try teaming up with a she-cat who is chasing down a missing zoo cat," David said, holding her close.

"Yeah, on a nondangerous mission."

"The next one won't be a mission," David said. "Strictly fun in the jungle—in Costa Rica."

"Do they have waterfall pools?"

"Yeah, just for us."

"We'd better train those kids quick. But after the theater?"

"Hmm?" David said as they took their seats next to Wade and Maya and Connor and Kat.

"Tonight it's time for another bubble bath." She smiled as David's face flushed a little while Wade chuckled. She rested her head on David's arm. "I love a man who can enjoy a bubble bath with a she-cat."

"I love a she-cat that is all wild," David said and kissed the top of her head as he settled down to watch *Annie*.

Before the show started, she wondered... "You didn't put the kids up to requesting me to help train them, did you?"

He just smiled.

She shook her head at that devilish look. "I love you anyway." And she'd definitely get him back. Maybe with the teens' help.

"Good, because we have lots of unfinished business," David said and wrapped his arm around her shoulders. Years and years of unfinished business, he thought. And all because of a zoo cat that went missing.

Annie was singing her heart out on stage, but all he could think of was Tammy and his next move...another bubble bath and lots more loving. Though the notion of joining Tammy in another waterfall pool definitely had him thinking up ways to finish up the teens' training ASAP.

Acknowledgments

Thanks to Loretta Melvin for her invaluable research, and to her, Donna Fournier, and Dottie Jones for being my beta readers. Thanks to Deb Werksman for helping to make the books even better, and Danielle Jackson for all her help in promotions. And thanks to the cover artist gods who wow me and all my readers with their gorgeous covers.

About the Author

Bestselling and award-winning author **Terry Spear** has written more than fifty paranormal romance novels and four medieval Highland historical romances. Her first werewolf romance, *Heart of the Wolf*, was named a 2008 *Publishers Weekly* Best Book of the Year, and her subsequent titles have garnered high praise and hit the *USA Today* bestseller list. A retired officer of the U.S. Army Reserves, Terry lives in Crawford, Texas, where she is working on her next werewolf romance and continuing her new series about shape-shifting jaguars. For more information, please visit www.terryspear.com, or follow her on Twitter, @TerrySpear. She is also on Facebook at www.facebook.com/terry.spear. And on Wordpress at:

Terry Spear's Shifters
terryspear.wordpress.com/

the extent that people in it have meaningful opportunities to take part in the formation of public policy. There are a lot of different ways in which that can be true, but insofar as it's true, the society is democratic.

A society can have the formal trappings of democracy and not be democratic at all. The Soviet Union, for example, had elections.

The US obviously has a formal democracy with primaries, elections, referenda, recalls, and so on. But what's the content of this democracy in terms of popular participation?

Over long periods, the involvement of the public in planning or implementation of public policy has been quite marginal. This is a business-run society. The political parties have reflected business interests for a long time.

One version of this view which I think has a lot of power behind it is what political scientist Thomas Ferguson calls "the investment theory of politics." He believes that the state is controlled by coalitions of investors who join together around some common interest. To participate in the political arena, you must have enough resources and private power to become part of such a coalition.

Since the early nineteenth century, Ferguson argues, there's been a struggle for power among such groups of investors. The long periods when nothing very major seemed to be going on are simply times when the major groups of investors have seen more or less eye to eye on what public policy should look like. Moments of conflict come along when groups of investors have differing points of view.

During the New Deal, for example, various groupings of private capital were in conflict over a number of issues. Ferguson identifies a high-tech, capital-intensive, export-oriented sector that tended to be quite pro-New Deal and in favor of the reforms. They wanted an orderly work force and an opening to foreign trade.

A more labor-intensive, domestically oriented sector, grouped essentially around the National Association of Manufacturers, was strongly anti-New Deal. They didn't want any of these reform measures. (Those groups weren't the only ones involved, of course. There was the labor movement, a lot of public ferment and so on.)

You view corporations as being incompatible with democracy, and you say that if we apply the concepts that are used in political analysis, corporations are fascist. That's a highly charged term. What do you mean?

I mean fascism pretty much in the traditional sense. So when a rather mainstream person like Robert Skidelsky, the biographer of [British economist John Maynard] Keynes, describes the early postwar systems as modeled on fascism, he simply means a system in which the state integrates labor and capital under the control of the corporate structure.

That's what a fascist system traditionally was. It can vary in the way it works, but the ideal state that it aims at is absolutist—top-down control with the public essentially following orders.

Fascism is a term from the political domain, so it doesn't apply strictly to corporations, but if you look at them, power goes strictly top-down, from the board of directors to managers to lower managers and ultimately to the people on the shop floor, typists, etc. There's no flow of power or planning from the bottom up. Ultimate power resides in the hands of investors, owners, banks, etc.

People can disrupt, make suggestions, but the same is true of a slave society. People who aren't owners and investors have nothing much to say about it. They can choose to rent their labor to the corporation, or to purchase the commodities or services that it produces, or to find a place in the chain of command, but that's it. That's the totality of their control over the corporation.

That's something of an exaggeration, because corporations are subject to some legal requirements and there is some limited degree of public control. There are taxes and so on. But corporations are more totalitarian than most institutions we call totalitarian in the political arena.

Is there anything large corporate conglomerates do that has beneficial effects?

A lot of what's done by corporations will happen to have, by accident, beneficial effects for the population. The same is true of the government or anything else. But what are they trying to achieve? Not a better life for workers and the firms in which they work, but profits and market share.

That's not a big secret—it's the kind of thing people should learn in third grade. Businesses try to maximize profit, power, market share and control over the state. Sometimes what they do helps other people, but that's just by chance.

There's a common belief that, since the Kennedy assassination, business and elite power circles control our so-called democracy. Has that changed at all with the Clinton administration?

First of all, Kennedy was very pro-business. He was essentially a business candidate. His assassination had no significant effect on policy that anybody has been able to detect. (There *was* a change in policy in the early 1970s, under Nixon, but that had to do with changes in the international economy.)

Clinton is exactly what he says he is, a pro-business candidate. The *Wall Street Journal* had a very enthusiastic, big, front-page article about him right after the NAFTA vote. They pointed out that the Republicans tend to be the party of business as a whole, but that the Democrats tend to favor big business over small business. Clinton, they said, is typical of this. They quoted executives from the Ford Motor Company, the steel industry, etc. who said that this is one of the best administrations they've ever had.

The day after the House vote on NAFTA, the *New York Times* had a very revealing front-page, pro-Clinton story by their Washington correspondent, R.W. Apple. It went sort of like this: People had been criticizing Clinton because he just didn't have any principles.

He backed down on Bosnia, on Somalia, on his economic stimulus program, on Haiti, on the health program. He seemed like a guy with no bottom line at all.

Then he proved that he really was a man of principle and that he really does have backbone—by fighting for the corporate version of NAFTA. So he does have principles—he listens to the call of big money. The same was true of Kennedy.

Radio listener: I've often wondered about people who have a lot of power because of their financial resources. Is it possible to reach them with logic?

They're acting very logically and rationally in their own interests. Take the CEO of Aetna Life Insurance, who makes $23 million a year in salary alone. He's one of the guys who is going to be running our health-care program if Clinton's plan passes.

Suppose you could convince him that he ought to lobby against having the insurance industry run the health-care program, because that will be very harmful to the general population (as indeed it will be). Suppose you could convince him that he ought to give up his salary and become a working person.

What would happen then? He'd get thrown out and someone else would be put in as CEO. These are institutional problems.

Why is it important to keep the general population in line?

Any form of concentrated power doesn't want to be subjected to popular democratic control—or, for that matter, to market discipline.

That's why powerful sectors, including corporate wealth, are naturally opposed to functioning democracy, just as they're opposed to functioning markets...for themselves, at least.

It's just natural. They don't want external constraints on their capacity to make decisions and act freely.

And has that been the case?

Always. Of course, the descriptions of the facts are a little more nuanced, because modern "democratic theory" is more articulate and sophisticated than in the past, when the general population was called "the rabble." More recently, Walter Lippmann called them "ignorant and meddlesome outsiders." He felt that "responsible men" should make the decisions and keep the "bewildered herd" in line.

Modern "democratic theory" takes the view that the role of the public—the "bewildered herd," in Lippmann's words—is to be spectators, not participants. They're supposed to show up every couple of years to ratify decisions made elsewhere, or to select among representatives of the dominant sectors in what's called an "election." That's helpful, because it has a legitimizing effect.

It's very interesting to see the way this idea is promoted in the slick PR productions of the right-wing foundations. One of the most influential in the ideological arena is the Bradley Foundation. Its director, Michael Joyce, recently published an article on this. I don't know whether he wrote it or one of his PR guys did, but I found it fascinating.

It starts off with rhetoric drawn, probably consciously, from the left. When left liberals or radical activists start reading it, they get a feeling of recognition and sympathy (I suspect it's directed at them and at young people). It begins by talking about how remote the political system is from us, how we're asked just to show up every once in a while and cast our votes and then go home.

This is meaningless, the article says—this isn't real participation in the world. What we need is a functioning and active civil society in which people come together and do important things, not just this business of pushing a button now and then.

Then the article asks, How do we overcome these inadequacies? Strikingly, you don't overcome them with more active participation in the political arena. You do it by abandoning the political arena and joining the PTA and going to church and getting a job and going to the store and buying something. That's the way to become a real citizen of a democratic society.

Now, there's nothing wrong with joining the PTA. But there are a few gaps here. What happened to the political arena? It disappeared from the discussion after the first few comments about how meaningless it is.

If you abandon the political arena, somebody is going to be there. Corporations aren't going to go home and join the PTA. They're going to run things. But that we don't talk about.

As the article continues, it talks about how we're being oppressed by the liberal bureaucrats, the social planners who are trying to convince us to do something for the poor. They're the ones who are really running the country. They're that impersonal, remote, unaccountable power that we've got to get off our backs as we fulfill our obligations as citizens at the PTA and the office.

This argument isn't quite presented step-by-step like that in the article—I've collapsed it. It's very clever propaganda, well designed, well crafted, with plenty of thought behind it. Its goal is to make people as stupid, ignorant, passive and obedient as possible, while at the same time making them feel that they're somehow moving towards higher forms of participation.

In your discussions of democracy, you often refer to a couple of comments of Thomas Jefferson's.

Jefferson died on July 4, 1826—fifty years to the day after the Declaration of Independence was signed. Near the end of his life, he spoke with a mixture of concern and hope about what had been achieved, and urged the population to struggle to maintain the victories of democracy.

He made a distinction between two groups—aristocrats and democrats. Aristocrats "fear and distrust the people, and wish to draw all powers from them into the hands of the higher classes." This view is held by respectable intellectuals in many different societies today, and is quite similar to the Leninist doctrine that the vanguard party of radical intellectuals should take power and lead the stupid masses to a bright future. Most liberals are aristocrats in Jefferson's sense. [Former Secretary of State] Henry Kissinger is an extreme example of an aristocrat.

Democrats, Jefferson wrote, "identify with the people, have confidence in them, cherish and consider them as the most honest and safe, although not the most wise, depository of the public interest." In other words, democrats believe the people should be in control, whether or not they're going to make the right decisions. Democrats do exist today, but they're becoming increasingly marginal.

Jefferson specifically warned against "banking institutions and monied incorporations" (what we would now call "corporations") and said that if they grow, the aristocrats will have won and the American Revolution will have been lost. Jefferson's worst fears were realized (although not entirely in the ways he predicted).

Later on, [the Russian anarchist Mikhail] Bakunin predicted that the contemporary intellectual classes would separate into two groups (both of which are examples of what Jefferson meant by aristocrats). One group, the "red bureaucracy," would take power into their own hands and create one of the most malevolent and vicious tyrannies in human history.

The other group would conclude that power lies in the private sector, and would serve the state and private power in what we now call state capitalist societies. They'd "beat the people with the people's stick," by which he meant that they'd profess democracy while actually keeping the people in line.

You also cite [the American philosopher and educator] John Dewey. What did he have to say about this?

Dewey was one of the last spokespersons for the Jeffersonian view of democracy. In the early part of this century, he wrote that democracy isn't an end in itself, but a means by which people discover and extend and manifest their fundamental human nature and human rights. Democracy is rooted in freedom, solidarity, a choice of work and the ability to participate in the social order. Democracy produces real people, he said. That's the major product of a democratic society—real people.

He recognized that democracy in that sense was a very withered plant. Jefferson's "banking institutions and monied incorporations" had of course become vastly more powerful by this time, and Dewey felt that "the shadow cast on society by big business" made reform very difficult, if not impossible. He believed that reform may be of some use, but as long as there's no democratic control of the workplace, reform isn't going to bring democracy and freedom.

Like Jefferson and other classical liberals, Dewey recognized that institutions of private power were absolutist institutions, unaccountable and basically totalitarian in their internal structure. Today, they're far more powerful than anything Dewey dreamed of.

This literature is all accessible. It's hard to think of more leading figures in American history than Thomas Jefferson and John Dewey. They're as American as apple pie. But when you read them today, they sound like crazed Marxist lunatics. That just shows how much our intellectual life has deteriorated.

In many ways, these ideas received their earliest—and often most powerful—formulation in people like [the German intellectual] Wilhelm von Humboldt, who inspired [the English philosopher] John Stuart Mill and was one of the founders of the classical liberal tradition in the late eighteenth century. Like [the Scottish moral philosopher] Adam Smith and others, von Humboldt felt that at the root of human nature is the need for free creative work under one's own control. That must be at the basis of any decent society.

Those ideas, which run straight through to Dewey, are deeply anticapitalist in character. Adam Smith didn't call himself an anticapitalist because, back in the eighteenth century, he was basically precapitalist, but he had a good deal of skepticism about capitalist ideology and practice—even about what he called "joint stock companies" (what we call corporations today, which existed in quite a different form in his day). He worried about the separation of managerial control from direct participation, and he also feared that these joint stock companies might turn into "immortal persons."

This indeed happened in the nineteenth century, after Smith's death [under current law, corporations have even more rights than individuals, and can live forever]. It didn't happen through parliamentary decisions—nobody voted on it in Congress. In the US, as elsewhere in the world, it happened through judicial decisions. Judges and corporate lawyers simply crafted a new society in which corporations have immense power.

Today, the top two hundred corporations in the world control over a quarter of the world's total assets, and their control is increasing. *Fortune* magazine's annual listing of the top American corporations found increasing profits, increasing concentration, and reduction of jobs—tendencies that have been going on for some years.

Von Humboldt's and Smith's ideas feed directly into the socialist-anarchist tradition, into the left-libertarian critique of capitalism. This critique can take the Deweyian form of a sort of workers'-control version of democratic socialism, or the left-Marxist form of people like [the Dutch astronomer and political theorist] Anton Pannekoek and [the Polish-German revolutionary] Rosa Luxemburg, or [the leading anarchist] Rudolf Rocker's anarcho-syndicalism (among others).

All this has been grossly perverted or forgotten in modern intellectual life but, in my view, these ideas grow straight out of classical, eighteenth-century liberalism. I even think they can be traced back to seventeenth-century rationalism.

Keeping the rich on welfare

A book called A*merica: Who Pays the Taxes?,* written by a couple of *Philadelphia Inquirer* reporters, apparently shows that the amount of taxes paid by corporations has dramatically declined in the US.

That's for sure. It's been very striking over the last fifteen years.

Some years ago, a leading specialist, Joseph Pechman, pointed out that despite the apparently progressive structure that's built into the income tax system (that is, the higher your income, the higher your tax rate), all sorts of other regressive factors end up making everyone's tax rate very near a fixed percentage.

An interesting thing happened in Alabama involving Daimler-Benz, the big German auto manufacturer.

Under Reagan, the US managed to drive labor costs way below the level of our competitors (except for Britain). That's produced consequences not only in Mexico and the US but all across the industrial world.

For example, one of the effects of the so-called free trade agreement with Canada was to stimulate a big flow of jobs from Canada to the southeast US, because that's an essentially nonunion area. Wages are lower; you don't have to worry about benefits; workers can barely organize. So that's an attack against Canadian workers.

Daimler-Benz, which is Germany's biggest conglomerate, was seeking essentially Third World conditions. They managed to get our southeastern states to compete against one another to see who could force the public to pay the largest bribe to bring them there. Alabama won. It offered hundreds of millions of dollars in tax benefits, practically gave Daimler-Benz the land on which to construct their plant, and agreed to build all sorts of infrastructure for them.

Some people will benefit—the small number who are employed at the plant, with some spillover to hamburger stands and so on, but primarily bankers, corporate lawyers, people involved in investment and financial services. They'll do very well, but the cost to most of the citizens of Alabama will be substantial.

Even the *Wall Street Journal*, which is rarely critical of business, pointed out that this is very much like what happens when rich corporations go to Third World countries, and it questioned whether there were going to be overall benefits for the state of Alabama. Meanwhile Daimler-Benz can use this to drive down the lifestyle of German workers.

German corporations have also set up factories in the Czech Republic, where they can get workers for about 10% the cost of German workers. The Czech Republic is right across the border; it's a Westernized society with high educational levels and nice white people with blue eyes. Since they don't believe in the free market any more than any other rich people do, they'll leave the Czech Republic to pay the social costs, pollution, debts and so on, while they pick up the profits.

It's exactly the same with the plants GM is building in Poland, where it's insisting on 30% tariff protection. The free market is for the poor. We have a dual system—protection for the rich and market discipline for everyone else.

I was struck by an article in the *New York Times* whose headline was, "Nation considers means to dispose of its plutonium." So the nation has to figure out how to dispose of what was essentially created by private capital.

That's the familiar idea that profits are privatized but costs are socialized. The costs are the nation's, the people's, but the profits weren't for the people, nor did they make the decision to produce plutonium in the first place, nor are they making the decisions about how to dispose of it, nor do they get to decide what ought to be a reasonable energy policy.

One of the things I've learned from working with you is the importance of reading *Business Week, Fortune* and the *Wall Street Journal.* In the business section of the *New York Times,* I read a fascinating discussion by a bureaucrat from MITI [Japan's Ministry of International Trade and Industry] who trained at the Harvard Business School.

One of his classes was studying a failed airline that went out of business. They were shown a taped interview with the company's president, who noted with pride that through the whole financial crisis and eventual bankruptcy of the airline, he'd never asked for government help. To the Japanese man's astonishment, the class erupted into applause.

He commented, "There's a strong resistance to government intervention in America. I understand that. But I was shocked. There are many shareholders in companies. What happened to his employees, for example?" Then he reflects on what he views as America's blind devotion to a free-market ideology. He says, "It is something quite close to a religion. You cannot argue about it with most people. You believe it or you don't." It's interesting.

It's interesting, in part, because of the Japanese man's failure to understand what actually happens in the US, which apparently was shared by the students in his business class. If it was Eastern Airlines they were talking about, Frank Lorenzo, the director, was trying to put it out of business. He made a personal profit out of that.

He wanted to break the unions in order to support his other enterprises (which he ripped off profits from Eastern Airlines for). He wanted to leave the airline industry less unionized and more under corporate control, and to leave himself wealthier. All of that happened. So naturally he didn't call on government intervention to save him—things were working the way he wanted.

On the other hand, the idea that corporations don't ask for government help is a joke. They demand an extraordinary amount of government intervention. That's largely what the whole Pentagon system is about.

Take the airline industry, which was created by government intervention. A large part of the reason for the huge growth in the Pentagon in the late 1940s was to salvage the collapsing aeronautical industry, which obviously couldn't survive in a civilian market. That's worked—it's now the United States' leading export industry, and Boeing is the leading exporter.

An interesting and important book on this by Frank Kofsky just came out. It describes the war scares that were manipulated in 1947 and 1948 to try to ram spending bills through Congress to save the aeronautical industry. (That wasn't the only purpose of these war scares, but it was a big factor.)

Huge industries were spawned, and are maintained, by massive government intervention. Many corporations couldn't survive without it. (For some, it's not a huge part of their profits at the moment, but it's a cushion.) The public also provides the basic technology—metallurgy, avionics or whatever—via the public subsidy system.

The same is true just across the board. You can hardly find a functioning sector of the US manufacturing or service economy which hasn't gotten that way and isn't sustained by government intervention.

The Clinton administration has been pouring new funds into the National Bureau of Standards and Technology. It used to try to work on how long a foot is but it will now be more actively involved in serving the needs of private capital. Hundreds of corporations are beating on their doors asking for grants.

The idea is to try to replace the somewhat declining Pentagon system. With the end of the Cold War, it's gotten harder to maintain the Pentagon system, but you've got to keep the subsidy going to big corporations. The public has to pay the research and development costs.

The idea that a Japanese investigator could fail to see this is fairly remarkable. It's pretty well known in Japan.

Health care

I don't suppose you can see the Boston skyline from your home in Lexington. But if you could, what would be the two tallest buildings?

The John Hancock and the Prudential.

And they happen to be two types of what?

They're going to be running our health-care program if Clinton has his way.

There's a general consensus that the US health-care system needs to be reformed. How did that consensus evolve?

It evolved very simply. We have a relatively privatized health-care system. As a result, it's geared towards high-tech intervention rather than public health and prevention. It's also hopelessly inefficient and extremely bureaucratic, with huge administrative expenses.

This has gotten just too costly for American business. In fact, a bit to my surprise, *Business Week*, the main business journal, has come out recently with several articles advocating a Canadian-style, single-payer program. Under this system, health care is individual, but the government is the insurer. Similar plans exist in every industrial country in the world, except the US.

The Clinton plan is called "managed competition." What is that, and why are the big insurance companies supporting it?

"Managed competition" means that big insurance companies will put together huge conglomerates of health-care institutions, hospitals, clinics, labs and so on. Various bargaining units will be set up to determine which of these conglomerates to work with. That's supposed to introduce some kind of market forces.

But a very small number of big insurance conglomerates, in limited competition with one another, will be pretty much in charge of organizing your health care. (This plan will drive the little insurance companies out of the market, which is why they're opposed to it.)

Since they're in business for profit, not for your comfort, the big insurance companies will doubtlessly micromanage health care, in an attempt to reduce it to the lowest possible level. They'll also tend away from prevention and public health measures, which aren't their concern. Enormous inefficiencies will be involved—huge profits, advertising costs, big corporate salaries and other corporate amenities, big bureaucracies that control in precise detail what doctors and nurses do and don't do—and we'll have to pay for all that.

There's another point that ought to be mentioned. In a Canadian-style, government-insurance system, the costs are distributed in the same way that taxes are. If the tax system is progressive—that is, if rich people pay a higher percentage of their income in taxes (which all other industrial societies assume, correctly, to be the only ethical approach)—then the wealthy will also pay more of the costs of health care.

But the Clinton program, and all the others like it, are radically regressive. A janitor and a CEO pay the same amount. It's as if they were both taxed the same amount, which is unheard of in any civilized society.

Actually, it's even worse than that—the janitor will probably pay more. He'll be living in a poor neighborhood and the executive will be living in a rich suburb or a downtown high-rise, which means they'll belong to different health groupings. Because the grouping the janitor belongs to will include many more poor and high-risk people, the insurance companies will demand higher rates from it than the one the executive belongs to, which will include mostly wealthier, lower-risk people.

According to a Harris poll, Americans prefer the Canadian-style health-care system by a huge majority. That's kind of remarkable, given the minimal amount of media attention the single-payer system has received.

The best work I know on this is by [Professor] Vicente Navarro [of Johns Hopkins]. He's discovered that there's been quite consistent support for something like a Canadian-style system ever since polls began on this issue, which is now over forty years.

Back in the 1940s, Truman tried to put through such a program. It would have brought the US into line with the rest of the industrial world, but it was beaten back by a huge corporate offensive, complete with tantrums about how we were going to turn into a Bolshevik society and so on.

Every time the issue has come up, there's been a major corporate offensive. One of Ronald Reagan's great achievements back in the late 1960s was to give somber speeches (written for him by the AMA) about how if the legislation establishing Medicare was passed, we'd all be telling our children and grandchildren decades hence what freedom used to be like.

Steffie Woolhandler and David Himmelstein [both of Harvard Medical School] also cite another poll result: When Canadians were asked if they'd want a US-style system, only 5% said yes.

By now, even large parts of the business community don't want it. It's just too inefficient, too bureaucratic and too costly for them. The auto companies estimated a couple of years ago that it was costing them about $500 extra per car just because of the inefficiencies of the US health system—as compared with, say, their Canadian operations.

When business starts to get hurt, then the issue moves into the public agenda. The public has been in favor of a big change for a long time, but what the public thinks doesn't matter much.

There was a nice phrase about this sort of thing in the *Economist* [a leading London business journal]. The *Economist* was concerned about the fact that Poland has degenerated into a system where they have democratic elections, which is sort of a nuisance.

The population in all of the East European countries is being smashed by the economic changes that are being rammed down their throats. (These changes are called "reforms," which is supposed to make them sound good.) In the last election, the Poles voted in an anti-"reform" government. The *Economist* pointed out that this really wasn't too troublesome because "policy is insulated from politics." In their view, that's a good thing.

In this country too, policy is insulated from politics. People can have their opinions; they can even vote if they like. But policy goes on its merry way, determined by other forces.

What the public wants is called "politically unrealistic." Translated into English, that means the major centers of power and privilege are opposed to it. A change in our health-care system has now become politically more realistic because the corporate community wants a change, since the current system is harming them.

Vicente Navarro says that a universal and comprehensive health-care program is "directly related to the strength of the working class and its political and economic instruments."

That's certainly been true in Canada and Europe. Canada had a system rather like ours up until the mid-1960s. It was changed first in one province, Saskatchewan, where the NDP [the New Democratic Party, a mildly reformist, umbrella political party with labor backing] was in power.

The NDP was able to put through a provincial insurance program, driving the insurance companies out of the health-care business. It turned out to be very successful. It was giving good medical care and reducing costs and was much more progressive in payment. It was mimicked by other provinces, also under labor pressure, often using the NDP as an instrument. Pretty soon it was adopted across Canada nationally.

The history in Europe is pretty much the same. Working-class organizations have been one of the main (although not the only) mechanisms by which people with very limited power and resources can get together to participate in the public arena. That's one of the reasons unions are so hated by business and elites generally. They're just too democratizing in their character.

So Navarro is surely right. The strength and organization of labor and its ability to enter into the public arena is certainly related— maybe even decisively related—to the establishment of social programs of this kind.

There may be a parallel movement going on in California, where there's a ballot initiative to have single-payer health care.

The situation in the US is a little different from what Navarro described, because business still plays an inordinate role here in determining what kind of system will evolve. Unless there are significant changes in the US—that is, unless public pressure and organizations, including labor, do a lot more than they've done so far—the outcome will once again be determined by business interests.

Much more media attention has been paid to AIDS than to breast cancer, but a half a million women in the US will die from breast cancer in the 1990s. Many men will die from prostate cancer. These aren't considered political questions, are they?

Well, there's no vote taken on them, but if you're asking if there are questions of policy involved, of course there are. You might add to those cancers the number of children who will suffer or die because of extremely poor conditions in infancy and childhood.

Take, say, malnutrition. That decreases life span quite considerably. If you count that up in deaths, it outweighs anything you're talking about. I don't think many people in the public health field would question the conclusion that the major contribution to improving health, reducing mortality figures and improving the quality of life, would come from simple public health measures like ensuring people adequate nutrition and safe and healthy conditions of life, clean water, effective sewage treatment, and so on.

You'd think that in a rich country like this, these wouldn't be big issues, but they are for a lot of the population. *Lancet,* the British medical journal—the most prestigious medical journal in the world—recently pointed out that 40% of children in New York City live below the poverty line. They suffer from malnutrition and other poor conditions that cause very high mortality rates—and, if they survive, they have very severe health problems all through their lives.

The *New England Journal of Medicine* pointed out a couple of years ago that black males in Harlem have about the same mortality rate as people in Bangladesh. That's essentially because of the extreme deterioration of the most elementary public health conditions, and social conditions.

Some people have linked the increase in breast cancer and prostate cancer to environmental degradation, to diet, and to the increase of additives and preservatives. What do you think about that?

It's doubtless some kind of a factor. How big or serious a factor it is I'm not sure.

Are you at all interested in the so-called natural or organic food movement?

Sure. I think there ought to be concerns about the quality of food. This I would say falls into the question of general public health. It's like having good water and good sewage and making sure that people have enough food and so on.

All these things are in roughly the same category—they don't have to do with high-technology medical treatment but with essential conditions of life. These general public-health issues, of which eating food that doesn't contain poisons is naturally a part, are the overwhelming factors in quality of life and mortality.

Crime and punishment

There's been a tendency over the last few years for local TV news programs to concentrate on crimes, rapes, kidnappings, etc. Now this is spilling over into the national network news programs.

That's true, but it's just a surface phenomenon. Why is there an increase in attention to violent crime? Is it connected to the fact that there's been a considerable decline in income for the large majority of the population, and a decline as well in the opportunity for constructive work?

But until you ask why there's an increase in social disintegration, and why more and more resources are being directed towards the wealthy and privileged sectors and away from the general population, you can't have even a concept of why there's rising crime or how you should deal with it.

Over the past twenty or thirty years, there's been a considerable increase in inequality. This trend accelerated during the Reagan years. The society has been moving visibly towards a kind of Third World model.

The result is an increasing crime rate, as well as other signs of social disintegration. Most of the crime is poor people attacking each other, but it spills over to more privileged sectors. People are very worried—and quite properly, because the society is becoming very dangerous.

A constructive approach to the problem would require dealing with its fundamental causes, but that's off the agenda, because we must continue with a social policy that's aimed at strengthening the welfare state for the rich.

The only kind of responses the government can resort to under those conditions is pandering to the fear of crime with increasing harshness, attacking civil liberties and attempting to control the poor, essentially by force.

Do you know what "smash and grab" is? When your car is in traffic or at a stop light, people come along, smash in the window and grab your purse or steal your wallet.

The same thing is going on right around Boston. There's also a new form, called "Good Samaritan robbery." You fake a flat tire on the highway and when somebody stops to help, you jump them, steal their car, beat them up if they're lucky, kill them if they're not.

The causes are the increasing polarization of the society that's been going on for the past twenty-five years, and the marginalization of large sectors of the population. Since they're superfluous for wealth production (meaning profit production), and since the basic ideology is that a person's human rights depend on what they can get for themselves in the market system, they have no human value.

Larger and larger sectors of the population have no form of organization and no viable, constructive way of reacting, so they pursue the available options, which are often violent. To a large extent, those are the options that are encouraged in the popular culture.

You can tell a great deal about a society when you look at its system of justice. I was wondering if you'd comment on the Clinton crime bill, which authorizes hiring 100,000 more cops, boot camps for juveniles, more money for prisons, extending the death penalty to about fifty new offenses and making gang membership a federal crime—which is interesting, considering there's something about freedom of association in the Bill of Rights.

It was hailed with great enthusiasm by the far right as the greatest anticrime bill ever. It's certainly the most *extraordinary* crime bill in history. It's greatly increased, by a factor of five or six, federal spending for repression.

There's nothing much constructive in it. There are more prisons, more police, heavier sentences, more death sentences, new crimes, three strikes and you're out.

It's unclear how much pressure and social decline and deterioration people will accept. One tactic is just drive them into urban slums—concentration camps, in effect—and let them prey on one another. But they have a way of breaking out and affecting the interests of wealthy and privileged people. So you have to build up the jail system, which is incidentally also a shot in the arm for the economy.

It's natural that Clinton picked up this crime bill as a major social initiative, not only for a kind of ugly political reason—namely, that it's easy to whip up hysteria about it—but also because it reflects the general point of view of the so-called New Democrats, the business-oriented segment of the Democratic Party to which Clinton belongs.

What are your views on capital punishment?

It's a crime. I agree with Amnesty International on that one, and indeed with most of the world. The state should have no right to take people's lives.

Radio listener: Does this country have a vested interest in supporting the drug trade?

It's complicated; I don't want to be too brief about it. For one thing, you can't talk about marijuana and cocaine in the same breath. Marijuana simply doesn't have the lethal effects of cocaine. You can debate about whether marijuana is good or bad, but out of about sixty million users, I don't think there's a known case of overdose. The criminalization of marijuana has motives other than concern about drugs.

On the other hand, hard drugs, to which people have been driven to a certain extent by the prohibitions against soft drugs, are very harmful—although nowhere near the harm of, say, tobacco and alcohol in terms of overall societal effects, including deaths.

There are sectors of American society that profit from the hard drug trade, like the big international banks that do the money laundering or the corporations that provide the chemicals for the industrial production of hard drugs. On the other hand, people who live in the inner cities are being devastated by them. So there are different interests.

Gun control

Advocates of free access to arms cite the Second Amendment. Do you believe that it permits unrestricted, uncontrolled possession of guns?

It's pretty clear that, taken literally, the Second Amendment doesn't permit people to have guns. But laws are never taken literally, including amendments to the Constitution or constitutional rights. Laws permit what the tenor of the times interprets them as permitting.

But underlying the controversy over guns are some serious questions. There's a feeling in the country that people are under attack. I think they're misidentifying the source of the attack, but they do feel under attack.

The government is the only power structure that's even partially accountable to the population, so naturally the business sectors want to make that the enemy—not the corporate system, which is totally unaccountable. After decades of intensive business propaganda, people feel that the government is some kind of enemy and that they have to defend themselves from it.

It's not that that doesn't have its justifications. The government *is* authoritarian and commonly hostile to much of the population. But it's partially influenceable—and potentially very influenceable—by the general population.

Many people who advocate keeping guns have fear of the government in the back of their minds. But that's a crazy response to a real problem.

Do the media foster the feeling people have that they're under attack?

At the deepest level, the media contribute to the sense that the government is the enemy, and they suppress the sources of real power in the society, which lie in the totalitarian institutions—the corporations, now international in scale—that control the economy and much of our social life. In fact, the corporations set the conditions within which the government operates, and control it to a large extent.

The picture presented in the media is constant, day after day. People simply have no awareness of the system of power under which they're suffering. As a result—as intended—they turn their attention against the government.

People have all kinds of motivations for opposing gun control, but there's definitely a sector of the population that considers itself threatened by big forces, ranging from the Federal Reserve to the Council on Foreign Relations to big government to who knows what, and they're calling for guns to protect themselves.

Radio listener: On the issue of gun control, I believe that the US is becoming much more like a Third World country, and nothing is necessarily going to put a stop to it. I look around and see a lot of Third World countries where, if the citizens had weapons, they wouldn't have the government they've got. So I think that maybe people are being a little short-sighted in arguing for gun control and at the same time realizing that the government they've got is not exactly a benign one.

Your point illustrates exactly what I think is a major fallacy. The government is far from benign—that's true. On the other hand, it's at least partially accountable, and it can become as benign as we make it.

What's not benign (what's extremely harmful, in fact) is something you didn't mention—business power, which is highly concentrated and, by now, largely transnational. Business power is very far from benign and it's completely unaccountable. It's a totalitarian system that has an enormous effect on our lives. It's also the main reason why the government isn't benign.

As for guns being the way to respond to this, that's outlandish. First of all, this is not a weak Third World country. If people have pistols, the government has tanks. If people get tanks, the government has atomic weapons. There's no way to deal with these issues by violent force, even if you think that that's morally legitimate.

Guns in the hands of American citizens are not going to make the country more benign. They're going to make it more brutal, ruthless and destructive. So while one can recognize the motivation that lies behind some of the opposition to gun control, I think it's sadly misguided.

Becoming a Third World country

A recent Census Bureau report stated that there's been a 50% increase in the working poor—that is, people who have jobs but are still below the poverty level.

That's part of the Third-Worldization of the society. It's not just unemployment, but also wage reduction. Real wages have been declining since the late 1960s. Since 1987, they've even been declining for college-educated people, which was a striking shift.

There's supposed to be a recovery going on, and it's true that a kind of recovery is going on. It's at about half the rate of preceding postwar recoveries from recession (there've been half a dozen of them) and the rate of job creation is less than a third. Furthermore— out of line with earlier recoveries—the jobs themselves are low-paying, and a huge number of them are temporary.

This is what's called "increasing flexibility of the labor market." *Flexibility* is a word like reform—it's supposed to be a good thing. Actually, *flexibility* means insecurity. It means you go to bed at night and don't know if you'll have a job in the morning. Any economist can explain that that's a good thing for the economy—that is, for profit-making, not for the way people live.

Low wages also increase job insecurity. They keep inflation low, which is good for people who have money—bondholders, say. Corporate profits are zooming, but for most of the population, things are grim. And grim circumstances, without much prospect for a future or for constructive social action, express themselves in violence.

It's interesting that you should say that. Most of the examples of mass murders are in the workplace. I'm thinking of the various killings in post offices and fast-food restaurants, where workers are disgruntled for one reason or another, or have been fired or laid off.

Not only have real wages stagnated or declined, but working conditions have gotten much worse. You can see that just in counting hours of work. Julie Schor, an economist at Harvard, brought out an important book on this a couple of years ago, called *The Overworked American*. If I remember her figures correctly, by around 1990, the time she was writing, workers had to put in about six weeks extra work a year to maintain something like a 1970 real wage level.

Along with the increasing hours of work comes increasing harshness of work conditions, increasing insecurity and, because of the decline of unions, reduced ability to protect oneself. In the Reagan years, even the minimal government programs for protecting workers against workplace accidents and the like were reduced, in the interest of maximizing profits. The absence of constructive options, like union organizing, leads to violence.

Labor

[Harvard professor] Elaine Bernard and [union official] Tony Mazzocchi have been talking about creating a new labor-based party. What are your views on that?

I think that's an important initiative. The US is becoming very depoliticized and negative. About half the population thinks both political parties should be disbanded. There's a real need for something that would articulate the concerns of that substantial majority of the population that's being left out of social planning and the political process.

Labor unions have often been a significant force—in fact, the main social force—for democratization and progress. On the other hand, when they aren't linked to the political system through a labor-based party, there's a limit on what they can do. Take health care, for example.

Powerful unions in the US were able to get fairly reasonable health-care provisions for themselves. But since they were acting independently of the political system, they typically didn't attempt to bring about decent health conditions for the general population. Compare Canada, where the unions, being linked to labor-based parties, were able to implement health care for everybody.

That's an illustration of the kind of difference a politically oriented, popular movement like labor can achieve. We're not in the day any longer where the industrial workers are the majority or even the core of the labor force. But the same questions arise. I think Bernard and Mazzocchi are on the right track in thinking along those lines.

Yesterday was May 1. What's its historical significance?

It's May Day, which throughout the world has been a working-class holiday for more than a hundred years. It was initiated in solidarity with American workers who, back in the 1880s, were suffering unusually harsh conditions in their effort to achieve an eight-hour workday. The US is one of the few countries where this day of solidarity with US labor is hardly even known.

This morning, way in the back of the *Boston Globe,* there was a little item whose headline read, "May Day Celebration in Boston." I was surprised, because I don't think I've ever seen that here in the US. It turned out that there indeed was a May Day celebration, of the usual kind, but it was being held by Latin American and Chinese workers who've recently immigrated here.

That's a dramatic example of the efficiency with which business controls US ideology, of how effective its propaganda and indoctrination have been in depriving people of any awareness of their own rights and history. You have to wait for poor Latino and Chinese workers to celebrate an international holiday of solidarity with American workers.

In his *New York Times* column, Anthony Lewis wrote: "Unions in this country, sad to say, are looking more and more like the British unions...backward, unenlightened....The crude, threatening tactics used by unions to make Democratic members of the House vote against NAFTA underline the point."

That brings out Lewis's real commitments very clearly. What he called "crude, threatening tactics" were labor's attempt to get their representatives to represent their interests. By the standards of the elite, that's an attack on democracy, because the political system is supposed to be run by the rich and powerful.

Corporate lobbying vastly exceeded labor lobbying, but you can't even talk about it in the same breath. It wasn't considered raw muscle or antidemocratic. Did Lewis have a column denouncing corporate lobbying for NAFTA?

I didn't see it.

I didn't see it either.

Things reached the peak of absolute hysteria the day before the vote. The *New York Times* lead editorial was exactly along the lines of that quote from Lewis, and it included a little box that listed the dozen or so representatives in the New York region who were voting against NAFTA. It showed their contributions from labor and said that this raises ominous questions about the political influence of labor, and whether these politicians are being honest, and so on.

As a number of these representatives later pointed out, the *Times* didn't have a box listing corporate contributions to them or to other politicians—nor, we may add, was there a box listing advertisers of the *New York Times* and their attitudes towards NAFTA.

It was quite striking to watch the hysteria that built up in privileged sectors, like the *Times'* commentators and editorials, as the NAFTA vote approached. They even allowed themselves the use of the phrase "class lines." I've never seen that in the *Times* before. You're usually not allowed to admit that the US has class lines. But this was considered a really serious issue, and all bars were let down.

The end result is very intriguing. In a recent poll, about 70% of the respondents said they were opposed to the actions of the labor movement against NAFTA, but it turned out that they took pretty much the same position that labor took. So why were they opposed to it?

I think it's easy to explain that. The media scarcely reported what labor was actually *saying.* But there was plenty of hysteria about labor's alleged tactics.

The CIA

What about the role of the CIA in a democratic society? Is that an oxymoron?

You could imagine a democratic society with an organization that carries out intelligence-gathering functions. But that's a very minor part of what the CIA does. Its main purpose is to carry out secret and usually illegal activities for the executive branch, which wants to keep these activities secret because it knows that the public won't accept them. So even inside the US, it's highly undemocratic.

The activities that it carries out are quite commonly efforts to undermine democracy, as in Chile through the 1960s into the early 1970s [described on pp. 91–95]. That's far from the only example. By the way, although most people focus on Nixon's and Kissinger's involvement with the CIA, Kennedy and Johnson carried out similar policies.

Is the CIA an instrument of state policy, or does it formulate policy on its own?

You can't be certain, but my own view is that the CIA is very much under the control of executive power. I've studied those records fairly extensively in many cases, and it's very rare for the CIA to undertake initiatives on its own.

It often looks as though it does, but that's because the executive wants to preserve deniability. The executive branch doesn't want to have documents lying around that say, I told you to murder Lumumba, or to overthrow the government of Brazil, or to assassinate Castro.

So the executive branch tries to follow policies of plausible deniability, which means that messages are given to the CIA to do things but without a paper trail, without a record. When the story comes out later, it looks as if the CIA is doing things on their own. But if you really trace it through, I think this almost never happens.

The media

Let's talk about media and democracy. In your view, what are the communications requirements of a democratic society?

I agree with Adam Smith on this—we'd like to see a tendency toward equality. Not just equality of opportunity, but actual equality—the ability, at every stage of one's existence, to access information and make decisions on the basis of it. So a democratic communications system would be one that involves large-scale public participation, and that reflects both public interests and real values like truth, integrity and discovery.

Bob McChesney, in his recent book *Telecommunications, Mass Media and Democracy,* details the debate between 1928 and 1935 for control of radio in the US. How did that battle play out?

That's a very interesting topic, and he's done an important service by bringing it out. It's very pertinent today, because we're involved in a very similar battle over this so-called "information superhighway."

In the 1920s, the first major means of mass communication since the printing press came along—radio. It's obvious that radio is a bounded resource, because there's only a fixed bandwidth. There was no question in anyone's mind that the government was going to have to regulate it. The question was, What form would this government regulation take?

Government could opt for public radio, with popular participation. This approach would be as democratic as the society is. Public radio in the Soviet Union would have been totalitarian, but in, say, Canada or England, it would be partially democratic (insofar as those societies are democratic).

That debate was pursued all over the world—at least in the wealthier societies, which had the luxury of choice. Almost every country (maybe every one—I can't think of an exception) chose public radio, while the US chose private radio. It wasn't 100%; you were allowed to have small radio stations—say, a college radio station—that can reach a few blocks. But virtually all radio in the US was handed over to private power.

As McChesney points out, there was a considerable struggle about that. There were church groups and some labor unions and other public interest groups that felt that the US should go the way the rest of the world was going. But this is very much a business-run society, and they lost out.

Rather strikingly, business also won an ideological victory, claiming that handing radio over to private power constituted democracy, because it gave people choices in the marketplace. That's a very weird concept of democracy, since your power depends on the number of dollars you have, and your choices are limited to selecting among options that are highly structured by the real concentrations of power. But this was nevertheless widely accepted, even by liberals, as the democratic solution. By the mid- to late 1930s, the game was essentially over.

This struggle was replayed—in the rest of the world, at least—about a decade later, when television came along. In the US this wasn't a battle at all; TV was completely commercialized without any conflict. But again, in most other countries—or maybe every other country—TV was put in the public sector.

In the 1960s, television and radio became partly commercialized in other countries; the same concentration of private power that we find in the US was chipping away at the public-service function of radio and television. At the same time in the US, there was a slight opening to public radio and television.

The reasons for this have never been explored in any depth (as far as I know), but it appears that the private broadcasting companies recognized that it was a nuisance for them to have to satisfy the formal requirements of the Federal Communications Commission that they devote part of their programming to public-interest purposes. So CBS, say, had to have a big office with a lot of employees who every year would put together a collection of fraudulent claims about how they'd met this legislative condition. It was a pain in the neck.

At some point, they apparently decided that it would be easier to get the entire burden off their backs and permit a small and under-funded public broadcasting system. They could then claim that they didn't have to fulfill this service any longer. That was the origin of public radio and television—which is now largely corporate-funded in any event.

That's happening more and more. PBS [the Public Broadcasting Service] is sometimes called "the Petroleum Broadcasting Service."

That's just another reflection of the interests and power of a highly class-conscious business system that's always fighting an intense class war. These issues are coming up again with respect to the Internet [a worldwide computer network] and the new interactive communications technologies. And we're going to find exactly the same conflict again. It's going on right now.

I don't see why we should have had any long-term hopes for something different. Commercially run radio is going to have certain purposes—namely, the ones determined by people who own and control it.

As I mentioned earlier, they don't want decision-makers and participants; they want a passive, obedient population of consumers and political spectators—a community of people who are so atomized and isolated that they can't put together their limited resources and become an independent, powerful force that will chip away at concentrated power.

Does ownership always determine content?

In some far-reaching sense it does, because if content ever goes beyond the bounds owners will tolerate, they'll surely move in to limit it. But there's a fair amount of flexibility.

Investors don't go down to the television studio and make sure that the local talk-show host or reporter is doing what they want. There are other, subtler, more complex mechanisms that make it fairly certain that the people on the air will do what the owners and investors want. There's a whole, long, filtering process that makes sure that people only rise through the system to become managers, editors, etc., if they've internalized the values of the owners.

At that point, they can describe themselves as quite free. So you'll occasionally find some flaming independent-liberal type like Tom Wicker who writes, Look, nobody tells me what to say. I say whatever I want. It's an absolutely free system.

And, for *him,* that's true. After he'd demonstrated to the satisfaction of his bosses that he'd internalized their values, he was entirely free to write whatever he wanted.

Both PBS and NPR [National Public Radio] frequently come under attack for being left-wing.

That's an interesting sort of critique. In fact, PBS and NPR are elite institutions, reflecting by and large the points of view and interests of wealthy professionals who are very close to business circles, including corporate executives. But they happen to be liberal by certain criteria.

That is, if you took a poll among corporate executives on matters like, say, abortion rights, I presume their responses would be what's called liberal. I suspect the same would be true on lots of social issues, like civil rights and freedom of speech. They tend not to be fundamentalist, born-again Christians, for example, and they might tend to be more opposed to the death penalty than the general population. I'm sure you'll find plenty of private wealth and corporate power backing the American Civil Liberties Union.

Since those are aspects of the social order from which they gain, they tend to support them. By these criteria, the people who dominate the country tend to be liberal, and that reflects itself in an institution like PBS.

You've been on NPR just twice in 23 years, and on *The MacNeil-Lehrer News Hour* once in its almost 20 years. What if you'd been on *MacNeil-Lehrer* ten times? Would it make a difference?

Not a lot. By the way, I'm not quite sure of those numbers; my own memory isn't that precise. I've been on local PBS stations in particular towns.

I'm talking about the national network.

Then probably something roughly like those numbers is correct. But it wouldn't make a lot of difference.

In fact, in my view, if the managers of the propaganda system were more intelligent, they'd allow more leeway to real dissidents and critics. That would give the impression of broader debate and discussion and hence would have a legitimizing function, but it still wouldn't make much of a dent, given the overwhelming weight of propaganda on the other side. By the way, that propaganda system includes not just how issues are framed in news stories but also how they're presented in entertainment programming— that huge area of the media that's simply devoted to diverting people and making them more stupid and passive.

That's not to say I'm against opening up these media a bit, but I would think it would have a limited effect. What you need is something that presents every day, in a clear and comprehensive fashion, a different picture of the world, one that reflects the concerns and interests of ordinary people, and that takes something like the point of view with regard to democracy and participation that you find in people like Jefferson or Dewey.

Where that happens—and it has happened, even in modern societies—it has effects. In England, for example, you did have major mass media of this kind up until the 1960s, and it helped sustain and enliven a working class culture. It had a big effect on British society.

What do you think about the Internet?

I think that there are good things about it, but there are also aspects of it that concern and worry me. This is an intuitive response—I can't prove it—but my feeling is that, since people aren't Martians or robots, direct face-to-face contact is an extremely important part of human life. It helps develop self-understanding and the growth of a healthy personality.

You just have a different relationship to somebody when you're looking at them than you do when you're punching away at a keyboard and some symbols come back. I suspect that extending that form of abstract and remote relationship, instead of direct, personal contact, is going to have unpleasant effects on what people are like. It will diminish their humanity, I think.

Sports

In 1990, in one of our many interviews, we had a brief discussion about the role and function of sports in American society, part of which was subsequently excerpted in *Harper's.* I've probably gotten more comments about that than anything else I've ever recorded. You really pushed some buttons.

I got some funny reactions, a lot of irate reactions, as if I were somehow taking people's fun away from them. I have nothing against sports. I like to watch a good basketball game and that sort of thing. On the other hand, we have to recognize that the mass hysteria about spectator sports plays a significant role.

First of all, spectator sports make people more passive, because you're not doing them—you're watching somebody doing them. Secondly, they engender jingoist and chauvinist attitudes, sometimes to quite an extreme degree.

I saw something in the newspapers just a day or two ago about how high school teams are now so antagonistic and passionately committed to winning at all costs that they had to abandon the standard handshake before or after the game. These kids can't even do civil things like greeting one another because they're ready to kill one another.

It's spectator sports that engender those attitudes, particularly when they're designed to organize a community to be hysterically committed to their gladiators. That's very dangerous, and it has lots of deleterious effects.

I was reading something about the glories of the information superhighway not too long ago. I can't quote it exactly, but it was talking about how wonderful and empowering these new interactive technologies are going to be. Two basic examples were given.

For women, interactive technologies are going to offer highly improved methods of home shopping. So you'll be able to watch the tube and some model will appear with a product and you're supposed to think, God, I've got to have that. So you press a button and they deliver it to your door within a couple of hours. That's how interactive technology is supposed to liberate women.

For men, the example involved the Super Bowl. Every red-blooded American male is glued to it. Today, all they can do is watch it and cheer and drink beer, but the new interactive technology will let them actually participate in it. While the quarterback is in the huddle calling the next play, the people watching will be able to decide what the play should be.

If they think he should pass, or run, or punt, or whatever, they'll be able to punch that into their computer and their vote will be recorded. It won't have any effect on what the quarterback does, of course, but after the play the television channel will be able to put up the numbers—63% said he should have passed, 24% said he should have run, etc.

That's interactive technology for men. Now you're really participating in the world. Forget about all this business of deciding what ought to happen with health care—now you're doing something really important.

This scenario for interactive technology reflects an understanding of the stupefying effect spectator sports have in making people passive, atomized, obedient nonpartici-pants—nonquestioning, easily controlled and easily disciplined.

At the same time, athletes are lionized or—in the case of Tonya Harding, say—demonized.

If you can personalize events of the world—whether it's Hillary Clinton or Tonya Harding—you've succeeded in directing people away from what really matters and is impor-tant. The John F. Kennedy cult is a good example, with the effects it's had on the left.

Religious fundamentalism

In his book *When Time Shall Be No More,* historian Paul Boyer states that, "surveys show that from one third to one half of [all Americans] believe that the future can be interpreted from biblical prophecies." I find this absolutely stunning.

I haven't seen that particular number, but I've seen plenty of things like it. I saw a cross-cultural study a couple of years ago—I think it was published in England—that compared a whole range of societies in terms of beliefs of that kind. The US stood out— it was unique in the industrial world. In fact, the measures for the US were similar to pre-industrial societies.

Why is that?

That's an interesting question. This is a very fundamentalist society. It's like Iran in its degree of fanatic religious commitment. For example, I think about 75% of the US population has a literal belief in the devil.

There was a poll several years ago on evolution. People were asked their opinion on various theories of how the world of living creatures came to be what it is. The number of people who believed in Darwinian evolution was less than 10%. About half the population believed in a church doctrine of divine-guided evolution. Most of the rest presumably believed that the world was created a couple of thousand years ago.

These are very unusual results. Why the US should be off the spectrum on these issues has been discussed and debated for some time.

I remember reading something maybe ten or fifteen years ago by a political scientist who writes about these things, Walter Dean Burnham. He suggested that this may be a reflection of depoliticization—that is, the inability to participate in a meaningful fashion in the political arena may have a rather important psychic effect.

That's not impossible. People will find some ways of identifying themselves, becoming associated with others, taking part in something. They're going to do it some way or other. If they don't have the option to participate in labor unions, or in political organizations that actually function, they'll find other ways. Religious fundamentalism is a classic example.

We see that happening in other parts of the world right now. The rise of what's called

Islamic fundamentalism is, to a significant extent, a result of the collapse of secular nationalist alternatives that were either discredited internally or destroyed.

In the nineteenth century, you even had some conscious efforts on the part of business leaders to promote fire-and-brimstone preachers who led people to look at society in a more passive way. The same thing happened in the early part of the industrial revolution in England. E.P. Thompson writes about it in his classic, *The Making of the English Working Class.*

In a State of the Union speech, Clinton said, "We can't renew our country unless more of us—I mean, all of us—are willing to join churches." What do you make of this?

I don't know exactly what was in his mind, but the ideology is very straightforward. If people devote themselves to activities that are out of the public arena, then we folks in power will be able to run things the way we want.

Don't tread on me

I'm not quite clear about how to formulate this question. It has to do with the nature of US society as exemplified in comments like *do your own thing, go it alone, don't tread on me, the pioneer spirit—* all that deeply individualistic stuff. What does that tell you about American society and culture?

It tells you that the propaganda system is working full-time, because there is no such ideology in the US. Business certainly doesn't believe it. All the way back to the origins of American society, business has insisted on a powerful, interventionist state to support its interests, and it still does.

There's nothing individualistic about corporations. They're big conglomerate institutions, essentially totalitarian in character. Within them, you're a cog in a big machine. There are few institutions in human society that have such strict hierarchy and top-down control as a business organization. It's hardly *don't tread on me*—you're being tread on all the time.

The point of the ideology is to prevent people who are outside the sectors of coordinated power from associating with each other and entering into decision-making in the political arena. The point is to leave the powerful sectors highly integrated and organized, while atomizing everyone else.

That aside, there is another factor. There's a streak of independence and individuality in American culture that I think is a very good thing. This *don't tread on me* feeling is in many respects a healthy one—up to the point where it keeps you from working together with other people.

So it's got a healthy side and a negative side. Naturally it's the negative side that's emphasized in the propaganda and indoctrination.

The world

Toward greater inequality

In his column in the *New York Times,* Anthony Lewis wrote, "Since World War II, the world has experienced extraordinary growth." Meanwhile, at a meeting in Quito, Ecuador, Juan de Dias Parra, the head of the Latin American Association for Human Rights, said, "In Latin America today, there are 7 million more hungry people, 30 million more illiterate people, 10 million more families without homes, 40 million more unemployed persons than there were 20 years ago. There are 240 million human beings in Latin America without the necessities of life, and this when the region is richer and more stable than ever, according to the way the world sees it." How do you reconcile those two statements?

It just depends on which people you're talking about. The World Bank came out with a study on Latin America which warned that Latin America was facing chaos because of the extraordinarily high level of inequality, which is the highest in the world (and that's after a period of substantial growth). Even the things the World Bank cares about are threatened.

The inequality didn't just come from the heavens. There was a struggle over the course of Latin American development back in the mid-1940s, when the new world order of that day was being crafted.

The State Department documents on this are quite interesting. They said that Latin America was swept by what they called the "philosophy of the new nationalism," which called for increasing production for domestic needs and reducing inequality. The basic principle of this new nationalism was that the people of the country should be the prime beneficiary of the country's resources.

The US was sharply opposed to that and came out with an economic charter for the Americas that called for eliminating economic nationalism (as it's also called) in all of its forms and insisting that Latin American development be "complementary" to US development. That means we'll have the advanced industry and the technology and the peons in Latin America will produce export crops and do some simple operations that they can manage. But they won't develop economically the way we did.

Given the distribution of power, the US of course won. In countries like Brazil, we just took over—Brazil has been almost completely directed by American technocrats for about fifty years. Its enormous resources should make it one of the richest countries in the world, and it's had one of the highest growth rates. But thanks to our influence on Brazil's social and economic system, it's ranked around Albania and Paraguay in quality of life measures, infant mortality and so on.

It's true, as Lewis says, that there's been very substantial growth in the world. At the same time, there's incredible poverty and misery, and that's increased even more.

If you compare the percentage of world income held by the richest 20% and the poorest 20%, the gap has dramatically increased over the past thirty years. Comparing rich countries to poor countries, it's about doubled. Comparing rich people to poor people within countries, it's increased far more and is much sharper. That's the consequence of a particular kind of growth.

Do you think this trend of growth rates and poverty rates increasing simultaneously will continue?

Actually, growth rates have been slowing down a lot; in the past twenty years, they've been roughly half of what they were in the preceding twenty years. This tendency toward lower growth will probably continue.

One cause is the enormous increase in the amount of unregulated, speculative capital. The figures are really astonishing. John Eatwell, one of the leading specialists in finance at Cambridge University, estimates that, in 1970, about 90% of international capital was used for trade and long-term investment—more or less productive things—and 10% for speculation. By 1990, those figures had reversed: 90% for speculation and 10% for trade and long-term investment.

Not only has there been radical change in the nature of unregulated financial capital, but the quantity has grown enormously. According to a recent World Bank estimate, $14 *trillion* is now moving around the world, about $1 trillion or so of which moves every *day*.

This huge amount of mostly speculative capital creates pressures for deflationary policies, because what speculative capital wants is low growth and low inflation. It's driving much of the world into a low-growth, low-wage equilibrium.

This is a tremendous attack against government efforts to stimulate the economy. Even in the richer societies, it's very difficult; in the poorer societies, it's hopeless. What happened with Clinton's trivial stimulus package was a good indication. It amounted to nothing—$19 billion, but it was shot down instantly.

In the fall of 1993, the *Financial Times* [of London] trumpeted, "the public sector is in retreat everywhere." Is that true?

It's largely true, but major parts of the public sector are alive and well—in particular those parts that cater to the interests of the wealthy and the powerful. They're declining somewhat, but they're still very lively, and they're not going to disappear.

These developments have been going on for about twenty years now. They had to do with major changes in the international economy that became more or less crystallized by the early 1970s.

For one thing, US economic hegemony over the world had pretty much ended by then, and Europe and Japan had reemerged as major economic and political powers. The costs of the Vietnam War were very significant for the US economy, and extremely beneficial for its rivals. That tended to shift the world balance.

In any event, by the early 1970s, the US felt that it could no longer sustain its traditional role as—essentially—international banker. (This role was codified in the Bretton Woods agreements at the end of the Second World War, in which currencies were regulated relative to one another, and in which the de facto international currency, the US dollar, was fixed to gold.)

Nixon dismantled the Bretton Woods system around 1970. That led to tremendous growth in unregulated financial capital. That growth was rapidly accelerated by the short-term rise in the price of commodities like oil, which led to a huge flow of petrodollars into the international system. Furthermore, the telecommunications revolution made it extremely easy to transfer capital—or, rather, the electronic equivalent of capital—from one place to another.

There's also been a very substantial growth in the internationalization of production. It's now a lot easier than it was to shift production to foreign countries—generally highly repressive ones—where you get much cheaper labor. So a corporate executive who lives in Greenwich, Connecticut and whose corporate and bank headquarters are in New York City can have a factory somewhere in the Third World. The actual banking operations can take place in various offshore regions where you don't have to worry about supervision—you can launder drug money or whatever you feel like doing. This has led to a totally different economy.

With the pressure on corporate profits that began in the early 1970s, a big attack was launched on the whole social contract that had developed through a century of struggle and that had been more or less codified around the end of the Second World War with the New Deal and the European social welfare states. The attack was led by the US and England, and by now has reached continental Europe.

It's led to a serious decline in unionization, which carries with it a decline in wages and other forms of protection, and to a very sharp polarization of the society, primarily in the US and Britain (but it's spreading).

Driving in to work this morning, I was listening to the BBC [the British Broadcasting Company, Britain's national broadcasting service]. They reported a new study that found that children living in workhouses a century ago had better nutritional standards than millions of poor children in Britain today.

That's one of the grand achievements of [former British Prime Minister Margaret] Thatcher's revolution. She succeeded in devastating British society and destroying large parts of British manufacturing capacity. England is now one of the poorest countries in Europe—not much above Spain and Portugal, and well below Italy.

The American achievement was rather similar. We're a much richer, more powerful country, so it isn't possible to achieve quite what Britain achieved. But the Reaganites succeeded in driving US wages down so far that we're now the second lowest of the major industrial countries, barely above Britain. Labor costs in Italy are about 20% higher than in the US, and in Germany they're maybe 60% higher.

Along with that goes a deterioration of the general social contract and a breakdown of the kind of public spending that benefits the less privileged. Needless to say, the kind of public spending that benefits the wealthy and the privileged—which is enormous—remains fairly stable.

"Free trade"

My local newspaper, the Boulder [Colorado] *Daily Camera,* which is part of the Knight-Ridder chain, ran a series of questions and answers about GATT [the General Agreement on Tariffs and Trade]. They answered the question, Who would benefit from a GATT agreement? by writing, "Consumers would be the big winners." Does that track with your understanding?

If they mean rich consumers—yes, they'll gain. But much of the population will see a decline in wages, both in rich countries and poor ones. Take a look at NAFTA [the North American Free Trade Agreement], where the analyses have already been done. The day after NAFTA passed, the *New York Times* had its first article on its expected impact in the New York region. (Its conclusions apply to GATT too.)

It was a very upbeat article. They talked about how wonderful NAFTA was going to be. They said that finance and services will be particularly big winners. Banks, investment firms, PR firms, corporate law firms will do just great. Some manufacturers will also benefit—for example, publishing and the chemical industry, which is highly capital-intensive, with not many workers to worry about.

Then they said, Well, there'll be some losers too: women, Hispanics, other minorities, and semi-skilled workers—in other words, about two-thirds of the work force. But everyone else will do fine.

Just as anyone who was paying attention knew, the purpose of NAFTA was to create an even smaller sector of highly privileged people—investors, professionals, managerial classes. (Bear in mind that this is a rich country, so this privileged sector, although smaller, still isn't tiny.) It will work fine for them, and the general population will suffer.

The prediction for Mexico is exactly the same. The leading financial journal in Mexico, which is very pro-NAFTA, estimated that Mexico would lose about 25% of its manufacturing capacity in the first few years and about 15% of its manufacturing labor force. In addition, cheap US agricultural exports are expected to drive several million people off the land. That's going to mean a substantial increase in the unemployed workforce in Mexico, which of course will drive down wages.

On top of that, union organizing is essentially impossible. Corporations can operate internationally, but unions can't—so there's no way for the work force to fight back against the internationalization of production. The net effect is expected to be a decline in wealth and income for most people in Mexico and for most people in the US.

The strongest NAFTA advocates point that out in the small print. My colleague at MIT, Paul Krugman, is a specialist in international trade and, interestingly, one of the economists who's done some of the theoretical work showing why free trade doesn't work. He was nevertheless an enthusiastic advocate of NAFTA—which is, I should stress, not a free trade agreement.

He agreed with the *Times* that unskilled workers—about 70% of the work force—would lose. The Clinton administration has various fantasies about retraining workers, but that would probably have very little impact. In any case, they're doing nothing about it.

The same thing is true of skilled white-collar workers. You can get software programmers in India who are very well trained at a fraction of the cost of Americans. Somebody involved in this business recently told me that Indian programmers are actually being brought to the US and put into what are kind of like slave labor camps and kept at Indian salaries—a fraction of American salaries—doing software development. So that kind of work can be farmed out just as easily.

The search for profit, when it's unconstrained and free from public control, will naturally try to repress people's lives as much as possible. The executives wouldn't be doing their jobs otherwise.

What accounted for all the opposition to NAFTA?

The original expectation was that NAFTA would just sail through. Nobody would even know what it was. So it was signed in secret. It was put on a fast track in Congress, meaning essentially no discussion. There was virtually no media coverage. Who was going to know about a complex trade agreement?

That didn't work, and there are a number of reasons why it didn't. For one thing, the labor movement got organized for once and made an issue of it. Then there was this sort of maverick third-party candidate, Ross Perot, who managed to make it a public issue. And it turned out that as soon as the public learned anything about NAFTA, they were pretty much opposed.

I followed the media coverage on this, which was extremely interesting. Usually the media try to keep their class loyalties more or less in the background—they try to pretend they don't have them. But on this issue, the bars were down. They went berserk, and toward the end, when it looked like NAFTA might not pass, they just turned into raving maniacs.

But despite this enormous media barrage and the government attack and huge amounts of corporate lobbying (which totally dwarfed all the other lobbying, of course), the level of opposition remained pretty stable. Roughly 60% or so of those who had an opinion remained opposed.

The same sort of media barrage influenced the Gore-Perot television debate. I didn't watch it, but friends who did thought Perot just wiped Gore off the map. But the media proclaimed that Gore won a massive victory.

In polls the next day, people were asked what they thought about the debate. The percentage who thought that Perot had been smashed was far higher than the percentage who'd seen the debate, which means that most people were being told what to think by the media, not coming to their own conclusions.

Incidentally, what was planned for NAFTA worked for GATT—there was virtually no public opposition to it, or even awareness of it. It was rammed through in secret, as intended.

What about the position people like us find ourselves in of being "against," of being "anti-," reactive rather than pro-active?

NAFTA's a good case, because very few NAFTA critics were opposed to any agreement. Virtually everyone—the labor movement, the Congressional Office of Technology Assessment (a major report that was suppressed) and other critics (including me)— was saying there'd be nothing wrong with *a* North American Free Trade Agreement, but not this one. It should be different, and here are the ways in which it should be different— in some detail. Even Perot had constructive proposals. But all that was suppressed.

What's left is the picture that, say, Anthony Lewis portrayed in the *Times:* jingoist fanatics screaming about NAFTA. Incidentally, what's called the left played the same game. James Galbraith is an economist at the University of Texas. He had an article in a sort of left-liberal journal, *World Policy Review,* in which he discussed an article in which I said the opposite of what he attributed to me (of course—but that's typical).

Galbraith said there's this jingoist left— nationalist fanatics—who don't want Mexican workers to improve their lives. Then he went on about how the Mexicans are in favor of NAFTA. (True, if by "Mexicans" you mean Mexican industrialists and executives and corporate lawyers, not Mexican workers and peasants.)

All the way from people like James Galbraith and Anthony Lewis to way over to the right, you had this very useful fabrication—that critics of NAFTA were reactive and negative and jingoist and against progress and just wanted to go back to old-time protectionism. When you have essentially total control of the information system, it's rather easy to convey that image. But it simply isn't true.

Anthony Lewis also wrote, "The engine for [the world's] growth has been...vastly increased...international trade." Do you agree?

His use of the word "trade," while conventional, is misleading. The latest figures available (from about ten years ago—they're probably higher now) show that about 30% or 40% of what's called "world trade" is actually internal transfers within a corporation. I believe that about 70% of Japanese exports to the US are intrafirm transfers of this sort.

So, for example, Ford Motor Company will have components manufactured here in the US and then ship them for assembly to a plant in Mexico where the workers get much lower wages and where Ford doesn't have to worry about pollution, unions and all that nonsense. Then they ship the assembled part back here.

About half of what are called US exports to Mexico are intrafirm transfers of this sort. They don't enter the Mexican market, and there's no meaningful sense in which they're exports to Mexico. Still, that's called "trade."

The corporations that do this are huge totalitarian institutions, and they aren't governed by market principles—in fact, they promote severe market distortions. For example, a US corporation that has an outlet in Puerto Rico may decide to take its profits in Puerto Rico, because of tax rebates. It shifts its prices around, using what's called "transfer pricing," so it doesn't seem to be making a profit here.

There are estimates of the scale of governmental operations that interfere with trade, but I know of no estimates of internal corporate interferences with market processes. They're no doubt vast in scale, and are sure to be extended by the trade agreements.

GATT and NAFTA ought to be called "investor rights agreements," not "free trade agreements." One of their main purposes is to extend the ability of corporations to carry out market-distorting operations internally.

So when people like [Clinton's National Security Advisor] Anthony Lake talk about enlarging market democracy, he's enlarging something, but it's not markets and it's not democracy.

Mexico (and South Central LA)

I found the mainstream media coverage of Mexico during the NAFTA debate somewhat uneven. The *New York Times* has allowed in a number of articles that official corruption was—and is—widespread in Mexico. In fact, in one editorial, they virtually conceded that Salinas stole the 1988 presidential election. Why did that information come out?

I think it's impossible to repress. Furthermore, there were scattered reports in the *Times* of popular protest against NAFTA. Tim Golden, their reporter in Mexico, had a story a couple of weeks before the vote, probably in early November [1993], in which he said that lots of Mexican workers were concerned that their wages would decline after NAFTA. Then came the punch line.

He said that that undercuts the position of people like Ross Perot and others who think that NAFTA is going to harm American workers for the benefit of Mexican workers. In other words, the fact that they're *all* going to get screwed was presented as a critique of the people who were opposing NAFTA here!

There was very little discussion here of the large-scale popular protest in Mexico, which included, for example, the largest non-governmental trade union. (The main trade union is about as independent as the Soviet trade unions were, but there are some independent ones, and they were opposed to the agreement.)

The environmental movements and most of the other popular movements were opposed. The Mexican Bishops' Conference strongly endorsed the position the Latin American bishops took when they met at Santa Domingo [in the Dominican Republic] in December 1992.

That meeting in Santa Domingo was the first major conference of Latin American bishops since the ones at Puebla [Mexico] and Medellín [Colombia] back in the 1960s and 1970s. The Vatican tried to control it this time to make sure that they wouldn't come out with these perverse ideas about liberation theology and the preferential option for the poor. But despite a very firm Vatican hand, the bishops came out quite strongly against neoliberalism and structural adjustment and these free-market-for-the-poor policies. That wasn't reported here, to my knowledge.

There's been significant union-busting in Mexico.

Ford and VW are two big examples. A few years ago, Ford simply fired its entire Mexican work force and would only rehire, at much lower wages, those who agreed not to join a union. Ford was backed in this by the always-ruling PRI [the Institutional Revolutionary Party, which has controlled Mexico since the 1920s].

VW's case was pretty much the same. They fired workers who supported an independent union and only rehired, at lower wages, those who agreed not to support it.

A few weeks after the NAFTA vote in the US, workers at a GE and Honeywell plant in Mexico were fired for union activities. I don't know what the final outcome will be, but that's exactly the purpose of things like NAFTA.

In early January [1994], you were asked by an editor at the *Washington Post* to submit an article on the New Year's Day uprising in Chiapas [a state at the southern tip of Mexico, next to Guatemala]. Was this the first time the *Post* had asked you to write something?

It was the first time ever. I was kind of surprised, since I'm never asked to write for a national newspaper. So I wrote the article—it was for the *Sunday Outlook* section—but it didn't appear.

Was there an explanation?

No. It went to press, as far as I know. The editor who commissioned it called me, apparently after the deadline, to say that it looked OK to him but that it had simply been cancelled at some higher level. I don't know any more about it than that.

But I can guess. The article was about Chiapas, but it was also about NAFTA, and I think the *Washington Post* has been even more extreme than the *Times* in refusing to allow any discussion of that topic.

What happened in Chiapas doesn't come as very much of a surprise. At first, the government thought they'd just destroy the rebellion with tremendous violence, but then they backed off and decided to do it by more subtle violence, when nobody was looking. Part of the reason they backed off is surely their fear that there was just too much sympathy all over Mexico; if they were too up front about suppression, they'd cause themselves a lot of problems, all the way up to the US border.

The Mayan Indians in Chiapas are in many ways the most oppressed people in Mexico. Nevertheless, their problems are shared by a large majority of the Mexican population. This decade of neoliberal reforms has led to very little economic progress in Mexico but has sharply polarized the society. Labor's share in income has declined radically. The number of billionaires has shot up.

In that unpublished *Post* article, you wrote that the protest of the Indian peasants in Chiapas gives "only a bare glimpse of time bombs waiting to explode, not only in Mexico." What did you have in mind?

Take South Central Los Angeles, for example. In many respects, they are different societies, of course, but there are points of similarity to the Chiapas rebellion. South Central LA is a place where people once had jobs and lives, and those have been destroyed—in large part by the socio-economic processes we've been talking about.

For example, furniture factories went to Mexico, where they can pollute more cheaply. Military industry has somewhat declined. People used to have jobs in the steel industry, and they don't any more. So they rebelled.

The Chiapas rebellion was quite different. It was much more organized, and much more constructive. That's the difference between an utterly demoralized society like South Central Los Angeles and one that still retains some sort of integrity and community life.

When you look at consumption levels, doubtless the peasants in Chiapas are poorer than people in South Central LA. There are fewer television sets per capita. But by other, more significant criteria—like social cohesion—Chiapas is considerably more advanced. In the US, we've succeeded not only in polarizing communities but also in destroying their structures. That's why you have such rampant violence.

Haiti

Let's stay in Latin America and the Caribbean, which [former US Secretary of War and of State] Henry Stimson called "our little region over here which has never bothered anyone." Jean-Bertrand Aristide was elected president of Haiti in what's been widely described as a free and democratic election. Would you comment on what's happened since?

When Aristide won in December 1990 (he took office in February, 1991), it was a big surprise. He was swept into power by a network of popular grassroots organizations, what was called *Lavalas*—the flood—which outside observers just weren't aware of (since they don't pay attention to what happens among poor people). There had been very extensive and very successful organizing, and out of nowhere came this massive popular organization that managed to sweep their candidate into power.

The US was willing to support a democratic election, figuring that its candidate, a former World Bank official named Marc Bazin, would easily win. He had all the resources and support, and it looked like a shoe-in. He ended up getting 14% of the vote, and Aristide got about 67%.

The only question in the mind of anybody who knows a little history should have been, How is the US going to get rid of Aristide? The disaster became even worse in the first seven months of Aristide's office. There were some really amazing developments.

Haiti is, of course, an extremely impoverished country, with awful conditions. Aristide was nevertheless beginning to get places. He was able to reduce corruption extensively, and to trim a highly bloated state bureaucracy. He won a lot of international praise for this, even from the international lending institutions, which were offering him loans and preferential terms because they liked what he was doing.

Furthermore, he cut back on drug trafficking. The flow of refugees to the US virtually stopped. Atrocities were reduced to way below what they had been or would become. There was a considerable degree of popular engagement in what was going on, although the contradictions were already beginning to show up, and there were constraints on what he could do.

All of this made Aristide even more unacceptable from the US point of view, and we tried to undermine him through what were called—naturally—"democracy-enhancing programs." The US, which had never cared at all about centralization of power in Haiti when its own favored dictators were in charge, all of a sudden began setting up alternative institutions that aimed at undermining executive power, supposedly in the interests of greater democracy. A number of these alleged human rights and labor groups became the governing authorities after the coup, which came on September 30, 1991.

In response to the coup, the Organization of American States declared an embargo of Haiti; the US joined it, but with obvious reluctance. The Bush administration focused attention on Aristide's alleged atrocities and undemocratic activities, downplaying the major atrocities which took place right after the coup. The media went along with Bush's line, of course. While people were getting slaughtered in the streets of Port-au-Prince [Haiti's capital], the media concentrated on alleged human rights abuses under the Aristide government.

Refugees started fleeing again, because the situation was deteriorating so rapidly. The Bush administration blocked them—instituted a blockade, in effect—to send them back. Within a couple of months, the Bush administration had already undermined the embargo by allowing a minor exception—US-owned companies would be permitted to ignore it. The *New York Times* called that "fine-tuning" the embargo to improve the restoration of democracy!

Meanwhile, the US, which is known to be able to exert pressure when it feels like it, found no way to influence anyone else to observe the embargo, including the Dominican Republic next door. The whole thing was mostly a farce. Pretty soon Marc Bazin, the US candidate, was in power as prime minister, with the ruling generals behind him. That year—1992—US trade with Haiti was not very much below the norm, despite the so-called embargo (Commerce Department figures showed that, but I don't think the press ever reported it).

During the 1992 campaign, Clinton bitterly attacked the Bush administration for its inhuman policy of returning refugees to this torture chamber—which is, incidentally, a flat violation of the Universal Declaration of Human Rights, which we claim to uphold. Clinton claimed he was going to change all that, but his first act after being elected, even before he took office, was to impose even harsher measures to force fleeing refugees back into this hellhole.

Ever since then, it's simply been a matter of seeing what kind of finessing will be carried out to ensure that Haiti's popularly elected government doesn't come back into office. It doesn't have much longer to run [the next elections are scheduled for December, 1995], so the US has more or less won that game.

Meanwhile, the terror and atrocities increase. The popular organizations are getting decimated. Although the so-called embargo is still in place, US trade continues and, in fact, went up about 50% under Clinton. Haiti, a starving island, is exporting food to the US—about 35 times as much under Clinton as it did under Bush.

Baseballs are coming along nicely. They're produced in US-owned factories where the women who make them get 10¢ an hour—if they meet their quota. Since meeting the quota is virtually impossible, they actually make something like 5¢ an hour.

Softballs from Haiti are advertised in the US as being unusually good because they're hand-dipped into some chemical that makes them hang together properly. The ads don't mention that the chemical the women hand-dip the balls into is toxic and that, as a result, the women don't last very long at this work.

In his exile, Aristide has been asked to make concessions to the military junta.

And to the right-wing business community.

That's kind of curious. For the victim—the aggrieved party—to make concessions to his victimizer.

It's perfectly understandable. The Aristide government had entirely the wrong base of support. The US has tried for a long time to get him to "broaden his government in the interests of democracy."

This means throw out the two-thirds of the population that voted for him and bring in what are called "moderate" elements of the business community—the local owners or managers of those textile and baseball-producing plants, and those who are linked up with US agribusiness. When they're not in power, it's not democratic.

(The extremist elements of the business community think you ought to just slaughter everybody and cut them to pieces and hack off their faces and leave them in ditches. The moderates think you ought to have them working in your assembly plants for 14¢ an hour under indescribable conditions.)

Bring the moderates in and give them power and then we'll have a real democracy. Unfortunately, Aristide—being kind of backward and disruptive—has not been willing to go along with that.

Clinton's policy has gotten so cynical and outrageous that he's lost almost all major domestic support on it. Even the mainstream press is denouncing him at this point. So there will have to be some cosmetic changes made.

But unless there's an awful lot of popular pressure, our policies will continue and pretty soon we'll have the "moderates" in power.

Let's say Aristide is "restored." Given the destruction of popular organizations and the devastation of civil society, what are his and the country's prospects?

Some of the closest observation of this has been done by Americas Watch [a US-based human-rights monitoring organization]. They gave an answer to that question that I thought was plausible. In early 1993, they said that things were reaching the point that even if Aristide were restored, the lively, vibrant civil society based on grassroots organizations that had brought him to power would have been so decimated that it's unlikely that he'd have the popular support to do anything anyway.

I don't know if that's true or not. Nobody knows, any more than anyone knew how powerful those groups were in the first place. Human beings have reserves of courage that are often hard to imagine. But I think that's the plan—to decimate the organizations, to intimidate people so much that it won't matter if you have democratic elections.

There was an interesting conference run by the Jesuits in El Salvador several months before the Salvadoran elections; its final report came out in January [1994]. They were talking about the buildup to the elections and the ongoing terror, which was substantial. They said that the long-term effect of terror— something they've had plenty of experience with—is to domesticate people's aspirations, to make them think there's no alternative, to drive out any hope. Once you've done that, you can have elections without too much fear.

If people are sufficiently intimidated, if the popular organizations are sufficiently destroyed, if the people have had it beaten into their heads that either they accept the rule of those with the guns or else they live and die in unrelieved misery, then your elections will all come out the way you want. And everybody will cheer.

Cuban refugees are considered political and are accepted immediately into the US, while Haitian refugees are termed economic and are refused entry.

If you look at the records, many Haitians who are refused asylum in the US because they aren't considered to be political refugees are found a few days later hacked to pieces in the streets of Haiti.

There were a couple of interesting leaks from the INS [the Immigration and Naturalization Service]. One was from an INS officer who'd been working in our embassy in Port-au-Prince. In an interview with Dennis Bernstein of KPFA [a listener-supported radio station in Berkeley CA], he described in detail how they weren't even making the most perfunctory efforts to check the credentials of people who were applying for political asylum.

At about the same time, a document was leaked from the US interests section in Havana (which reviews applications for asylum in the US) in which they complain that they can't find genuine political asylum cases. The applicants they get can't really claim any serious persecution. At most they claim various kinds of harassment, which aren't enough to qualify them. So—there are the two cases, side by side.

I should mention that the US Justice Department has just made a slight change in US law which makes our violation of international law and the Universal Declaration of Human Rights even more grotesque. Now Haitian refugees who, by some miracle, reach US territorial waters can be shipped back. That's never been allowed before. I doubt that many other countries allow that.

Nicaragua

You recall the uproar in the 1980s about how the Sandinistas were abusing the Miskito Indians on Nicaragua's Atlantic coast. President Reagan, in his inimitable, understated style, said it was "a campaign of virtual genocide." UN Ambassador Jeane Kirkpatrick was a bit more restrained; she called it the "most massive human rights violation in Central America." What's happening now with the Miskitos?

Reagan and Kirkpatrick were talking about an incident in which, according to Americas Watch, several dozen Miskitos were killed and a lot of people were forcefully moved in a rather ugly way in the course of the contra war. The US terrorist forces were moving into the area and this was the Sandinista's reaction.

It was certainly an atrocity, but it's not even visible compared to the ones Jeane Kirkpatrick was celebrating in the neighboring countries at the time—and in Nicaragua, where the overwhelming mass of the atrocities were committed by the so-called "freedom fighters."

What's happening to the Miskitos now? When I was in Nicaragua in October 1993, church sources—the Christian Evangelical Church, primarily, which works in the Atlantic coast—were reporting that 100,000 Miskitos were starving to death as a result of the policies we were imposing on Nicaragua. Not a word about it in the media here. (More recently, it did get some slight reporting.)

People here are worrying about the fact that one typical consequence of US victories in the Third World is that the countries where we win immediately become big centers for drug flow. There are good reasons for that—it's part of the market system we impose on them.

Nicaragua has become a major drug transshipment center. A lot of the drugs go through the Atlantic coast, now that Nicaragua's whole governmental system has collapsed. Drug transhipment areas usually breed major drug epidemics, and there's one among the Miskitos, primarily among the men who dive for lobsters and other shellfish.

Both in Nicaragua and Honduras, these Miskito Indian divers are compelled by economic circumstances to do very deep diving without equipment. Their brains get smashed and they quickly die. In order to try to maintain their work rate, the divers stuff themselves with cocaine. It helps them bear the pain.

There's concern about drugs here, so *that* story got into the press. But of course nobody cares much about the working conditions. After all, it's a standard free-market tech-

nique. You've got plenty of superfluous people, so you make them work under horren-
dous conditions; when they die, you just
bring in others.

China

Let's talk about human rights in one of our major
trading partners—China.

During the Asia Pacific summit in Seattle [in
November, 1993], Clinton announced that we'd
be sending more high-tech equipment to
China. This was in violation of a ban that was
imposed to punish China for its involvement
in nuclear and missile proliferation. The executive branch decided to "reinterpret" the ban,
so we could send China nuclear generators,
sophisticated satellites and supercomputers.

Right in the midst of that summit, a little
tiny report appeared in the papers. In boom-
ing Kwangdong province, the economic miracle of China, 81 women were burned to death
because they were locked into a factory. A
couple of weeks later, 60 workers were killed
in a Hong Kong-owned factory. China's Labor
Ministry reported that 11,000 workers had
been killed in industrial accidents just in the
first eight months of 1993—twice as many as
in the preceding year.

These sort of practices never enter the
human rights debate, but there's been a big
hullabaloo about the use of prison labor—
front-page stories in the *Times*. What's the difference? Very simple. Because prison labor is

state enterprise, it doesn't contribute to private profit. In fact, it undermines private profit, because it competes with private industry. But locking women into factories where they burn to death contributes to private profit.

So prison labor is a human rights violation, but there's no right not to be burned to death. We have to maximize profit. From that principle, everything follows.

Russia

Radio listener: I'd like to ask about US support for Yeltsin vs. democracy in Russia.

Yeltsin was the tough, autocratic Communist Party boss of Sverdlovsk. He's filled his administration with the old party hacks who ran things for him under the earlier Soviet system. The West likes him a lot because he's ruthless and because he's willing to ram through what are called "reforms" (a nice-sounding word).

These "reforms" are designed to return the former Soviet Union to the Third World status it had for the five hundred years before the Bolshevik Revolution. The Cold War was largely about the demand that this huge region of the world once again become what it had been—an area of resources, markets and cheap labor for the West.

Yeltsin is leading the pack on pushing the "reforms." Therefore he's a "democrat." That's what we call a democrat anywhere in the world—someone who follows the Western business agenda.

Dead children and debt service

After you returned from a recent trip to Nicaragua, you told me it's becoming more difficult to tell the difference between economists and Nazi doctors. What did you mean by that?

There's a report from UNESCO (which I didn't see reported in the US media) that estimated the human cost of the "reforms" that aim to return Eastern Europe to its Third World status.

UNESCO estimates that about a half a million deaths a year in Russia since 1989 are the direct result of the reforms, caused by the collapse of health services, the increase in disease, the increase in malnutrition and so on. Killing half a million people a year— that's a fairly substantial achievement for reformers.

The figures are similar, but not quite as bad, in the rest of Eastern Europe. In the Third World, the numbers are fantastic. For example, another UNESCO report estimated that about half a million children in Africa die every year simply from debt service. Not from the whole array of reforms—just from interest on their countries' debts.

It's estimated that about eleven million children die every year from easily curable diseases, most of which could be overcome by treatments that cost a couple of cents. But the economists tell us that to do this would be interference with the market system.

There's nothing new about this. It's very reminiscent of the British economists who, during the Irish potato famine in the mid-nineteenth century, dictated that Ireland must export food to Britain—which it did right through the famine—and that it shouldn't be given food aid because that would violate the sacred principles of political economy. These policies always happen to have the curious property of benefiting the wealthy and harming the poor.

Historical background

How the Nazis won the war

In his book *Blowback,* Chris Simpson described Operation Paper Clip, which involved the importation of large numbers of known Nazi war criminals, rocket scientists, camp guards, etc.

There was also an operation involving the Vatican, the US State Department and British intelligence, which took some of the worst Nazi criminals and used them, at first in Europe. For example, Klaus Barbie, the butcher of Lyon [France], was taken over by US intelligence and put back to work.

Later, when this became an issue, some of his US supervisors didn't understand what the fuss was all about. After all, we'd moved in—we'd replaced the Germans. We needed a guy who would attack the left-wing resistance, and here was a specialist. That's what he'd been doing for the Nazis, so who better could we find to do exactly the same job for us?

When the Americans could no longer protect Barbie, they moved him over to the Vatican-run "ratline," where Croatian Nazi priests and others managed to spirit him off to Latin America. There he continued his career. He became a big drug lord and narco-trafficker, and was involved in a military coup in Bolivia—all with US support.

But Barbie was basically small potatoes. This was a big operation, involving many top Nazis. We managed to get Walter Rauff, the guy who created the gas chambers, off to Chile. Others went to fascist Spain.

General Reinhard Gehlen was the head of German military intelligence on the eastern front. That's where the real war crimes were. Now we're talking about Auschwitz and other death camps. Gehlen and his network of spies and terrorists were taken over quickly by American intelligence and returned to essentially the same roles.

If you look at the American army's counterinsurgency literature (a lot of which is now declassified), it begins with an analysis of the German experience in Europe, written with the cooperation of Nazi officers. Everything is described from the point of view of the Nazis—which techniques for controlling resistance worked, which ones didn't. With barely a change, that was transmuted into American counterinsurgency literature. (This is discussed at some length by Michael McClintock in *Instruments of Statecraft*, a very good book that I've never seen reviewed.)

The US left behind armies the Nazis had established in Eastern Europe, and continued to support them at least into the early 1950s. By then the Russians had penetrated American intelligence, so the air drops didn't work very well any more.

You've said that if a real post-World War II history were ever written, this would be the first chapter.

It would be a part of the first chapter. Recruiting Nazi war criminals and saving them is bad enough, but imitating their activities is worse. So the first chapter would primarily describe US—and some British—operations throughout the world that aimed to destroy the anti-fascist resistance and restore the traditional, essentially fascist, order to power. (I've also discussed this in an earlier book in this series, *What Uncle Sam Really Wants.*)

In Korea (where we ran the operation alone), restoring the traditional order meant killing about 100,000 people just in the late 1940s, before the Korean War began. In Greece, it meant destroying the peasant and worker base of the anti-Nazi resistance and restoring Nazi collaborators to power.

When British and then American troops moved into southern Italy, they simply reinstated the fascist order—the industrialists. But the big problem came when the troops got to the north, which the Italian resistance had already liberated. The place was functioning—

industry was running. We had to dismantle all of that and restore the old order.

Our big criticism of the resistance was that they were displacing the old owners in favor of workers' and community control. Britain and the US called this "arbitrary replacement" of the legitimate owners. The resistance was also giving jobs to more people than were strictly needed for the greatest economic efficiency (that is, for maximum profit-making). We called this "hiring excess workers."

In other words, the resistance was trying to democratize the workplace and to take care of the population. That was understandable, since many Italians were starving. But starving people were their problem—our problem was to eliminate the hiring of excess workers and the arbitrary dismissal of owners, which we did.

Next we worked on destroying the democratic process. The left was obviously going to win the elections; it had a lot of prestige from the resistance, and the traditional conservative order had been discredited. The US wouldn't tolerate that. At its first meeting, in 1947, the National Security Council decided to withhold food and use other sorts of pressure to undermine the election.

But what if the communists still won? In its first report, NSC 1, the council made plans for that contingency: the US would declare a national emergency, put the Sixth Fleet on alert in the Mediterranean and support paramilitary activities to overthrow the Italian government.

That's a pattern that's been relived over and over. If you look at France and Germany and Japan, you get pretty much the same story.

Nicaragua is another case. You strangle them, you starve them, and then you have an election and everybody talks about how wonderful democracy is.

The person who opened up this topic (as he did many others) was Gabriel Kolko, in his classic book *Politics of War* in 1968. It was mostly ignored, but it's a terrific piece of work. A lot of the documents weren't around then, but his picture turns out to be quite accurate.

Chile

Richard Nixon's death generated much fanfare. Henry Kissinger said in his eulogy: "The world is a better place, a safer place, because of Richard Nixon." I'm sure he was thinking of Laos, Cambodia and Vietnam. But let's focus on one place that wasn't mentioned in all the media hoopla— Chile—and see how it's a "better, safer place." In early September 1970, Salvador Allende was elected president of Chile in a democratic election. What were his politics?

He was basically a social democrat, very much of the European type. He was calling for minor redistribution of wealth, to help the poor. (Chile was a very inegalitarian society.) Allende was a doctor, and one of the things he did was to institute a free milk program for half a million very poor, malnourished children. He called for nationalization of major industries like copper mining, and for a policy of international independence—meaning that Chile wouldn't simply subordinate itself to the US, but would take more of an independent path.

Was the election he won free and democratic?

Not entirely, because there were major efforts to disrupt it, mainly by the US. It wasn't the first time the US had done that. For example, our government intervened massively to prevent Allende from winning the preceding election, in 1964. In fact, when the Church Committee investigated years later, they discovered that the US spent more money per capita to get the candidate it favored elected in Chile in 1964 than was spent by both candidates (Johnson and Goldwater) in the 1964 election in the US!

Similar measures were undertaken in 1970 to try to prevent a free and democratic election. There was a huge amount of black propaganda about how if Allende won, mothers would be sending their children off to Russia to become slaves—stuff like that. The US also threatened to destroy the economy, which it could—and did—do.

Nevertheless, Allende won. A few days after his victory, Nixon called in CIA Director Richard Helms, Kissinger and others for a meeting on Chile. Can you describe what happened?

As Helms reported in his notes, there were two points of view. The "soft line" was, in Nixon's words, to "make the economy scream." The "hard line" was simply to aim for a military coup.

Our ambassador to Chile, Edward Korry, who was a Kennedy liberal type, was given the job of implementing the "soft line." Here's how he described his task: "to do all within our power to condemn Chile and the Chileans to utmost deprivation and poverty." That was the soft line.

There was a massive destabilization and disinformation campaign. The CIA planted stories in *El Mercurio* [Chile's most prominent paper] and fomented labor unrest and strikes.

They really pulled out the stops on this one. Later, when the military coup finally came [in September, 1973] and the government was overthrown—and thousands of people were being imprisoned, tortured and slaughtered—the economic aid which had been cancelled immediately began to flow again. As a reward for the military junta's achievement in reversing Chilean democracy, the US gave massive support to the new government.

Our ambassador to Chile brought up the question of torture to Kissinger. Kissinger rebuked him sharply—saying something like, Don't give me any of those political science lectures. We don't care about torture—we care about important things. Then he explained what the important things were.

Kissinger said he was concerned that the success of social democracy in Chile would be contagious. It would infect southern Europe—southern Italy, for example—and would lead to the possible success of what was then called Eurocommunism (meaning that Communist parties would hook up with social democratic parties in a united front).

Actually, the Kremlin was just as much opposed to Eurocommunism as Kissinger was, but this gives you a very clear picture of what the domino theory is all about. Even

Kissinger, mad as he is, didn't believe that Chilean armies were going to descend on Rome. It wasn't going to be that kind of an influence. He was worried that successful economic development, where the economy produces benefits for the general population—not just profits for private corporations—would have a contagious effect.

In those comments, Kissinger revealed the basic story of US foreign policy for decades.

You see that pattern repeating itself in Nicaragua in the 1980s.

Everywhere. The same was true in Vietnam, in Cuba, in Guatemala, in Greece. That's always the worry—the threat of a good example.

Kissinger also said, again speaking about Chile, "I don't see why we should have to stand by and let a country go Communist due to the irresponsibility of its own people."

As the *Economist* put it, we should make sure that policy is insulated from politics. If people are irresponsible, they should just be cut out of the system.

In recent years, Chile's economic growth rate has been heralded in the press.

Chile's economy isn't doing badly, but it's based almost entirely on exports—fruit, copper and so on—and thus is very vulnerable to world markets.

There was a really funny pair of stories yesterday. The *New York Times* had one about how everyone in Chile is so happy and satisfied with the political system that nobody's paying much attention to the upcoming election.

But the London *Financial Times* (which is the world's most influential business paper, and hardly radical) took exactly the opposite tack. They cited polls that showed that 75% of the population was very "disgruntled" with the political system (which allows no options).

There is indeed apathy about the election, but that's a reflection of the breakdown of Chile's social structure. Chile was a very vibrant, lively, democratic society for many, many years—into the early 1970s. Then, through a reign of fascist terror, it was essentially depoliticized. The breakdown of social relations is pretty striking. People work alone, and just try to fend for themselves. The retreat into individualism and personal gain is the basis for the political apathy.

Nathaniel Nash wrote the *Times'* Chile story. He said that many Chileans have painful memories of Salvador Allende's fiery speeches, which led to the coup in which thousands of people were killed [including Allende]. Notice that they don't have painful memories of the torture, of the fascist terror—just of Allende's speeches as a popular candidate.

Cambodia

Would you talk a little about the notion of unworthy vs. worthy victims?

[*NY Newsday* columnist and former *New York Times* reporter] Sidney Schanberg wrote an oped piece in the *Boston Globe* in which he blasted Senator Kerry of Massachusetts for being two-faced because Kerry refused to concede that the Vietnamese have not been entirely forthcoming about American POWs. Nobody, according to Schanberg, is willing to tell the truth about this.

He says the government ought to finally have the honesty to say that it left Indochina without accounting for all the Americans. Of course, it wouldn't occur to him to suggest that the government should be honest enough to say that we killed a couple of million people and destroyed three countries and left them in total wreckage and have been strangling them ever since.

It's particularly striking that this is Sidney Schanberg, a person of utter depravity. He's regarded as the great conscience of the press because of his courage in exposing the crimes of our official enemies—namely, Pol Pot [leader of Cambodia's Khmer Rouge rebel army]. He also happened to be the main US reporter in Phnom Penh [Cambodia's capital] in 1973. This was at the peak of the US bombardment of inner Cambodia, when hundreds of thousands of people (according to the best estimates) were being killed and the society was being wiped out.

Nobody knows very much about the bombing campaign and its effects because people like Sidney Schanberg refused to cover it. It wouldn't have been hard for him to cover it. He wouldn't have to go trekking off into the jungle—he could walk across the street from his fancy hotel in Phnom Penh and talk to any of the hundreds of thousands of refugees who'd been driven from the countryside into the city.

I went through all of his reporting—it's reviewed in detail in *Manufacturing Consent*, my book with Edward Herman [currently editor of *Lies of Our Times*]. You'll find a few scattered sentences here and there about the bombing, but not a single interview with the refugees.

There is one American atrocity he did report (for about three days); *The Killing Fields*, the movie that's based on his story, opens by describing it. What's the one report? American planes hit the wrong village—a government village. That's an atrocity; that he covered. How about when they hit the right village? We don't care about that.

Incidentally, the United States' own record with POWs has been atrocious—not only in Vietnam, where it was monstrous, but in Korea, where it was even worse. And after WW II, we kept POWs illegally under confinement, as did the British.

World War II POWs

Other Losses, a Canadian book, alleges it was official US policy to withhold food from German prisoners in World War II. Many of them supposedly starved to death.

That's James Bacque's book. There's been a lot of controversy about the details, and I'm not sure what the facts of the matter are. On the other hand, there are things about which there's no controversy. Ed Herman and I wrote about them back in the late 1970s.

Basically, the Americans ran what were called "re-education camps" for German POWs (the name was ultimately changed to something equally Orwellian). These camps were hailed as a tremendous example of our humanitarianism, because we were teaching the prisoners democratic ways (in other words, we were indoctrinating them into accepting our beliefs).

The prisoners were treated very brutally, starved, etc. Since these camps were in gross violation of international conventions, they were kept secret. We were afraid that the Germans might retaliate and treat American prisoners the same way.

Furthermore, the camps continued after the war; I forget for how long, but I think the US kept German POWs until mid-1946. They were used for forced labor, beaten and killed. It was even worse in England. They kept their German POWs until mid-1948. It was all totally illegal.

Finally, there was public reaction in Britain. The person who started it off was Peggy Duff, a marvelous woman who died a couple of years ago. She was later one of the leading figures in the CND [the Campaign for Nuclear Disarmament] and the international peace movement during the 1960s and 1970s, but she started off her career with a protest against the treatment of German POWs.

Incidentally, why only German POWs? What about the Italians? Germany's a very efficient country, so they've published volumes of documents on what happened to their POWs. But Italy's sort of laid back, so there was no research on their POWs. We don't know anything about them, although they were surely treated much worse.

When I was a kid, there was a POW camp right next to my high school. There were conflicts among the students over the issue of taunting the prisoners. The students couldn't physically attack the prisoners, because they were behind a barrier, but they threw things at them and taunted them. There were a group of us who thought this was horrifying and objected to it, but there weren't many.

Miscellaneous topics

Consumption vs. well-being

The United States, with 5% of the world's population, consumes 40% of the world's resources. You don't have to be a genius to figure out what that's leading to.

For one thing, a lot of that consumption is artificially induced—it doesn't have to do with people's real wants and needs. People would probably be better off and happier if they didn't have a lot of those things.

If you measure economic health by profits, then such consumption is healthy. If you measure the consumption by what it means to people, it's very unhealthy, particularly in the long term.

A huge amount of business propaganda—that is, the output of the public relations and advertising industry—is simply an effort to create wants. This has been well understood for a long time; in fact, it goes back to the early days of the Industrial Revolution.

For another thing, those who have more money tend to consume more, for obvious reasons. So consumption is skewed towards luxuries for the wealthy rather than towards necessities for the poor. That's true within the US and on a global scale as well. The richer countries are the higher consumers by a large measure, and within the richer countries, the wealthy are higher consumers by a large measure.

Cooperative enterprises

There's a social experiment in Mondragón in the Basque region of Spain. Can you describe it?

Mondragón is basically a very large worker-owned cooperative with many different industries in it, including some fairly sophisticated manufacturing. It's economically quite successful, but since it's inserted into a capitalist economy, it's no more committed to sustainable growth than any other part of the capitalist economy is.

Internally, it's not worker-controlled—it's manager-controlled. So it's a mixture of what's sometimes called industrial democracy—which means ownership, at least in principle, by the work force—along with elements of hierarchic domination and control (as opposed to worker management).

I mentioned earlier that businesses are about as close to strict totalitarian structures as any human institutions are. Something like Mondragón is considerably less so.

The coming eco-catastrophe

Radio listener: What's happening in the growing economies in Southeast Asia, China, etc.? Is it going to be another example of capitalist exploitation, or can we expect to see some kind of change in their awareness?

Right now, it's catastrophic. In countries like Thailand or China, ecological catastrophes are looming. These are countries where growth is being fueled by multinational investors for whom the environment is what's called an "externality" (which means you don't pay any attention to it). So if you destroy the forests in Thailand, say, that's OK as long as you make a short-term profit out of it.

In China, the disasters which lie not too far ahead could be extraordinary—simply because of the country's size. The same is true throughout Southeast Asia.

But when the environmental pressures become such that the very survival of people is jeopardized, do you see any change in the actions?

Not unless people react. If power is left in the hands of transnational investors, the people will just die.

Nuclear power

At a conference in Washington DC, a woman in the audience got up and decried the fact that you're in favor of nuclear power. Are you?

No. I don't think anybody's in favor of nuclear power, even business, because it's too expensive. But what I am in favor of is being rational on the topic. That means recognizing that the question of nuclear power isn't a moral one—it's a technical one. You have to ask what the consequences of nuclear power are, versus the alternatives.

There's a range of other alternatives, including conservation, solar and so on. Each has its own advantages and disadvantages. But imagine that the only alternatives were hydrocarbons and nuclear power. If you had to have one or the other, you'd have to ask yourself which is more dangerous to the environment, to human life, to human society. It's not an entirely simple question.

For example, suppose that fusion were a feasible alternative. It could turn out to be nonpolluting. But there are also negative factors. Any form of nuclear power involves quite serious problems of radioactive waste disposal, and can also contribute to nuclear weapons proliferation. Fusion would require a high degree of centralization of state power too.

On the other hand, the hydrocarbon industry, which is highly polluting, also promotes centralization. The energy corporations are some of the biggest in the world, and the

Pentagon system is constructed to a significant degree to maintain their power.

In other words, there are questions that have to be thought through. They're not simple.

The family

You've suggested that, to further democracy, people should be "seeking out authoritarian structures and challenging them, eliminating any form of absolute power and hierarchic power." How would that work in a family structure?

In any structure, including a family structure, there are various forms of authority. A patriarchal family may have very rigid authority, with the father setting rules that others adhere to, and in some cases even administering severe punishment if there's a violation of them.

There are other hierarchical relations among siblings, between the mother and father, gender relations, and so on. These all have to be questioned. Sometimes I think you'll find that there's a legitimate claim to authority—that is, the challenge to authority can sometimes be met. But the burden of proof is always on the authority.

So, for example, some form of control over children is justified. It's fair to prevent a child from putting his or her hand in the oven, say, or from running across the street in traffic. It's proper to place clear bounds on children. They want them—they want to understand where they are in the world.

However, all of these things have to be done with sensitivity and with self-awareness and with the recognition that any authoritarian role requires justification. It's never self-justifying.

When does a child get to the point where the parent doesn't need to provide authority?

I don't think there are formulas for this. For one thing, we don't have solid scientific knowledge and understanding of these things. A mixture of experience and intuition, plus a certain amount of study, yields a limited framework of understanding (about which people may certainly differ). And there are also plenty of individual differences.

So I don't think there's a simple answer to that question. The growth of autonomy and self-control, and expansion of the range of legitimate choices, and the ability to exercise them—that's growing up.

What you can do

Radio listener: Taking it down to the individual, personal level, I got a notice in my public service bill that said they're asking for a rate hike. I work, and I really don't have the time to sit down and write a letter of protest. This happens all the time, and not just with me. Most people don't have time to be active politically to change something. So those rate hikes go through without anybody ever really pointing out what's going on. I've often wondered why there isn't a limitation on the amount of profit any business can make (I know this probably isn't democratic).

I think it's highly democratic. There's nothing in the principle of democracy that says that power and wealth should be so highly concentrated that democracy becomes a sham.

But your first point is quite correct. If you're a working person, you just don't have time—alone—to take on the power company. That's exactly what organization is about. That's exactly what unions are for, and political parties that are based on working people.

If such a party were around, they'd be the ones speaking up for you and telling the truth about what's going on with the rate hike. Then they'd be denounced by the Anthony Lewises of the world for being anti-democratic—in other words, for representing popular interests rather than power interests.

Radio listener: I'm afraid there may be a saturation point of despair just from knowing the heaviness of the truth that you impart. I'd like to strongly lobby you to begin devoting maybe 10% or 15% of your appearances or books or articles towards tangible, detailed things that people can do to try to change the world. I've heard a few occasions where someone asks you that question and your response is, Organize. Just do it.

I try to keep it in the back of my mind and think about it, but I'm afraid that the answer is always the same. There is only one way to deal with these things. Being alone, you can't do anything. All you can do is deplore the situation.

But if you join with other people, you can make changes. Millions of things are possible, depending on where you want to put your efforts.

To help you get started, Odonian Press has put together a list of 144 organizations that work to make the world a better place. It begins on the next page.

You may also find a couple of current books useful. Howard Zinn's *You Can't Be Neutral on a Moving Train* (Beacon, 1994) is well-written (as always) and has an optimistic message. Michael Albert's *Stop The Killing Train: Radical Visions for Radical Change* (South End, 1993) is also forward-looking and constructive.

Noam Chomsky

The organizations on this list were suggested by Noam Chomsky, Jane Maxwell, Chris Rosene, Davida Coady, Susan McCallister, Gar Smith, Sheila Katz, David Barsamian and myself. I've grouped them into the following categories:

- affordable housing
- anti-war, anti-military and economic conversion
- Canadian
- church groups
- civil rights
- communications and research (general)
- environmental
- funding
- general and miscellaneous
- health and reproductive rights
- human rights
- labor and community organizing
- Latin America
- Middle East
- political parties and groups
- Third World development
- women's issues

It's unlikely that any of us would agree with everyone else's choices, so please don't assail us with complaints about which organizations are—or aren't—included on the list. (Thanks.)

We all realize that there are *many, many* other worthwhile groups—particularly small, local ones. One way to find out about them is to ask any of the regional funding foundations on the list below for the names of the organizations they support.

Arthur Naiman

Affordable housing

**Fund for an Open
  Society**
311 S Juniper, #400
Philadelphia PA 19107
215 735 6915

Habitat for Humanity
121 Habitat St
Americus GA 31709
912 924 6935

South Shore Bank
7054 S Jeffery Blvd
Chicago IL 60649
312 288 1000

*Anti-war, anti-military
  and economic
  conversion*

**Campaign for Peace and
  Democracy**
Box 1640 Cathedral Station
New York NY 10025
212 666 5924

**Center for Defense
  Information**
1500 Massachusetts Ave
NW
Washington DC 20005
202 862 0700

**Center for Economic
  Conversion**
222 View St
Mountain View CA 94041
415 968 8798

**Central Committee for
  Conscientious Objectors**
(Western Region)
655 Sutter, #514
San Francisco CA 94102
415 474 3002

**Livermore Conversion
  Project**
Box 31835
Oakland CA 94604
510 832 4347

**Nevada Desert
  Experience**
Box 4487
Las Vegas NV 89127
702 646 4814

PeaceNet *(online)*
see Institute for Global
  Communications *in the
  Communications section*

**Veterans Speakers
  Alliance**
942 Market St, #709
San Francisco CA 94102
415 255 7331

War Resisters League
339 Lafayette St
New York NY 10012
212 228 0450

Canadian
Also see Church groups.

**Canadian Environmental
  Law Association**
517 College St, #401
Toronto, Ontario
M6G 4A2 Canada
416 960 2284

CCIC (Canadian Council
  for International
  Cooperation)
1 Nicholas St, #300
Ottawa, Ontario
K1N 7B7 Canada
613 241 7007

CUSO
135, rue Rideau St
Ottawa, Ontario
K1N 9K7 Canada
613 241 1264

Oxfam Canada
294 Albert St, #300
Ottawa, Ontario
K1P6E6 Canada
613 237 5236

Church groups

**American Friends
  Service Committee**
1501 Cherry St
Philadelphia PA 19102
215 241 7000

**Anglican Church of
  Canada**
600 Jarvis St
Toronto, Ontario
M4Y 2J6 Canada
416 924 9192

**Canadian Catholic
  Organization for Devel-
  opment and Peace**
5633 Sherbrooke E
Montréal, Québec
H1N 1A3 Canada
514 257 8711

**Maryknoll Mission
  Association of the
  Faithful**
Box 307
Maryknoll NY10545
914 762 6364

**National Council of
  Churches**
475 Riverside Dr
New York NY 10115
212 870 2511

**Unitarian-Universalist
  Association**
78 Beacon St
Boston MA 02108
617 742 2100

United Church of Canada
85 St. Clair Ave E
Toronto, Ontario
M4T 1M8 Canada
416 925 5931

Civil rights

**American Civil Liberties
  Union**
132 W 43rd St
New York NY 10036
212 944 9800

Asian Law Caucus
468 Bush St, 3rd flr
San Francisco CA 94108
415 391 1655

**Center for Constitutional
  Rights**
666 Broadway
New York NY 10012
212 614 6464

Drug Policy Foundation
4455 Connecticut Ave
  NW, #B-500
Washington DC 20008
202 537 5005

MALDEF (Mexican-Amer-
  ican Legal Defense and
  Education Fund)
634 S Spring St
Los Angeles CA 90014
213 629 2512

NAACP (National Association for the Advancement of Colored People)
4805 Mount Hope Dr
Baltimore MD 21215
410 358 8900

National Gay and Lesbian Task Force
2320 17th St NW
Washington DC 20009
202 332 6483

National Emergency Civil Liberties Committee
175 Fifth Ave
New York NY 10010
212 673 2040

National Urban League
500 E 62nd St
New York NY 10021
212 310 9000

Native American Rights Fund
1506 Broadway
Boulder CO 80302
303 447 8760

NORML (National Organization for the Reform of Marijuana Laws)
1001 Connecticut Ave NW, #1010
Washington DC 20036
202 483 5500

Southern Poverty Law Center
Box 2087
Montgomery AL 36102
205 264 0286

Communications and research (general)

Also see the publishers listed on pp. 118–19.

Center for Investigative Reporting
568 Howard St, 5th flr
San Francisco 94105
415 543 1200

Covert Action
1500 Massachusetts Ave NW, #732
Washington DC 20005
202 331 9763

Data Center
464 19th St
Oakland CA 94612
510 835 4692

FAIR (Fairness and Accuracy in Reporting)
130 W 25th St
New York NY 10001
212 633 6700

Institute for Global Communications
18 Deboom St
San Francisco CA 94107
415 442 0220
mother organization to EcoNet, LaborNet and PeaceNet

Institute for Media Analysis
145 W 4th St
New York NY 10012
212 254 1061
publishes Lies of Our Times

Institute for Policy Studies
1601 Connecticut Ave NW, #500
Washington DC 20009
202 234 9382

KFCF
Box 4364
Fresno CA 93744
209 233 2221

KPFA
1929 Martin Luther King Jr. Way
Berkeley CA 94704
510 848 6767

KPFK
3729 Cahuenga Blvd W
North Hollywood CA 91604
818 985 2711

KPFT
419 Lovett
Houston TX 77006
713 526 4000

The Nation Institute
72 Fifth Ave
New York NY 10011
212 463 9270 or
212 242 8400

Pacifica National News
700 H St NW
Washington DC 20001
202 783 1620
mother organization to KFCF, KPFA, KPFK, KPFT, WBAI and WPSW

The Progressive
409 E Main St
Madison WI 53703
608 257 4626

Public Media Center
466 Green St, #300
San Francisco CA 94133
415 434 1403

WBAI
505 Eighth Ave, 19th flr
New York, NY 10018
212 279 0707

WPSW
702 H St NW
Washington DC 20001
202 783 3100

Z Media Institute
18 Millfield St
Woods Hole MA 02543
508 548 9063

Environmental
Also see Canadian groups

Alliance for a Paving Moratorium
Box 4347
Arcata CA 95521
707 826 7775

Earth First!
Box 1415
Eugene OR 97440
503 741 9191

Earth Island Institute
300 Broadway, #28
San Francisco CA 94133
415 788 3666

EcoNet *(online)*
see Institute for Global Communications *above*

Greenpeace
1436 U St NW
Washington DC 20009
202 462 1177

Indigenous Environmental Network
Box 485
Bemidji MN 56601
218 751 4967

PEG (Political Ecology Group)
519 Castro St, Box 111
San Francisco CA 94114
415 641 7835

Student Environmental Action Coalition
Box 1168
Chapel Hill NC 27514
919 967 4600

Funding

The first listing is a national network office for progressive funds. The other listings are member funds, all of which (except Resist) have a regional focus.

Funding Exchange
666 Broadway, #500
New York NY 10012
212 529 5300

Appalachian Community Fund
517 Union Ave, #206
Knoxville TN 37902
615 523 5783

Bread and Roses Community Fund
1500 Walnut St, #1305
Philadelphia PA 19102
215 731 1107

Chinook Fund
2418 W 32nd Ave
Denver CO 80211
303 455 6905

Crossroads Fund
3411 W Diversey Ave, #20
Chicago IL 60647
312 227 7676

Fund for Southern Communities
552 Hill St SE
Atlanta GA 30312
404 577 3178

Haymarket People's Fund
42 Seaverns Ave
Jamaica Plain MA 02130
617 522 7676

Headwaters Fund
122 W Franklin Ave, #518
Minneapolis MN 55404
612 879 0602

Liberty Hill Foundation
1316 Third St Promenade, #B-4
Santa Monica CA 90401
310 458 1450

McKenzie River Gathering Foundation
3558 SE Hawthorne
Portland OR 97214
503 233 0271

North Star Fund
666 Broadway, 5th flr
New York NY 10012
212 460 5511

People's Fund
1325 Nuuanu Ave
Honolulu HI 96817
808 526 2441

Resist
One Summer St
Somerville MA 02143
617 623 5110

Three Rivers Community Fund
100 N Braddock Ave, #207
Pittsburgh PA 15208
412 243 9250

Vanguard Public Foundation
383 Rhode Island, #301
San Francisco CA 94103
415 487 2111

Wisconsin Community Fund
122 State St, #508
Madison WI 53703
608 251 6834

General and miscellaneous

Center for Ethics and Economic Policy
2512 9th St, #3
Berkeley CA 94710
510 549 9931

Center for Living Democracy
Rural Route 1
Black Fox Rd
Brattleboro VT 05301
802 254 1234

Davis-Putter Scholarship Fund
744 Broad St, #2500
Newark NJ 07102

Gray Panthers
2025 Pennsylvania Ave NW, #821
Washington DC 20006
202 466 3132

INFACT
256 Hanover St
Boston MA 02113
617 742 4583

Neighbor to Neighbor
2601 Mission, #400
San Francisco CA 94110
415 824 3355
also DC, 202 543 2429

People for the American Way
2000 M St NW, #400
Washington DC 20036
202 467 4999

Physicians for Social Responsibility
1101 14th St NW, #700
Washington DC 20036
202 898 0150

Public Citizen
2000 P St NW, #700
Washington DC 20036
202 833 3000

Quixote Center
Box 5206
Hyattsville MD 20782
301 699 0042

Rosenberg Fund for Children
1145 Main St, #408
Springfield MA 01103
413 739 9020

Women's International League for Peace and Freedom
1213 Race St
Philadelphia PA 19107
215 563 7110

Health and reproductive rights

Advocates for Youth
1025 Vermont Ave NW, #200
Washington DC 20005
202 347 5700

Coalition for the Medical Rights of Women
558 Capp St
San Francisco CA 94110
415 647 2694

Hesperian Foundation
2796 Middlefield Rd
Palo Alto CA 94306
415 325 9017

NARAL *(National Abortion Rights Action League)*
1156 15th St NW, #700
Washington DC 20005
202 828 9300

Partners in Health
113 River St
Cambridge MA 02139
617 661 4564

Planned Parenthood
810 Seventh Ave
New York NY 10019
212 541 7800

Seva Foundation
8 N San Pedro Rd
San Rafael CA 94903
415 492 1829

Human rights

Amnesty International USA
322 Eighth Ave
New York NY 10001
212 807 8400

Coalition for Immigrant and Refugee Rights and Services
995 Market St, #1108
San Francisco CA 94103
415 243 8215

East Timor Action Network
Box 1182
White Plains NY 10602
914 428 7299
also San Francisco, 415 387 2822, and Vancouver, 604 264 9973

Human Rights Watch
(includes Americas Watch, Africa Watch, Asia Watch, etc.)
485 Fifth Ave, 3rd flr
New York NY 10017
212 972 8400

Physicians for Human Rights
100 Boylston St, #702
Boston MA 02116
617 695 0041

Labor and community organizing

Center for Third World Organizing
1218 E 21st St
Oakland CA 94606
510 533 7583

Industrial Areas Foundation
36 New Hyde Park Road
Franklin Square NY 11010
516 354 1076

LaborNet *(online)*
see Institute for Global Communications *in the Communications section*

Labor Party Advocates
Box 53177
Washington DC 20009
202 319 1932

Latin America

Barricada International
Box 410150
San Francisco CA 94141
415 621 8981

CISPES (Committee in Solidarity with the People of El Salvador)
19 W 21st St, #502
New York NY 10010
212 229 1290

CHRICA (Committee for Health Rights in Central America)
347 Delores St , #210
San Francisco CA 94110
415 431 7760

Disarm/Cuban Medical Project
36 E 12th St
New York NY 10003
212 475 3232

Documentation Exchange
Box 2327
Austin TX 78768
512 476 9841

Global Exchange
2017 Mission, #303
San Francisco CA 94110
415 255 7296

GNIB (Guatemalan News and Information Bureau)
Box 28594
Oakland CA 94604
510 835 0810

Guatemala Partners
945 G St NW
Washington DC 20001
202 783 1123

Inter-Hemispheric Education Resource Center
Box 4506
Albuquerque NM 87196
505 842 8288

MADRE
121 W 27th St, #301
New York NY 10001
212 627 0444

NACLA (North American Congress on Latin America)
475 Riverside Dr, #454
New York NY 10115
212 870 3146

Nicaragua Network
1247 E St SE
Washington DC 20003
202 544 9355

NISGUA (Network in Solidarity with the People of Guatemala)
1500 Massachusetts Ave NW, #214
Washington DC 20005
202 483 0050

Office of the Americas
8124 W Third St, #202
Los Angeles CA 90048
213 852 9808

International Peace for Cuba Appeal
39 W 14th St, #206
New York NY 10011
212 633 6646
also San Francisco, 415 821 6545

Pueblo to People
2105 Silber Rd, #101
Houston TX 77055
713 956 1172

Resource Center of the Americas
317 17th Ave SE
Minneapolis MN 55404
612 627 9445

San Carlos Foundation
1065 Creston Road
Berkeley CA 94708
510 525 3787

Witness for Peace
2201 P St NW
Washington DC 20037
202 797 1160

WOLA (Washington Office on Latin America)
110 Maryland Ave NE, #404
Washington DC 20002
202 544 8045

Middle East

Jewish Peace Lobby
8604 Second Ave, #317
Silver Spring MD 20910
301 589 8764

Middle East Children's Alliance
905 Parker St
Berkeley CA 94710
510 548 0542

Middle East Justice Network
Box 495
Boston MA 02112
617 542 5056

Search for Justice and Equality in Palestine/Israel
Box 3452
Framingham MA 01701
508 877 2611

Political parties and groups

Democratic Socialists of America
180 Varick St, 12th flr
New York NY 10014
212 727 8610

Green Party USA
Box 30208
Kansas City MO 64112
816 931 9366

New Party
227 W 40th St, #1303
New York NY 10018
212 302 5053

Third World development

Also see Canadian groups

Food First (Institute for Food and Development Policy)
398 60th St
Oakland CA 94618
510 654 4400

Center for International Policy
1755 Massachusetts Ave NW, #312
Washington DC 200365
202 232 3317

Oxfam America
26 West St
Boston MA 02111
617 482 1211

Results
236 Massachusetts Ave NE, #300
Washington DC 20002
202 543 9340

World Neighbors
4127 NW 126th
Oklahoma City OK 73120
405 946 3333

Women's issues

Also see Health and reproductive rights

Coalition of Labor Union Women
1126 16th St NW
Washington DC 20036
202 466 4610

Connexions
Box 14431
Berkeley CA 94712
510 549 3505

Ms. Foundation
120 Wall St, 33rd flr
New York, NY 10005
212 742 2300

9to5, National Association of Working Women
238 W Wisconsin Ave, #700
Milwaukee WI 53203
414 274 0925

NOW (National Organization of Women) **Legal Defense and Education Fund**
99 Hudson St
New York NY 10013
212 925 6635

WOW (Wider Opportunities for Women)
815 15th St NW, #916
Washington DC 20005
202 638 3143

Other books
by Noam Chomsky

These two pages list Noam Chomsky's other political books in reverse chronological order (alphabetically within years). His books on linguistics aren't included unless they contain some political material; neither are shorter works or collections of essays by various authors. Addresses and phone numbers for the smaller publishers are given the first time they're mentioned.

World Orders Old and New. Columbia University Press, 1994.

Letters from Lexington: Reflections on Propaganda (letters). Common Courage (Box 702, Monroe ME 04951; 800 497 3207), 1993.

The Prosperous Few and the Restless Many (compiled from interviews with David Barsamian). Odonian Press (Box 32375, Tucson AZ 85751; 602 296 4056 or 800 REAL STORY), 1993.

Rethinking Camelot. South End Press (116 St Botolph St, Boston MA 02115; 617 266 0629 or 800 533 8478), 1993.

Year 501: The Conquest Continues. South End, 1993.

Chronicles of Dissent (interviews with David Barsamian). Common Courage (Box 702, Monroe ME 04951; 800 497 3207), 1992.

What Uncle Sam Really Wants (compiled from talks and interviews). Odonian, 1992.

Deterring Democracy. Verso (29 W 35th St, New York NY 10001; 212 244 3336), 1990; updated edition, Hill & Wang (NY), 1991.

Necessary Illusions: Thought Control in Democratic Societies. South End, 1989.

The Culture of Terrorism. South End, 1988.

Language and Politics. Edited by C.P. Otero. Black Rose Books (distributed by the University of Toronto Press, 340 Nagel Dr, Cheektowaga NY 14225, 716 683 4547), 1988.

Manufacturing Consent (Edward S. Herman, principal author). Pantheon Books (NY), 1988.

Pirates and Emperors: International Terrorism in the Real World. Black Rose, 1986; new edition, Amana (Box 678, Brattleboro VT 05301; 802 257 0872), 1988.

The Chomsky Reader. Edited by James Peck. Pantheon, 1987.

On Power and Ideology: the Managua Lectures. South End, 1987.

Turning the Tide: U.S. Intervention in Central America and the Struggle for Peace. South End, 1985.

The Fateful Triangle: The United States, Israel and the Palestinians. South End, 1983.

Towards a New Cold War. Pantheon, 1982.

Radical Priorities. Black Rose, 1981.

After the Cataclysm: Postwar Indochina and the Reconstruction of Imperial Ideology [The Political Economy of Human Rights, Part II] (with Edward S. Herman). South End, 1979.

Language and Responsibility (interviews with Mitsou Ronat). Pantheon, 1979.

The Washington Connection and Third World Fascism [The Political Economy of Human Rights, Part I] (with Edward S. Herman). South End, 1979.

Peace in the Middle East? Reflections on Justice and Nationhood. Pantheon, 1974 (out of print).

For Reasons of State. Pantheon, 1973 (out of print).

The Pentagon Papers, Volume 5, Analytic Essays and Index (edited with Howard Zinn). Beacon, 1972 (out of print).

Problems of Knowledge and Freedom (the Russell Lectures). Vintage Books (NY), 1972 (out of print).

At War with Asia: Essays on Indochina. Pantheon, 1970 (out of print).

American Power and the New Mandarins. Pantheon, 1969 (out of print).

Index

If you liked this book, check out some of our others:

The CIA's Greatest Hits — Mark Zepezauer

In crisply written, two-page chapters, each accompanied by a cartoon, this book describes the CIA's many attempts to assassinate democracy all over the world. *95 pp. $6.* *Just out.*

What Uncle Sam Really Wants — Noam Chomsky

A brilliant overview of the real motivations behind US foreign policy, from the man the *New York Times* called "arguably the most important intellectual alive." Chomsky's most popular book, it's full of astounding information. *111 pp. $5.* *Highly recommended. —Booklist*

69,000 copies in print

The Prosperous Few and the Restless Many — Noam Chomsky

A wide-ranging state-of-the-world report that covers everything from Bosnia to NAFTA. Chomsky's fastest-selling book ever, it was on the *Village Voice Literary Supplement's* bestsellers list for six months running. *95 pp. $5.* *Calmly reasoned. Most welcome. —Newsday*

54,000 copies in print

The Decline and Fall of the American Empire — Gore Vidal

Gore Vidal is one of our most important—and wittiest—social critics. This delightful little book is the perfect introduction to his political views. *95 pp. $5.* *Acerbic, deliciously, maliciously funny.*
—New York Times Book Review

The Greenpeace Guide to Anti-environmental Organizations — Carl Deal

A comprehensive guide to more than 50 industry front groups that masquerade as environmental organizations. The deception is amazing. *110 pp. $5.* *Fascinating. A must. —New Orleans Times-Picayune*